RANDOM
HOUSE
LARGE
PRINT

Barbara Taylor Bradford

WHERE YOU BELONG

RANDOM HOUSE
LARGE PRINT

Library of Congress Cataloging-in-Publication Data
Bradford, Barbara Taylor, 1933–
Where you belong : a novel /
Barbara Taylor Bradford.
p.   cm.
ISBN 0-375-72797-3
1. Kosovo (Serbia)—History—Civil War, 1998—
Fiction.   2. Women photographers—Fiction.
3. Photojournalism—Fiction.   4. Young
Women—Fiction.   5. Large type books.   I. Title

PS3552.R2147   W48   2000b
813'.54—dc21   99-087930
                                              CIP

Printed in the United States of America

1   3   5   7   9   10   8   6   4   2

This Large Print Edition published in accord
with the standards of the N.A.V.H.

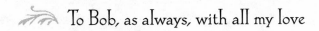 To Bob, as always, with all my love

Contents

Where You Belong

Part One

A MATTER OF
ℐNTEGRITY

Chapter 1

I

Kosovo, August 1998 ⋄ The three of us sat in a small copse situated at the far end of the village, taking shelter from the blistering heat. It was bosky and cool on this scorching summer's day.

The jeep was parked out on the road nearby, and I peered toward it, frowning slightly, wondering what had happened to Ajet, our adviser, guide, and driver. He had gone on foot to the village, having several days before arranged to meet an old school friend there, who in turn would take us to see the leaders of the K.L.A. According to Ajet, the Kosovo Liberation Army had their main training camp in the vicinity of the village, and Ajet had assured us in Peć, and then again on the drive here, that the leaders would be in the camp, and that they would be more than willing to have their photographs taken for transmission to newspapers and magazines around the world. "Everyone should know the truth, should know about our cause, our just and rightful cause," Ajet had said to us time and again.

When he had left the copse ages ago, he had been smiling cheerfully, happy at the idea of meeting his old friend, and I had watched him step out jauntily as he walked down the dusty road in a determined and purposeful manner. But that had been over three hours ago, and he had still not returned, and this disturbed me. I could not help wondering if something unforeseen, something bad, had happened to the friendly young Kosovar who had been so helpful to us.

I rose and walked through the trees, shading my eyes with my hand and looking down the dirt road. There was no sign of Ajet, and, in fact, there was very little activity at all. But I waited for a short while longer, hoping he would appear at any moment.

My name is Valentine Denning, and I'm a New Yorker born and bred, but now I base myself in Paris, where I work as a photojournalist for Gemstar, a well-known international news-photo agency. With the exception of my grandfather, no one in my family ever thought I would become a

photojournalist. When I was a child, Grandfather had spotted my desire to record everything
I saw and bought me my first camera. My parents
never paid much attention to me, and what I
would do when I grew up never seemed to cross
their minds. My brother Donald, to whom I was
much closer in those days and tended to bully
since he was younger, was forever after me to
become a model, a job that held no attraction for
me whatsoever. Donald kept pointing out that I
was tall and slim, with long legs and an athletic
build, as if I didn't know my own body. I know
I'm not pretty enough, but at least I don't look too
bad in the pictures Jake and Tony have taken of
me. But I'm not much into clothes; I like T-shirts,
khaki pants, white cotton shirts, and bush jackets,
workmanlike clothes that are perfect for the life I
lead.

I'm thirty-one years old, constantly traveling,
living out of a suitcase, and then there are the
crazy hours, the lack of comfort, even of the most
basic of amenities, when I'm on the front lines
covering wars and other disasters, not to mention
the danger I often find myself facing. But I prefer
this life to walking down a catwalk, showing off
Paris couture.

Turning away from the road at last, I went
back through the trees to rejoin Jake Newberg
and Tony Hampton, comrades-in-arms, as Tony
calls us. I think of these two men as my family;

we've worked together for several years now and we're inseparable. Jake is my best friend, and Tony has graduated from best friend to lover in the past year. The three of us go everywhere together, and we always make sure we are on the same assignments for our news-photo agencies.

I gazed at Tony surreptitiously for a moment, thinking how fit and healthy he looked as he sat on part of a felled tree trunk, loading two of his cameras with rolls of new film. Tony, who is British, is ten years older than me. Stocky and muscular, he inherited his mother's Black Irish good looks, and he is a handsome and charismatic man. But it's his masculinity, his potent sexuality, that women find most appealing, even overwhelming, and certainly irresistible, as I have discovered.

Considered to be one of the world's great war photographers, of the same ilk as the late Robert Capa, he is something of a risk taker when it comes to getting his pictures. This does not unduly worry me, although I know it gives Jake Newberg cause for concern; he has discussed it with me frequently of late.

I eyed Jake, sitting on the grass with his back to a tree, looking nonchalant as he made notes in the small blue leather notebook he always carries with him. Jake is also an American, "a Jew from Georgia" is the way he likes to describe himself. At thirty-eight, he is also one of the top war photographers, a prizewinner like Tony. I've won many awards myself but I've never attempted to put myself in their league, although Tony and Jake say I belong there, that I'm just as good as they are.

Jake is tall, lean, with a physical toughness about him that makes him seem indestructible; anyway, that is the way I view him. He's an attractive man with an expressive face, blondish curly hair, and the most vivid blue eyes I've ever seen. Yet despite his puckishness and the mischievous twinkle that often glints in those eyes, I long ago discovered that Jake is the most compassionate of men. And I've come to appreciate his understanding of the complexities of the human heart and the human frailties we are all afflicted with.

Tony glanced up as he became aware of me hovering over him. "What is it?" he asked, frowning slightly. "Is something wrong?"

"I hope Ajet's all right, Tony, he's been gone—"

"I'm sure he is," Tony cut in quickly with a certain firmness, and then he gave me a reassuring smile. "It's very quiet, peaceful out there, isn't it?"

I nodded. "There's hardly any sign of life."

"Doesn't surprise me. I think the village is probably half deserted by now. It's more than likely that a lot of locals have already left, are moving south ahead of the Serbian army, crossing the border into Albania as fast as they can."

"You're probably right." I sat down on the grass and fell silent, ruminating.

Jake glanced at me and then pinned his eyes thoughtfully on Tony. He said in a brisk tone, "Let's abandon this shoot, get the hell out of here, Tony. I've suddenly got a bad feeling."

"But we won't get this chance again," I felt bound to point out, sitting up straighter, staring at Jake.

Before either man could address my comment, Ajet suddenly reappeared. He came wandering in from the road looking as if he had no cares in the world. Not only did he seem unperturbed, he actually looked pleased with himself, almost smug.

"Everything's set up," he announced in his perfect English, learned during the eight years he had lived and worked in Brooklyn, where his uncle and cousin still lived. "I saw my guy," he continued, "I talked to him at length. We drank coffee. He has just closed his shop, gone out to the farmhouse in the fields at the other side of the village. The farmhouse is the K.L.A.'s headquarters now. He is going to bring the top leaders here—" Ajet broke off, looked at his watch, a cheap copy of a Rolex he had bought on the streets of Manhattan. He nodded to himself and finished,

"One more hour. Yes, in one hour approximately they will come to the village. We will meet them at the shop. Now we relax, we wait here."

"Good man!" Tony exclaimed, beaming at the young Kosovar. "And since we've got an hour to kill, we should eat. Let's get the bottled water and the sandwiches from the jeep." Jumping up, Tony started to walk toward the road.

Ajet exclaimed, "No, no, Tony, please sit down! *Please.* Do not trouble yourself. I will go for the box of sandwiches and the water."

I murmured, "I'm not hungry, but I would love some water."

"No food for me either," Jake said. "Just water, like Val."

The young man hurried off, and I looked at Tony and then at Jake. "I might go down the road to the village, mosey around a bit. What do you think?"

Jake nodded but made no comment.

Tony walked over to me, took hold of my hand, and pulled me up from the grass. "I don't like you being out of my sight on a shoot like this, Val, especially since we don't really know the lay of the land around here. But I think it's okay; certainly Ajet doesn't appear to be worried. So go for a walk if you want."

Slipping his arm around my waist, he brought me closer to him, held me in a loving embrace. Against my hair he murmured, "I'd like to get back to Belgrade tonight, Vee. There's something about your room at the hotel that I find most appealing."

"It's because I'm in it," I answered, laughing, and I kissed his cheek. "At least, that *better* be the reason."

"You know it is." Holding me away from him, he smiled, his black eyes dancing, and then almost immediately his expression turned serious. "When you get down there, keep your eyes peeled and stay on the perimeters of the village. That way you can get back here quickly, should it be necessary."

I leaned into him. "Don't worry so much, I'll be fine. By the way, I haven't told you today that I love you, have I? But I do."

"I love you too, Val."

Ajet came back to the copse carrying a cardboard box. After placing it on the rocks, he opened it with a bit of a flourish and began to hand out the bottles of water, offering us the wrapped sandwiches from the hotel in Peć. He went on fussing around us and behaving as though he were serving us at a grand banquet, and Tony and Jake exchanged amused, knowing looks and laughed.

I had been loading my camera, and I looked from one to the other and asked, "Am I missing something? What's the joke?"

"No joke," Tony said, and blew me a kiss.

II

I focused my Leica 35mm on the ragtag collection of children ahead of me, a short way down the road. There were five of them in all, sitting together against a ruined wall. As I peered through my lens, I took in their pallor, their haunted expressions, and the fear clouding their innocent young eyes.

A heartbreaking little band, I thought, so forlorn on this bright, sunny day. A day for playing. Not a day for war. I repressed a sigh and began taking pictures.

A flurry of unexpected activity had begun to erupt all around me . . . exploding bombs, mortar fire, the rumble of tanks in the distance. The sound of gunfire was breaking the quietness of the afternoon, and I instantly abandoned the shots of the children. Closer by, I heard screams, the sound of running feet, people scattering, seeking safety. And then more screams filled the air, along with the staccato rat-a-tat of machine guns, and guns not so far away at that.

All of my senses were alerted to danger, and my chest tightened, and I sucked in my breath sharply when I saw Tony rushing out of the copse just behind me. I had left him there only a few minutes before, sitting on the rocks with Jake, eating a sandwich.

Now he was sprinting toward the line of fire.

I raced after him in his wake. And dimly, in the distance, I heard Jake behind us, shouting, "Val! Val! Don't follow him, for God's sake. *It's too dangerous.*"

I paid no attention.

Tony was our leader, and as always he was hell-bent on getting the best pictures, whatever war we were covering and no matter what the cost. Taking risks meant nothing to him. He seemed to thrive on danger, as well I knew. Tony was consistently in harm's way, and so were we because of him, although, as he frequently reminded us, we did have a choice of whether or not to follow him into the fray.

Once again Jake's voice carried to me above the noise of exploding shells and deafening artillery. "*Val! Stop!* Don't follow Tony."

I did not stop. Nor did I look back. I was hard on Tony's heels, my camera held tightly in my hands, my mind, my entire being, concentrated on one thing: Doing my job as professionally as possible and getting the best pictures I could.

I could hear Jake coming after me and Tony. I realized his warnings of a moment earlier had been pushed to one side, indeed probably forgotten altogether. What he always wanted was to reach me, grab hold of me, and pull me out of danger.

Kalashnikovs were spraying bullets from all

sides and the shelling was rapidly growing heavier; the summer air was thick with smoke and dust, the smell of cordite mingling with that of blood. And the stench of death was suddenly all-pervasive, numbing, and I wished we had never come here.

We had arrived late that morning to take a few simple photographs of the Kosovo Liberation Army's leaders; now, unexpectedly, we found ourselves in the midst of this violent battle between the K.L.A. and Serbian troops. I couldn't help wondering if this was a deadly ambush, a trap we had walked into with our eyes wide open. And where was Ajet? I hoped the young Kosovar had been smart enough to stay in the copse, and that hopefully he had driven the jeep into the trees for safety.

I knew that Serbian troops had been moving south for days, keeping up the deadliest fighting along the way, brutally driving the Kosovars out of their villages and towns. Thousands of terrified civilians were already on the move, a steady stream of humanity being cruelly driven from their homes and homeland, seeking safety across the borders in Albania and Macedonia.

Unexpectedly, a small boy appeared as if from nowhere, and began to totter forward on his thin little legs, heading directly into the line of fire, oblivious of the fighting and the melee spinning around him. I saw him out of the corner of my eye and reacted instantly. Veering to my right, I sped over to the child and threw myself on top of him, all of my instincts compelling me to protect him no matter what.

Bombs continued to explode, and pieces of shrapnel were swirling like deadly snowflakes. I covered the child with my body, put my arms around him, and held him tightly. He was shaking, and this did not surprise me one bit. I detested the sound of the guns and bombs myself; they were discordant and frightening, and most especially to a small child.

After a moment, I lifted my head and glanced up.

The sky was a perfect cerulean blue, without cloud, and the sun was shining brilliantly. Summer, I thought; I ought to be on vacation with Tony, not spread-eagle on the ground with my face pressed into the dirt in some obscure village in the Balkans.

Small rubbery legs and arms began to wriggle, eel-like, under me, and I finally rolled off the child, jumped up, and pulled him to his feet.

He gazed up at me soulfully with a faint, perplexed smile; I smiled back and gave him a little push toward a young woman who was rushing toward us, calling out something I did not understand. With a nod to me and the words "Thank you" spoken in carefully pronounced but accented English, the young woman grabbed the boy's arm and dragged him away. It was obvious that she was scolding him as the two of them moved away from the shelling and went behind one of the houses on the side of the road.

I was glad to see the child taken to safety; at least I hoped he was safe. Many of the nearby houses and shops had been bombed, had crumbled into heaps of stones and bricks, and there were fires flaring everywhere.

Wondering where Tony and Jake were, I glanced around, suddenly saw their backs disappearing down a narrow side street. Immediately I jogged after them, trying to catch up, not wanting to be left behind.

The shelling had now reached a crescendo, and I knew Tony and Jake were heading right into the maelstrom, their cameras poised. I followed them into the fray, but for once, much to my surprise and consternation, I realized I did so against my better judgment. I had to admit to myself that for the first time in my association with Tony and Jake I had certain misgivings about following Tony's lead. A curious sense of foreboding swept over me, and this feeling was so unfamiliar, so unprecedented, I was startled, and I stopped in my tracks, discovering that for a split second I was unable to move forward. I was rooted to the spot.

Then the moment I'd had nightmares about, had forever dreaded, was suddenly and frighteningly upon me. Tony was going down, his camera flying out of his hands as he was struck by a stream of bullets. He was thrown backward by the impact, lay sprawled on the cobbled street, still and unmoving.

"Tony! Tony!" I screamed, and began to run to him.

Jake, who was closer, also shouted his name, and went on. "I'm coming to you, Tony, hang in there!" But the words had hardly left Jake's mouth, when he toppled forward and fell to the ground, hit by a sniper's bullets.

Without thinking about safety, I pressed on through the curtain of gunfire and shrapnel, heading toward my friends, knowing I must do something to help them, although I was not certain what I *could* do under these horrific circumstances.

Out of breath and panting, I paused momentarily next to Jake, bent over him, and gasped, "How bad are you?"

"I've been hit in my leg and hip, but I'm okay, don't worry about me. It's Tony I'm concerned about."

"Me too," I muttered, and sprinted away. When I reached Tony, I dropped to my knees next to him. "Darling, it's me." As I spoke, I moved a strand of black hair away from his damp forehead and stared down into his face.

Finally he opened his eyes. "Go, Val. Find cover. Dangerous here," he told me in a low, strangled voice.

"I'm not going to leave you," I answered, looking him over swiftly. I was appalled at his gunshot wounds, and I felt myself filling with dread. He had been hit in his chest, his shoulder, and his legs, and seemingly other parts of his body as well, as far as I could make out. I was frightened and alarmed by all the blood; he was covered in it, as if he had been riddled with bullets. Oh God, oh God, he might not make it. I swallowed the cry that rose in my throat. It took all my self-control not to break down; I leaned over him, brought my face close to his. "I'm not leaving you, Tony," I repeated, endeavoring to keep my voice as steady as possible.

"Go," he whispered. Summoning all of his strength, he managed to say, "Get out. For me." His voice was very shaky.

Realizing that Tony was becoming unduly agitated by my continuing presence, and knowing that I must try to find help for both men, I finally acquiesced. "All right, I'll go," I murmured against Tony's face. I stroked his cheek. "Just stay calm, lay still. I won't be long. I'll be back with help very soon."

I kissed him lightly and began to crawl away on my hands and knees, keeping low and close to the ground in an effort to dodge the flying bullets. I was making for a small building nearby, one of the few that remained standing, and I had almost reached it, when I felt the impact of a bullet slamming into my thigh. I slumped down in a heap, wincing in pain and clutching my Leica to my chest. Then I glanced down at my leg; blood was already oozing through my khaki pants, and it occurred to me that I wasn't going to be much use to either Tony or Jake.

Turning my head, I glanced over at Jake. "How're you doing?"

"Okay. Are you hurt very badly, Val?"

"I don't think so," I replied, and hoped this was really the case. Although deep down I was fairly certain it wasn't, I nevertheless had a need to reassure Jake.

He asked over the battery of noise, "What about Tony?"

"He's not good," I said, and my voice wobbled. "He's terribly shot up and in need of medical attention, urgent need of it, and much more than we are. I saw a Red Cross ambulance up on the ridge over there, and let's hope the medics get here quickly. Tony's losing masses of blood . . ." I swallowed. "It's . . . it's touch and go with him . . . I think. . . ."

For a moment Jake could not speak. He was obviously distressed by my words. At last he said, "Tony's going to be all right, Val. He's tough, and don't forget he's always said he has the luck of the Irish."

"He also says he's blessed by the saints," I replied tensely. "I hope he's right."

Jake called back, "Just keep cool, hang in there, honey."

I could hardly hear him. His words were almost but not quite drowned out by the explosions and the thunder of mortar fire, which seemed to be closer than ever. In a few minutes troops were swarming everywhere, both the K.L.A. and the Serbians; they were filling the village, running through the streets, fighting. I wasn't sure who was who. I looked for distinguishing emblems on their uniforms but without success, then remembered that those who wore the black paratrooper berets were the Kosovars. They seemed to be outnumbered. I closed my eyes, hoping I would be taken for dead and overlooked. I knew there was no longer any possibility of dragging myself over to Tony. My spirit was more than willing, but I was just too weak physically, and the troops were converging now.

So I resigned myself to wait for the Red Cross ambulance I had seen not long before. Surely it would drive down into the village soon. Putting my hand under my T-shirt, I found the gold chain on which I'd hung Tony's ring. He had given it to me only a couple of weeks earlier, when we had been in Paris together. Suddenly tears were dangerously close to the surface as memories of those happy days rushed back to flood my mind.

My fingers closed around the ring. I began to pray: Oh God, please let Tony be all right. Please don't let him die. Please, please, let him live. I went on praying silently, and the fighting raged on around me unabated.

III

White light, very bright white light, was invading my entire being, or so it seemed. I was suffused in the bright white light until I became part of it; I was no longer myself, but the light . . .

I opened my eyes and blinked rapidly. The light was harsh, startling, and I felt disoriented. And for a moment I thought I had not really woken up, but was still in my dream, living the dream. As I blinked again, came slowly awake, I wondered where I was; still somewhat disoriented, I glanced around in puzzlement. The white walls and ceiling and the white tile floor, in combination with the brilliant sunlight flooding through the windows, created a dazzling effect . . . echoing the bright white light that had dominated my strange and haunting dream.

Shifting slightly in the bed, I winced as a sharp pain shot up my thigh, and immediately I remembered everything. Of course, I was in a hospital room. In Belgrade. After the three of us had been shot, we had subsequently been rescued by the Red Cross and patched up by the doctors on a temporary basis, so that we could travel. We had then been taken to Peć in the ambulance I had seen in the village when the fighting had first started.

As I'd suspected, Jake and I had not been as seriously injured as Tony, who was in critical condition, having lost a lot of blood. Fortunately, the medics in Peć had been able to give him a blood transfusion before the three of us were flown out.

Details of the flight came back to me as my mind finally began to clear. Tony had been on a stretcher in the transport plane, and I sat next to him all the way, holding his hand, talking to him, begging him to keep fighting. The one good thing was that the medics were hopeful he would pull through; they had told me and Jake that Tony had a better than average chance of making it. He had slept through most of the flight while Jake and I kept a vigil by his side; our hopes soared as we had headed toward Belgrade because he was holding his own so well.

But when *was* the flight? Yesterday? The day before? Or even earlier than that?

Glancing at my wrist, expecting to see the time, I discovered I was not wearing my watch. My eyes strayed to the utilitarian metal nightstand, but it was not there either. The top of the stand was entirely empty.

I pushed aside the bedclothes, and, moving gingerly, inched myself into an upright position, and then maneuvered my body onto the edge of the bed. My bandaged thigh was still quite sore from the gunshot wound, but I managed, nonetheless, to stand up, and I was surprised and relieved to discover that I was relatively steady on my feet and had only the slightest amount of discomfort when I walked.

In the cramped bathroom attached to the hospital room, I ran cold water into the sink and splashed my face with it, patted myself dry with a paper towel, and peered into the mirror. My reflection didn't please me. I looked lousy, done in. But then, what else could I expect? My pallor was unusual—normally I have such good color— and there were violet smudges under my eyes.

Moving slowly, I made it back to the bed, where I sat on the edge, fretting about Tony and Jake, and wondering what to do next. My main concern was Tony, whose injuries were the worst. Where the hell was he in this hospital? And where was Jake? My clothes had apparently been taken away, and since I was wearing only a skimpy cotton hospital gown tied at the back, I couldn't very well go wandering around in search of them. My eyes scanned the room for a phone. There wasn't one.

A sudden loud knocking on the door startled me, and I glanced toward it just as it was pushed open, and Jake, heavily bandaged and supporting himself on a pair of crutches, hobbled in. He was unshaven and looked crumpled in hospital-issue pajamas and an equally creased cotton robe.

"Hi," he said, and propping the crutches against the wall near the nightstand, he half hopped, half limped to the bed, where he sat down next to me. "How're you doing, Val?"

"Well, I'm obviously not going dancing *ce soir*," I said, glancing down first at my bandaged thigh, which bulged under the cotton gown, and then at him. "I'll give you a rain check. And you seem to be doing okay with your balancing act on those crutches."

He nodded.

"How's Tony? Have you seen him yet? Where is he? When can I go and see him?"

Jake did not answer me.

I stared at him.

He gazed back at me, still not saying a word.

I saw then how pale he was, and haggard-looking, and noticed that his bright blue eyes were clouded, bloodshot, as if he'd been crying. Inside I began to shrivel, scorched by an innate knowledge I dare not admit existed. But it did. *Oh yes.*

Jake cleared his throat and looked at me intently.

My heart dropped. I knew instinctively what he was going to say; an awful sense of dread took me in its stranglehold, and I felt my throat closing. Clasping my hands tightly together, I braced myself for bad news.

"I'm afraid Tony didn't make it, Val darling," Jake said at last, his tone low, almost inaudible. And final. "He'd become far too weakened before we arrived here, and he'd lost such a great deal of blood initially—" Jake paused when his voice broke, but eventually he went on. "It's devastating . . . I never thought it could happen, I—" Very abruptly, he stopped again and, unable to continue, he said nothing more, simply sat there helplessly, gazing at me, shaking his head. His sorrow was reflected in his face, which was gray, bereft.

I was speechless. Finally, I opened my mouth to speak, but no words came out. There was a long, silent scream echoing through my brain, and I snapped my eyes shut, wishing I could block it out, wishing I could steady myself. Instead, I fell apart, began to shake uncontrollably as shock engulfed me.

A second later I felt Jake's strong arms encircling me, and I clung to him, sobbed against his shoulder. Jake wept also, and we held on to each other for a long time. And together we mourned the loss of a man we both loved who had died before his time.

Chapter 2

I

Paris, September ⋅ I have always loved my apartment on the Left Bank where I've lived for the last seven years. It is spacious, light, and airy, with six large windows in its three main rooms, all of which are of good proportions. These rooms open onto each other, and this enfilade gives it a lovely flowing feeling that appeals to my sense of order and symmetry, traits inherited from my grandfather, who was an architect.

But ever since my return from Belgrade in August, I've been experiencing an overwhelming feeling of claustrophobia, one which I am still finding hard to dispel. Although I can't quite understand why I should feel this way, every day

I have the constant need to flee my apartment as soon as I awaken.

It's not that it holds any heart-wrenching memories of Tony, because it doesn't. Friends for a long time though we were, we did not become emotionally involved with each other until twelve months ago; besides which, he hardly ever spent any time at my place, being constantly on the move for work, or in London, where he lived.

I was aware that my urge to get out had more to do with my own innermost feelings of despair than anything else; I've been unnaturally agitated inside and filled with a weird restlessness that propels me into the street, and as early as dawn sometimes.

The streets of Paris are my solace, and part of my healing process physically in a very real sense. First, the constant walking every day is therapeutic because it strengthens my damaged leg; second, being outside in the open air, among crowds of people bustling about their business, somehow soothes my troubled soul, lifts my spirits, and helps to diminish my depression.

Today, as usual, I got up early. After coffee and a croissant at my local café on the corner, I set off at a steady pace, taking my long daily walk. It's become a ritual for me, I suppose, something I find so very necessary. At least for the time being. Soon I hope my leg will be completely healed so that I can return to work.

It was a Friday morning in the middle of September, a lovely, mild day. The ancient buildings were already acquiring a burnished sheen in the bright sunlight, and the sky was an iridescent blue above their gleaming rooftops. It was a golden day, filled with crystalline light, and a soft breeze blew across the river Seine. My heart lifted with a little rush of pleasure, and for a moment, grief was held at bay.

Paris is the only place I've ever wanted to live, and for as long as I can remember; I fell in love with it as a child, when I first came on a trip with my grandparents, Cecelia and Andrew Denning. I used to tell Tony that it was absolutely essential to my well-being, and if Jake happened to be present, he would nod, agreeing, and pointing out that he lived there for the same reason as I did.

I always thought it odd that Tony would merely frown, looking baffled, as if he didn't understand what I meant. Tony was born in London, and it was there that he lived all his life. And whenever the three of us would have this discussion about the merits of the two cities, he would laugh and shake his head. "London is essential to me because it's a man's city," he would remark, and wink at Jake.

I had supposed he was alluding to those very British private clubs for men filled with old codgers reading *The Times,* the male-dominated pubs, cricket at Lords, football at Wembley, and the Savile Row tailors who appealed to his desire for sartorial elegance when not on the battlefront covering wars. He had never really discussed it in depth, but then, he had been like that about a lot of things, an expert at brushing certain matters aside if he didn't want to talk about them.

Thoughts of Tony intruded, swamped me, instantly washing away the mood of a few moments earlier, when I had felt almost happy again. I came to a stop abruptly, leaned against the wall of a building, taking deep breaths, willing the sudden surge of anguish to go away. Eventually it did recede, became less acute, and taking control of my swimming senses, I walked on purposefully.

It struck me as being rather odd, the way I vacillated between bouts of mind-boggling pain at his loss and the most savage attacks of anger.

There were those tear-filled days when I believed I would never recover from his death, which had been so sudden, so tragic, when grief was like an iron mantle weighting me down, bringing me to my knees. At these times it seemed that my sorrow was unendurable.

Miraculously, though, my heartbreak would inexplicably wash away quite unexpectedly, and I would feel easier within myself, in much better spirits altogether, and I was glad of this respite from pain, this return to normality. I was almost like my old self.

It was then that the anger usually kicked in with a vengeance, shaking me with its intensity. I was angry because Tony was dead when he should have been alive, and I blamed him for his terrible recklessness, the risks he had taken in Kosovo, risks that had ultimately cost him his life. Unnecessary risks, in my opinion.

Destiny, I thought, and came to a halt. As I stood there in the middle of the street, frowning to myself, I suddenly understood with the most stunning rush of clarity that if character is destiny, then it had been Tony's fate to die in the way he had. Because of his character . . . and who and what he was as a man.

II

After crossing the Place Saint-Michel, I made my way toward the Rue de la Huchette and walked down that narrow street, which long ago had been immortalized in a book by the American writer Elliot Paul, very aptly entitled *A Narrow Street.* After reading the book, I had been drawn to this particular area of Paris, and for the three years I was a student at the Sorbonne I had lived right there on the street, in a quaint little hotel called the Mont Blanc.

The hotel came into my line of vision almost immediately, and as I strolled past, I glanced up at the room that had been mine, and I remembered those days in a swirl of unexpected nostalgia.

Thirteen years ago now. Not so long really. But in certain ways they seemed far, far away, light-years away, those youthful days when things had been infinitely simpler in my life.

So much had happened to me in the intervening years; I had lived a lifetime in them, and I had become a woman. A grown-up woman, mature and experienced.

Glancing across the street, I eyed the El Djazier, the North African restaurant that had once been my local hangout . . . what a habitué I had been of that strange little nightspot full of colorful characters.

Sandy Lonsdale, an English writer who had lived in the hotel at the same time as I did, had constantly predicted I would disappear one night, never to be seen again, whipped off to some disreputable brothel in Casablanca or Tangier by one of the seedy guys who lurked in the restaurant most nights.

But of course that had never happened, the seedy men being perfectly innocuous in reality, and I had taken enormous pleasure in teasing Sandy about his vivid imagination and its tendency to work overtime. "You'll make a great novelist," I used to tell him, and he had merely grinned at me and retorted, "You'd better be right about that."

On numerous occasions I had taken Tony and Jake there, and they had enjoyed it as much as me, their taste buds tantalized by the couscous and the piquant Moroccan sauce called Harissa, not to mention the erotic belly dancers in their flimsy costumes and tinkling ankle bracelets.

On these evenings, when we were back in Paris for a bit of relaxation and rest from covering wars, Jake would usually invite us to one of the jazz joints after dinner at the El Djazier. There were several spots on the Rue de la Huchette, where many of the greats of American jazz came to play or listen to others play.

Jake was a jazz aficionado and could happily spend long hours in these smoke-filled places, sipping a cognac and tapping his foot, lost in the music, lost to the world for a short while.

I ambled up the street and glanced around as I walked. I never tired of wandering around this particular part of Paris, which I knew so well. It was full of picturesque cobblestone streets, ancient buildings, Greek and North African restaurants, art galleries, and small shops selling colorful wares from some of the most exotic places in the world. Aside from anything else, it brought back memories of the time I had attended the Sorbonne, such a happy time for me, perhaps the happiest of my life.

III

My grandfather Andrew Denning had been alive when I decided I wanted to study in Paris. Later, he had often come here to visit me, defying my mother, who had forbidden any contact between us once I had made the decision. My mother was angry with me because I had chosen to study in France, although I never understood her attitude, since she had been indifferent to me from the day I was born. So why did it matter where I studied?

Grandfather Denning didn't have much time for his daughter-in-law; in fact, he privately thought she was a cold, unfeeling woman, and he had never paid any attention to what she said. He had reminded her that I was the only daughter of his only son, and his only female grandchild, and he was damned if he would let anyone stand in the way of his visiting me and whenever he wished to do so. As an afterthought, he had added in no uncertain terms that no one told him what to do or how to spend his money, least of all his son's wife. And that had been that, apparently. Grandfather had told me all about it later; we kept no secrets from each other. I thought of him as being more like a pal than a grandfather, perhaps because he was so young in appearance and had the most youthful of spirits.

To my mother's great consternation and frustration, she had not been able to influence him one iota, let alone control him, and she had apparently ranted and raved about her father-in-law for months after their original confrontation. This I had heard from my brother, the family gossip, who only reinforced my opinion of him when he became the sidekick to a gossip columnist. According to Donald, my mother had screamed blue murder, but my father had, as was customary, remained totally mute. For years I suspected that this state of being had afflicted Father since the day he entered into so-called wedded bliss with Margot Scott. Until the day he died he hardly ever said a word, perhaps because he couldn't get one in edgewise.

It was my grandfather who supported me financially and morally once I had decided to study in Paris, and in those days he had been my best friend.

My mother had never forgiven him, or me, for that matter. But then, I believe my mother has never forgiven me for being born, although I don't know why this should be so. However, from that day to this she has never shown me any love or given me much thought. It is not that Margot Scott Denning doesn't like children; everyone knows she dotes on my sibling,

Donald the Great, as I used to call him when we were children. It is I she has an aversion to, whom she tends to avoid most of the time, and whenever she possibly can.

Grandfather and I were always aware of that, and he had often expressed concern about the situation. I had taught myself not to care. I still don't. He has been dead for five years now, and I still miss him. He gave me the only sense of family I ever had; certainly my parents never managed to induce that sentiment in me. Quite the opposite. I wished Grandfather were here with me now, walking these streets; I always found such comfort in his words, his understanding, his kindness, and his wisdom. He was the only person other than Grandma and Tony who had loved me. Now all three of them were gone.

Was that the reason I had chosen to walk around this particular area today? Because he had been so partial to it, and because it made my happy memories of him and of our time spent together here so vivid in my mind's eye?

"Teaching you Paris," Grandfather used to say as he took me around the different arrondissements of the city. Gradually, I had come to learn about many of the great buildings, the architects who had brought them into being, the historical significance of each one, not to mention the many different architectural features.

When I reached the top of the Rue de la

Huchette, I crossed into the Rue de la Bûcherie, which was more like an open square than a street. It had flower-filled little gardens fronting onto cafés lined up along one side of the square, and overshadowing them was the Cathedral of Notre Dame. This magnificent edifice outlined against the azure September sky stood on the Île de la Cité, one of the islands in the Seine, and on the spur of the moment I decided to go over to the cathedral. I had not visited it in years. In fact, the last time I had been there had been with my grandfather.

Andrew Denning had enjoyed an extremely successful career as an architect in New York, and he had had an extraordinary eye for beautiful buildings, whether modern or ancient. In particular, he had been an admirer of the cathedrals of Europe, forever marveling at their majesty and grandeur, the soaring power inherent in them and in their design and structure.

And so whenever he came to visit me in Paris he made a point of taking me on excursions to see some of his favorites—Rouen and Chartres in France, and, across the English Channel, St. Paul's and Winchester; and, up in Yorkshire, Ripon Cathedral and York Minster, the latter being my own favorite. It is from my grandfather that I have inherited my eye, which serves me so well as a photographer; that's what I think anyway, and as it happens, I've also grown to love cathedrals as much as he did.

Within minutes I was across the bridge and standing in front of the three huge portals that lead into Notre Dame. I chose to enter through the one on the right because the door stood ajar, beckoning to me, I thought.

Once inside, I caught my breath and stood perfectly still . . . I was utterly mesmerized. I had forgotten how awe-inspiring this place was, with its beauty and size; its absolute stillness overwhelmed me.

There were hardly any tourists there, the cathedral was practically empty, and as I began to slowly walk down the center aisle, my footsteps echoed hollowly against the stone floor.

Glancing up, I gaped at the apse, that enormous, intricate, domed ceiling, flung so high, it seemed to disappear into infinity. "Soaring up to heaven," Grandfather used to say of it.

He and I had visited many of the smaller churches in Paris and the surrounding countryside, and we had taken part in the services as best we were able. We both spoke enough French to follow the Catholic service; being Protestant, we were not exactly familiar with the rituals, but somehow we managed. We also made trips to other European countries, as well as to North Africa and Israel, where we visited mosques and synagogues. Grandfather was fascinated by places of worship whatever the religion being practiced in them.

I heard his voice reverberating in my head: "It doesn't matter whose house you sit in, Val, as long as you love God." He had once remarked to me, "In my Father's house there are many mansions: if it were not so I would have told you. I go to prepare a place for you." With those words of St. John's Gospel ringing in my ears, I continued down the aisle and took a chair, sat staring up at the high altar in front of me.

Sunlight was filtering in through the many windows above the altar. It was a light that subtly changed color as it seeped in through the stained glass panes in those breathtaking windows, changing from blue to green to pearl, and then to a soft yellow and a lovely lambent rose.

It was the most tranquil light that seemed to tremble visibly on the air, and dust motes rose up into the shafts of sunlight. The peacefulness was a balm, and how cool it was within these thick and ancient stone walls. Cool, restful, restorative, a welcome refuge, far away from the turbulence and violence of the world I lived in when I was working.

I closed my eyes, let myself fall down into myself, and eventually, as was inevitable in this quiet place of worship, I began to think of Tony, of his death, and of the future. And I asked myself yet again, for the umpteenth time, how I was going to go on without him, how I would manage without him by my side. I had no answers.

It seemed to me that all of my energy ebbed away, leaving me deflated, and I just sat there, collapsed in the chair, with my eyes closed, for the longest time. I had no appointments, nowhere to go, no one waiting for me or worrying where I was. Time passed. And after a long while, just sitting there in the silence of the cathedral, I heard my grandfather speaking to me as if from a great distance. His voice was so very clear when he said, "Always remember this, Val, God never gives us a burden that is too heavy to carry."

IV

The phone was ringing loudly as I let myself into my apartment an hour later. I snatched it up and exclaimed, "Hullo?" only to hear the receiver clattering down at the other end.

Too late, I had gotten it on the last ring, and sticking out my good leg, I slammed the front door shut with my foot. Swinging around, I went into my tall, narrow kitchen, a place I'd always enjoyed but which I had not occupied very much of late. I like cooking, in fact, it's a sort of hobby of mine, a way to be creative, to relax when I'm back from covering wars and the like. But because of my grief and misery, I had abandoned the kitchen, having no desire to be in it to cook only for myself.

I had hardly eaten a thing these last few weeks, and I had lost weight. But suddenly, today, I felt really hungry and I opened the refrigerator, frowned at the contents, or, rather, the lack of them, and swiftly closed the door in frustration. Of course there was nothing worthwhile to eat in there, I hadn't been shopping. I would have to make do with a mug of green tea and a couple of cookies, and later I would go to the corner store and pick up a few things for dinner.

A moment or two after I'd put the kettle on, the phone began to shrill once again, and I lurched toward it, grabbed hold of it before the caller had a chance to hang up. As I spoke, I heard Jake's voice at the other end.

"Where've you been all day?" He sounded both put out and worried at the same time.

"Walking. I've been out walking, Jake."

"Again. I can't believe it. I bet if someone locked you up in an empty room and told you to draw a detailed map of Paris and its environs, you could do so without batting an eyelid. And all from memory."

"Yes, I guess I could. But you do a lot of walking too, so why are you picking on me?"

"I'm not. I called to invite you to dinner tonight. I haven't seen you for a week. Too long, Val."

"True, and I'd love to have dinner. I'll cook

for you," I said. Hearing his voice had instantly cheered me up, and I'd missed him while he had been in the South; anyway, he was my biggest fan when it came to my culinary skills.

"That's a great offer, but I prefer to take you out . . . it's much more relaxing for you."

"Okay, it's a deal."

Jake cleared his throat several times, and his voice was a bit more subdued when he added, "I had a call from London today. From Tony's photo agency. About a memorial service for him. They've planned one and they want us to come."

This news so startled me, so threw me off balance, I was rendered silent, and when I finally did speak, all I could manage was a weak "Oh."

"We have to go, Val."

"I'm not sure . . . I don't think I'm up to it," I began, and faltered, unable to continue.

"We were his closest friends," Jake countered. "His intimates. His comrades-in-arms, he called us."

"We were, I know, but it's hard for me."

Jake fell silent, then after a moment or two he said softly, "The whole world is aware that we were with him in Kosovo when he was killed . . . that *we* came out alive. How will it look if we don't show?"

I stood there, gripping the receiver, utterly mute, as if I'd been struck dumb, shaking like the proverbial leaf as I weighed the odds. Should I risk Jake's disapproval, everyone's disapproval, by not going? Or should I go and expose myself to a large amount of pain and heartache? And could I handle that? I just didn't know. For weeks I had tried very hard to get my turbulent feelings under control, and I was not so sure I could face a memorial service. Not now. It would open up so much and it would just . . . do me in emotionally.

"Are you still there, Val?" Jake asked, cutting into my swirling thoughts.

"Yes."

"You seem reluctant to go."

"I'm not . . . I'm just . . . thinking it through."

He said nothing. I could hear him waiting at the other end of the line, could practically hear him breathing.

Finally, realizing he was waiting for me to say something, I muttered, "I couldn't bear to hear the world eulogizing him. . . . It would be so painful for me, I'd be in floods of tears through the entire service. I'm trying to come to grips with my grief."

"I understand what you're saying. If you want to know the truth, I'm not so keen to live through it myself. But we don't have a choice. And Tony would want us to be present."

"I guess he would . . ." My voice trailed off.

"We'll talk about it tonight."

"All right," I agreed, my heart sinking.

"Good girl. I'll be there about eight to pick you up. See ya, Kid."

He had hung up before I could say another word, and for a second or two I stood there, clutching the receiver, chastising myself under my breath. I was so dumb. Absolutely stupid. I ought to have realized that Tony's agency would hold a memorial service for their fallen colleague, one who had been their biggest star—and their hero. If only I'd thought it through properly, and earlier, I would have been far better prepared.

I banged the receiver into the cradle and stared at the kettle absently, thinking it was taking a long time to boil. I turned up the gas automatically and let out a heavy sigh. I'd been caught off guard. And now there was no way out. I would have to go to the memorial service for appearance's sake. And I could easily come face-to-face with *her*.

That was it, of course. That was at the root of my discomfort and reluctance to go to the memorial. I didn't want to run into Fiona Hampton. Tony's ex-wife. It struck me then that it was unlikely she would be there, in view of their recent divorce and the searing bitterness that had existed between them. Of course she wouldn't go to hear him lovingly eulogized by his friends and colleagues. That would be out of character. She was a hard woman whose contentiousness had driven him away from her and the marriage, and sympathy and compassion did not exist in her makeup.

Remembering how unpleasant things had been between them convinced me I was right and eased my anxiety about going myself. I made the mug of green tea, took out a packet of cookies, and stood at the counter, munching on a couple and sipping the tea, suddenly feeling more relaxed.

Of course, I had no way of knowing that indeed Fiona would attend the memorial, and that encountering her would change my life irrevocably, and so profoundly, it would never be the same again.

Chapter 3

I

After my long morning walks through the streets, I always felt tired in the afternoons and invariably had to rest. Today was no exception; in fact, I felt more fatigued than usual. I went into my bedroom, took off my cotton trousers and shirt, slipped into a dressing gown, and lay down on the bed.

My head had barely touched the pillow, when the phone next to my ear shrilled loudly. I reached for it and pushed myself up on the pillows as I said, "Hullo?"

"It's me, Val," Mike Carter announced in his warm, affectionate midwestern voice. He was the head of the Paris bureau of Gemstar, one of the founders actually, and a very old, very dear friend. "How're you feeling, honey?"

"I'm fine, Mike, thanks. A lot better. Well, coping at least. What's happening?"

"Oh just the usual stuff . . . you know, wars, terrorist attacks, hijackings, serial murders, famine, earthquakes, floods. Disasters by the cartload, in other words." He laughed, but it was a hollow laugh. "I guess one day the world will blow itself up, but in the meantime, what's happening is what I call the small stuff." He chuckled again in that macabre way of his and asked, "Know what I mean?"

"I do," I answered, laughing with him. Mike's black sense of humor appealed to me, as did his penchant for practical jokes. But these things aside, he had always been my strongest ally, a great supporter of mine ever since I'd joined the agency seven years ago. Over the years a close friendship had developed between us. My grandfather had been very taken with him, and Mike had been smitten in much the same way, and the two had remained good friends until the day Grandfather died.

Mike went on. "I'm not calling to lure you back into the fray, Val. Whenever you want, come on in. But take as much time as you need. It's your call. We all understand how you feel, me most especially."

"I know that. Maybe in a couple of weeks," I

murmured, and surprised myself with this answer. Two weeks was not so far away; I'd actually planned on taking three months off, and here I was, shortening it. I was amazed at my unexpected response to him.

"Well, that's great!" Mike said. "You're sorely missed around here. But listen, sweetie, the reason I called is because Qemal, the brother of Ajet, got in touch with the agency today. He asked for you, so he was put through to me. He wanted you to know that Ajet's safe. In Macedonia."

"I'm so glad to hear that!" I cried, genuinely relieved and pleased to have news of the young Kosovar at last. What had happened to him, what his fate had been, had troubled me and Jake for weeks. When we'd attempted to reach his brother, there was never any reply at his Paris apartment. "Jake and I thought Ajet had been killed, Mike," I explained. "Where has he been all these weeks? Did his brother say?"

"Yes, he told me Ajet had been wounded the day he was with you outside Peć. Apparently he left the wood where he was waiting for you with the jeep once the fighting started. He actually went looking for the three of you, but he was shot before he could make contact. After he was injured, he was left for dead in the streets, but later he was rescued by some of the locals. They went out into the countryside a couple of days later and found soldiers from the K.L.A. who were able to get medical help for Ajet. The Kosovar soldiers then took him to Albania, God help him, I've heard the hospital conditions there are primitive. Eventually Ajet got to Macedonia, although his brother didn't say how. You'd written the agency number on a bit of paper and given it to him, and the kid kept it. He asked Qemal to let us know he was safe. He especially wanted you to know that, Val."

"I'm glad he's safe, and recovered. And it was a fluke he made it."

"I know, I know. Everything's in the lap of the gods in the long run. That's my belief, at any rate. As Bogie once said, it's a cockeyed world we live in." Mike half sighed, half coughed, and hurried on. "I gotta go, honey. Let's talk next week, or when you feel like it. I'm here if you need me, whenever you need me, day or night. Just give me a shout and I'll be there."

"Thanks, Mike, for everything, and especially for caring about me, and for your friendship. . . ." I found myself choking up and left the sentence unfinished.

"Feel better soon," he murmured into the phone.

We hung up and I lay back against the pillows. Mike Carter was one of the good guys, and he'd seen it all. After knocking around the world as a photojournalist, he and several of his colleagues had founded Gemstar, an agency very similar to

Magnum, which had been started years before, in the late 1940s, by Robert Capa.

When Mike's wife Sarah had been killed in a freak automobile accident outside Paris, he had given himself a desk job at Gemstar in order to stay put so that he could bring up his two young children himself, with the help of a nanny. He was no stranger to sudden death, to unspeakable loss. And grief and sorrow were old companions of his, as I well knew. But he somehow managed to hide his pain behind the gruff heartiness and a genuine warmth. Still, I knew how much he had suffered after Sarah's unexpected and untimely death ten years ago.

Now my thoughts turned to Ajet and that fateful day near Peć, the memory of it still terribly vivid in my mind. Almost immediately, I pushed the violent images away, smothered them. I closed my eyes, needing desperately to sleep. That was the ultimate refuge from heartache. Very simply, I wanted to blot out everything, everyone, the whole damn world.

II

I must have dozed off and slept for a very long time, because when I awakened with a start, the room was no longer filled with the bright sunlight of early afternoon.

Gray shadows lurked everywhere, curled around the bookshelves and the big Provençal armoire, slid across the ceiling and spilled down onto the walls.

The overwhelming grayness gave my normally cheerful bedroom a gloomy look, and involuntarily I shivered. Someone walked over my grave, I thought, as gooseflesh speckled my arms, and then I couldn't help wondering why I'd thought of that particular and rather morbid analogy.

Glancing at the bedside clock, I saw that it was almost six. I couldn't believe I'd been asleep for over four hours. Slipping off the bed, I went and looked out the big bay window.

The beautiful Paris sky of earlier was cloud-filled now and darkening rapidly, the sunny blue entirely obscured. Rain threatened. Perhaps there would be a storm. I turned on the lamp that stood on the desk, and bright light flooded across the photograph of Tony in its silver frame. It had been taken by Jake the previous year, when we had been on vacation together in southern France. I stared down at it for a moment, and then I turned away, filled with sadness.

Sometimes I couldn't bear to look at it. He was so full of life in this particular shot, his hair blowing in the wind, his teeth very white and gleaming in his tanned face, those merry black eyes narrowed against the sunlight as he squinted back at the camera.

Tony stood on the deck of the sloop on which we were sailing that vacation, the white masts above him billowing out in the breeze. How carefree he looked, bare-chested in his white tennis shorts. A man in his prime, obviously loving that he was so virile. You could see this just by looking at the expression on his face, the wide, confident smile on his mouth.

I sighed under my breath and reached out to steady myself against the desk, and then I moved slowly across the floor, retreating from the window area.

His son Rory had taken possession of Tony's body once it had arrived in England, and the boy had taken it on to Ireland. To County Wicklow. There Tony had been buried next to his parents.

Rory would be at the memorial service, wouldn't he?

That question hovered around in my head for a moment. Of course he would, I eventually answered myself. And so perhaps I would finally get to meet the son Tony had had such pride in and loved so much.

I lay down on the bed again and curled up in a ball, thoughts of Tony uppermost once more. Absently, I twisted his ring on my finger, then glanced down at it. A wide gold band, Grecian in design, set with aquamarines.

"The color of your eyes," he'd said the day he'd chosen it, not so long ago. "They're not blue, not gray, not green, but pale, pale turquoise. You have sea eyes, Val, eyes the color of the sea."

Pushing my face in the pillow, I forced back the tears that were welling suddenly.

"Mavourneen mine," I heard him whisper against my cheek, and I sighed again as I felt his hand touching my face, my neck, and then smoothing down over my breast. . . .

Snapping my eyes wide open, I sat up with a jolt, got off the bed, hurried into the bathroom. Pressing my face against the glass wall of the shower stall, I told myself I must pull myself together, must stop thinking about him in *that* way . . . stop thinking about him sexually. I've got to get over him, he's not coming back. He's dead. And buried. Gone from this life. But I knew I couldn't help myself. I knew that his memory would be always loitering in my mind, lingering in my heart.

III

I took off my dressing gown and the rest of my clothes and stepped into the shower, let the hot water sluice down over my body, and then I dumped loads of shampoo on top of my head and thoroughly washed my hair.

After stepping out of the shower and toweling myself dry, I wrapped a smaller towel in a turban around my head. And then I examined my wound. I did this every day. There was a funny puckering around it, but that would go away eventually; that's what my doctor here in Paris had told me.

I'd been very fortunate, he'd explained when I'd first gone to see him, in that the bullet had missed muscle and bone and gone right through flesh. Where it had exited, it had left a gaping hole originally, and the main problem for the doctors in Belgrade had been picking out the bits of cloth from my clothes that had been blown into the open wound. They had apparently done an excellent job, according to Dr. Bitoun, and I had healed well.

There was no question about it in my mind, luck had been running with me that day. Just as it had with Jake. The two of us had somehow been protected.

IV

The storm broke as I finished dressing.

Thunder and lightning rampaged across the sky, and I turned on additional lights in my bedroom before going into the living room.

A master switch controlled all the lamps in

there, and a second after I'd hit it with my finger, the room was bathed in a lambent glow. I glanced around, my eyes taking in everything.

Although I knew this room so well, it always gave me pleasure whenever I looked at it. My grandfather had put it together, created the decorative scheme, and his choices in furniture, all gifts from him to me, were superb. Even the lamps and paintings had been his selections, and the room had a cohesion and a quiet beauty that was very special.

Janine, the wonderfully efficient and motherly Frenchwoman who looked after the apartment—and me when I was in it—had been very visible all day yesterday. She had cleaned and polished and fussed around in general, and had even arrived bearing a lovely gift . . . the masses of pink roses that she had arranged in various bowls around the living room.

And tonight the room literally shone from her efforts. The antique wood pieces were warm and mellow in the lamplight, gleamed like dark ripe fruit; how beautifully they stood out against the dark pink walls, while the silk-shaded porcelain lamps threw pools of soft light onto their glistening surfaces.

Like the rest of the apartment, the floor in the living room was of highly polished wood and left bare, as the floors in the other rooms were. The latter were decorated more simply, since I'd done them myself; it was Grandfather's room, as I called it, that looked the best.

After admiring it from the doorway for a moment longer, I then stepped inside, went over and straightened a few cushions on the deep-rose linen-covered sofa near the fireplace before bending over to sniff Janine's flowers. For once they had a perfume, which was unusual these days. Most bought flowers had no scent at all.

I went into the kitchen, checked that there were bottles of white wine in the refrigerator, and returned to my bedroom. For a minute or two I studied myself in the long mirror on a side wall, thinking that I looked much better than I had for days. Healthy, in fact. But that was merely an illusion, one very cleverly created by my artifice with cosmetics; a golden-tinted foundation camouflaged my deathly pallor, hid the dark smudges under my eyes. The latter I'd enhanced with a touch of eye shadow and mascara, while a hint of pink blush and pink lipstick helped to bring a little additional life to my wan face.

The real truth was that I'd looked quite ill for the past week, haggard, white-faced, and red-eyed from crying, and I hadn't wanted Jake to see me looking that way tonight. He worried enough about me as it was.

I wasn't sure where we were going to dinner, so I'd chosen one of my basic outfits, composed of black gabardine pants, a white silk shirt, and a black blazer. My blond-streaked hair was pulled back in a ponytail, and, as I regarded myself objectively, I thought: plain Jane and then some.

Turning around, I went to the desk, opened the drawer, and took out a pair of small pearl earrings. I was putting them on, when the doorbell rang.

I hurried into the hall, eager to see Jake, who had been gone for the past week.

"Aren't you a sight for sore eyes," he drawled when I flung open the door to let him in.

"Likewise," I answered, and we stood there, staring at each other.

Then he reached out eagerly and pulled me into his arms, enveloping me in a tight bear hug. And he held me so close to him, I was momentarily startled.

V

When Jake finally let go of me, he gave me an odd little smile that seemed a bit self-conscious to me. Then he abruptly swung around and closed the front door.

For a moment I believed that he, too, was startled by the fervor and length of his embrace, and then I changed my mind. He was my best friend and we had been close for years, so why wouldn't he hug me excessively when he'd just returned

from a trip? And especially under the circumstances.

"It's not raining," I murmured.

"No, it's not," he answered, turning to look at
me. "The storm seems to have blown away before
it got started."

I nodded and headed for the kitchen to open a
bottle of his favorite Pouilly-Fuissé.

Jake followed me.

"I'll do that," he said when I took the bottle of
white wine from the refrigerator. He opened a
drawer where he knew I kept the bar utensils and
found a corkscrew. While he deftly pulled the
cork, I took two wineglasses out of the cupboard
and set them on the counter next to him, and a
second later he was pouring wine for us.

He handed me a glass, and I said, "I've got
good news, Jake. Mike heard from Ajet's brother.
Qemal told him Ajet is safe and well in
Macedonia."

"Hey, that's great!" he exclaimed, and clinked
his glass to mine. "Here's to Ajet. Thank God he
made it okay."

I nodded. "To Ajet."

We took our drinks into the living room,
where Jake lowered himself into a chair near the
fireplace and I sat down in the corner of the sofa,
as I always did.

"What's the full story?" Jake asked, peering
across at me over the rim of his glass.

After I told him the whole story, I settled back, studying Jake, thinking how well he looked after a week's rest in the South. He'd asked me to go with him to Saint-Jean-Cap-Ferrat, but I'd declined, and I suddenly wondered if that might have been a mistake on my part. A vacation would have obviously done me good. His few days in the sun had given him a golden tan, turned his streaky hair more blond than ever, and he was in glowing health. Tonight he was wearing a blue cotton shirt with his gray sport jacket and slacks, and his eyes looked more vividly blue than ever.

"You're staring at me," he said. "What's wrong?" That was Jake, who was always questioning me about everything in my life. It had been that way since we'd first met in Beirut.

"Nothing's wrong," I replied at last. "It's just that you look in such great shape, I think I ought to have accepted your invitation."

"Yes, you should have," he quickly replied. He spoke softly enough, but I detected a certain undertone of vehemence in his voice. He took a swallow of white wine and then sat nursing his drink, staring down into the glass, his face thoughtful.

When he looked up at me, he said, "You needed a holiday, and even though you think you look great, you don't really. The makeup doesn't deceive *me*. And you've lost weight."

So much for my efforts with the cosmetic pots, I thought, and said, "Black makes me look thin."

"It's me you're talking to," he answered. "I know you better than everyone, even better than you know yourself." He put the glass down on the coffee table and seemed about to get up but suddenly leaned back against the rose-colored-linen cushions and closed his eyes.

After a couple of minutes, I ventured to ask, "Are you feeling all right, Jake?"

Opening his eyes, he said, "Yep. But I worry about you, Val."

"Oh, please don't," I said. "I'm fine. I haven't lost a pound," I lied. *"Nothing. Nada. Zilch."*

He shook his head. "Has Mike said anything about your going back to work?"

"He said I was welcome back anytime I felt like coming in, but to take my time, that it was my call."

"The sooner you get back to the agency, the better, in my opinion. You need to be busy, occupied, Val, not walking around the streets of Paris every day and sitting here alone in the apartment afterward. I know you're suffering. I am too. Tony was my best buddy, but we've got to go on, that's what he would want."

"I'm trying hard, I really am, Jake. And the walking helps. I'm not sure why, but it does."

"You're less alone when you're out there in the streets. They make you feel more alive because they're full of life, people, traffic, noise, activity. The streets are the world. Did I ever tell you about John Steinbeck and what he did when he heard that Robert Capa had been killed in Indochina?"

I frowned. I wasn't certain whether he'd told me or not, and yet at the back of my mind I thought that perhaps he had. Or was it Tony who had told me? Certainly we all revered Capa, the greatest war photographer who had ever lived. I said, "I'm not sure, you might have. But tell me again."

"Capa was killed in 1954, on May twenty-fifth, actually. And of course within hours, news of his death spread around the world. Steinbeck, who was a good friend of Capa's, was in Paris when he heard. He was so shaken up, he went out and walked the streets for fourteen hours straight. I guess he just couldn't believe it. And he couldn't sit still. He had to be on the move. And you're doing something very similar, but you're doing it every day, Val."

"No, I'm not, I don't walk the streets for fourteen hours!"

Jake sighed and said nothing, just gave me one of those penetrating looks of his that always made me reexamine everything I said to him. I shrugged, and finally admitted, "Okay, you're right, I guess I am doing the same thing. And you did tell me the story. It was on one of those days when you were ticked off with Tony because you thought he was too reckless. You were comparing him to Capa."

"No, I wasn't." Jake sat up straighter and gave me a hard stare. "Capa wasn't reckless in the way that Tony was. Those who knew Capa always said he was very cautious. Don't forget, he was an expert when it came to taking *calculated* risks. When he went to Indochina, it was his fifth war, and only a photojournalist of his great experience would know how to properly calculate when something was truly dangerous or not. From what I know about him, he measured the risks, especially when he had to walk across exposed areas, and he was always cautious, did not take risks unnecessarily. But if he saw the possibility of a great photograph and there was a calculated risk, then he took the risk. Tony just rushed in without—" He cut himself off and took a swallow of his wine, obviously feeling disloyal.

"Without thinking," I finished for him, stood up, and headed toward the kitchen.

"Where are you going?"

"To get the bottle of wine," I answered. When I came back, I filled his goblet, and then mine, and put the bottle down on the glass coffee table. "What about the memorial service?" I said, getting right to the heart of the matter. "Do you know when it is?"

"Next week. On Tuesday."

"I see. Where's it being held?"

"At the Brompton Oratory at eleven o'clock."

I was silent, looked down at the drink in my hands.

Jake said, "I've booked us in at the Milestone in Kensington. I know you like that hotel."

I nodded. He had surprised me with the information about the memorial. Events seemed to be moving more quickly than I'd anticipated, and I wasn't prepared at all. Only four days away. And then I'd be sitting there among all of his friends and colleagues, many of them my colleagues, in fact, and listening to the world talk about the man I was still grieving. I was suddenly appalled at the idea, and I sat back jerkily.

Jake was telling me something else, and I blinked and tried to concentrate on his words. He was saying, "I've spoken to Clee Donovan, and he's definitely going to be there, and I've left messages for the Turnley brothers. I know they'll come too if they're able."

I gazed at him blankly. I was feeling overwhelmed, and the prospect of going to London frightened me, filled me with tension and anxiety.

"What's wrong?" Jake asked.

I swallowed. "I'm . . . *dreading* it. There'll be so many people there," I said.

Jake made no response for a split second, and then he said, "I know what you mean, but let's be

glad and proud that so many people want to celebrate Tony's life. Because that's what a memorial is, Val, a celebration that the person was ever
alive. We are showing our gratitude that Tony
was born and was among us for as long as he
was."

"Yes."

He got up and came and sat next to me on the
sofa, took hold of my hand in the most loving
way. "I know it's tough . . . but he's dead, Val,
and you've got to accept that because—"

"I do," I cut in, my voice rising slightly.

"You've got to get yourself busy, start working.
You can't just . . . *drift* like this."

I stared at him. There he was, being bossy again
in that particular very macho way of his, and before
I could stop myself, I exclaimed, "You've not done
very much yourself since we came back from
Belgrade." And I could have bitten my tongue off
as soon as these dreadful words left my mouth; I
felt the flush of embarrassment rising from my
neck to flood my face.

"I wish I *had* been able to work, but my leg's
been pretty bad, and it's taken longer to heal than
I expected."

I was furious with myself. "I'm sorry, Jake, I
shouldn't have said that. I know your injuries
were more severe than mine. I'm so thought-
less."

"No, you're not, and, listen, let's make a pact

right now. To help each other go forward from where we are tonight, to get ourselves *moving*. Let's get started again, Val, let's pick up our cameras and get on with the job."

"I don't think I could go back to Kosovo."

"God, I wasn't meaning that! I don't want to go there either, but there are other things we can cover as well as wars."

"But we're best known for doing *that*," I reminded him.

"We can pick and choose our assignments, Val darling."

"I suppose so," I said.

Jake's eyes changed, turned darker blue, became reflective, and after a moment he adroitly changed the subject, remarked, "I've booked us on a plane to London on Monday night, okay?"

I simply nodded. Reaching for my glass, I took a sip of wine, then put the glass down and exclaimed with forced cheerfulness, "Tell me about your trip to the South of France."

"It was really great, Val, I wish you'd been with me—" Jake stopped and glanced at the phone as it started to ring.

I extracted my hand from his, got up, and went to the small desk on which it stood. "Hullo?"

VI

To my utter amazement, it was my brother, Donald, calling from New York, and I sat down heavily. I was flummoxed at hearing his voice, although after we'd exchanged greetings, I quickly pulled myself together and listened to what he had to say. Donald had always been tricky; deviousness was second nature to him.

Once he had finished his long speech, I said, "I just can't get away right now. I have to go to London next week, to a memorial service for a colleague, and I've also got loads of assignments stacking up."

I listened again as patiently as possible, and once more I said, "I'm sorry, I can't make the trip at this time. And listen, I really can't stay on the phone, I have guests and I've got to go. Thanks for calling." In his typical selfish fashion, determined to get all his points across, Donald went on blabbering at me, and short of banging the receiver down rudely, I had no option but to hear him out. When he finally paused for breath, I saw my opportunity and jumped in, repeated that I could not leave Europe under any circumstances for the time being. After saying a quick good-bye, I hung up.

Returning to the sofa, I sat down and said, "What a nerve! I can't believe he called me!"

"*Who?* And what did *he* call you about to get you so heated up?"

I turned toward Jake and explained. "It was my brother, Donald, calling from New York. To tell me my mother's not well. I should say *his* mother, because she's never been a mother to me. He wanted me to fly to New York. What cheek!"

"What's wrong with her? Is she very sick?"

I saw the frown, the baffled, almost confused look in his eyes, and I instantly realized that he'd never truly understood the relationship I'd had with my mother. But then, how could he understand when I couldn't either. From what Jake had told me about himself during the years we'd known each other, he came from a marvelously warm, loving, close-knit Jewish family, and he had been raised with a lot of love, understanding, and tremendous support from his parents, grandparents, and sisters. Whereas I'd been an orphan within the bosom of the Denning family. If it hadn't been for my father's parents, and Grandfather in particular, I would have withered away and died a young death from emotional deprivation. I asked myself then why I even thought in terms of having a relationship with Mother, because there had never been a relationship between us.

Iceberg Aggie, my grandfather had called her, and he had often wondered out loud to me what his son, my father, had ever seen in her. She had been very beautiful, of course. Still was, in all probability, although I hadn't seen her for years, not since my Beirut days.

Cutting into my thoughts, Jake asked me again, "Is your mother very ill, Val?"

"Donald didn't really explain. All he said was that she wasn't well and that she had told him she wanted to see me. He was relaying the message for her. But it can't be anything serious, or he would have told me. Donald's her pet, Jake, and very much under her thumb. Still, he never fools around with the truth when it comes to her well-being, or anything to do with her. He'd definitely have told me if there were real problems, I've no doubts about that."

"Maybe she wants to make amends," Jake suggested, and raised a brow as he added, "A rapprochement perhaps?"

I shook my head vehemently. "No way. She hasn't given a damn about me for thirty-one years. And I'm not going to New York."

"You could phone her."

"There's nothing to say, Jake. I told you about her years ago." I bit my lip and shook my head slowly. "I can't feel anything for a woman who has never felt anything for me."

Jake did not respond, and a long silence fell between us. But at last he said quietly and with some compassion, "Jesus, Val, I've never been able to understand her attitude toward you. It seems so unnatural for a mother not to love her child. I mean, what could she possibly have had against a newborn baby?"

"Beats me," I answered, and lifted my shoulders in a light shrug. "My Denning grandparents could never fathom it either, and as far as my mother's mother was concerned, I really didn't know her very well. My grandmother Violet Scott was an enigma to me, and she avoided me." I laughed harshly. "I used to think I was illegitimate when I was younger, and that my mother had become pregnant by another man before she married my father. But the dates were all wrong, they didn't jell, because she'd been married to my father for over a year when I was born."

"Maybe she slept with somebody else *after* she married your father," Jake suggested.

"I've thought of that as well, but I look too much like my grandmother Cecelia Denning when she was my age. Grandfather always commented on it."

I jumped up, opened the bottom desk drawer, and took out a cardboard box. Carrying it over to the sofa, I handed it to Jake. "Take a look at these," I said as I sat down next to him again.

He did so, staring for a few minutes at the old photographs of my grandmother that he had removed from the box. "Yes, you're a Denning all right, and a dead ringer for Cecelia. If it weren't for her old-fashioned clothes, she could be you as you are today." He shuffled through the other photographs in the box and chuckled. "I took this one!" he cried, waving a picture of me at me.

"Hey, let me see that!"

Still laughing, he handed it to me. I couldn't help smiling myself as I stared back at my own image. There I was in all my glory, standing outside the Commodore Hotel in Beirut, which is where I'd first set eyes on Jake. I was wearing my safari jacket and pants, and a collection of assorted cameras were slung haphazardly around my neck. It was obvious from my solemn expression that I took myself very seriously indeed. I was looking too self-important for words, and I gave a mock shudder. "I must have really fancied myself, but God, how awful I looked in those days."

"No, you were the most gorgeous thing on two legs I'd ever seen!" he exclaimed, and then stopped with suddenness; a startled expression crossed his face, as if he had surprised himself with his words. Clearing his throat, Jake returned to the conversation about my mother when he said, "It *is* very odd, Val, the way your mother has always treated you. With all of your accomplishments, she should be proud of you."

I sighed and made a small moue with my mouth. "It's a mystery. And one I have no intention of solving. I just can't be bothered. Now, how about taking me to dinner?"

Chapter 4

I

He drew to a standstill, but I didn't dare mention the limp or ask him how he felt, since he'd practically bitten my head off last night when I'd worried out loud about his wounds. Instead, I took hold of his arm, leaned into him, and kissed his cheek.

He gave me a faint smile and said, "Sorry I kept you waiting. Now we're running late, so we'd better get going."

The heavens opened up the moment Jake and I started to walk down the front steps of the hotel. The uniformed doorman hurried after us, wielding a large umbrella, and the two of us huddled under it as he led us to the waiting chauffeur-driven car Jake had ordered.

Once we were seated in the car, Jake said quietly, "It'll be all right, Val, try not to worry so much. It'll soon be over." Reaching out, he took hold of my hand and squeezed it reassuringly.

Being a very private person, especially when it came to my feelings, I'd never worn my emotions on my sleeve. And so I preferred to grieve for Tony in my own way, in the quiet of my home, not in a public place like the Brompton Oratory, although it was apparently a very beautiful Roman Catholic church—the Vatican of London, was the way someone had once described it to me years ago.

After a few minutes of staring out at the rain-sodden streets, as the car plowed its way through the heavy London traffic, I turned away from the window. Taking a cue from Jake, who was huddled in the corner of the seat with his eyes closed, I did the same thing. And I did not open them until the car slid to a standstill outside the church.

I sat up, smoothed one hand over my hair, which I'd sleeked back into a neat chignon, and straightened the jacket of my black suit. Then I took a deep breath and made up my mind to get through the service with quiet dignity, and as much composure as I could muster.

II

There was such a crowd of people going into the Brompton Oratory, it was hard to pick out friends and colleagues, or recognize anyone at a quick glance, for that matter. Everyone was dressed in black or other somber colors, and faces were etched with solemnity or sorrow, or both.

I had wisely clamped on a pair of sunglasses before exiting the car, and these made me feel as if I were incognito, and also protected, if not actually invisible. Nonetheless, despite the concealing dark glasses, I clutched Jake's arm as we mingled with the others filing sedately into the church.

We had just entered, when I felt someone behind me tap me lightly on the shoulder. I glanced around to find myself staring into the lovely face of Nicky Wells, the Paris bureau chief of ATN, the most successful of all the American cable news networks.

She and I had been together in Tiananmen Square in Beijing when the students had demonstrated against the Chinese government. That had been in 1989, and Nicky had been very helpful to me, since I was a beginner at the time. Fifteen years older than I, she had frequently taken me under her wing when I was such a novice.

We had remained friends ever since those early days and would occasionally socialize in Paris. Standing next to Nicky was her husband Clee

Donovan, another renowned war photographer, who had founded the agency Image some years ago. After the birth of their first child, Nicky had left the field as a war correspondent, deeming it wiser and safer to remain in Paris, covering local stories.

Jake and Clee had been good friends for many years, bonded as American expats, war photographers, and also as winners of the Robert Capa Award. This prize had been established in 1955, just after Capa's death, by *Life* magazine and the Overseas Press Club of America, and was awarded for "the best photographic reporting from abroad requiring exceptional courage and enterprise."

I knew that both men treasured this particular award as their proudest possession, Capa being a god to them, indeed to all of us in the business of being photojournalists covering wars.

The four of us hung back and spoke for a few moments about Tony and the sadness of the occasion, and then we arranged to make a date for dinner once we were all in Paris at the same time and for more than a couple of days.

As we began to move again, it was Clee who said, "We can't go to the wake afterward, Jake. Nicky and I have to head back to Paris immediately after the service ends. Are you going?" He looked from Jake to me.

I was so taken aback, I couldn't speak.

Jake cleared his throat, rather nervously I thought, and muttered something I didn't quite catch. Then he added, "We're in the same situation as you, Clee, we've got to get back too. Commitments to meet. But we might drop in for a few minutes, just to pay our respects."

Nothing else was said, since the four of us were suddenly being edged forward by the throngs pressing in behind us. I held on to Jake's hand, but in the crush we became separated from Nicky and Clee. And a second or two later we found ourselves being ushered down one of the aisles and into a pew by a church official.

Once we were seated, I grabbed Jake's arm ferociously, pulled him closer to me, and hissed, "You never told *me* anything about a wake."

"I thought it better not to, at least not until we got here," he admitted in a whisper.

"Who's giving the wake?" I demanded, but kept my voice low, endeavoring to curb my anger with him.

"Rory and Moira." He glanced at me swiftly, and again nervously cleared his throat. "I have the distinct feeling we won't be going, will we, Val?"

"You bet we won't," I snapped.

III

It was just as well other people came into our pew at this precise moment, because it prevented a continuation of our conversation, which could have easily spiraled out of hand.

I was furious with Jake for not telling me about the wake before then, not to mention irritated with myself for not anticipating that there would be one.

Tony, after all, had been Irish; on the other hand, a wake was usually held after a funeral and not a memorial, wasn't it? But the Irish were the Irish, with their own unique rules and rituals, and apparently a wake today was deemed in order, perhaps because the funeral had been held in Ireland. A wake was an opportunity for family and friends to get together, to comfort each other, to reminisce and remember, and to celebrate the one who had died. I was fully aware I wouldn't be able to face the gathering. Coming on top of the memorial, it would be too much for me to handle. What I couldn't understand was why Jake didn't realize this.

The sound of organ music echoed through the church, and I glanced around surreptitiously. Here and there among the crowd I caught glimpses of familiar faces—of those we had worked with over the past couple of years.

There were also any number of famous photographers and journalists, as well as a few celebrities, none of whom I knew, but instantly recognized because of their fame.

It was an enormous turnout, and Tony would have been gratified and pleased to know that so many friends and members of his profession had come to remember him, to honor him today.

I went on peering about me, hoping to see Rory. I felt quite positive that I would recognize him, since Tony had shown me so many photographs of his son, and of his daughter, Moira. They were nowhere to be seen, yet they had to be there. It struck me then that they would be sitting in the front pew, facing the altar, and that was out of my line of vision.

I sat back, bowed my head, and tuned myself in to the organ music. It was mournful but oddly soothing. I closed my eyes for a moment, and I was filled with relief that I was keeping my feelings in check. Well, for the moment at least.

When the organ music stopped, I opened my eyes at once and saw a priest standing in front of the altar. Immediately, he began to pray for Tony's soul, and we all knelt to pray with him and then we rose automatically and sat in our seats again. The priest continued to speak, this time about Tony and his life and all that he had done with it, and what he had accomplished.

And I took refuge by sinking down into myself, only half listening, absently drifting along with the proceedings, and endeavoring to remain uninvolved. Instinctively, I was scared to be a participant for fear of making a fool of myself by displaying too much emotion or weeping. Yet, tears had risen to the surface, were rapidly gathering behind my eyes, and I struggled desperately to control myself.

Soon the priest drew to a close and glided over to one side of the altar, and as if from far, far away a lone choirboy's voice rang out. It was an extraordinary voice, a high-pitched soprano that seemed to emanate from the very rafters of the church. The voice was so pure, so thrilling, it sent chills down my spine, and I sat up straighter and listened, enraptured.

The Minstrel Boy to the war is gone,
In the ranks of death you'll find him.
His father's sword he has girded on,
And his wild harp slung behind him . . .

Hearing the young choirboy singing so beautifully literally undid me. My mouth began to tremble uncontrollably, and as my face crumpled, I covered it with my hand. I shrank into the corner of the pew and discovered, a split second later, that I wasn't able to quell the tears. They rolled down my cheeks unchecked, slipping out from under my dark glasses and dropping down onto my hand, which was clutching the lapel of my jacket.

Jake put his arm around me, drew me closer, wanting to comfort me. Leaning against him gratefully, I swallowed hard, compressed my lips, and finally managed to get my swimming senses under control. The ballad came to an end at last, and that lilting soprano was finally silent. I hoped there would not be too much of this kind of thing, because I knew it would be unbearable for me.

But of course there was more. First Tony's brother Niall eulogized him; he was followed by Tony's oldest friend in the business, Eddie Marsden, the photo editor at Tony's agency, who spoke at length. And finally, it was Rory who was standing there in the pulpit, looking for all the world like a young Tony, strong and courageous in his grief. He had inherited his father's handsome Black Irish looks, his mannerisms, and his voice was so similar, it was like listening to Tony himself speaking.

Rory's words came truly from the heart, were eloquent and moving. He reminded us of Tony's great charm and his talent as a photographer, of his modesty and his lack of conceit, of his abhorrence of violence, his humanity, and his condemnation of the wars he covered. Rory talked of his father's Irish roots, his love of

Ireland and of family. He spoke so lovingly about his father, I felt the tears rising in my throat once more.

Rory went on. "He was too young a man to die . . . and yet he died doing what he loved the most, recording history in the making. And perhaps there's no better way to die than doing that, doing what you love the most. . . ."

But he could have lived a long life, I thought as young Rory's voice continued to wash over me. If he hadn't taken such terrible risks, none of us would be here today grieving over him. The instant these thoughts formed, I hated myself for thinking them. But it *was* the truth.

IV

Rory spotted us as we came slowly up the central aisle. He was waiting to speak to friends of his father's as they left the church, his eyes lit up as soon as they settled on Jake. Moira was positioned next to him, and on his other side stood a slender red-haired woman who even from this distance appeared to be quite beautiful. I knew at once it was Fiona, Tony's former wife. I began to shake inside.

Jake had no way of knowing I had been seized

by this internal shaking; nevertheless, he took hold of my elbow to steady me as though he did know.

Fiona was smiling warmly at him, obviously glad to see him, and it was apparent they were old friends. Moving toward her, Jake let go of me only when we came to a standstill in front of her. He wrapped his arms around Fiona and gave her a big bear hug, then hugged Moira and Rory.

Bringing me forward into the group, he introduced me. "Fiona, this is Val—Val Denning."

"Hello, Val," she said warmly in a soft voice, and she gave me a small half-smile and thrust out her hand.

I took hold of it and said "Fiona," and inclined my head, trying not to stare at her. She had a lovely face, with high cheekbones, a dimpled chin, and smooth brow. Her skin was that pale milky white that Irish redheads seem to be blessed with, but it was liberally peppered with freckles across the bridge of her nose and her cheekbones. Her hair, cut short and curly, was flame-colored and her eyes were dark, black as coal, in fact. A true Celt, I thought.

"I'm so glad you were able to come to London," Fiona was saying to Jake in her lilting brogue that bespoke her heritage. "To be honest, I'd worried that you might both be off on assignments, that you wouldn't make the memorial service. Thanks for coming." She looked at me, and then back at Jake, and said, "So you'll be joining us at the house to take a bite with us?"

Jake hesitated uncertainly, gave me a quick glance, and said to Fiona, "Val hasn't been feeling well since we got here last night, have you, Val?"

· He had adroitly thrown the ball into my court, and I had no option but to go along with him. "No, I haven't, not really. I think I must be coming down with something."

Fiona's face dropped. "Oh, that's such a disappointment, 'tis indeed, Val. And here I was, wanting to give you both something of Tony's. As a memento, you know. There's so much at the house, all of his possessions collected over the years. I thought you could choose something, Val, and you, Jake, something personal, like a camera, or maybe a pair of cuff links." She paused and shook her head, and a wry smile touched her mouth. "Well, as far as Tony's concerned, there would be nothing more personal than a camera I'm thinking, since every camera he ever owned was part of him."

"We do want you to come, Jake, you worked alongside Dad for so long. And you should come too," Rory cut in, looking directly at me. "If you feel up to it. It's not a real wake, you know. It's a sort of . . . well, it's just a gathering of friends remembering my father with his family, in his home—"

"It won't be the same without you," Fiona

interjected. "Why, Jake, you were so close to him these last few years, I thought at times that you were joined at the hip. Please come to the house. It means so much to me and the children."

Jake said something, but I wasn't paying attention. Instead, I was staring at Fiona. And I knew with absolute certainty that she was not Tony's ex-wife. Fiona was still his wife. Or, rather, his widow.

Chapter 5

I

"Tony came to me at the end of July and said he was divorced. Why didn't you tell me he wasn't?" I asked as evenly as possible, trying to keep my voice level and controlled.

"Because I didn't know he wasn't," Jake answered, returning my stare with one equally penetrating.

"But *why* didn't you know? You were his best buddy, and you seem very pally with Fiona. You must have known something, known what was going on in their life together!" I exclaimed, my voice rising slightly.

Jake did not answer.

We stood facing each other in my room at the

Milestone, where we had returned after leaving the Brompton Oratory. When truth and reality had suddenly hit me in the face at the church, I had hurriedly excused myself to Fiona, hinting in a vague way that I really wasn't well and had to leave. Under pressure from her, Jake had finally agreed to go to her house once he had dropped me off at the hotel. On the way here in the car, he had tried to talk to me, asking me why I had rushed out so abruptly. But I'd hushed him into silence, explaining that we must wait to have our discussion in private.

Now we were having it. He suddenly reached out, as if to take me in his arms. But as he moved toward me, I took a step backward. "Don't try to comfort me right now," I said swiftly. "I'm not in the mood, Jake, and anyway, I want to talk this out with you." I shook my head. "I always thought you were my friend, my best friend, actually, but now . . ." I let my sentence trail off.

Instantly I saw that I had annoyed him. His mouth tightened into a thin line, and his bright blue eyes, usually so benign, had turned flinty and cold. "Don't you dare question my friendship and loyalty!" he said. "And stop being so damned accusatory, Val. I haven't done anything to hurt you, I'm only an innocent bystander. Now listen to me for a moment."

"I'm listening."

He took a deep breath and said, "Although

Tony and I were close, he never confided in me about his private life, only ever hinted at things. I knew there were lots of women—" He cut himself off, looked chagrined, and eyed me carefully before continuing.

I knew Jake would never willfully hurt me, and I guessed that he was now worrying he had just caused me a degree of pain. But that wasn't so. "It's okay, Jake, keep going," I said in what I hoped was a reassuring voice.

He nodded. "Val, you have to face up to the fact that you weren't the first, there were others before you. But he never left Fiona. She was always there in the background, his childhood sweetheart, his child bride, as he called her, and the mother of his children. She was inviolate in a sense. At least, that's what *I* believed. As I told you, we never discussed his marriage or his love affairs, just as I didn't talk about my personal life or my divorce from Sue Ellen. We touched on those things only in the most peripheral way. Very casually. Then he got involved with you last year, and eventually I began to think the unthinkable, that he was going to break up with Fiona. Not that he ever said so. Nor did he discuss you. However, when he came to Paris in July, he announced out of the blue that he was divorced—"

"And you were gobsmacked, as the English say," I interrupted with some acidity.

Ignoring my sarcasm, Jake continued. "You're right, in one sense, yes. Because he was such a dyed-in-the-wool Catholic, I'd always thought a divorce was out of the question. And then again, he'd done something I'd never expected him to do. He'd broken the mold. Mind you, Val, I understood on another level why he would want to be free. It was for you. Yes, I understood that aspect of it very well."

"He lied to both of us. He wasn't divorced."

"We don't really know that," Jake answered in a reasonable tone.

"Oh yes we do. At least I do."

"I'd like you to consider a couple of things. First, think about Fiona and her demeanor today. She isn't playing the grieving widow. She seems a bit sad, I'll grant you that, but she's not distraught. And second, she's having only a small gathering at the house, just a few friends. In other words, she's not making a big deal out of the memorial."

"I don't think those are very good arguments."

"Are you making the assumption they were not divorced just because she talked about Tony's possessions being at the house, and because Rory spoke about Tony as if he lived in the bosom of his family, and very happily so?"

"Perhaps."

"But those things don't add up to Tony still being married to Fiona when he was killed.

Think about it, Val. Even if they were divorced, no one would bring it up *today,* least of all his *son.* It just wouldn't have been appropriate or very nice, and anyway, there was no reason to do so. It was a memorial service given by people who loved Tony, and the legal status of their marriage didn't figure into it at all."

"I guess not," I admitted. "On the other hand, there's Fiona's attitude toward me. If there'd been a divorce, why was she so nice to me? So pleasant?"

"Because she didn't know you were involved with Tony, that's why."

"I see."

"Please don't make the mistake of using her attitude toward you as a yardstick, Val. That would be very flawed judgment on your part."

I bit my lip and thought for a moment before saying, "Well, I guess the best way, perhaps the only way, to get to the truth is to ask Fiona if she and Tony were divorced."

"You wouldn't do that!"

"No, I wouldn't. But *you* could ask her, Jake."

"Oh, no, not me. And certainly not today of all days."

I sat down on a chair and dropped my head into my hands. After a minute or two, I looked up at him intently. "Jake, I'm going to ask you a question, and I want you to answer it as truthfully as you can. It's this: Do you really believe Tony and Fiona were divorced?"

Jake lowered his long, lean frame into the other chair. "Yes, I do," he answered after giving it some thought. And then he slowly shook his head. A doubtful expression flickered in his eyes. He said, "You know, Val, if I'm absolutely honest, I just don't know whether they were divorced or not. On the other hand, why would he announce it to me as well as to you?" Jake lifted his hands in a helpless sort of gesture and shook his head again. "Why would he invent that? What was his purpose?"

"I don't know. But trust a woman's instincts. The *other woman's* instincts. They weren't divorced."

II

I wound up going with Jake to Fiona's house in Hampstead.

He wasn't too happy about this because he was nervous at first, worried that I would verbally accost Fiona. But I promised I wouldn't do that, and he knew I never broke a promise. Also, he understood very well that I would never create an embarrassing scene either.

By the time Jake was leaving my room, I knew I had to go with him, there were no two ways about it. I had to get to the bottom of the situation, find out everything I could without actually asking any direct questions.

It had occurred to me on the drive up to Hampstead with Jake that their home, whether Tony had vacated recently or not, would also tell me a great deal about their relationship. And then there were the children, eighteen-year-old Rory, and Moira, who was twenty. In my experience, children frequently said a lot about their parents, and without actually meaning to they invariably revealed a few secrets. I hoped this would be the case today.

III

Where was the monster? Where was the harridan? Where was the disturbed woman Tony had complained about so often?

Certainly not present today, as far as I could ascertain, not unless Fiona was a superb actress or suffering from a split personality. Could she be a Dr. Jekyll and Mrs. Hyde? I was rather doubtful of that. In fact, she appeared to be a pleasant sort of woman who seemed perfectly normal to me.

I knew she was forty, but she didn't look her age at all. A pretty woman, it was her coloring that was the most striking thing about her, and her natural flame-colored hair and bright, dark eyes gave her a kind of vivid radiance. Of me-

dium height and build, she had an innate grace-
fulness that was most apparent now as she moved
around the room, tending to the needs of her
guests. Including Fiona and her children, there
were eleven of us altogether, since only Niall, his
wife, Kate, and several really close friends and
colleagues had been invited to the intimate buffet
lunch.

I sat on the sofa alone, facing the French
doors that led to the garden. Jake was off in a
corner, deep in conversation with Rory and
Moira, and so I took this opportunity to catch
my breath, to relax and review the past few
hours. It had been a wild morning. Emotional.
Disturbing. And in many ways more dismaying
than I'd anticipated.

Outside the windows the scene was pastoral,
and I was enjoying sitting there looking at it,
enjoying this moment of quietness and solitude
in the midst of the gathering. Everyone was
engaged in conversation, but this did not bother
me; I was part of them, yet separate. I might easily have been in the depths of the country, and
not in Hampstead, although parts of this area of
London were bucolic, I knew that.

From my position on the sofa I could see a
number of large trees, including an oak and a
sycamore, and a verdant lawn that was held in
check by herbaceous borders. There was an
ancient fountain spraying arcs of shimmering

water up into the air, and beyond this, a high, old stone wall into which had been set a wrought-iron gate with an elaborate scroll design.

This gate led to an apple orchard, so Fiona had told me a moment ago, and she had added, "Tony's favorite spot. He did love his garden so."

Nodding, smiling, I had not uttered a word on hearing this. It was something that seemed so unlikely; but I had taken a fast sip of the sherry Jake had poured for me earlier, to be followed quickly by several more sips. Her words had startled me. I had no idea how to respond, and then realized that no response was necessary.

When did *he* have time to sit in a garden? I asked myself, frowning at Fiona's retreating figure as she flitted away to serve more drinks and questioning the veracity of her remark. Yet there was no reason for her to make this comment if it were not true. What did she have to gain? Nothing, of course. Anyway, it had been said almost offhandedly, as if no thought had been given to it. Nonetheless, I found it curious.

Almost instantly it struck me that he'd had plenty of time to spend in the garden, because he had always hotfooted it to London at the end of an assignment, leaving me and Jake to make our way back to France together.

And Tony had usually had plenty of good reasons for rushing off, ready excuses on the tip of his tongue; he had to check in with his agency, spend time there, see his kids, have lunch with his brother, get a doctor's checkup, go to the dentist. No, he had never been at a loss when it came to explaining away his absence from my life when we were not working.

Tony had been in London through June and most of July, and certainly he could have easily done a lot of garden sitting then. He had not joined us in Paris until the last few days of July, just before we set off for Kosovo in August to cover the war.

Do we ever really know another person? Until earlier today I had believed I knew everything there was to know about Tony Hampton. Not so, it seemed.

I'd had a bit of a shock in the Brompton Oratory, when it had suddenly hit me, and with some force, that I was actually standing next to Tony's widow and not his ex-wife, as I had believed her to be. But the shock had receded somewhat, and I had begun to regain some of my equilibrium.

When I'd rushed out of the church I'd been full of rage; but as the anger had subsided I had accepted the fact that I'd been duped. Not only that, I could also admit to myself that Tony had purposely set out to beguile me last year, and I had been foolishly sucked in, captivated by his Irish charm—if anyone had kissed the Blarney Stone, he had. I had been bowled over by his sudden and rather intense interest in me; it had been so unexpected. After all, he had known me for several years and had always treated me as a pal. Suddenly I was the focus of his romantic and sexual interest, and for a while I was baffled. But he was charismatic, and of course I had not been able to resist his looks, his humor, his cleverness, his sexuality. I had been a sitting duck. . . .

There was something else. I trusted my gut instinct absolutely, and earlier today it had told me Tony had died a married man. I was convinced I was right about that, even if Jake was wavering on this point.

I was baffled by Tony's behavior at the end of July. Why had he unexpectedly announced to Jake that he was divorced? And why had he told me exactly the same thing? I'd certainly not been bugging him about marriage. And who could fathom out a blatant lie like that? What was the motivation behind it? What was the reason for the lie? What had he hoped to gain?

All kinds of other questions jostled for prominence in my mind as I sat there in his house in Hampstead with his widow playing hostess; I went on sipping her dry sherry and pondering my love affair with him.

Had Tony been playing for time? Had he been intending to marry me, as he had often said he would, and in doing so commit bigamy? Had he merely been stringing me along, hoping that

Fiona would leave him? Or that I would tire of waiting? Had he found himself in so deep with me, he didn't know how to extricate himself, and therefore had invented the divorce and given me the Grecian ring as . . . *pacifiers?* Had he been hoping that something would happen to solve his problems?

Tony had had a favorite expression, one he used frequently. "Life has a way of taking care of itself," he would say to me and others constantly.

Well, life had indeed taken care of itself in the end. Had he always known he would die covering a war? Had he had a presentiment about this? An icy shiver shot through me at this appalling thought, and I immediately put it out of my head. Otherwise, I might start thinking that his recklessness had in some way been calculated. A feeling of dismay mingled with the frustration lodged in the pit of my stomach as I recognized that I would never know what had been in Tony's mind.

IV

Not wishing to wrestle any further with the puzzle of Tony's marital status and his terrible game playing, if that *was* what he had been doing, I focused my eyes on the garden for a short while longer. It was so tranquil, filled with such a calm beauty, I took a measure of peace from it. And again I was thankful that nobody was disturbing me with their idle chatter.

The slashing rain had long since stopped and the day had turned sunny; airy white clouds floated across a soft periwinkle-blue sky, and it had become one of those lovely September afternoons that are so endemic to England.

Suddenly that bright sunlight was pouring into the room. Yellow was the predominant color, and the result was magical; the whole room acquired a shimmer to it, a warm golden glow that appeared to make everything gleam. My eyes roamed around, taking everything in for the first time since I'd arrived.

There were some attractive modern paintings on the walls, and a number of handsome Georgian antiques were on display. But essentially it was a room that had been furnished rather than decorated, because there was no cohesive decorative theme to it. Beautiful things were dotted here and there, but they looked as if they had been gathered somewhat indiscriminately and then placed around haphazardly. The room did have comfort and there was more than a hint of refined taste at work, but very little of Tony was in evidence. This setting had been created solely by Fiona, I was sure of that.

Jake moved away from the corner of the room at last, sauntered over to me, and looked down.

He said, "You seem a bit pensive. Are you all right?"

"I'm fine. I've just been sitting here, thinking. Thinking things through."

Jake nodded, gave me a small lopsided smile. "We'll talk later. In the meantime, how about coming into the dining room, getting a little food? You should try to eat something, Val, before we go to the airport."

I agreed.

V

In the end it was the study that told the real story.

Jake and I had just finished eating when Fiona came over. Leaning closer to us, she said in a low, confidential voice, "Let's slip away. I want you to choose something of Tony's as a memento."

I jumped up at this invitation. Jake and I followed her out of the dining room, up the stairs, down the corridor, and into the long, rather spacious room that had been Tony's private abode.

The moment I stepped inside, I knew that no one else could possibly have occupied it; his own unique imprint was stamped on it everywhere.

The first thing I noticed was the baseball cap, and my stomach lurched.

How could I miss it? I had bought it for him last year, on our vacation in the South of France.

There were a number of other hats hanging on the antique mahogany hat stand near the door, but my baseball cap had been his favorite. The way it hung there now, a bit lopsidedly, made me catch my breath. He might have just flung it onto the peg a moment before.

Feeling decidedly queasy, I glanced away and moved farther into the room.

Along one wall, a series of built-in cupboards ran down toward the window, and I guessed that this was his filing system; those cabinets more than likely housed hundreds of his photographs and all his records. And God knows what else. I wished I could get into them, but there was no hope of that, I knew.

Stacks of magazines, piles of books, and a selection of very expensive cameras were carefully arranged on top of the cabinets, and above the long countertop the wall was lined with cork. Onto this Tony had pinned a lot of photographs. Including some of mine, I noticed with a small jolt of surprise.

Walking closer, I looked at them, remembering. Remembering so much.

I instantly closed my mind to those memories. With a rush of irritation I knew he had put them up there as souvenirs of our vacation in France. All of them had been taken near St. Tropez, where we had spent a week sailing. Seascapes. Empty beaches. Sunsets. Shots of the endless sky.

Close-ups of flowers, trees, birds, nature in all its forms. Beautiful shots, which were a relief for me to take after the horrors of war. They were unidentified, but they were mine all right.

Then my gaze fell on the camera I had given him. A Leica.

Automatically, I reached for it, held it in my hand, thinking of Tony, suddenly angry with him again. I felt betrayed and used by him.

Fiona must have seen me pick it up, because she exclaimed, "If you want the camera, please take it, Val dear. Rory and Moira have chosen the ones they prefer. I'm so pleased she's taking after Tony, following in his footsteps. I'm sure she's told you all about her plans, Jake, hasn't she?"

I turned around to face the two of them.

Fiona stood near the big partners desk in the middle of the room, and she was looking up at Jake.

He said, "Yes, she has been filling me in, and she's very excited that she's going to join Tony's agency next year."

As I continued to look at them, it struck me suddenly that Jake looked very tired, as if the day had affected him as deeply as it had me. Also, I couldn't help wondering what Moira and Rory had been talking to him about. Their father, no doubt.

Picking up the camera, I went to join them

both. Jake put his arm around me, drew me closer to him, almost protectively, I thought.

"Thanks, Fiona, I'd like the camera," I murmured, although I didn't want it at all. But I thought it would look churlish, perhaps even odd, if I didn't take something of his, since we had worked together.

Looking pleased, Fiona now picked up a small leather box that was on the desk and opened it. She showed the contents to us; it held a pair of cuff links. Glancing at Jake, she said, "I thought you might like to have these as a memento of Tony. They're good ones, you know. They're made of eighteen-karat gold, and lapis, as you can see."

"Thanks," he said, taking them from her. He studied them for a moment, closed the box, and put it in his jacket pocket without another word.

"Would you like to select one or two of Tony's cameras?" she asked him.

Jake shook his head. "I've got so many of my own, honey, but thanks for offering."

Sitting down at the desk, Fiona opened the center drawer, took out an office-sized checkbook, and turned the pages. "Tony must've owed you money, Jake. Five hundred pounds, to be exact." Her expression was questioning, and then she went on. "He made out this check to you, dated and signed it, then forgot to tear it out before he left for Paris at the end of July. I found it the other day, when I'd finally screwed up the courage to go through his desk."

Jake was obviously not surprised by her words. Nodding, he explained, "Tony told me he'd left the check behind by mistake. I said he should forget it, that it didn't matter." Jake cleared his throat and added, "I'd loaned him some money to buy film when we were in Jordan in March. Look, it's not important, Fiona."

"No, no, I insist you take it," she exclaimed, tore out the check, and handed it to Jake. Since I was standing next to him, I couldn't help noticing that the check came from a joint account. An account bearing Fiona's name as well as his.

Well, so much for that, I thought. She had a joint account with him. She has his children. His house. His garden. A whole life with him to remember.

As for me, what did I have?

Chapter 6

I

Jake did not have much to say on the way to the airport. In fact, he was not only silent but rather glum. In contrast, I was brimming with thoughts, theories, and comments and desperately wanted to talk to him. But in the end I remained silent, deeming it wiser to hold my tongue for the moment.

It was obvious to me that he didn't want to talk about Tony and Fiona, or Rory and Moira either, with whom he had spent a lot of time at the lunch. Nor did he want to discuss that lunch, which we had just left, or the memorial service of earlier. I didn't blame him. Everything had become as painful for Jake as it had for me, or so I believed.

Heathrow was as busy as it always was, crowded with people, and as we pushed our way through the bustling throngs heading for all corners of the world, I got the distinct feeling Jake couldn't wait to get back to Paris. I hurried along next to him, hauling my one piece of luggage, a fold-over bag that had traveled the world with me, while endeavoring to keep my large tote on my shoulder.

"Hey, honey, let me help you with your stuff," he suddenly said, becoming aware of the difficulties I was having with the large bag slung over one shoulder.

"I can manage, Jake. Please don't worry, you've enough to carry of your own," I replied, but I was still struggling, and before I could protest further, he grabbed the fold-over bag out of my hands.

"I'm sorry, Val, I should have carried this for you all along. No excuse for me, except that I've been preoccupied." He gave me a faint smile, and finished with "I've been very neglectful."

"Please, it's okay!" I exclaimed. "I'm a strong, tough girl who can carry her own luggage and take care of herself in any situation."

Staring down at me, he gave me an odd look and muttered, "I'm not so sure about that, Kid."

I didn't answer. I simply trotted along next to him, trying to keep up with his long strides. After a second or two I remarked, "Anyway, I know what you mean about being preoccupied. I'm on overload myself at the moment."

He nodded, gave me a swift glance, and said, "Yes, you are. Emotional overload. The point is, we're *both* top-heavy with a lot of crap, a lot of disturbing and conflicting feelings. I just need to clear my head, Val, so that I can look at . . . things as clearly as possible."

"I understand," I answered, "and I realize now is not the right time to talk, since we're rushing through an airport like maniacs, trying to make a plane. But we should sit down and chat, Jake. We need to understand about Tony and Fiona. Whenever you want, but we really must do it," I insisted.

When he made no response whatsoever, I eyed him worriedly and pressed, "At the lunch you said we'd talk later, remember? And we have to make sense out of Tony's behavior, you know."

"I guess we do," he muttered, and his face became closed, his mouth grimly set. He plunged ahead, making for the gate, deftly handling our luggage.

I sighed under my breath. So much for that illuminating conversation, I muttered to myself, and ran after him to board the plane to Paris.

II

The flight across the English Channel was short, just over an hour, and I spent most of that time wondering why Jake was still so silent, wrapped up in his own thoughts. I'd tried to make small talk with him, but to no avail. He barely responded, seemed reluctant to say anything at all. And when he did reply to the odd question or comment of mine, his answers were brief and to the point.

If I didn't know better, I would have said he was being sulky, but that wasn't his nature. Jake was not a moody man, nor was he temperamental, and like me he was usually on an even keel. Quite aside from that, I always thought of him as being straightforward, honest, and dependable. The salt of the earth: and my best friend, the one I relied on.

His quietness, his unexpected reserve, puzzled me a bit, and I wondered if something else was bothering him, something other than Tony Hampton.

Now I stole a look at him. His head was thrown back against the plane seat and his eyes were closed, but even in repose his expression was troubled. His mouth had relaxed, but there was a tautness in his face, a tenseness in his body, even though he dozed. Poor Jake, I thought, I've put him through hell these past few weeks since Tony's death. I suddenly felt very guilty about that. We had both loved Tony in our different ways, and losing him had traumatized us. Commiserating, we had tried to help each other along, while continuing to miss him.

But as of today we had a different Tony Hampton to contemplate and contend with, a Tony much less noble, a man without honor as far as I was concerned.

I asked myself why I had never realized that, never spotted this flaw in him? I prided myself on my integrity, and I found it hard to relate to those who lacked this quality. My grandfather had always held integrity very dear, and he had drilled its importance into me, reminding me about the value of honor, honesty, trustworthiness, and decency. I have tried to live by Grandfather's rules and standards, and I believe I have succeeded.

Once, long ago, my little slug of a brother Donald had told me that my standards were too high, that I expected too much from people, that no one could live up to my highfalutin expectations, going on to inform me that the world was full of rotten people. "And most people *are* rotten, whatever *you* think, Val Denning," he had exploded, his rage spilling over. "They stink. They cheat, they steal, they lie. They commit adultery and murder, and they're shit! Yes, the whole world is full of shitty people, and the sooner you realize that, the better off you'll be."

I had gaped at him in astonishment at the time, wondering what rock he had crawled out from under, and then I turned away in disgust. Over the years I constantly endeavored to avoid confrontations with my brother as best I could, but I hadn't always succeeded. Ever since childhood I loathed getting embroiled with him because he was so opinionated, and he never ever listened. I can't remember now what had set Donald off that particular day, but whenever he started to rant, I usually did a disappearing act.

I suddenly remembered that Tony had also once said my standards were too high, and like Donald he had pointed out that very few people could live up to my expectations of them. I wondered now if he'd been thinking of himself that day. Of course I would never know; and the enigma of Tony would puzzle me for the rest of my life.

III

Jake suddenly awakened, stretched, and turned to me. "Well, I've not been much company, have I, Val?" He made a face. "Sorry about that, honey, but I felt bushed when we got on the plane. I just had to grab a bit of sleep."

I nodded my understanding. "Do you feel better?"

Jake grimaced. "Not really. London's been a tough trip, especially for you, and we *will* talk about Tony and Fiona, I promise. But later, okay? I'm just not up to it tonight."

"Whenever you can, Jake, because it is important to me."

"I'm aware of that. It's just as important to me, and in more ways than you can imagine." He reached over, took hold of my hand, and squeezed it. "I'll drop you off at your apartment, and I'll call you tomorrow, Val."

"All right," I murmured, feeling disappointed. I'd hoped to have dinner with him that night, so I could discuss Tony. But apparently that wasn't to be. Never mind, I could bide my time until he was ready.

Chapter 7

I

Paris, September ◆ The persona Tony Hampton
had presented to the world had been dazzling.
Intrepid war photographer, one of the most brilliant photojournalists of this decade, courageous,
charismatic, a handsome and divine ladies' man,
raconteur par excellence, bon vivant, and most
generous host.

But there had been another side to him. He
had been a liar and a cheat and he had undoubtedly led a double life. This is what I now truly
believed even though I had only my own intuition to go on.

Maybe Jake wouldn't entirely agree with me, but
I felt quite certain there had been a much darker

side to Tony. Being in the bosom of his family at the memorial service earlier today had convinced me of this. And I was now absolutely positive he had never been divorced from Fiona. From his family's behavior, and all that they had said, I placed him right in their midst until he left London in July. It was then he had come to Paris to pick us up, so that we could head out to Kosovo together. And he had been *happily* ensconced in their midst, from what I deducted.

I was sitting at the desk in my bedroom, and I reached out, picked up the photograph of Tony in its silver frame. I held it in both hands, staring at his face. He stood there on the deck of the sloop anchored off St. Tropez last year, squinting in the summer sunshine. So dashing, so debonair . . . so enigmatic . . .

And I couldn't help wondering about him, wondering about his complicated life and what it had been all about in the end.

He would have been a psychiatrist's dream, I thought. Put him on a couch for analysis and God knows what he would have spilled. Or would he? Psychotics didn't always do that, did they?

Psychotic.

The word hung there. Silently, I repeated it in my head, considered it carefully, asking myself why it had popped into my mind. And yet it did seem appropriate, didn't it? Tony *was* psychotic, wasn't he?

I put the photograph back in its given place on the desk, leaned back in my chair, and stared off into space. In the far reaches of my mind I'd had Tony Hampton under a mental microscope for a good part of the day, and I didn't like what I'd seen; nor did my conclusions about him elate me.

He was not just a liar telling small white lies— didn't we all do that at times?—but a pathological liar telling real whoppers, lies that were dangerous because they could conceivably do damage to people, cause them great heartache, and change their lives, and not always for the best.

That deep-seated lying had probably become a way of life for him. He couldn't stop because he couldn't help himself. Then again, he had needed to lie for his own protection. He had spun a web of deceit he couldn't crawl out of; he had entrapped himself with his complex machinations.

Then there was his adultery. It had been compulsive, excessive, a dominant force in his life, and it had obviously grown out of hand over the years. It became an addiction, I was sure.

I hadn't needed Jake to inform me today about the many women Tony had been involved with before me. I was well aware of his countless affairs; after all, we'd worked together, traveled together on various assignments.

Naturally Tony had tried to keep these women under wraps, and a secret, because his private life was his private life. It was none of my business, in his opinion. Nor was it Jake's business either, and so he had striven for privacy.

However, I could put two and two together and come up with six, just like everyone else. Tony had always underestimated me, and so had Jake. Just because I never discussed Tony's international sexual dalliances didn't mean that I didn't know they existed. I did know, and I didn't care. After all, I wasn't in love with him then, not involved in that way. This knowledge hadn't changed my opinion of him in those days. I thought he was a great guy, a good human being, and naturally I admired his talent as a photojournalist. It was more than that really; I considered it an honor to work alongside him.

But to think Jake believed I hadn't known about Tony's very busy love life . . . how ludicrous that was. I was much smarter than he imagined, than Tony imagined. I suddenly wanted to laugh out loud at the mere idea of it.

All those women . . . and one in particular whom I had known and disliked. I thought of her now. . . .

II

It was April 1996, and for once Tony and I were on assignment without Jake. He had gone to

New York to deal with his divorce from Sue Ellen Jones, the famous model, and Tony and I had flown out to the Middle East for our respective news-photo agencies. We were in Lebanon to cover the new hostilities that had erupted between the Israelis and Hezbollah.

The long civil war was over by that time and things were beginning to mend, beginning to get back to normal, and then the skirmishing had unexpectedly started once more.

For the first time in fourteen years the Israelis had attacked Beirut directly, using laser-homing Hellfire missiles shot from four helicopter gunships off the coast.

The Israelis were not the aggressors though. They were actually responding to Hezbollah's recent bombing of their country. And that war of attrition had started up again because Hezbollah had then retaliated after the missile attack, sending forty rockets smack into the middle of Israel. And so it went. . . .

One lovely spring day—late in the afternoon, actually—Tony and I were sitting in the bar of the Marriott Hotel in the Hamra district of Beirut. I suppose I'll never forget that day, because we had had such bad news about a colleague of ours, Bill Fitzgerald of CNS, one of the American cable television networks. He had disappeared several days earlier, and none of us knew what had happened to him. We were all a bit nervous and concerned, and afraid for Bill.

Two of his crew, who had been with him out on the streets, had seen him grabbed by three young men, who had hustled him into a waiting Mercedes and then driven off at breakneck speed. The two crew members had been alert, and at once they jumped into their car and followed in furious pursuit. But the Mercedes disappeared—into thin air.

Since then there had been no news about Bill, and none of the terrorist organizations claimed his kidnapping. Who had snatched him, and for what purpose, we did not know.

But as we sat around in the bar that day, drinking with a group of international correspondents, all of us were offering theories, and speculation was rampant.

III

"Islamic Jihad," I had said all of a sudden, glancing around the table at my companions. "They've got him."

"But why would they have grabbed him?" Tony had asked. "And if it is them, what have they got to *gain,* Val? Listen, snatching a newsman just doesn't make sense."

"It might. They've managed to make use of

hostages before," I'd shot back. "And don't forget, Islamic Jihad is the terrorist arm of Hezbollah. Its members are extremely dangerous, unpredictable, and nuts."

Tony had given me a strange look, but he had said nothing else.

Frank Petersen, of *Time* magazine, had exclaimed, "I agree with you, Val, Islamic Jihad *is* full of real wackos. And it's got to be them, in my opinion. They're the ones who took Terry Anderson and William Buckley, and they're not known for their fast releases."

"Terry Anderson was a hostage for seven years," I had muttered. "Jesus, this is just awful. Does anyone know what Bill's network is doing about finding him?"

"There's not a lot they can do, Val."

I had looked across at Joe Alonzo as he spoke. He had just arrived, and he was Bill Fitzgerald's soundman, had been on the streets with Bill when he was taken. Sitting down at the table with us, Joe went on. "Bill's photo has been circulated throughout Beirut, throughout Lebanon in fact. Pressure has been put on the Lebanese and Syrian governments, and on the White House too. But until somebody claims responsibility for the kidnapping, there's not much else CNS can do. Our network doesn't know who to deal with, Val."

At that moment Allan Brent, the Middle East

bureau chief for CNN, had hurried into the bar, glanced around, and made a beeline for our table. His face was extremely grim. "We've just had a news flash. About Bill. Hezbollah did it. Well, they're *claiming* they've got him."

"Oh, shit," Tony had said, and shaken his head in dismay. "I still don't get it . . . why would they grab a newsman . . ." His voice had trailed off weakly.

The CNS correspondent who was covering for Bill Fitzgerald had also arrived at our table. His name was Mark Lawrence, and it was apparent he was distressed. "I guess you've heard it from Allan. Islamic Jihad just announced Bill is their captive." He looked about to burst into tears.

"That group is so unstable, so fanatical, I think Bill has to be in very grave danger," I had murmured gloomily. And later, very sadly, I was proven to be correct in this prediction. Bill never did make it out alive.

As the others had gone on talking about Bill's predicament, speculating about his fate in concerned voices, Tony leaned closer to me and stared into my face in the most peculiar way. He was actually studying me very intently. For a few seconds I hadn't been able to fathom the meaning of this close scrutiny, until it struck me he was actually giving me the once-over. And in the most appraising manner. It was as if he were suddenly seeing me differently, objectively, and in a new light.

"What's wrong?" I finally asked him, irritated. He had begun to make me feel uncomfortable, nervous even, and I didn't appreciate those feelings. He had never acted like this before, and I was puzzled and annoyed with him.

"Nothing's wrong," he had answered lightly, leaning back, balancing his chair precariously on its two back legs. "Where do you want to go to dinner tonight, Val? I've invited Anne Curtis to join us. We'll have a good meal, go to a club afterward, go dancing. If you like, I'll ask Frank to come along. We can make it a foursome, Val."

I had been thunderstruck, and I had stared at him speechlessly, unable to comprehend how he could speak so nonchalantly about having a social evening when we were all so devastated, so worried about Bill's kidnapping. Who the hell cared about dinner, for God's sake, when a man's life was at stake, I had thought indignantly. But the words hadn't left my mouth; they'd remained stuck in my throat, although more from disgust with him than reticence on my part.

Tony was being insensitive and callous, and I was suddenly very, very angry with him. But before I'd had a chance to chastise him for his heartlessness, Anne Curtis herself came over to join us.

She was English, but so dark of complexion and coloring I'd always thought she must have Mediterranean or Middle Eastern ancestry. She was with the BBC World Service, and was a brilliant radio journalist. On various occasions she'd tried to be friendly, but I'd never warmed to her. There was something about her that struck me as being untrustworthy, although I had nothing specific to go on. It was just an instinctive feeling on my part.

But it was quite obvious she had warmed to Tony.

She had squeezed in between the two of us when Frank had very gallantly pulled up a chair for her, and although Tony had remained cool and detached, the look in her eyes had told me plenty.

I had guessed at once that they were embroiled in a hot affair; this suspicion was confirmed later that evening, when we did finally go out to dinner, dragging Frank Petersen along with us. Anne had left little to anyone's imagination. The manner in which she had drooled over Tony, in the most disgusting and juvenile way, had telegraphed everything to me. And to Frank, who had appeared to be somewhat embarrassed by her performance. Yet I'd had to hand it to Tony that night. He hadn't batted an eyelash; what's more, he had appeared so completely indifferent to her, it was quite amazing. He deserves an Academy Award, I thought at the time.

The following day I'd run into Anne in the lobby of the Commodore Hotel, and she had attacked me verbally, berating me in the worst way and accusing me of being a spoilsport. "You don't have to tell me you didn't enjoy the evening," she had announced, glaring at me. "It was written all over your face. You made us all suffer, constantly going on about Bill Fitzgerald. Poor Frank didn't know how to cope. He *is* Bill's best friend, you know."

"Of course Frank knew how to handle it," I'd exclaimed, glaring back at her. "Mostly I think he was cringing at your behavior."

"You can't have him, my dear," she had cried heatedly, leaning into me almost threateningly. "Tony belongs to me. He's mine and I intend to keep him. *Permanently*. So just keep your jealous little paws off him, Valentine. Understand me, kiddo?"

I remember I had stared at her aghast, told her she'd gotten it all wrong, and then hurried off mortified. I was furious not only with her, but with Tony as well, for putting me in such an untenable position.

And I had continued to seethe about that evening for quite a while. Anne's accusations didn't particularly bother me in the long run, since they were patently ridiculous, but what did

upset me was Tony's callousness, his lack of concern for Bill Fitzgerald.

I began to despise myself for going to that dinner, for being a party to it under the circumstances. I also continued to be disturbed by Tony's
behavior, his thoughtlessness that night. But
eventually I let it go, and soon I found myself
making excuses for him . . . as war photographers we lived with constant danger, took terrible
chances when we hurled ourselves into the fray
on the front lines or in disaster areas. And so, in a
certain way, we did become inured to tragedy,
perhaps because there was so much of it around
us. Tragedy was commonplace for journalists like
us, human suffering the norm.

IV

Reaching for Tony's photograph once more, I
gave it a quick glance, then opened a drawer in
the desk and placed it inside. Sometimes it
seemed to me that his brilliant dark eyes followed
me as I moved around my bedroom. It was most
disconcerting.

Perhaps I ought to take it out of the frame and
tear it up. Yes, I would do that, I decided. I would
tear up every one of his photographs and destroy
those little notes and letters and cards he'd sent
me this past year. Tomorrow though, not tonight.

I was far too tired, exhausted actually. It had been a very long day, and emotionally draining.

But there was one thing I *could* do now.

I glanced down at my right hand and then I pulled off the Grecian ring with the aqua stones, held it in my hand for a moment, studying it. I was about to throw it in the wastepaper basket and then I changed my mind. Janine was coming to clean the apartment the next day; she would undoubtedly find it and put it on my desk, not understanding that I had deliberately thrown it away.

I went into the kitchen, dropped the ring in the trash can, emptied the used coffee grains on top of it, and then added a lump of wet paper towels to the mess. That way, Janine would never find it, not unless she scrabbled through my kitchen garbage, which I very much doubted.

I went back to the desk in my bedroom and sat down again. My brain still raced. I knew deep down within myself that my ultimate conclusions about my dead lover were absolutely accurate. Right on the mark.

Furthermore, I accepted now that I'd been used, abused in a sense, and played for a fool. The first time Tony had taken me out on an actual date, he had confided that he had started divorce proceedings against Fiona. Not true. And he'd never intended to marry me.

A long sigh escaped me. I knew I must pull

myself together, start over again, make an effort somehow to get on with my life. But before I could do that, I had to unburden myself, get all of this off my chest. I had to talk to Jake, that was imperative. No one else would understand my turbulent feelings, my distress, my terrible hurt inside. And certainly no one else cared in the way that he did. He was my best friend, wasn't he?

Chapter 8

I

The following morning Jake called me as he had promised he would during our flight back to Paris. We made a date to have lunch.

Several hours later I met him at the Bar des Théâtrés on the avenue Montaigne, a little bit down the street from the Hôtel Plaza Athénée. It was one of his favorite haunts, since it was frequented by the gorgeous models who worked at the Balmain haute couture salon on the rue François 1ᵉʳ nearby.

I couldn't help thinking how much better he looked today as he stood up to greet me. The tan he had acquired in the South of France last week gave him a healthy look anyway; but it was his eyes that were different. They were bright and alert again, and he was smiling broadly. It was quite a change from the day before. In London he had been so gloomy, and introspective on the plane, had appeared weary, worn out, and not a bit like the Jake I'd come to know. He was usually so outgoing, energetic, and vital.

After giving me a quick peck on the cheek, he said, "You look wonderful, Val, the white suit is great on you. Much better than black."

Well, I'm not in mourning anymore, I thought with some acerbity, but I didn't say a word. I simply smiled back at him and murmured, "You don't look so bad yourself."

Once we were seated opposite each other at the table, he asked, "What would you like to drink?"

"Not sure . . ."

"I'm thinking of having a dry martini. Want to try one?"

I hesitated but only fractionally. "Why not?" Then quickly I added, "But I might get drunk if I do."

"You don't have to worry, you know I always look after you."

I shook my head. "Perhaps I'd better not have a martini, Jake. It's far too strong. A glass of white wine instead, please."

He grinned at me. "And I'll have the same,

you're right about the martini. It *is* too potent, especially at lunchtime."

Once Jake had ordered the drinks, he turned to me and began. "I know you have the pressing need to talk to me about Tony, and I'm ready to listen. Now, or later after lunch, whatever you prefer."

"Yes—" I paused and sighed. "I've had a sleepless night, running everything through my mind again and again, going over every detail. But whichever way I twist and turn, I keep coming up with the same answers, and—" I broke off, shook my head.

"And what?" he prompted.

"I know that certain things are true, without the benefit of anyone giving me information or telling me anything. Tony was a liar, Jake, and he *did* lead a double life, playing other women off against Fiona. Who now has my pity, by the way. He wasn't divorced from her, nor was he intending to be. Tony wanted his cake and he wanted to eat it. I know I'm not wrong."

"I tend to agree with you. And it's a very male characteristic, isn't it, Val?" He looked at me intently. Then he went on. "Tony wanted a wife and a mistress apparently. And there's nothing new about that, is there? Mistresses have been around for centuries, since the beginning of time. And if you're going to have a wife and a mistress and lead a double life, then you have to be a liar, and a damned good one. Because it seems to me the two go hand in glove."

"That's true." I cleared my throat. "I want you to know something else, Jake."

"Go ahead, tell me."

I was silent for a split second; the waiter had arrived with our drinks. But once we were alone again, I continued. "Just over a year ago, before Tony and I became involved, before he'd even invited me out on a date, he confided in me over lunch one day . . . he said he'd just gotten a legal separation from Fiona, that he was in the process of divorcing her."

"I'd no idea he'd said a thing like that," Jake replied, looking surprised. Picking up his glass, he said "Cheers" and took a sip of the white wine.

"Cheers," I answered, and tasted the Sancerre. "I now believe that that was a downright lie, that he invented the story. He knew I would never go out with him because he was a married man. He knew what I felt about married men. They were verboten as far as I was concerned."

"Yes, he did know that. We both did."

"In the end it's all a matter of integrity, isn't it?" I shook my head sadly. "Tony Hampton didn't have any integrity, although until yesterday I thought he did."

"So did I," Jake muttered in a low voice. "Yes, well, he had integrity in his work, of course, but not in his personal life. Obviously."

"Correct."

Jake settled back in the chair, his expression reflective.

I sipped my wine, watching him closely. Waiting. He seemed to be mulling something over in his mind.

Finally, after a few more moments of deep reflection, Jake said, "Your intuition was correct yesterday. In the Brompton Oratory, I mean, when you suddenly *knew* in your bones that Fiona was his widow and not his ex-wife."

"She told you!" I cried, sounding a bit triumphant, I must admit. I fixed my eyes on him expectantly.

"No," he said. "No, she didn't, Val. But I'm certain of it, after talking to Rory and Moira at the lunch. They were both full of Tony, singing his praises, telling me what a good father he'd been to them, and right until the end. Rory explained that Tony had spent a wonderful six-week period with them in June and July before going off to Kosovo. And Moira became very weepy for a few seconds; she told me how glad they all were they'd been able to have this special time with him. And that he'd taken her to his photo agency and gotten her a job and she was starting there next year."

Although Jake was merely confirming what I already believed to be the truth, I still crumpled a bit, slumped down in my chair. I felt my eyes filling up.

Jake leaned forward, grabbed my hand, and said in a concerned tone, "Don't get upset, Val. Please. You've done enough weeping about him. And he's not worth it."

"He was a bastard," I whispered.

II

"Let's look at the menu and order lunch." As he spoke, Jake motioned to the waiter, who was at his side in an instant.

"What're your specials today, Antoine?"

The waiter told us, and Jake, looking across the table at me, said, "How about the green salad, entrecôte, and French fries? Sounds good to me."

I wasn't very hungry, but I nodded in agreement, not wanting to argue with him.

After giving the waiter instructions about how he wanted the steaks cooked, Jake added, "And let's have two more glasses of wine, please, Antoine."

"*Oui,* Monsieur Newberg," Antoine responded, smiled, and hurried off.

"Got to put some flesh on you," Jake murmured, and grinned at me.

I grimaced and sipped my wine. After a

moment I said, "You were very quiet on the plane last night. Preoccupied, you said. Was that because of Rory and Moira? And what they'd said to you about Tony?"

Jake sighed. "Yup, that was it. I suddenly realized your instincts were correct, and I was appalled at what he'd done to you."

"There's something else, Jake. I think Tony's apartment on the King's Road was just a place for him to develop film and seduce women. I could never reach him there. The answering machine was always on, I was forever leaving messages. He'd call back, of course, but always hours later. Sometimes I tried him on his cell phone, but a lot of the time that was turned off. I know the flat was properly furnished and all that, and he did have clothes and stuff there, but now I think it was just a front. I bet you anything he really lived at the house in Hampstead with Fiona."

Jake was silent for a minute or two, and then he said very quietly, "You're probably right, Val. It's true, he never picked up the phone at his flat. And basically, I have the same problem as you—believing he lived there, I mean. I could hardly ever reach him in London because his cell phone *was* turned off more than it was on. I left countless messages with his photo agency when I really needed to get him."

"We were *both* duped by him," I muttered,

giving Jake a hard stare. "I'm glad it wasn't just me."

III

After lunch we went for a walk along the Seine. It was a nice afternoon, quite balmy, and although the sun wasn't shining, the sky was a clear, gentle blue dotted with pale clouds.

We ambled along, heading toward the Pont des Arts, the only metal bridge in Paris, not talking very much, lost in our own thoughts. Jake and I were comfortable together; we didn't have to keep up a nonstop conversation.

I was the first one to break our compatible silence when I suddenly stopped, turned to Jake, and said, "Do you think Tony was psychotic?"

Also coming to a standstill, he stared at me and exclaimed, "Val, that's an odd thing to say! And off the top of my head, no, I don't think he was psychotic. From what you and I *think* we know about him, I'll grant you he was a sexual predator and a very clever liar, but not sick in the head. At least, not the way you're suggesting. He always had his wits about him, knew what he was doing, what he was saying. Yes, he was smart—and very devious. But psychotic?" Jake shook his head.

I opened the black satchel thrown over my

shoulder, took out a piece of paper, and explained. "Listen to this . . . I looked in the dictionary this morning. *Psychotic:* Of, relating to, or affected by psychosis. *Psychosis:* A severe mental disorder, with or without organic damage, characterized by derangement of personality and loss of contact with reality. Don't you think he'd lost contact with reality, telling us both he was divorced, asking me to marry him?"

"Only if he believed his own lies, Val. *That* would be a loss of contact with reality. I think Tony lived in the real world, I really do. There's nothing more real than war, as you well know, and he was always out there, shooting film, looking for the greatest picture, just as we were. No, I can't say he was psychotic. Just a *son of a bitch!*"

"Yes, he was, and then some. But he had to be off the wall to a certain extent, mentally unbalanced, doing what he did to me. Jesus, Jake, he was nuts thinking he could get away with it."

"I agree with you. But even so, I can't really explain his behavior or his reasoning, because he never confided in me. Perhaps he fully intended to lead a double life with you. Many men have gotten away with that! Fiona in London. You in Paris. Captain's paradise."

"And a bigamous marriage with me? Is that what you mean?"

"Maybe, Val. I just don't know."

"We'll never know."

Jake put his arm around me and we walked on in silence. After a moment he said softly, "I didn't sleep much myself last night, turning all this over in my mind. I even thought at one point that I should go back to London to see Fiona, to try to find out the state of their marriage when he was killed. Just so you and I would really know the truth. But I changed my mind. Without actually coming out and asking her if they were divorced, I don't think I'd be able to glean very much having a roundabout conversation with her . . ." He didn't finish, just half shrugged and looked down at me, making a small grimace.

"Oh, just leave it alone, Jake! It's all yesterday's news!" I exclaimed, and I was startled at the shakiness of my voice.

"Hey, Val honey, I didn't mean to upset you." Jake wrapped both arms around me and hugged me close. "You're right, it is old news. And I've got a great idea."

"What?" I whispered against his shoulder, blinking back incipient tears.

"Let's go down to Cap-Ferrat this weekend. To Peter Guiseborn's house. I've got the use of it until he comes back from New York."

"I don't know if I want to go, Jake."

He held me away from him and looked at me intently. "It'll do us both good. We can relax, get the sun, have some delicious meals, not that you ever eat, but you won't be able to resist the food there. Simone, Peter's housekeeper, is a great cook. And what are you going to do this weekend anyway, Val? Tramp the streets of Paris, sit alone in your apartment thinking about Tony, getting angry with him. Come on, Val, say you'll come with me. Listen, you've got to move forward now, look to the future."

"Okay," I mumbled, giving in, too weary to resist. "I guess it will help to get away from Paris for a few days."

Grinning at me, he hugged me to him again, and then he took hold of my hand, making for the steps near the bridge. These led up to the Quai Malaquais in Saint-Germain-des-Prés, and just beyond the quai was the Rue Bonaparte, where I lived.

As he hurried me along with him, I couldn't help noticing again how badly he was limping, and this worried me. But I didn't dare ask him how his wounds were healing; he usually snapped at me when I did so.

And then I thought: But at least he's alive, and I'm alive, and he's right, I have a whole future ahead of me.

And I made up my mind to bury the dead.

Part Two

THE VALUE OF
*T*RUTH

Chapter 9

I

Saint-Jean-Cap-Ferrat, September • The house hung on a hillside in Cap-Ferrat, overlooking gardens filled with an abundance of flowers, and beyond, stretching to the horizon, was the glittering deep-blue Mediterranean.

I sat on the terrace of the house, looking out toward the sea, content to drift along with my thoughts, enjoying the perfect stillness, unbroken except for the occasional trilling of the birds, the faint buzzing of a bee. It was a glorious morning, and even though it was sunny and warm, a light breeze blew up intermittently. It rippled through the trees, making the leaves dance, and gave the morning air its freshness.

Called Les Roches Fleuries, the villa was aptly named, since so many flowers spilled down over the rocks upon which the house had been built. It was long and rambling, made of a local stone washed pale pink, with a typical Provençal roof of red-slate tiles and green-painted shutters at the many windows.

On the plane to Nice on Thursday, Jake had told me all about the villa. Even so, I hadn't expected anything quite like this. And although he had described it well, I'd teased him and said, "Well, it's true what they say, you know, about a picture being worth a thousand words. Better stick to snapping the old Polaroid."

"Only too true, Val," he'd laughed as he had taken me on a grand tour. I had at once been captivated by the house, which pleased Jake, since he loved it himself; he felt lucky and privileged to be able to use it whenever he wished. It belonged to his old friend Peter Guiseborn, who had moved from Paris to work in New York for a year, and Peter had told Jake to take advantage of his absence. Jake was also flattered and touched because Peter had not extended this invitation to any of his other friends.

The interiors were cool and restful. All of the rooms had white walls, wood-beamed ceilings, and terra-cotta tile floors, and they were furnished with wonderful Provençal antiques made of polished dark woods. There was very little clutter in the rooms, which added to the feeling of restfulness.

Color, bright rafts of it, was introduced in the vibrant paintings hanging on the walls and in the huge bunches of flowers arranged in large stone pots and placed in almost every room.

"I could move in and live here forever," I'd enthused. "And so could I," he'd agreed.

When we arrived we had received a warm welcome from Simone and Armand Roget, the caretakers, who lived in a small house on the property. It was Simone who kept the place so immaculate and sparkling, and the pantry well stocked with her delicious food.

Her husband, Armand, was responsible for the upkeep of the property and the gardens, which were filled to overflowing with bougainvillea, frangipani, honeysuckle, night-blooming jasmine, azaleas, geraniums, and many different species of roses. The flower gardens were set off by velvety green lawns, while a long line of twenty-five stately cypress trees stood guard in the background, dark sentinels silhouetted against the azure sky.

Over dinner on our first night here, Jake had told me the story of the house, at least what little he knew about it. Les Roches Fleuries had been built in the 1930s by a French duke for his English mistress, a beautiful opera singer called Adelia Roland. After her retirement from the stage she had made it her permanent home, had lived there until she died at the age of ninety in 1990. In her will she had left the villa and almost everything else she owned to her great-nephew Peter, Jake's pal from his Oxford days.

I was intrigued by the story of Adelia and the duke, but Jake didn't know much more than he'd already told me. Neither did the Rogets have a great deal to impart to me when I quizzed them about her. They had been at Les Roches Fleuries for twenty years; for eight of these they had worked for Peter, once he had inherited the property. The preceding twelve years had been spent in the employment of Adelia Roland, but by that time she was already an old lady, and the duke had long been dead. They said she had been charming but cool and reserved. And very mysterious.

Earlier that morning, when I'd strolled out-side holding a cup of coffee in my hand, I had spotted Armand working in the garden. Walking over, I had started to chat to him about the house and about Adelia. Suddenly, unexpectedly, he had turned garrulous, and he confided that it had been Adelia herself who had been the brains and driving force behind the planning and execution of these most extraordinary gardens.

Apparently, she had toiled on them herself, and religiously so, had thought nothing of working alongside the various gardeners who had helped her fulfill her plans over the years. The gardens had been ruined during the German Occupation of France, in the Second World War, but she had restored them later, once the war had ended; now they were an exotic paradise.

II

I glanced around when I heard footsteps, and I saw Jake walking along the terrace. I waved to him and he waved back, and a moment later he was standing over the chaise where I lay shaded by an umbrella, looking down at me, smiling broadly.

"This is what I like to see!" he exclaimed.

"And what's that?"

"You lying here like this, relaxing, taking it easy, and looking so contented." He lowered himself onto the edge of the chaise next to mine as he spoke.

"I certainly feel relaxed, Jake. It's just so beautiful here, and the tranquillity's hard to beat, isn't it?"

He merely nodded, and smiled again.

I went on. "I feel . . . well, I feel really peaceful *inside* . . . for the first time in many weeks." I genuinely meant every word I said. I *did* feel so much better, and after only a couple of days.

There was a moment's silence before he

remarked, "So do I, Val. This house has always had a restorative effect on me in the past . . . it's a benign house, full of love and good vibes. The only other one I've known with exactly the same atmosphere was my grandparents' house in Georgia. I always looked forward to going there as a child, I felt enveloped by love, so safe and secure. I still derive pleasure from going there, in fact."

How I envied Jake. The truth was, I'd never felt safe or secure in my life except when I was with my grandparents.

"How is your grandmother doing, Jake?" I now asked, knowing how much he loved the old lady. Actually, I think he loved her in much the same way I had loved Andrew Denning.

"Still going strong. She's really quite amazing. Very bright, not a bit senile, and in great health."

"She's living there alone at the house?"

"Oh, yes. Well, there's help living there with her. A couple of old retainers who've been devoted to her for forty years or more. It would be hard to get her to leave, practically her whole life has been lived out there. It's an old plantation house, not that big really, but beautiful. An antebellum house, redolent of the Old South that once was. You don't see much of *that* anymore, except in a few remote places. Anyway, her place is not too far from Atlanta, and my parents now go there almost every weekend. They worry

about her . . . but they shouldn't, in my opinion."

"Why not?"

"She makes everybody else I know look de-
crepit!"

I smiled. "But she's quite old, isn't she?"

"Eighty-eight. Going on thirty-five though!
And she's independent, opinionated, and very,
very feisty. You'd love her."

Jake started to laugh again, and his bright blue
eyes sparkled with sudden merriment.

"What is it?"

"I was wondering how to describe her physically, and I can say only this . . . she reminds me
of an old movie actress from the 1930s and '40s by
the name of Maria Ouspenskaya. Do you know
who I mean?" He went on chuckling and then
added, "You're looking mystified, Val."

"I am, I'm afraid I *don't* know her."

"Ouspenskaya was petite, fragile-looking,
white-haired, and she spoke with the slightest of
accents, more than likely Russian with a name
like hers. Granmutti Hedy, as we call her, had a
bit of a German accent, but it's very slight now.
Here's something that might just jog your memory about Ouspenskaya. Did you ever see an old
movie called *Love Affair*?"

I shook my head.

"Well, Ouspenskaya was in it, playing an old

lady, of course, and the stars were Charles Boyer and Irene Dunne, and it was about—"

"Wait a minute, I have seen it!" I exclaimed, cutting in as I suddenly recalled the film. "And I *do* know what Ouspenskaya looked like. Incidentally, wasn't that the original version of a later movie called *An Affair to Remember* with Cary Grant and Deborah Kerr?"

"Exactly! And so if you think of Ouspenskaya, you'll know what my grandmother Hedy looks like. She's an extraordinary woman, and she was so strong and vital when she was younger. A marvel, even though I say so myself. She is also very cultured, well read, full of knowledge about art and music. And she was a very, very wonderful grandmother to a little boy and his two sisters."

III

As Jake had been speaking so lovingly about his grandmother, I'd noticed a change in his voice. It was ever so slight, but it was there nonetheless; a soft southern drawl had crept in to diffuse the transatlantic accent he had acquired from years of living in Paris and, before that, Oxford.

Now he was saying, "Don't you think that's a great idea, Val? We'll watch some old movies tonight. Peter has stacks of them, there's quite a wide video selection in his library and there are lots of choices."

"I wonder if he has *Love Affair?*" I said, thinking out loud.

"He might. I know he's got *Casablanca* and many of the other classics from the thirties, forties, and fifties. He's even got *Gone With the Wind.* I wouldn't mind watching *that* again."

I started to laugh.

"What's the matter?" he asked, raising a brow quizzically.

Continuing to laugh, I said, "Are you feeling homesick for Atlanta, Jake?"

Laughing with me, he nodded. "I'm always homesick for Georgia in one way or another, but it just happens to be a really fabulous movie. Let's watch it, okay?"

"Anything you want," I answered. Out of the corner of my eye I could see Simone coming toward us. "I guess lunch is ready," I murmured to Jake, and glanced at my watch. I couldn't believe it was already past one-thirty. Time seemed to fly at Les Roches Fleuries with Jake. The last couple of days had gone by in the blink of an eye.

Pushing himself to his feet, Jake stretched out his hand to me. I took it and he pulled me up from the chaise, led me down the terrace.

"We're coming, Simone," he called out, and she smiled at us, turned on her heel, and went back to the arbor at the far end of the terrace. This little shaded area was just a stone's throw from the kitchen, and it was there she stood, waiting for us.

Within seconds Jake and I were seated opposite each other under the vine-covered arbor, and Simone was saying to us, "Mademoiselle Denning, Monsieur Jake, I found a beautiful *rouget* at the fish market this morning. I've grilled it for you, and I shall bring it now with a dish of vegetables."

"Thanks, Simone, it sounds delicious," Jake replied.

She inclined her head, hurried off to fetch the fish, and Jake lifted the bottle of chilled *vin rosé,* which he loved to drink with lunch, and poured it into the large glasses.

"I'm not planning to go back to Paris on Tuesday after all," he suddenly said, glancing at me across the table. "It's so restful here, the weather's wonderful, and I'm seriously thinking of spending next week at the house. Won't you stay on too, Val?"

"Yes, I'd love to," I answered immediately without even having to think about it. "Why not? I don't have anything pressing to do," I added.

"That's great. I'm glad you'll stay and keep me company."

"What are best friends for?" I asked, returning his smile.

Chapter 10

I

And so I stayed on at Les Roches Fleuries with Jake.

It seemed to me that time just sped by, even though we didn't do anything very special. In the first few days we were there together we fell into a routine, a pattern that was built on a number of little rituals and which we both discovered we enjoyed.

I think the reason we found enjoyment in them is that we lived such a helter-skelter life when we were out on assignment and never knew what was going to happen from one day to the next, or where we might end up.

But at the villa on the hillside, our days rarely

varied, and neither of us minded this at all. In fact, we thought of it as a blessing.

Every morning Jake and I had breakfast together, sitting at the round table under the vine-covered arbor. The weather was still glorious, and the shady arbor offered us protection from the early morning sun. Neither of us ate very much at breakfast, nor were we inclined to talk, so we were, as usual, compatible and at ease with each other.

After breakfast I usually read for a short time while Jake sunbathed, swam in the pool, and occasionally called his photo agency for messages; on other mornings he would spend time writing in his notebook.

Sometimes I would take a swim with Jake but not always. However, I did go to the basement gym with him at exactly eleven o'clock every day, where I fast-walked on the treadmill. Because of his wounds, Jake avoided the treadmill, but he enjoyed lifting weights.

After about half an hour in the gym, we went off to our rooms to shower and change into cool cottons, then we took the car and drove down into the little town of Beaulieu-sur-Mer.

I knew Beaulieu quite well, since my grandparents had frequently stayed at La Réserve, a lovely pink-and-white hotel in the town. It sat on a wedge of land at the edge of the sea, was renowned for its elegance and its wonderful restaurant. When my grandparents had come to France to see me in the summer, they went down to the South after a week in Paris. I always joined them in Beaulieu, once the Sorbonne was on summer recess.

Because of his frequent sojourns at Peter's villa, Jake was also well acquainted with this charming little town, and we liked to walk around, buying the French and English newspapers and magazines, visiting the antique dealers we liked, and picking up the odd items we needed at the local shops. But our most favorite spot was the open-air fruit and vegetable market right in the heart of Beaulieu.

Inevitably our mouths started watering when we stopped to look at the baskets of raspberries, red currants, strawberries, blackberries, plums, peaches, and the fragrant melons from Cavaillon, which we both knew from experience were the very best. Everything on the market stalls looked so luscious and tempting; but we never dared buy anything to take back to the house, for fear of offending Simone. She prided herself on her careful selection of produce for the delicious meals she created for us.

There was a small port in Beaulieu, where sailboats and yachts were at anchor in the quiet harbor. It was a charming, picturesque spot, and there were all manner of bistros, cafés, and boutiques centered around the port. We loved to

linger there, whiling away the time as we mean-
dered along the quais.

Just before lunch we went to La Réserve for an
aperitif, since the hotel was close to the old port.
If we didn't stop there, then we would end up at
the Grand Hotel du Cap-Ferrat on our way
home to the villa. We had discovered that the
outside bar on the tree-shaded terrace of the hotel
was a cool place for a Kir Royale or a simple
citron pressé.

This kind of leisurely morning, devoid of the
drama, stress, and death we were accustomed to
coping with, was so unusual for us, we got a
tremendous kick out of it. "Being normal, living
normal," Jake called it, and he was right. Most of
our working days were spent watching people
being blown up, maimed, or killed while we
plied our trade as war photographers.

After our visit to the Grand Hotel, we would
then drive on, up the winding hill and through
the woods, making it back to Les Roches Fleuries
just in time for lunch.

The afternoons were very lazy.

Jake read and slept. I did the same, or listened
to music. Neither of us ever thought of turning
on the television set and tuning in to CNN. We
didn't want to hear the bad news, to know about
wars, terrorism, earthquakes, hurricanes, floods,
fires, or famine.

This kind of quiet, uneventful time was rare

for us, and therefore seductive . . . we wanted to make it last. And so we were never tempted to venture out in the evening; certainly we had no desire to visit the chic spots in Monte Carlo, Nice, and Cannes. For the most part, Jake and I stayed close to the villa, which we were very partial to and enjoyed to the fullest. It seemed to us that there was no reason to go anywhere else. The extraordinary peacefulness was our idea of bliss, and we made the most of it.

II

One morning at the end of my first week at the villa, I woke up and discovered that I felt different.

I lay in bed for a moment, watching the sunlight slither in through the slats of the wooden blinds, wondering *why* I felt this way, and then, in an instant, I *knew*.

It was because I hadn't thought about Tony Hampton for several days. And because I hadn't thought about him, or what he'd done to me, I wasn't angry or hurt.

I was just *me* . . . Valentine Denning. The Val Denning of old again. It was a great feeling.

A second or two later I was standing in front of the bathroom mirror, staring at myself. To my astonishment, I even looked different. The violet smudges under my eyes had all but disappeared, and the grayish tinge to my skin had been replaced by a lovely golden glow. Without actually sunbathing, I had somehow managed to catch the sun, had acquired a light tan; even my hair was sun-streaked. I hadn't looked so healthy for a long time, and suddenly I was very pleased.

This miraculous and unexpected change in my appearance gave me a huge boost, a sense of renewed energy, and I threw off my nightgown, stepped into the shower, and turned on the water. After lathering myself with shower gel and then shampooing my hair, I rinsed off, stepped out, and toweled myself dry.

Within minutes I was tying my hair in a ponytail, then pulling on a swimsuit; I found a white cotton-voile shirt in the wardrobe, pushed my feet into a pair of flat mules, jammed on my dark glasses, and went in search of Jake.

I found him sitting at the edge of the swimming pool with his feet dangling in the water, his ear pressed to his cell phone. He was listening intently. When he saw me coming down the steps to the pool, he merely raised his hand in greeting then beckoned me to join him.

After a moment or two of listening, he said, "Okay, Jacques. Thanks. Call me back if you think I can be of help." Listening again, he reached for the notepad next to him. His eyes scanned it quickly, then he said, "Yup, I got it. See ya, Jacques."

Once he had clicked off the phone, I walked over and gave him a kiss on the cheek. "Good morning."

"And top o' the morning to you."

I smiled at him. "In our Irish mode, are we?"

"I guess so. Perhaps because I had a call at the photo agency from Fiona. She's in Dublin. At the Shelbourne Hotel. She wants me to call her."

I frowned. "I wonder why?"

"God knows," Jake murmured, and glanced down at his cell phone and then the notepad, and began to dial. A moment later he was asking for Mrs. Fiona Hampton. He waited for a couple of seconds, then said, "Thanks very much," and clicked off. Turning to face me, he explained, "She's checked out. No forwarding address."

"She's probably gone back to London. To the house in Hampstead."

"I guess."

"Did Jacques have anything else to say?"

"He wanted to know if I'd like to go back to Rwanda. To do another story on the gorillas. I said no. He's going to ask Harry Lennox if he wants to do it. I told him I'd help with Harry if it was necessary. But I don't think it will be. Harry's ambitious, even if he is a bit of an innocent abroad, so to speak. He'll jump at the assignment."

"Perhaps," I murmured. I wasn't sure about Jake's assessment of Harry. I thought he was much more worldly than Jake gave him credit for. In my opinion, Harry Lennox was also devious, possibly even treacherous as well. He had always reminded me of my brother, Donald the Great.

"You sound dubious, Valentine. What's your problem?" he asked in his breezy way.

"I think you underestimate Harry Lennox. He's made dissembling a fine art. And he's a jealous little bugger. Especially jealous of you."

Jake threw back his head and laughed. "Oh, come on, Val, don't be ridiculous."

"I'm not being ridiculous, and listen, I know his type. He's like my sneaky little brother . . . I wouldn't trust either of them as far as I could see them. And that's a fact—" I broke off as I saw Simone hurrying down the steps to the pool. She was as white as bleached bone and obviously distressed.

III

"Simone, what's wrong?" Jake said. And as he spoke he pulled his legs out of the pool and scrambled to his feet.

She drew to a standstill in front of us and I saw at once that she was on the verge of tears. I reached out, put my hand on her arm. "Whatever is it?" I asked.

"It is my daughter, Françoise," Simone began, and then her voice quavered. After a moment she recovered, and continued in a rush of words. "She had a bad fall this morning. Down the stairs. Olivier, her husband, has taken her to the hospital. They are worried about the baby."

"My God, that's terrible!" I exclaimed. "Is there anything we can do?"

Simone shook her head, looking distracted and worried, then brushed her hand across her eyes. "Olivier, he just phoned," she added.

Jake said, "You must go to Marseilles, Simone, with Armand. We can manage here. And you'll only worry if you don't go."

She nodded. "That is true, I will. *Merci,* Monsieur Jake. Please come, the breakfast is ready."

IV

The three of us walked up to the vine-covered arbor at the far end of the terrace, and Simone disappeared through the door to the kitchen.

Jake and I sat down, staring at each other worriedly. Jake sounded concerned when he said, "I believe Françoise's about seven or eight months pregnant with her first baby. I hope she hasn't injured herself and the child, that they're going to be all right."

"So do I . . . but what are they doing in Marseilles? I thought their daughter lived in Cannes?"

"That's Solange, the younger daughter."

"I see." I picked up the crystal jug of fresh orange juice that stood on the table and filled our glasses. Before I got a chance to say anything else, Simone was back with a large pot of coffee and a jug of hot milk for the *café au lait* we both preferred.

Returning to the kitchen, she came out a second later carrying a basket of warm croissants and brioches. She said: "Armand is telephoning the Nice airport, Monsieur Jake. There's a plane to Marseilles at one o'clock. I will attend to the beds, clean the kitchen—"

Cutting in, Jake said, "You'll do no such thing, Simone. I told you, we can manage. Go and get ready, I know how anxious you must be. Once you're packed, I'll drive you to the airport."

"But, Monsieur Jake—"

"No buts," he interrupted again, holding up his hand, taking charge. "Go and do as I say, and we'll leave whenever you want."

"Merci, Monsieur Jake, c'est gentil de votre part."

When we were alone, Jake said, "How about coming with me to the airport in Nice?" He poured coffee and hot milk into his large cup, then looked across at me.

"Well . . ." I cocked my head on one side and murmured, "Maybe it's better I stay here, tidy the kitchen, do a few chores, be domesticated for a change." I smiled at him. "And I'll prepare a lovely lunch."

He nodded. "Okay, but only if you let me fix dinner."

"Southern style?" I demanded.

He laughed. "You're on."

V

Once they had left, it didn't take me very long to stack the dishwasher and mop the kitchen floor; I then went to make the beds and tidy up our bathrooms.

When all these jobs were finished, I returned to the kitchen and went directly to the walk-in pantry near the refrigerator. I was amazed when I saw how beautifully kept it was. Everything was arranged so neatly, the glass jars of bottled vegetables, fruits, and pickles carefully labeled and dated by Simone.

There were stacks of canned goods on higher shelves, and on the long countertop were most of the ingredients I needed for our lunch. A bowl of large brown eggs, a big wooden board holding different local cheeses, and a straw basket containing tomatoes, lettuce, and cucumbers. I picked this up and took it out to the sink.

After washing and drying the lettuce leaves, I wrapped them in paper towels and put them back in the pantry. I peeled and sliced half of a long cucumber, then sliced two large tomatoes. Once I had arranged these slices on a platter, I covered it with plastic wrap. This, too, went into the pantry.

All I would have to do later was arrange the ingredients in a salad bowl and add Simone's famous vinaigrette dressing, which stood on the shelf right in front of my eyes.

The eggs for the omelette could be beaten later, once Jake had returned from the airport. At that time I would also warm a baguette and bring out the cheese board. Everything was on hand, and ready to prepare at the last moment.

Walking to the far end of the kitchen, I pulled open the door leading down to the basement, which ran the full length of the house. The first flight of six steps stopped at a wide landing fitted with large stone shelves, and it was here other foodstuffs were stored. A second flight of stone steps continued on to the actual basement, where there was a wine cellar, one much appreciated by Jake, since it contained some rare vintage wines. Peter had given him the run of this.

It was dark and I switched on a light before

descending into the murkiness. I shivered slightly, it was so cold, and glanced around. Simone had arranged things as neatly here as she had in the other pantry. On one of the stone shelves I found small trugs of berries, bowls of fresh figs, several melons—Cavaillon—lots of vegetables, and a big basket of apples. Certainly there was plenty to choose from, and we weren't going to starve during Simone's absence in Marseilles.

I stood for a moment, my hand resting on the stone shelf, thinking again of Simone's sudden and unexpected departure a short while ago. How white-faced and anxious she had been when she had come to the kitchen to say good-bye to me.

"I'm sure everything's going to be all right, that Françoise is fine," I'd murmured, wanting to reassure her. I had given her a quick hug, and discovered how tense her body was.

Nodding, Simone had bravely tried to smile but without much success. "*Ma petite fille,* my little girl . . . I must go to her. She needs me, I know."

Catching her hand in mine, I'd squeezed it, and agreed. "Yes, she does need you, Simone, but you'll be with her soon. Try not to worry."

Again Simone attempted to give me another smile, but this, too, had wavered and she left with Jake and Armand, who looked as worried as his wife.

I stood at the kitchen door, waving good-bye to them as Jake backed the car out. A loving mother, a good mother, I had thought as I'd turned to go back inside. And I hoped that Françoise had not lost the child she was carrying, and that she herself was not in any danger.

Chapter 11

I

Climbing the stairs from the pantry, I went back to the kitchen.

After pouring myself a large glass of water, I went out to the terrace and walked down the steps, making for a favorite spot of mine.

This was located in one of the smaller gardens of the villa which was mostly composed of green lawn surrounded by flowering shrubs. The lawn ran to the tip of the property, where steep craggy rocks fell precipitously down to the sea.

I felt as though I were on a ship whenever I sat here on the wrought-iron bench that had been placed under an ancient cedar. I leaned back, closing my eyes, enjoying the warmth of the morning air and the early sun filtering through the wide-splayed branches of the tree.

When I finally opened my eyes a few minutes later, I blinked. Brilliant sunshine was now filling the pale blue sky with incandescent light, and the sea spread out before me glittered like dark-blue glass shot through with golden veins.

A boat came into my line of vision, its white sails billowing out in the morning breeze. What an idyllic scene it was, and so very familiar to me . . . a lone ship etched against the blue horizon where sea and sky merged, sailing along . . . carrying whomever to where? I had often wondered that. It was mysterious, yet oddly intimate in my mind's eye. I'd seen other sailboats just like this so many times before in the past. . . .

II

A rush of memories assailed me.

Memories of those days spent here in the South of France with my grandparents, when I was studying at the Sorbonne in Paris. I had always joined them on summer recess from the university. Just a girl I'd been then.

Cecelia and Andrew Denning . . . they had been so good to me. All of my life. Until the day they died. She had gone first, very sadly, and then him. But thankfully I'd had the comfort of my grandfather for a few years longer.

The three of us a team, three against the world, my gran used to say with a light, cheery laugh. She was spirited and vivacious, even when she was old, and she had told me so many times that I must always spit in the eye of trouble, keep my back ramrod straight, my head high, and my heart wide open to receive all the good things that were coming my way.

They had loved me very much, and, more important perhaps, they had been able to show that love to me. It had been a shield after they were gone.

How very badly they had wanted to make up for the deficiencies of their son. "Henpecked," my grandmother had frequently muttered, and a trifle disdainfully at that, her sharp blue eyes glinting like steel, her generous mouth narrowed in disgust at the thought of her weak-kneed son.

What she'd said about him being henpecked was true, I think. My father had never been able to stand up to my mother, who had behaved as if I didn't exist. And therefore so had he.

I would still ponder this from time to time, wonder why my mother had behaved so strangely. There had to be a reason, didn't there? But what could it be?

This question had haunted me most of my life, and I'd never been able to come up with a proper answer for myself. Yet deep inside I was certain I was innocent of any wrongdoing. What *could* I have done to offend her when I was still a small baby?

Why would a mother hate her own child?

Once again the question hung there in front of my eyes, staring back at me balefully.

I sighed under my breath. Perhaps *hate* was too strong a word. She had shown no *interest* in me ever, but she hadn't *hated* me, had she?

No, I didn't think she had. Disliked me, perhaps. My mother had certainly never mistreated me or abused me. At least, not physically. Nor had she abused me verbally either; that was not her way. Still, in one sense she had been abusive to me, because she had behaved as if I weren't there. No wonder I was insecure, always longing to find a safe harbor for myself.

I wondered, all of a sudden, why I was a war photographer, constantly flinging myself into the face of danger, putting myself in harm's way. I didn't have an answer to that, and I never would. Perhaps only a psychiatrist would be able to provide one.

What a mess I would have been, I thought now, if it hadn't been for my grandparents, especially my grandfather. He had made me what I am, and he was the best part of me. Without him in my life, and with such constancy, without his guidance, love, and caring, I would have been nothing; I would have achieved nothing.

Unexpectedly, I thought of Tony Hampton. I almost laughed out loud. Here was I, seemingly always seeking a secure place to land, and yet I had become involved with him. Why *him?* He was as likely to offer me security and safety as a violent terrorist holding a gun to my head. So why had I chosen him? Because he had charmed me into a love affair, had truly convinced me he was madly in love with me. And because I hadn't known he was a two-timing, double-dealing lothario who didn't understand the meaning of truth, integrity, fidelity, or loyalty.

I pushed the image of him away from me, crushed it under my feet until it no longer existed. And silently I repeated my resolutions like a litany:

I had buried the dead.

I was not about to resurrect the dead.

I had started afresh with a clean slate.

I was interested only in the future.

Lolling back against the bench, I closed my eyes, drifting with my myriad thoughts. Out of the blue, Fiona Hampton came into my mind. Yesterday she had phoned Jake at his agency in Paris. Yet again, I couldn't help wondering why. Perhaps just to say hello? To cling to memories? . . . the past? . . . an old friendship? . . . her husband's best friend? I wasn't sure. Nor did it matter. If she really needed to speak to Jake, she'd call again. It had nothing to do with me, nor was it any of my business.

Without knowing, Fiona had enabled me to shake off my searing grief. And she had helped me to bury the dead. Her dead as much as mine, as it so happened.

It was through her that I'd had a moment of the greatest insight, had seen everything the way it actually was, and not as I imagined it to be.

I had seen the truth, looked it in the face.

And I suddenly understood the reality of her life. And the reality of mine. She was the wife, I the mistress. Sharing the same man without knowing that we were. Both of us lied to and misled. Sisters under the skin. Linked emotionally without either of us realizing this.

At least, she didn't know it. I did. Now.

Meeting Fiona Hampton had changed my life, and irrevocably so. And I was glad of that. It was she who had given me a future in a certain sense.

The nightmare of the memorial service had fortunately been just that—a very bad dream. And like most bad dreams, it had gone away. The burden had been lifted off me.

And now I was truly free.

Opening my eyes, I lifted my face, glanced up at the blue translucent sky. I was as free as that lone bird flying so high up there in the sky . . .

higher and higher it seemed to soar . . . until it finally disappeared from sight. Yes, I *was* as free as a bird on the wing. My spirits lifted at this thought.

Rising, I turned away from the glittering sea, slowly made my way back along the flagged path, heading up to the villa. As I walked along, I wondered if I would ever fall in love again, have a good relationship with a man, get a chance of lasting happiness with someone someday, in the not too distant future? I laughed hollowly to myself at the mere idea. It would take a miracle to make that happen, and I surely didn't believe in miracles. Again I laughed dismissively, not realizing that I would soon discover how wrong I was.

Especially when it came to miracles.

III

There was no sign of Jake when I got back to the house. I glanced at my watch, saw that it was almost twelve-thirty. He had been gone for several hours now, and it wasn't that far to Nice. Looking up at the kitchen clock on the wall, I checked the time. My watch was five minutes fast, but that was all.

He'll be back soon, I thought, shrugging lightly as I went to the sink, where I washed the glass I was carrying, and my hands. I then decided I might as well start to prepare lunch.

After retrieving the parcel of lettuce and the platter of cucumber and tomatoes from the pantry, I got out the green cabbage-leaf salad bowl, a glass mixing bowl, and a whisk. I put all of these items on the worktable near my parcel of lettuce; after opening it up and patting the leaves dry with paper towels, I tore them into pieces and dropped them into the cabbage-leaf bowl. I then added the slices of cucumber and tomatoes to the lettuce.

I remembered Simone's vinaigrette dressing, and I ran to the pantry to get it. I shook the jar several times before unscrewing the lid and looking at it. The dressing was a little thick from being in the cold pantry, and it needed to stand for a while to liquefy a bit more. Taking it over to the table, I left the lid off and returned to the pantry. I brought out the bowl of eggs and went back for the wooden board holding the selection of cheeses; there was just enough room for all of this on the table.

My first task was to whip up the eggs for the omelette. I broke six into the glass mixing bowl, decided this was not enough, added two more, threw away the shells, picked up the whisk, and began to beat them. Once they were smooth and creamy-looking, I reached for the pepper mill and the container of fines herbs. I added dashes of both to the eggs, along with several pinches of salt.

Suddenly the door flew open, and I looked up quickly as Jake pushed his way into the kitchen. At least, I assumed it was Jake, since his face was largely hidden by the paper bags of groceries he held in his arms. A muffled "Hi, Kid" emanated from behind the bags.

"Hi to you too," I replied, and went to help him with the bags, grabbed one from him, as he explained. "Couldn't get everything I needed for my genuine, authentic southern dinner, but enough to give you a sampling tonight, honey."

"I wondered where you were," I muttered, peering into the bag I'd placed on the countertop near the sink. "Oh, Jake!" I cried. "You went and bought fruit without me, and after all the mouth-waterings we shared!"

He grinned at me and set his bags down on the counter. "Don't be mad at me. I wasn't going to do it, I know how you've been longing to shop at the open-air market, but I was already there when I remembered that. It saved time, Val, I couldn't really drive back to get you."

"I know. Anyway, it's almost redundant, the fruit, I mean. There's all sorts of stuff in the second pantry down the steps to the basement."

"That figures, knowing Simone."

"They got off all right, I assume."

"Sure did. Well, I guess the berries'll keep for

another meal. I'm certain Simone and Armand won't be back for a couple of days or so. What's that?" He was now staring at my bowl of beaten eggs.

"Your lunch. Soon it will be an *omelette fines herbs.*"

"Great." He opened the refrigerator door and began to empty the bags into it. I noticed him placing chicken and other items on the shelves, then I turned away and went to get a skillet.

When the bags had been emptied, Jake said, "I'll bring up some rosé from the wine cellar," and headed for the door to the basement. He was back in a couple of minutes carrying two bottles. These he put in the refrigerator. "Now what can I do?"

"Can you hand me the butter, please?"

"Sure can." He went over to the refrigerator.

"Thanks," I said when he gave it to me. I walked to the stone jar that stood on a chest at the far end of the kitchen; it was in this large stone olive jar with its wooden lid that Simone kept her baguettes. She purchased these fresh every day at the bakery in Beaulieu. I took one of the long loaves out of the jar, but it didn't feel too fresh. And I realized she had not gone to the bakery that morning because of the phone call from Marseilles.

Taking the baguette to the sink, I wet it under the tap and put it in the oven. Later, once the omelette was ready, I would turn on the oven, set it at low, and in five or six minutes the bread would be warm, and as fresh as if it had just been made. Simone had shown me this little trick only the other day, and now I was pleased she had.

Jake poured himself a glass of water, then sat down on a stool and watched me making lunch, not saying very much but looking thoughtful.

And then quite out of the blue, he said slowly, in a muffled sort of voice, "I'm worried about Simone."

I glanced across at him. "What do you mean?" I quickly turned back to the omelette, not wanting it to spoil.

"She was very strange on the way to the airport, barely spoke at all, and she was extremely anxiety ridden and tense. Actually, she was sort of rigid with fright in the car. At least, that's what I thought."

"Well, she *was* worried when she got the news, Jake. A fall like that can be very dangerous to a pregnant woman, especially one who is seven or eight months gone," I pointed out.

"I realize that. But Simone's worry, her fear, seemed somehow a bit abnormal. Over the top, in a way."

"What about Armand, how was he?"

"Relatively silent, but then, he's not talkative, a

quiet sort of guy. Always has been. Simone's much more outgoing."

Jake sighed so heavily, I turned around swiftly, the spatula in my hand, and stared at him. "You're getting at something, Jake." I stared at him more intently, saw the genuine worry etched on his face, and then it hit me. "Oh my God, you don't think Simone's daughter was pushed down the stairs, do you?"

He shook his head. "I kinda think Simone believes that's what happened."

"What makes *you* think *she* thinks such a thing?" I asked, and felt the gooseflesh spring up on my neck and arms. "Did she tell you that?"

"Not in so many words, Val, no." Jake bit his lip. "But she said some really odd things. At one point she muttered to Armand about Olivier. I didn't quite catch it completely, but it was something like *I'll kill him if he did that.* And Armand gaped at her. He was startled, aghast, and shook his head, as if to warn her not to speak in front of me. Although obviously she knows I speak French. When we got to the ticket counter at the airport, Armand was busy buying the tickets, and I tried to talk to her again. Sort of soothe her, Val. She was so uptight, I thought she was going to explode. I finally gave up. I didn't want her to think I was prying. I told her to take as long as she wanted. After all, we're just guests here. It's Peter who's her employer."

I nodded. "Let's continue our conversation over lunch," I suggested. "Everything's ready now."

Chapter 12

I

Between mouthfuls of omelette, Jake said, "What made you ask me if I thought Françoise could have been pushed down the stairs? I mean, what exactly did I say to convey this to you?"

"It wasn't anything you said, but, rather, the expression on your face, Jake. It suddenly struck me that you might possibly be thinking along those lines. Spousal abuse is rampant these days."

He nodded. "Don't say *these days* like that, Val, there's nothing new about wife beating. It's always been with us. We just hear more about it now . . . in the way that we know more about everything, from wars and other disasters, to the infidelities of politicians. Chalk it up to the age we live in, the media age. Instant wars . . . seen on television as they're happening. Instant news. Instant everything on television . . . and on the Internet. Yup, the age of information . . . and misinformation."

"I guess you're right," I answered. "Is Simone going to call us later today? Let us know how her daughter is doing?"

"She promised she would once they'd been to the hospital, seen Françoise, and talked to the doctors. I heard her say something to Armand about bringing her back here to recuperate. And I must admit, I did think that was odd." He took a swallow of the wine, then added, "It's as if she wants Françoise to be out of Olivier's way, don't you think?"

"Perhaps . . ." I leaned back in my chair and thought for a moment before continuing. "Or it could be she just wants to look after her daughter herself. Unless Françoise has a lot of injuries. I mean, you don't fall down a flight of stairs and stand up unscathed, do you? Look, Jake, the doctors might keep her in the hospital for a while. Because of her pregnancy."

"You're right, and if they do let her go home because her injuries are minor, she would still probably need looking after. And Olivier's at work all day."

"What does he do?"

"He's a cop," Jake replied, and looked at me knowingly.

"Oh," I muttered. "Well, that doesn't mean anything." I grimaced. "Cops have been known to be wife beaters, you know, and some even think they're above the law."

"He could be that type," Jake muttered.

"Oh, have you met him, then?"

"Briefly, with Françoise. When I was down here with Peter. They were staying with Simone and Armand for a few days, and Peter introduced us. He's very fond of Simone, and of course Françoise and Solange grew up here at Les Roches Fleuries, so he's known them for years."

"How old is Françoise?"

"About twenty-six, and Solange is twenty-three, maybe twenty-four. Not sure. But they're both nice girls." Jake lifted his glass and took another long swallow of the *vin rosé*.

"You know, I never understand spousal abuse, Jake. How can a man be so brutal to the woman he loves and is married to? It just takes my breath away."

Jake gaped at me and put his glass down. "I can't believe that *you* of all people are saying this to me." He shook his head, and his blue eyes were tight on mine. "You know better than anybody how wicked and cruel human beings are. Just think about the atrocities and brutalities you've witnessed. You know as well as I do that man is evil, Val. In the Balkans alone you've seen men mowing each other down indiscriminately, men who were friends and neighbors once, and doing it without thinking twice. And what about the tortured and maimed we've both photographed?" Bafflement, bewilderment even, had settled on his face.

I felt a cold chill sweep through me as I stared back at him. And then I glanced away, suddenly not wanting to look into Jake's eyes any longer. Everything he said was true. The problem was I didn't want to remember or contemplate any of it. Not today, at any rate. I did not wish to focus on Kosovo and the other horrific wars I'd covered. I just couldn't bear to do so. I was sickened by it all, weary of war and all the killing. I suddenly wondered if I was burnt out; I frowned and sat up straighter in the chair. I had never thought anything like this before. The idea that I could be burnt out scared the hell out of me. And so I pushed the idea away.

I said slowly, "Nothing's changed in the world since medieval times, has it? Man hasn't learned anything, has he, Jake?"

"No. Nor will he ever, Val. Human beings will never be any different, not unless some scientist finds a way to give us all a different type of DNA, give us new genes. We are what we are because of our genes. James Watson discovered that when he discovered DNA. And so over the centuries man has gone on doing the same things over and over again, committing the same acts of cruelty, the same heinous crimes. It's in our genes, it's our nature. I don't think man has altered much since the beginning of time as we know it, since the day he got up on two legs and started to walk upright."

"Are you saying there's no hope for human beings?"

"That's correct. And there isn't."

"Let me understand this. You are telling me that as humans we are always going to fight wars, kill each other, commit murder and all manner of horrendous crimes, become child and wife beaters, adulterers, whatever? Is that what you believe, Jake?"

"Absolutely. History has proven to me time and again that it *is* cyclical . . . it just keeps repeating itself, and Homo sapiens, modern humans, keep repeating themselves over the centuries . . . endlessly . . . because they *are* humans."

I studied him intently. Jake was a Rhodes scholar, had read history at Oxford University, and had graduated with very high honors. History was his bailiwick, and he took it very seriously. And so I knew he meant every word.

"That's awful . . ." I said eventually, and then my voice trailed away. I was at a loss, I didn't know what else to say.

Jake smiled at me. "It's just the way it is, Val, and the way it's always been. And will always *be*.

You can't change it. I can't change it. No one can. We are what we are."

"What a frightening world we live in, when you think about it."

"That's true, but there's nowhere else to go. I'm afraid we're stuck with planet earth. And anyway, living here is better than the alternative."

"What's that?" I asked.

"Not to be alive at all, Val."

II

He changed the subject then, and began to tell me about the wonderful dinner he was going to make; later he helped me to clear away the dishes.

We were both stacking the dishwasher in the kitchen, when the phone rang. Jake went to answer it, and I knew at once that it was Simone calling.

I stood next to the dishwasher, looking across at Jake as he picked up the phone.

"Hullo?" he said, and listened for a split second before exclaiming, "That's great, Simone!" He gave me the thumbs-up sign, and went on. "We've been concerned. It's a relief to know that Françoise isn't seriously injured."

I relaxed against the countertop, and it struck me how worried I'd been for Françoise, a girl I'd never even met and didn't know. But I had grown to like her mother in the time I had been at the villa, and I empathized with Simone. And in any case, violence against women disturbed and alarmed me. Not that I knew there *had* been any violence in this particular case, but seemingly Simone had her suspicions.

Jake was still listening, but after a moment he said, "Yes, I will, Simone, and please, don't rush back. Do what you have to do. Just attend to Françoise and be sure she's all right before you leave. *Au revoir*."

As soon as he hung up, Jake glanced at me and explained, "Simone asked me to thank you for being so nice this morning."

I nodded. "From what I was hearing, Françoise is okay and she didn't lose the baby, thank God."

"She is, and no, she didn't miscarry. Apparently Françoise is very bruised and has a sprained ankle, but it wasn't such a bad accident after all. Simone thought she had fallen down the staircase from the second floor, but she'd misunderstood Olivier. Françoise stumbled when she was going down three steps into the pantry. She hit her head against a wall, but there was no concussion, just a big bump on her forehead and some other bruising. But nothing broken, and mother and baby perfectly okay."

"She was lucky," I remarked. "How did Simone sound?"

"Strange, I must admit. Uptight. I felt she was still worried in some way."

"But that's only natural under the circumstances, Jake. Anyway, it's hard to really know what she feels. I've noticed that her English is very . . . *precise*, I guess that's the best word. But it's also a bit quaint at times. She doesn't always express herself well."

"She sounds stilted," Jake said, and laughed. "She learned English from Adelia Roland all those years ago, and I think that's why she sometimes sounds . . . well, a bit old-fashioned, quaint, as you say. But getting back to Françoise, Simone might be overreacting. Perhaps she doesn't like her son-in-law."

"Did she imply that?"

He shook his head. "No, she didn't. She just said she'd misunderstood, that the fall hadn't been serious. She said she and Armand would come back tonight, but as you heard, I told her not to rush. She'll be calling us tomorrow."

III

We finished cleaning up the kitchen, and Jake sat down at the countertop to phone his agency in Paris to check for messages and discuss business.

Jacques Foucher was Jake's partner, along with Harvey Robinson in New York and Matt Logan in the Far East. The four photographers had started Photoreal some nine years ago, and Jacques ran the Paris office, preferring to be out of the field these days. He and Jake had been close buddies for about twelve years, and Jake relied on Jacques to handle the business end of the agency in Paris. They employed four other photographers at the bureau, but Jake was the big star.

While he talked on the phone, I sat at the kitchen table turning over the pages of the Paris edition of the *New York Herald Tribune,* which Jake had brought back with him from the Nice airport. But I did so halfheartedly, not really interested in the news. Most of it was bad anyway, if the headlines were anything to go by.

I was enjoying being at Les Roches Fleuries. It was like hiding away in a sense, but at this point I needed the break from the turbulent, danger-ous, and disturbing world I lived in most of the time. I believe we both did. I was also worried about Jake going out on assignment. His wounds looked as if they had healed, but sometimes he limped badly, and this was cause for concern, I thought. I still had not dared to broach the sub-ject, but I was going to when the opportunity pre-sented itself in the next couple of days.

Eventually Jake hung up and said, "Nothing

very important happening at the agency, Val. So I can relax a bit longer here. Well, I guess I'd better give Fiona a call in London." As he spoke, he was already dialing the number. It rang and rang, and then Jake said, "Hello, Fiona. Jake here. I'm returning your call. I'm in Cap-Ferrat." He left the number of the villa and signed off with a breezy good-bye.

Looking over at me, he asked, "A machine again. I'm beginning to hate them. Incidentally, have you spoken to Mike Carter?"

"Yes, the other day, when I decided to stay on here with you. I wanted to give him this number. He's still saying I should take my time about going back to work."

"He's right. Kosovo remains troublesome, but there's not much else for us to cover at the moment, so we might as well take it easy while we can."

Chapter 13

I

"I didn't know it was as steep as this," Jake said, peering down over the craggy rocks that fell into the sea far below. "It's stupendous here. And what a sheer drop!"

"Don't get so near the edge, it's dangerous!" I exclaimed. "There should be a railing there, somebody could easily fall over the edge."

"Yup, you're right about that, Val," Jake said, swinging around, walking over to join me on the wrought-iron bench in my favorite spot. We had been strolling around the garden following a long-drawn-out lunch, and had ended up here.

Now he said, "But I don't think Peter would come to this part of the gardens, or anyone else, for that matter. Only you, Kid, so nobody's in danger of falling off the edge. I'll say this, it's a fabulous view."

"Yes, you can see for miles." I moved slightly on the bench, leaned forward, and went on. "Tony loved danger, loved being near the vortex of it—" Abruptly, I stopped speaking, wondering why I had brought up his name. I was mad at myself for doing so.

Jake simply nodded but said nothing at all, as if he also wondered why I had mentioned Tony. I stared into his lean and expressive face, at a sudden loss for words, and forced a small smile.

Then, wanting to change the subject, I found myself blurting out, "Jake, I'm worried about you. I mean about the way you're limping. Don't you think you ought to see a doctor when we get back to Paris?"

"I saw the doctor before we came down here. He said I'm fine, that it's just a matter of time. It's sort of . . . well, I guess it's a slow healing process . . . inside the leg, I mean. Anyway, I don't always limp. Only occasionally."

"You limp a lot," I corrected him, giving him a stern and knowing glance.

"Not that much, only when it feels a bit tender." He took hold of my hand and held it in his. "Stop being such a Jewish mother." He was laughing as he said this, and then he added,

"Please stop fussing, Val honey. Honestly, I'm really okay. Fit and well and on top of my form."

I shook my head. "I can't help worrying, I care about you. You're my best friend, the only family I have."

"I'm glad I'm important to you. After all, I care about *you* very much."

There was a tender look in his eyes as he said this and a lot of love written across his face, and I was both startled and taken aback. All I could do was nod silently.

Finally, he added, "I hope *you're* on the mend, that you're not . . . dwelling on Tony and his shenanigans anymore. He's not worth it."

"Of course I'm not dwelling on him, or the past year! I want to forget it, believe me. Anyway, being here has been wonderful, such a treat, and a great rest for me. I haven't enjoyed myself so much since we were in Beirut. We've always had a lot of fun together, and it's great being with you, Jake."

"Likewise, Val, I feel the same way." He stood up, stretched several times, and flexed his arms. Then he announced, "This kind of indolent life of luxury is very addictive. I could easily become accustomed to it."

"Not you, my friend," I immediately shot back, glancing up at him, shaking my head knowingly. "You're a war photographer born and bred.

You'd miss the action too much, and if anything is addictive, *action* is."

"Oh, I don't know . . ." He didn't finish his sentence, just shrugged and leaned against the cedar tree.

"Trust me, *I* know." I studied him, my head on one side. "Why *did* you become a war photographer, Jake? I'm curious about that."

"Because I wanted to record history . . . when it was actually happening, when history was being made. I didn't want to learn about it after the event, I guess I wanted to be *part* of it, in one sense. I also wanted to capture the truth on film. I wanted my pictures to do more than merely inform, I needed them to *mean* something as well. It's a funny thing to say, perhaps, but I thought it was important to make people *feel* something about war, to make them conscious of its cruelty and viciousness, and also fully aware of its inhumanity. I hoped people would feel compassion for the dead when they saw my photographs. What I mean is, I wanted them to feel strongly about dead *strangers,* about people they'd never known. I guess I wanted to make them *care* about those people. Do you understand that, Val?"

"Absolutely, and you wanted to prove that your pictures were meaningful, that they could touch and move people. I hope we both achieve that,

Jake, otherwise what we do for a living wouldn't be worth doing, would it?"

"No, it wouldn't. And what about you? I know everything there is to know about you, I think, and yet I don't know why *you* decided to be a war photographer. You never said."

"I wanted to be where the action was, in the middle of it, actually. I thought it would be exciting, and let's admit it, there *is* always that rush of adrenaline when we're in the thick of the fighting. But when I was a child I just enjoyed being behind a camera, I may have been hiding, you know, pretending to be someone else. It's funny, Jake, but I always thought of my camera as being my third eye. Christopher Isherwood wrote *I Am a Camera*, and I guess I still feel that about myself. I am a camera, and my third eye has always been an accurate eye. It records the truth. I suppose, like you, I'm a seeker of the truth at heart. My grandfather said I was very observant as a child, that I didn't miss a trick when I was growing up, and I'm sure that's true," I finished, settling back on the bench.

"Being behind a camera, taking pictures of everyone, should have given you a great sense of power as a child," Jake now said, eyeing me carefully, a thoughtful look in his eyes.

"Do you think so?" I stared back at him, frowning at this idea.

He nodded. "Sure I do. Haven't you ever

thought of it that way? Thought of that aspect of it?"

"No," I said, shaking my head. "Never." And this was true, I hadn't ever thought of photography in terms of power over a person, only as a powerful tool with the public.

"You've always told me your parents, especially your mother, didn't pay attention to you, that they weren't concerned about you or what you were doing when you were growing up. I think that must have been a pretty lousy feeling to have, Val."

He was staring hard at me again, and there was such compassion on his face, I was touched by his empathy and concern. He really was a true friend and a good person. I wondered suddenly what I would have done without him in my life.

Jake continued. "Think of how *powerful* it must have been for you, as a child, to have a camera in your hands, recording everyone, having *their* images on *your* reel of film. It gave you an advantage, don't you think, Val?"

"I guess so, yes, I guess you're right, but I never thought of it in that way." I laughed. "Still, it's true I was never without my camera, Jake. I shot everything from the dog throwing up to Donald the Great stealing cigarettes from my father's cigarette case—"

I stopped with sudden abruptness and looked up. A large spot of rain had just hit my arm. I saw at once that the sky had turned a cold, steely gray and yet there was a curious luminosity behind that grayness. It was an ominous sky that threatened bad weather. I was wondering if a *mistral* was about to blow up, when the rain started to pelt down.

"I have a feeling there's going to be a helluva storm," I exclaimed, getting to my feet. "Come on, Jake, we'd better get going."

Together we hurried up the path through the gardens, and within seconds we were running as fast as we could. The rain was falling in torrents, and it was a heavy, slashing rain that drenched us through to the skin. As we ran past the swimming pool and up the steps to the terrace, there was a loud crack of thunder. Flashes of lightning were illuminating the darkening afternoon sky, and I felt the cool touch of the *mistral* blowing over my body as we stumbled on toward the villa.

II

By the time Jake dragged me into the kitchen, we were both sodden to the skin. Water ran off us and pooled around our feet on the terra-cotta floor.

Grabbing hold of the kitchen towel, he dabbed my face with it.

"Hey, stop!" I cried. "It's a dirty towel, Jake."

"Sorry." He started to laugh as he grabbed the roll of paper towels, tore some off, and reached for me again.

I backed away, holding up my hands, laughing with him. "We need proper towels," I told him, pushing my wet hair out of my face. "We're both soaked."

Without a word Jake dashed through the kitchen door; I struggled out of my dripping voile shirt and threw it on the floor, then stepped out of my ruined sandals.

A second later Jake was back with an armful of towels. After cocooning me in a large bath sheet, he picked up a smaller towel and began to rub my hair. Snatching up a towel myself, I leaned forward to do the same to him. In the process of drying each other off, we were becoming a tangle of arms and towels; Jake couldn't stop laughing, and neither could I.

III

The laughter died in us both at precisely the same moment.

All of a sudden Jake and I were very sober, gazing at each other intently, motionless and silent in the middle of the kitchen. We might have been struck by the lightning bouncing off the windows outside. Maybe we had been.

After a prolonged moment of total silence, Jake took a jerky step backward, and he seemed about to say something. Apparently he changed his mind, since he remained mute, but his eyes were very intense and most revealing.

He did not need to say anything to me. What he was thinking was written not only in his eyes but all over his face. Desire and longing were etched there . . . for the first time in our friendship I finally understood how much he cared about me as a woman.

As for me, I had the oddest feeling I was sloughing off a dead skin, shedding forever my old self. Even the events of the past year tumbled away from me as if they had never happened. I experienced a sense of enormous liberation.

I stood there, rooted to the spot, mesmerized by his unblinking blue gaze, and unexpected desire flared in me. This startled me. I realized I was seeing Jake Newberg differently, in a way I had never seen him before, not as my comrade-in-arms or my best friend, but as a man I desired sexually and with whom I wanted to make the most passionate love.

I took a step toward him, every part of me wanting him now. I was certain he felt the same.

At exactly the same moment, as if he had read my mind, he was moving toward me, reaching out for me.

I stepped into his arms, and I knew as I did so

that this was where I belonged, had always belonged. He clung to me, and I held on to him tightly, wondering if he could hear the thundering of my heart.

Eventually he tilted my face to his, looking deeply into my eyes, impaling me with his. Again his expression told me everything I needed to know, and it was confirmation of what I was feeling for him. He brought his mouth down to mine and kissed me gently, tenderly, at first. But almost instantly his passion spiraled upward, and he began to kiss me with greater urgency and an eagerness that inflamed me further.

I found myself responding to him with a rush of ardor, my hands pressing on the back of his neck, reaching up into his hair. My body cleaved to his; I felt the light touch of his tongue on mine, seeking, seeking. He ran his hands down my back and onto my buttocks, pulled me tighter to him, pressed me closer. Clinging together in this way, we shared a moment of total and complete intimacy I had never known before.

It was then I knew that I was his, would always be his. Perhaps I'd even been his from the first moment we'd met without my knowing it.

There was a sudden stillness about Jake now as he murmured softly against my neck, "Come on, Val, come with me. Let's be together."

IV

Arms around each other, we moved out of the kitchen, climbed the stairs, and went into his bedroom. Outside the huge window the sky was dark, almost as black as night, and the rain slashed down against the glass, driven hard by the wind.

Jake closed the door behind us with one hand without letting go of me and led me over to the bed. "Take this off," he muttered, touching my wet swimsuit. Stepping away from me, he swiftly shed his soaking trousers and shirt.

He wrapped the bath sheet he had brought upstairs around his waist, picked up the one I'd dropped on the floor, and tied it on me toga-style. Without a word we lay down next to each other. Neither of us spoke. My heart was racing.

Suddenly Jake raised himself on one elbow and gazed down at me.

My eyes stayed on his face expectantly.

"I never thought this would happen. I've waited so long for you, Val," he said in a quiet voice thick with emotion, and his face was congested with desire.

"Oh, Jake, I—"

He cut me off. "Don't say anything. Not now."

It was apparent he had an overwhelming physical need for me, as I did for him, and we reached out, clutched at each other, devoured each other with our mouths. Our tongues grazed, touched, caressed, and then lay still. Unexpectedly, Jake pulled away from me, tugged at the towel knotted around me. It fell open, and he brought his mouth to my neck and then my breast. He sucked on my nipple and at the same time he was stroking my inner thigh.

I could feel his mounting excitement. His heart was slamming against mine and I held him tighter, pressing my hands on his back and his shoulder blades. I moved my fingers up onto the nape of his neck, and they were strong and supple against his skin.

When we broke away at last, we were gasping, out of breath.

"My beautiful Val," he murmured, and leaned over me, his fingers seeking to know me fully. I stiffened as he touched the core of me, and he whispered, "Relax, darling, let me love you like this." And he slid down the bed, rested his head against my thigh, and eventually his mouth joined his fingers in his search for the center of my womanhood. I found myself relaxing as he had asked, and I opened myself up to him completely. It seemed to me that I floated away on waves of ecstasy of a kind I'd never known before. And then at that moment he pulled himself on top of me and took me to him. "Mine," he said. "You're mine now."

We made love for a long time, absorbed in each other and our bodies. I was reeling from amazement, startled by the passionate and erotic feelings he aroused in me, and reveling in them as well.

Finally spent and exhausted, our desire for each other sated at last, we lay still and unmoving on the bed. Half groaning, half sighing, Jake eventually slid off me and flopped against the pillows, "Oh God, Val," he muttered, and then he reached for my hand and held it tightly before bringing it up to his lips and kissing it with tenderness.

Then suddenly he was half on me again, flinging one leg and part of his body over mine, pulling me closer to him. "I'm never going to let you go. Not ever, Val."

V

I made no response to this statement of his.

I just lay there next to him, still filled with awe at our amazing lovemaking. I felt euphoric; I was also luxuriating in the sense of wonder and joy he had wrought in me.

"Who would've ever thought we would be so passionate with each other," I murmured at last.

"I would," he answered swiftly, and pushed

himself up on his arm, looked down at me. "I knew it from the first. At least, I knew how *I* felt."

"You did!" I said, surprised.

"Sure. When I met you in Beirut, I thought who the hell is this chick who's strolled along into my life? Who *is* this tall, long-legged, blue-eyed creature with sun-streaked hair and the face of an angel? I was immediately smitten, instantly undone." He paused and grinned at me. "I guess I was gobsmacked, to use your favorite expression."

"About me?"

"Of course about you. Who else?"

"But you didn't show it, didn't say it!" I exclaimed, staring at him intently.

"How could I? And that's not my way, I was married then, remember? Still struggling with Sue's emotional upset about her miscarriage, fighting off her demands that I go back and live with her in New York, give up being a war photographer, so I could baby-sit her while she pursued her modeling career and I put mine on hold. . . . Val, you *know* what those few years were like. Hell on earth for me. Looking back, I realize she was off the wall in certain ways, and actually not cut out for marriage. Not marriage to me anyway. It was a big mistake, our being together. Those were bad years for me, and I didn't think I should get involved with you until I had sorted out my mess. And I did eventually sort it out. Suddenly I was free at last—divorced, available. And where were you? Involved with Tony, to my dismay." He sighed. "I was out in the cold and there wasn't much I could do about it."

"Oh, Jake, if only I'd known."

"What difference would it have made?"

"A big difference, I think. If I'd known how you felt before, I'm sure I wouldn't have even looked at Tony. He and I had . . . well, quite a few problems when we were together, and there was a lot to be desired in our relationship. And for lots of reasons . . . some of which we now know."

"Yep, that's true, I was well aware things weren't always great between the two of you. But I don't go around snatching my best buddy's girl, that's just not me."

I nodded. "But I always had a . . . bit of a yen for you, Jake," I admitted softly, suddenly feeling a little shy with him. "You were in such a tangled web with Sue, I just tried to be your friend, and sort of disappeared into the woodwork, I guess."

"I wish you hadn't," he muttered, sounding regretful.

"So do I." As I said this, I couldn't help thinking how different my life would've been if Jake and I had been together. What a lot of heartache and pain I would have avoided ultimately; I felt sure I would have found a great deal more happiness with Jake than I had with Tony. He was a much more compassionate and decent man. And unlike Tony, he had integrity, and certainly he was honest and straightforward. Basically, what you saw was what you got as far as Jake was concerned.

Jake was saying, "Listen, that was then, this is now. '*Que sera, sera,* whatever will be, will be' . . . it's our time now. Anyway, I hope it is, Valentine Denning." His bright blue eyes searched my face questioningly. "It is, isn't it?"

"Oh, yes, Jake, it is!" I reached out, put my arms around his neck, and pulled him down to kiss me. It was a lingering kiss, and we embraced for a long time, finding pleasure in just holding each other close.

Outside, the storm was raging. The rain sounded like nail heads hitting the windows, sharp and metallic against the glass, and the wind was so fierce, I knew that the *mistral had* blown up. But I felt secure there with Jake, safe in his arms. And I, who didn't believe in miracles, knew that one had just happened to me. My miracle was Jake Newberg.

VI

Much later, after we had showered and put on trousers and sweaters, we went down to the kitchen.

Earlier, Jake had put a bottle of Dom Pérignon in the refrigerator, and after opening it he poured two glasses and said, "Here's to you and me, sweetheart."

We clinked glasses, and as I took a sip of the champagne, Jake added, "And now I'm about to bowl you over."

"You just did. And then some. But I'd be happy for you to do it again."

He laughed, planted a kiss on my forehead, and walked over to the refrigerator. "Now, sit down like a good girl while I prepare the southern dinner I've been promising you."

"I'm not going to move an inch," I answered, parking myself on one of the tall stools. "In this instance, I don't mind that you're being bossy."

"Me bossy?" He swung around, raised an eyebrow. "Never. Just authoritative."

"We're into semantics again," I muttered, and chuckled with him.

He was quick and deft, and knew exactly what he was doing, I soon realized, as I watched him moving around the kitchen with speed and grace. "I couldn't get everything I needed," he explained at one moment. "No okra, so I'll have to substitute zucchini in the gumbo. Have you ever eaten gumbo, Val?"

I shook my head. "No, and I'm not even sure what it is."

"A casserole of rice, tomatoes, and okra, but

it'll taste just as good with the zucchini, I'm sure. I couldn't find the ingredients for corn bread either, so I can't make us any hush puppies—that's fried round corn bread, Val—and you'd love it. But we'll have that in Georgia, when I take you home to meet my folks," he finished, and went on expertly working with the food he had spread out on the worktable.

I didn't say a word or acknowledge his comment, just sat there sipping the champagne and watching him, and knowing that I was going to fall hopelessly in love with him. I think I was a little already, always had been actually. How little we know ourselves, I thought unexpectedly, how little we understand our real feelings, our true feelings. We masked so much because we were afraid of looking foolish or of being rejected. At least, I did.

VII

"You can always be a chef if you ever get tired of being a war photographer," I joked later as we sat at the dining room table, eating Jake's southern dinner. "This is all wonderful food, delicious."

"I'm tired already," he said, surprising me.

"So you won't be going back to Kosovo, then, will you?"

"No, because you won't go there, and I want to be where you are, Val my Val."

"Likewise," I murmured, and smiled at him.

He smiled back and exclaimed, "I'm glad you like my southern cooking, and it's great to see you eating properly for once."

"Well, I've worked up an appetite, don't you know," I shot back and leered at him.

"So have I," he replied with a small self-satisfied smile, and helped himself to some more of the mashed potatoes and fried green tomatoes.

"You're much too smug, Newberg," I said, and took a piece of fried chicken. Biting into it, I went on. "You'll have to teach me how to cook some of these dishes. Your sweet potato pie is heavenly."

"Wait until you taste the dessert . . . my peach cobbler is as good as my mother makes. But I'll let you be the judge of that."

I raised a brow and asked, "Do you mean it? Are you really going to take me to Georgia to meet your parents and your grandmother?"

"You bet," he responded with a grin, and glanced at the fire. "I'm glad you decided to light that, Val, we'd be cold without it. The weather's turned lousy tonight. It's the *mistral*." Rising, he picked up the bottle of Saint-Émilion, came and poured me a glass, managing to kiss the top of my head as he did. "You're very special," he said against my hair. "Don't ever forget that."

I took hold of his hand resting on my shoulder

and squeezed it, but I didn't say anything. He lingered close to me, and finally I looked up at him. And I saw such a look of anxiety on his face, I was taken aback. I exclaimed, "Whatever's wrong, Jake?"

He stood there mute, staring down at me, and then at last he let out a long sigh and said, "I don't want anything to come between us, least of all the memory of Tony. He's not going to haunt you, is he?"

Pushing back my chair, I got up, put my hands on his shoulders, stood staring deeply into his eyes. I said quietly but in a firm voice, "He won't haunt me, Jake, I promise you that. As it turns out, he was a louse, so how could I let that happen?"

"I don't know, some women might, and the memory of a dashing lover cut down in his prime can be very powerful."

"You don't have to worry about Tony, not after what he did to me!" I reminded him.

"I guess we'll never know what was in his head, Val, or why he did what he did to you. He's dead, so he can't tell us. Nobody can."

I continued to stare at him, saying nothing. But Jake was wrong about this, as we were later to find out. Someone did know about Tony, and that person had all the answers. At least answers that would satisfy me. But this was yet to come. It was in the future.

VIII

After dinner we sat in front of the fire in the living room, sipping a large cognac each and talking endlessly about everything. About ourselves and our childhoods, about the years when we didn't know each other, about our first meeting in Beirut, and about all those missed chances of being together.

"Now *is* the perfect time for us, the right time, Jake, just as you said before. I'm much more grown-up and mature, better for you now."

"You were always better for me, Val, better than anyone else. We were destined to be together. Don't you know that?"

"Yes, I do," I said, meaning this, and knowing that he had meant every word he had said. I leaned my head against his shoulder and closed my eyes, but after a moment he took me in his arms and held me close, stroking my hair. And I knew that at last I had found my safe haven, the place where I was meant to be for the rest of my life. And for the first time in years I was at peace with myself.

Chapter 14

I

Two days after they had left for Marseilles, Simone and Armand returned to Les Roches Fleuries. They arrived in the late morning, as Simone had said they would when she had called the day before, and they came with their daughter Françoise.

I happened to be in the kitchen, making a pot of coffee and wondering what to prepare for Jake's lunch, when Simone appeared in the doorway, very suddenly and unexpectedly, dragging Françoise in her wake.

"*Mademoiselle Denning, bonjour!*" she exclaimed.

"*Bonjour,* Simone. I'm glad you're back, and

you arrived just in time to help me." I grinned at her. "I was looking around for inspiration—wondering what to prepare for Monsieur Jake's lunch."

"*Ah, Mademoiselle, c'est pas nécessaire maintenant.* I am here, it is not necessary for you to cook." She smiled warmly in her usual good-natured way, and then taking hold of her daughter's hand, she brought her forward.

The girl had been hanging back, had positioned herself behind Simone, and she appeared to be a little shy, I thought. But I realized, as she came into the sunny, light-filled kitchen, that she was badly bruised on her face; this was probably the reason she was reluctant to show herself to a stranger. She was a lovely-looking young woman, slender and fair of coloring, with blond hair and light gray eyes.

"This is my daughter," Simone said. "And, Françoise, this is Mademoiselle Denning."

"I am pleased to meet you," Françoise murmured quietly in excellent English, shaking my outstretched hand.

I smiled at her. "And it's nice to meet you too."

Françoise endeavored to smile back, but she was finding this difficult, no doubt because there were bruises around her mouth as well as on her forehead and cheekbone.

"I'm so glad you're all right, that nothing serious happened to you and the baby when you fell," I remarked, wanting to put her at ease.

"I was lucky," she replied in the same low voice.

Sensing that they would both feel better if I vacated the kitchen, I gestured at the coffeepot and said to Simone, "I'll be back in a minute or two for the coffee."

"No, no, rest *tranquil*. I will bring it to you and Monsieur Jake in a moment. *Avec du lait.*"

"*Merci,* Simone, and I'll tell Monsieur Jake you're back." I went outside and walked along the terrace to talk to Jake, who was relaxing on a chaise under an umbrella. "Simone's here," I announced, "and Françoise is with her." I leaned against the table, stared over at him, and then, pulling a chair out, I sat down.

Glancing up at me, looking surprised, Jake put down the book he was reading and said, "Odd she didn't mention Françoise would be coming when she phoned me last night. How does Françoise look?"

"Bruised. On her face. She's a lovely-looking girl though, isn't she?"

"A beauty. Maybe Simone and Armand decided it was wise to bring her back here with them to keep her safe from Olivier."

"Or perhaps to recuperate from her fall," I suggested gently. "She's not necessarily a battered wife."

"No. But you did say her face was bruised. And

I'm not so sure your face gets bruised when you fall down steps."

"Yes, I guess she could be battered. Only she knows the truth, and her mother perhaps."

"Simone would never mention anything to us. But she's a wise woman from what I know of her, and she'll do everything she can to protect Françoise from Olivier, if that's what is needed," he said.

"I'm sure you're right—" I began, and then paused when I saw Simone walking toward us, carrying a tray. "Here she is now," I added *sotto voce*.

Jake pushed himself up off the chaise just as Simone arrived at our side. She placed the tray of coffee on the table where I was seated and said, "*Bonjour, Monsieur* Jake."

"Hello, Simone," he replied, grasped her hand, and shook it. "I hear Françoise is with you."

"*Oui, Monsieur*. It will be good for her to relax here with us for a few days, to recover from her . . . fall."

"You're absolutely right. It's the perfect place, and we're glad she's here with you and Armand. Just let me know if there's anything I can do for you, Simone, or for Françoise, and thanks for bringing the coffee."

With a nod and a small pleased smile, she disappeared down the terrace.

Jake said to me slowly, thoughtfully, "She and

Armand were so insistent about taking a cab from the airport. They didn't want me to pick them up, maybe because Françoise was with them. . . ." He looked at me and made a face, then, sitting down at the table, he lifted the coffeepot and poured for both of us, saying, "I guess everybody's got to do their own thing."

"That's true, and *we* can't intrude on them. After all, they've lived here for twenty years, the girls grew up at Les Roches Fleuries, and this is their home. We're just Peter's guests here, Simone and Armand *belong*."

"Talking of being Peter's guests, when do you want to leave, Val?"

"Never," I answered, smiling across at him, reaching out, taking his hand in mine. "Les Roches Fleuries is the best place I've ever been, Jake."

"And why do you think that is?"

"Because you're here, and because we're together in the best sense of that word." I threw him a flirtatious look and added, "But anywhere with you would be marvelous. Still, this is such a fabulous house."

He laughed softly. "I feel the same way as you do about this house. And I adore *you,* and I don't want to leave either, there's something very special about Les Roches Fleuries . . . it's very romantic, perhaps that's what's so appealing about it."

"The atmosphere *is* happy," I remarked. "And I think that this goes back to Adelia Roland. After all, she's the only person who's lived in it other than Peter. She created a unique villa and extraordinary gardens. And I've always believed that people who inhabit a house give it a certain feeling, either *good* or *bad*. Don't you think that?"

He nodded. "I do."

"Anyway, perhaps Peter will let us come back one day."

"Anytime you wish."

"We will have to leave *soon,* I suppose, go back to work, earn our living. So what actually are your plans?" I asked. "When we leave here?"

"Not sure. Well, that's not exactly true, Val. To be honest, I'm thinking of going to New York for a couple of weeks."

"Oh." Flabbergasted to hear this, I gaped at him.

"Don't look so surprised," he said swiftly. "Listen, I've been meaning to speak to you about something. About a book I want to do. That's the reason I may be heading to New York. To talk to a publisher. Harvey Robinson has one in mind. In fact, he's already broached the idea to them, and they're very interested. They've told Harvey they want to see me."

"And you never even told me!" I exclaimed, staring at him somewhat reproachfully.

"I'm telling you now."

Realizing I had sounded hurt in the most

childish way a moment before, I now spoke in a more positive mature voice when I said, "I think that's terrific, Jake. A wonderful idea."

"It will be if you work on the book with me, Val."

He had surprised me again, and I didn't say anything for a moment, then I asked, "What will the book be about? And why do you need me?"

"It's about war, to answer the first part of your question. And I need you as a collaborator because I need your pictures, plus your help with the text. You're a great reporter, Val, the best, and you write so well. Far better than I do."

I couldn't help but be pleased with his compliments, and I said, "That's nice of you to say so, but as far as the book's concerned, I just don't know." I frowned as I added, "Anyway, what exactly do you mean when you say *a book about war*?"

"Not war per se, but, rather, it would be a book about the children of war. And not the dead children either, but those who managed to survive, who are the future of their countries, the flowers of their countries, the flowers of war in a sense, who offer hope to the world. You've got loads of dramatic shots of children—before, during, and in the aftermath of war. Because that's always been your speciality, not mine, not Tony's." He leaned closer. "Come on, honey, say you'll do it."

Wanting to hedge for a couple of seconds, I said, "That's a good title."

"What is?"

"*Flowers of War.*" I put great emphasis on the words.

"Jesus, you're right! You see, I *do* need you."

"I sincerely hope so," I murmured, and blew him a kiss.

"Is it a *yes,* Val?" he pressed, his eyes fastened on mine.

I smiled enigmatically. "It could be . . . it just depends on . . ."

"On what?" he demanded.

"How well you treat me."

"I'll love you to death," he promised.

"Then it's a deal."

Obviously delighted that I had agreed, he exclaimed, "And it really will be a proper deal, you know, fifty-fifty partners, a split right down the middle on any advance and on the royalties. How does that sound?"

"Great, Jake."

"We'll have some fun." He grinned at me, looking like a little boy who had just won the biggest prize of his life.

II

As usual, Simone made a wonderful lunch.

We started with vichyssoise, followed by an extraordinary Niçoise salad, served along with finely sliced *charcuterie* and warm *baguettes.* For dessert Simone presented us with our favorite Cavaillon melon topped with red currants mixed with raspberries.

All through lunch, as we ate the delicious food and sipped *vin rosé,* Jake talked about what had now become *our* book. His excitement about it was infectious.

I also liked the idea because I felt that working on it would keep Jake away from Kosovo. Although he had said he didn't want to go anywhere without me, I was nevertheless a bit worried that Jacques would pressure him into covering the war again. And if not that particular war in the Balkans, then another one somewhere; there were always wars to cover these days, and after all, Jake was a war photographer, as I was. But I had lost my taste for this dark side of journalism, at least for the time being anyway. I prayed he had too.

And so we talked about the pictures we'd taken, what we had in our files, and which ones would work; we even got down to outlining some of the chapters. With his particular brand of enthusiasm, he made the project sound both exciting and challenging, and by the time we had finished lunch, I discovered I was as committed to the book as he was.

III

We went upstairs to take an afternoon nap. But in the privacy of my room, resting seemed to be the last thing on Jake's mind. Very slowly, he undressed me, peeling off my shirt, bra, and cotton shorts; and then he shed his own clothes. Leading me over to the bed, he gently pushed me onto it, lay down next to me, and took me in his arms.

"Oh, Val, my darling Val," he whispered against my neck, stroking my hair. "We're so lucky to have found each other . . . we have so much together."

"Yes, I know we do."

He brought his face to mine and kissed me softly. I held him tightly, my arms around his neck. Finally, in a low voice, he said, "I adore you. Val. I have ever since the first day, but much more now."

"I feel the same way, Jake."

"Let's not lose this . . . let's try to keep it, keep it as long as we can . . ." His voice tapered off. He looked deeply into my eyes, as if he were seeing into my soul, and his own were very, very blue, reflecting his desire for me, and his love.

"For always. Let's keep it always," I responded.

"If we possibly can," he murmured. "*Always* is

a long time . . . but we can aim for it, can't we?" Without waiting for a response, he kissed me again, and then very tenderly and gently he began to make love to me.

But as usual our passion swiftly flared, and we clutched at each other, devoured each other, were unable to get enough of each other. And then afterward, wrapped in each other's arms, we fell asleep, at ease and content, knowing we belonged together.

Chapter 15

I

Jake went downstairs to call his photo agency, as he did every day. He sat at the big, beautiful antique desk in the window area of the room, which overlooked the gardens, and talked at length to Jacques Foucher. As one of the owners of the agency in Paris, Jake liked to know what business they were doing, what assignments were coming in and from which magazines and newspapers.

Knowing he would be occupied for quite a while, I went for a walk in the gardens, as I often did in the late afternoon. The furious storm of two days before had wreaked havoc and wrought a vast change in the vegetation and foliage. So many plants and flowers had been damaged by the rain and wind, and I had seen Armand walking around earlier today, looking crestfallen, glum, and concerned as he assessed the damage, especially to the azaleas and rosebushes.

The weather had changed as well since the storm. It was not as sunny as it had been, and the air was much cooler. Even the sky had altered in appearance. The vivid blueness had faded away, and this afternoon it was etiolated, a bleached-out sky the color of celery. In fact, the halcyon days of summer, which we had enjoyed for almost two weeks, had been replaced with a hint of fall. But I did not mind this change, or the cooling down, since I was happy being with Jake at Les Roches Fleuries.

As I came around the edge of the rosebushes, making for my favorite spot under the cedar tree, I stopped dead in my tracks when I saw Françoise. She was standing so near to the edge of the cliff, looked to be in such a precarious position, I thought she would fall off at any moment. My heart began to pound against my rib cage; I was scared. And I did not know what to do.

I felt panic rising in me, but I managed to push it back, knowing that I must keep a cool head and think very clearly. I dare not move abruptly or with suddenness. If I did, I might easily startle her, and that could prove fatal.

And so I just stood there, watching her, endeavoring to keep calm, wondering what my next move ought to be. After a couple of minutes I decided to make a few small noises, light sounds that might catch her attention without frightening her.

One false step on her part, and only one, and she would be tumbling over the edge. I couldn't help asking myself what she was doing there in the first place. I hoped to God she wasn't planning to commit some awful and irreversible act. I wondered again if she was indeed a battered wife, as Jake seemed to believe she was.

Suddenly she moved.

I held my breath, and my eyes closed involuntarily. Immediately I snapped them open. Thankfully Françoise was still there; my heart was racing faster than ever and I felt a terrible fear settling in the pit of my stomach. How could I stop her from jumping, if that was her intention? My mouth went dry.

Taking complete control of myself, I reached out and shook the nearest bush, but the rustling of the leaves did not draw her attention. She seemed oblivious of everything; in fact, she still stood there as unmoving as a statue with her back to me, staring down at the rocks.

Very carefully, and with stealth, I stepped backward, moved away from the cedar tree, until I was out of sight behind the hedge. Then I turned and hurried down the lawn. I paused in the middle of the grass, took a deep breath, and then began to sing. Not too loudly, which would have startled her, but just loud enough for her to hear me, for her to be aware of my presence in the distance, to know it was me and not anyone else. I hoped a distant voice would break into her contemplation of that steep drop to the sea, and without scaring her into doing something rash.

"Dance, in the old-fashioned way. . . . Dance, in the old fashioned way. . . . / Come close where you belong. . . ." It was the only popular song I knew the words to, and this old Charles Aznavour classic was my favorite.

As I sang the words over again, I moved forward more rapidly, going back down the lawn toward her. And as I stepped through the flowering rosebushes I saw to my relief that she had turned around, that she had been alerted to my presence. She was rooted to the same spot on the edge of the cliff, staring at me blankly through troubled eyes.

I stopped and stared back at her, wanting to appear normal, casual, unconcerned.

"Françoise, hello, hello!" I exclaimed in a soft voice. "I hope I didn't startle you with my awful singing." I forced laughter onto my lips and went on. "I don't have a very good voice, I'm afraid." I laughed once more, hoping to make light of the situation.

But there was no response. She just went on standing there, gaping at me as if she didn't know who I was. But thank God she hadn't taken a false step. Believing that behaving normally with her was my best bet, I began to walk very slowly toward the iron bench under the cedar tree.

In a conversational sort of way, I said, "You know, this is my favorite spot, Françoise. I love it here. And what a coincidence—I guess it must be your favorite place too."

She blinked and seemed to rouse herself at last from her trance. She said slowly, hesitantly, "I came here often with Madame Adelia. When I was a child."

"Please sit down with me, Françoise, talk to me about her. She fascinates me," I explained, striving for normalcy.

Françoise hesitated, then she swiveled her head and looked down at the rocks and the sea far below her, swaying slightly.

Once more I held my breath, trembling inside. Fear made my throat close. But I said nothing, made no move, simply sat there quietly.

Unexpectedly, she swung around and my stomach lurched, so sudden and swift were her movements, and then to my great relief she actually stepped away from the edge of the precipice and slowly walked toward me. I felt limp as the fear ebbed.

Swallowing, I said, "Madame Adelia was your friend, then?"

Françoise now stood in front of me. She nodded. "Yes . . . she was a very special woman."

I rose, took hold of her hand. "Please sit and talk to me." And as I led her to the iron bench she did not resist. But she did not say anything further, just sat down next to me, gazing out into space, that preoccupied look continuing to glaze her eyes.

I decided to remain silent.

Eventually she broke the silence when she confided, "I feel safe here."

"Do you mean here in this particular part of the gardens?"

"*Oui, oui.* Madame Adelia is here . . . her spirit is here. I am close to her here. She helps me."

Very gently I asked, "Do you want to talk to me about your problems, Françoise?"

Looking at me closely, intently, she repeated, "*Problems?*" and she frowned, seemed puzzled.

I nodded.

She did not speak.

"Sometimes it's easier to talk to a stranger. An American playwright, Tennessee Williams, once wrote, '*I have always depended on the kindness of strangers.*' So why don't you?"

A deep sigh escaped her, and she looked out into space, and it seemed to me that she saw something I could not see and that she was disturbed by what she saw. At last she muttered, "I . . . I . . . don't want to go back . . . I am . . . very afraid . . ."

"Of your husband?"

She chose not to answer, turned her head away from me.

"Of Olivier?" I asked very softly.

She inclined her head, but she was still avoiding my eyes.

"Then you must stay here at Les Roches Fleuries."

"No, no, I cannot. I must go. Far away."

"Because he'll come here looking for you, is that it, Francoise? Is that what you mean?"

"Yes."

"You must talk to your mother. I am sure she must know about Olivier's treatment of you. Or suspect that he abuses you."

"*C'est possible,*" she agreed. Tears suddenly welled in her lovely pellucid gray eyes. "I came here to think. To listen to Madame Adelia's voice. But I became so afraid, I could not hear her voice."

"We must act very calmly, use our heads," I said, taking her hand in mine again.

She turned to face me again and gave me a long, sorrowful look. "That is what she would have said to me." A sigh escaped again. "Madame Adelia died here."

Startled, I asked, "Do you mean here in this spot?"

"*Oui*. There was a wooden chaise longue here, and my father put many cushions on it every morning. Madame Adelia rested here. This was her memory place. That is what she told me. And one day she died. Right here. And then she went to the duke."

"Her spirit, you mean," I said, and wondered why I myself had been so attracted to this corner of the gardens.

"Yes," Françoise answered, "her spirit. I do not want to return to Marseilles. I am afraid. I would be better off dead. And the baby."

"No, no, you mustn't say that!" I tightened my grip on her hand. "And you mustn't make a habit of standing over there at the edge of the cliff. It is a dangerous place. I was so afraid for you a few moments ago. I thought how easy it would be for you to take a false step and fall over the edge. Yes, it's very dangerous to walk around over there."

"Yes, I know." She looked into my eyes, searched my face, and there was a plea in hers. "Mademoiselle Denning, please do not tell *Maman* . . . that I was on the edge of the precipice. It will frighten her. And worry her."

"All right, I won't."

"Promise?"

"I promise. But you must make a promise to me."

"What do you wish for me to promise to you?"

"You must promise not to even think of harming yourself or the baby."

"But I cannot go back to him. He is crazy when he drinks. One day he will kill me. I know. Why should I wait for him to do that? Why should I suffer? It is better I do kill myself. *Maintenant*. And the child. I think it would be less painful. Yes?"

"No, you mustn't even think in that way. We must make a plan. I will come up with an idea, an idea where you can go, where you will be safe."

Sudden hope flashed across her face, and then it disappeared just as quickly as it had appeared. "He will find me. He is a *flic* . . . a cop, Mademoiselle Denning."

"I know. Do you mind if I talk to Monsieur Jake?"

She looked frightened and shook her head. "No! You must not. He will speak with *Maman*. He will tell her."

"No, he won't, not if I ask him not to, Françoise," I reassured her. "He will respect your wishes. He is a man of integrity . . . a man of honor, and he has much compassion, you must trust me on that."

Folding her hands in her lap, Françoise sat there for a few moments, lost to the world, as she tried to come to a decision. "It is all right," she answered finally. "You can tell Monsieur Jake.

Please be kind, ask him not to say one word to my mother."

"I will. And you can trust him just as you can trust me. I have an idea already, Françoise. Let me think about it, think it through. Now, come, we must go inside. Your mother must be wondering where you are."

II

When I walked into the library, Jake was standing by the desk. He swung around and said, "Hi, I was just coming out to find you—" Abruptly he broke off, frowning, and asked, "What's wrong? You're looking mighty strange."

"You were right about Françoise being an abused wife," I said, hurrying across the floor, flopping down into a chair near the fireplace. "She's just admitted to me that she's afraid of Olivier, and that she thinks she'd be better off dead now rather than waiting to get killed by him at a later date. And suffering until that actually happens."

Jake sucked in his breath and stared at me. After a beat, he exploded, "Jesus, Val! How the hell did this all come out so suddenly?" He dropped into the opposite chair, obviously both startled and dismayed.

Leaning forward, I quickly told him what had

occurred in the garden while he had been on the phone to his Paris office. He listened attentively, as he always did, and I could see from the expression on his face that he was appalled at what he was hearing.

When I had finished recounting everything in detail, he said nothing, remained absolutely quiet. I became aware of the stillness in him, all around him. It was an internal patience, and I knew it well by then, and it was one of the things I'd always loved about him. He had this ability to become very calm and focused in times of trouble or crisis. Jake never panicked or flew off the handle; he was a cool guy who played it cool.

III

I could see that he was deep in thought, and I sat back and waited, trying to be as patient as he was. At last he said slowly, "Tell Françoise I won't say anything to Simone. Although I'm sure her mother knows she's being battered, beaten up. Simone's nobody's fool, and, anyway, mothers know these things instinctively, don't they?"

"How would I know, I never had a mother."

I saw him wince, but I couldn't help what I'd said, and I certainly wasn't going to retract it. The words had popped out automatically, and they did happen to be the truth.

"Oh God, Val, I forgot! Mike Carter called a few minutes ago, just before you walked in. Your brother's been on the phone to him. This afternoon. He's looking for you. Mike wouldn't give him this number, but he told him he'd try to get a message to you. Apparently your brother wants you to call him. He explained to Mike that it's urgent, important that he speaks to you."

I really didn't care, and I didn't want to return the call, but I muttered, "I wonder what that's all about?"

"I guess he didn't give any other explanation to Mike, Val, and I wrote the number on the pad by the phone," Jake was saying.

"Thanks," I replied, but I made no move to get up.

Pushing himself to his feet, Jake walked over to the French doors, stood looking out at the terrace and the gardens beyond. After a second or two, he remarked, as he turned to face me, "You said you told Françoise you'd had an idea . . . what is it?"

"It occurred to me that she would be safe with me in Paris. She could stay at my apartment, there's a daybed in my office, as you know. Besides, *I'll* probably be off on an assignment somewhere, or with you. I mean, I could camp out with you at a pinch, couldn't I?"

"I'll have to think about that."

I smiled, knowing he was teasing me, and continued. "Olivier doesn't know me. And as long as Simone and Armand keep quiet, he'll never be able to find Françoise. She'll be safe."

Jake sighed. "True. But he'll put pressure on them, I reckon."

"They'll never tell him where she is!" I exclaimed, and rushed on a bit heatedly. "Simone's strong and tough, and I'd pit her against anybody anytime, even a *flic.*"

He nodded. "So would I, and Armand's no pushover either. He was in the Resistance during the Second World War, during the German Occupation, he told me once. He was just a kid, of course, but he said it toughened him up, that he learned a lot about life and about people." Jake now focused his vivid blues on me steadily, unblinkingly, and asked, "Why would you take Françoise in, Val? Just like that." He snapped his thumb and second finger together and went on. "It's very nice of you to make the offer, but she's a stranger, you just met her today, and you hardly know her parents."

"I like Simone a lot," I replied. "In fact, I've become rather attached to her. She's so motherly; Mother Earth, the salt of the earth, to me at any rate. This is a terrible predicament for Simone and Armand, and for Françoise, to be in. What a tragedy for them all. And Françoise being pregnant and getting battered is unconscionable. I think I can help them, so why wouldn't I? We see so much suffering and pain, you and I, Jake, and it's suffering we haven't been able to do anything about, at least not much. Look how many times we've rescued kids and their mothers, and pregnant women from bad situations, dangerous situations, and then we've had to leave them to fend for themselves. I just want to rescue her, see something through for once. And I can't bear the thought of that beautiful young woman being battered to death, which is what will happen eventually. If she's not removed from Olivier's grasp, taken out of that hideous marriage."

"You're right—in everything you say, and it's very admirable of you to want to help Françoise, and you know I'll pitch in, do anything I can. Yup, we should go for it."

"Thanks, Jake, I'm so glad you agree with me."

"I do . . . and there's something else, something I'm curious about."

"Tell me."

"What made you think of making noises, off-stage, so to speak? What gave you the idea to sing? How did you know these antics of yours would work?" An arched brow rose quizzically, and he shook his head. "I don't think I'd have ever thought of doing such things."

"I honestly don't know why I did what I did. Common sense, I guess. I realized that if I startled her, she could easily fall off the edge of the cliff, or that she might just go ahead and jump. I suppose I wanted to distract her, turn her away from her purpose, but in a gentle way. That's why I tried to act so normal. Any other kind of behavior on my part could have pushed her . . . literally over the edge, so I believe."

"Is that what you really think? That she was intending to jump?" Jake seemed suddenly perturbed.

I thought about this question for a moment and then I nodded. "I do, Jake. She told me she'd gone there to hear Madame Adelia's voice, but that she was so afraid of Olivier, she hadn't been able to hear her. I'm pretty sure she would have killed herself this afternoon. If I hadn't come along when I did."

"Oh Jesus," he said, and came over to sit on the chair next to me. "You saved her life."

"I think so, and I want to save her some more, get her out of Olivier's clutches, get her safely to Paris. She can have the baby there."

"He's a cop, Val, Simone and Armand will have to be careful, and about a lot of things, especially phone calls."

I gaped at him, frowning slightly, not understanding what he was getting at. "Phone calls?"

"Well, I don't know whether cops can get hold of phone records in France or not, but they sure can in the States. I will have to warn them, they're going to have to use public phones, and mostly Françoise will have to call them. And talking of phone calls, perhaps you ought to get in touch with your brother. Don't you think?"

"I guess," I reluctantly agreed, and rising, I walked over to the desk. I seated myself in the chair and picked up the piece of paper with Donald's number written on it. And as I read it, I realized how much I really did detest the idea of calling him. For deep within myself I knew it had something to do with Margot Scott Denning. My mother, so called.

IV

It took me ages to pick up the receiver, but finally I did. As I dialed, I hoped Donald the Great would be out and then I would have an easy escape. I could leave a message. No such luck. It was Donald himself who answered, exclaiming, "Okay, Eliane, shoot."

"It's Val," I said.

"Oh, gee, hi, Val. I thought it was Eliane, one of my contacts. I just hung up on her and she said she'd call me back right away. So, how're you doing, sis?"

"I'm fine, Donald. I understand you tried to reach me earlier today. I was told it was urgent, important."

"It is. You've got to come home. Immediately.

Right away. Mom needs to talk to you," he said in a rush of words.

"I'm not sure I can come, Donald, not at this time, and at your whim. Or hers. And furthermore, New York is not my home, and for another, I've no desire to listen to a woman who's not paid me a blind bit of notice since the day I was born. What could *I* possibly have to say to *her*?" I felt like adding, *or you,* but I refrained.

"Don't be like that. She's been very ill!" he said, sounding slightly hysterical.

"Really." I held the phone a little tighter and pursed my lips.

"Yeah, sis, she's just had another heart attack, and you've got to come home. You didn't come when I asked you a few weeks ago, and if you delay again, it could be too late."

"Do you think she might die, Donald?"

"I do, and this is about her *will*. Her last will and testament. It affects me as well as you."

I sat back in the chair and glanced at Jake. He frowned at me, and I knew then that he would never truly understand about my family, at least not about my parents and Donald, because his family was so very different.

Donald was blabbering into the phone again, "I'm telling you, the stakes are high, sis, and I'm going to get screwed if you don't get your ass over here as soon as possible. If she dies and we haven't cleared this mess up, then I'm up shit creek without a paddle."

"Donald, you're not making a case for yourself, not with your crudeness and vulgarity. And who's *she?* The cat's mother? Or your mom, as you usually call her. Usually you're the doting son."

"Aw, come on, don't be such a pain, Val. Relax. What you need is a good f—"

"Donald," I cut in sharply, thus cutting him off. "Don't say it, or I'll hang up."

"Okay, okay, so come on, give me a date. This is important. Blood's thicker than water, sis."

"*Really.* How come this is the first time I've heard *that* sentiment expressed in the Denning family?"

"The old guy left you *everything,*" he said. "I got nothing . . . *now* it's my turn."

"How can you say you got nothing? Grandfather left you a very nice trust." I knew this statement of mine would be like a red rag to a bull, so I took a deep breath and rushed on before he could respond. "What this is all about is Margot Denning's will as far as I can ascertain from your conversation. And I can't imagine why you need *me.* I'm sure you're featured in it and not I. She's barely acknowledged me for thirty-one years. So why would she do so now?"

"Look, Val, I honestly don't understand what it's all about," Donald said. "What I do know is that somehow my inheritance is attached to yours, tied up with it. Why won't you just say when you're coming, so I can tell Mom?"

"Donald, I'll have to get back to you."

"But when? *When?* Come on, don't do this to me!"

"I'll call you at this time tomorrow."

"Okay, okay. Talk to you then."

He slammed the phone down and I continued to sit in the chair, still holding the receiver in my hand, staring at it. I slowly replaced it in the cradle, and then I told Jake what had just happened. And I must admit, I did so with a sense of sadness for my brother. Like my mother, he had never had much time for me. Until now.

Chapter 16

I

New York, October ⬩ If anyone had told me that I
would be sitting in the middle of Manhattan a
week after that conversation with Donald, I
would have laughed in their face.

But here I was, at my grandfather's old desk,
staring out across the East River at the giant
Pepsi-Cola sign anchored in Long Island City, on
the other side of the water.

It had been a lovely October day. Now, in the
late afternoon, I was whiling away the time, waiting for Jake to come back from a meeting with
the publisher. An editor at this well-established
house was interested in publishing *Flowers of
War,* the tentative title of the coffee table book.

That it would be a joint venture between the two of us was now a foregone conclusion: I would write some of the text as well as provide a selection of my pictures.

Earlier today he had asked me to go to the meeting with him and Harvey, but I had declined. It had always been Jake's deal, not mine, and he was much more famous than I. Also, I wanted time to catch my breath and relax for a day. I was really praying they would agree on the terms, since I knew the book was dear to his heart. Also, it would anchor Jake in one place, keep him from rushing off to Kosovo or other dangerous parts of the world, and this thought continued to please me no end.

As I sat gazing across the river, which gleamed in the fading afternoon sunlight, I realized how much had happened in the past eight days.

Following my revelations about Françoise to Jake, we had had a long talk with her, during which I had invited her to stay with me in Paris. She was at first rather shy, had been hesitant about this, but when Jake had suggested we take her parents into our confidence, she had instantly agreed, surprising us both. Simone and Armand had been somewhat taken aback by my invitation, then they had quickly seen the wisdom of such a move and had convinced their daughter to accept. And so the next day we flew back to Paris, taking Françoise along with us.

Before we left Les Roches Fleuries, Jake had had a serious talk with the Rogets, explaining to them that they must not phone Françoise in Paris, either from their own home or the villa. "As a cop, Olivier might be able to get the phone records for both places and trace the number in Paris to an address," he had pointed out. "It is much safer and wiser for Françoise to call you." And they had been in agreement with him, seeing the sense of this. But when we left Saint-Jean-Cap-Ferrat, I was suddenly worried about Simone and Armand; Jake had been extremely reassuring though, reminding me several times how strong they both were, also tough-minded and not easily pushed around.

Jake and I had been back in Paris for only one day when Harvey Robinson had called from New York, to tell him that the editor was eager to meet with him to discuss the book. And as soon as possible. Harvey had had another surprise in store for Jake. A well-known SoHo art gallery wanted to have an exhibition of his pictures of war, and they wished to talk to him in person as well.

"Let's go, Val. Next week," he had said to me that evening, obviously excited by these prospects. But I had not been very enthusiastic about flying to New York so unexpectedly, at the drop of a hat. "Anyway, if I'm there, I'll probably feel obligated to see Donald, and I don't want to do that," I'd muttered, realizing that I'd sounded sullen, which was not like me.

"Why don't you see him? Why don't you see your mother as well?" Jake had suggested. "Get to the bottom of this last will and testament business. And you should have it out with her, Val. Confront her, find the reason for this attitude of hers, find out why she's treated you the way she has all these years. Get it over with once and for all. You'll probably feel heaps better for it. It would be liberating, I think, Kid."

I was ambivalent about doing this, and I just couldn't make my mind up about going to New York. I was also a bit concerned about leaving Françoise alone—and unprotected so to speak. I mentioned this to Mike Carter the following morning, when I'd gone into Gemstar for the first time since late August, and he had solved the problem for me. Out of the blue, he had volunteered to keep an eye on her, and had convinced me to call her at the apartment and invite her to lunch with us. "So we can become acquainted," he had said.

Mike had been his usual warm and easygoing self over lunch, and Françoise had relaxed in his presence. In fact, I was surprised the way the two of them got along so well. She became positively gay in the restaurant, and for once that sad and sorrowful look had left her lovely gray eyes. At least for a short while.

That night, when I saw Jake for dinner, he announced that he had bought our tickets, and that we were leaving in a couple of days. He was taking charge as usual, in that macho way of his. I found myself being swept along by his charm and enthusiasm; I also realized that he was determined to go and make these deals no matter what, and I wanted to be with him. We had become very close in the South of France, and I didn't want absence and distance to break the euphoric mood that existed between us.

II

Jake and I were staying at my aunt's apartment in midtown Manhattan, a traditional, spacious place just off First Avenue in the fifties, and I knew it well.

Aunt Isobel had inherited it from my grandfather, and one day it would be mine, a stipulation written into his will. If I survived her, that is.

My grandfather had wanted to do the correct thing by his daughter, but he had also wanted me to have a home in New York, even if I rarely used it, and my aunt had concurred with this. Grandfather had called it my safety net, a place of refuge if I ever got tired of wielding my camera on the front lines.

My aunt was my grandparents' only daughter,

my father's older sister, although she and he had never been close. Her main home was about two and a half hours away, in the upper reaches of Connecticut, which is where she lived most of the time. She only occasionally stayed at the apartment, about once or twice a month for a night or two, and she had repeatedly told me to make use of it whenever I wished. In the meantime, she paid for its upkeep.

Isobel Denning Cox was a renowned interior designer with offices in Greenwich and New York and clients all over the world. Grandfather used to describe her as the Floral Queen, because she favored so much chintz in many of the interiors she designed. English antiques of the Georgian period were a specialty of hers, and together with the floral fabrics, she created the popular cozy, cluttered English country house look. She had made this her own, as had Mario Buatta, another great designer who had also perfected this style.

But she was an expert on eighteenth-century French furniture and works of art as well, and some of her settings looked as if they had been transported lock, stock, and barrel from several *châteaux* in the Loire Valley. I had always admired her for her brilliance and talent, her ability to produce such diverse, beautiful, and tasteful homes for her clients.

Her husband, James Mallard Cox, was a

retired banker, and something of an invalid these days. Sadly, their only child, Johnny, a playboy who had never married, had been tragically killed eight years before, when the small plane he was piloting himself had crashed in the French Alps in a thunderstorm.

She and I did not see each other very often unless she came to Paris on a buying trip and I was there and not shooting photographs of a war somewhere. Then we would get together for lunch or dinner.

We liked each other a lot, and had always been friendly. Aunt Isobel had been forever exasperated with my mother and had mostly taken Grandfather's side against her.

Opinionated and outspoken, my aunt was the most self-confident person I had ever met. Colorful phrases were never far from her lips, and she had once described my father as "a spineless twerp who needs his brains washed, preferably in disinfectant, and then hung out to dry in a sharp wind."

Whenever I thought of Aunt Isobel, I laughed to myself, remembering this description, which had forever endeared her to me; certainly it had made my grandfather chuckle, and for days on end.

My aunt had had white hair, sleek and thick, for as long as I could recall, and she was a tall, imposing woman, good-looking and elegant, with the finest taste in clothes as well as in antiques and art. She had a marvelous sense of humor and great wit; but she was also down to earth and genuinely kind of heart, all of which made her a very special woman in my eyes. Certainly a woman to look up to and admire, as I did.

Once I had decided to come to New York with Jake, I had telephoned my aunt at her Greenwich office, which is where she worked most of the time.

I had been put through to her secretary, who told me she was in New York, and that I would find her at the Beekman Place apartment. It was there that I had reached her a few minutes later, and she had been thrilled to hear that I wanted to stay at the flat.

"I'm not likely to be here again for several weeks, Val, so do please come and make yourself at home." She had burst into laughter. "What am I saying? It *is* your home." She had gone on to add, "And if I do have to come in for a night, there's plenty of room for us all. You do have your key, don't you?"

I had assured her that I did. And she had explained that she would tell Molly, her house-keeper, to come in three times a week instead of twice, for as long as we were staying at the apartment.

When we had arrived the night before, it was

obvious that Molly had been there in the morning. Everything sparkled, cushions were plumped up, and flowers graced the many vases. There was even a fresh supply of milk and other staples in the refrigerator.

Jake had walked around, whistling under his breath, looking impressed. He had said he felt as though he had just strolled into an English country house in the Cotswolds, and then announced that that was all right by him though.

"It's Aunt Isobel's trademark look," I had explained, laughing with him, and we had both agreed it was comfortable as well as charming, and a pleasant place to be.

"And certainly much nicer than staying in a hotel," Jake had murmured as he had lowered himself into an overstuffed sofa covered with a red-rose-green-leaf print, one my aunt often favored in her decorating schemes.

Leaping up suddenly, he had dashed to the big bay window, exclaiming about the panoramic view and the life on the river. For at that moment there were a number of barges and boats moving slowly along the waterway. "It's a very busy thoroughfare," I told him. "I remember it well from my childhood."

III

Naturally, it was full of nostalgic memories for me, and since my grandparents had owned this apartment for over forty years before their deaths, I had spent some very happy childhood times here. They were the only really happy days I could actually recall from those miserable years when I had been growing up in New York.

Once Jake and I had unpacked last night, we had gone out for a walk, needing to breathe some fresh air after being cooped up in the plane. And Jake had remarked about the charm of Beekman Place, a quiet, tree-lined enclave I had always been partial to, and which I knew so well from those long-ago days of my youth.

Later, we had wandered up First Avenue, had gone to Neary's pub on East Fifty-seventh Street, where Jimmy Neary, the owner and host, had greeted me like a long-lost daughter. Having three of his own, he was a very fatherly type, and he welcomed me with a huge smile that was warm, genuine, and very sincere.

After his retirement from the architectural firm he had founded, my grandfather had gone to Neary's several times a week for lunch, and he often took my grandmother there for supper. And so Jimmy had known them for many years, and known them quite well. After a drink at the bar, Jimmy gave us a cozy table for two in a corner, where we had had our dinner.

"Just like old home week for you, I reckon," Jake said as we walked down First Avenue after a hearty supper of homemade Irish stew and a bottle of good red wine. Arms around each other, we were happy to be together on this balmy night, sheltered by a high-flung dark-velvet sky littered with stars twinkling like diamond chips. "Lucy in the sky with diamonds," Jake warbled softly as we ambled along, making for Beekman Place. It was the loveliest return to New York I had ever experienced, and most especially later that night, when we had climbed into my grandparents' big old four-poster and made love.

IV

The phone jangled, interrupting my train of thought, and I jumped, startled out of my reverie, as I reached for it swiftly. "Hello?"

"It's Françoise," she said in the soft, lilting voice I had come to know.

"Hello, Françoise, hello!" I exclaimed, thinking how close she sounded. "Is everything all right? And how are you feeling?"

"It is all okay, Mademoiselle," she answered. "I

am feeling well. But it is Olivier, he has been to see my parents at Les Roches Fleuries—"

"Oh my God, are they all right?" I cut in worriedly. "Has he been pestering them?"

"*Oui* . . . but they are strong. They will not tell him where I am . . ."

Suddenly, abruptly, Françoise stopped speaking, and I heard muttered asides, another voice at her end of the phone. I assumed she was calling from my apartment, since it was now about ten-thirty at night in Paris. I couldn't help wondering who was with her.

"Françoise, Françoise," I said loudly into the receiver. "Are you there? Are you all right?"

Still she did not respond.

I was about to say her name again, when Mike Carter exclaimed, "Hi, Val, it's me, honey."

"Mike, is Françoise upset? Is everything okay with her parents? I'm sure Olivier's being a pest, and I'm being kind when I call him that."

Mike chuckled. "You're right, pest *is* too mild a word to describe that son of a bitch. Let's just say he's been pretty difficult with them, but they're holding up okay. All of this blew up yesterday afternoon when her husband showed up at the villa in Cap-Ferrat. You were flying over the Atlantic by that time. I think the parents have things pretty much under control. They've assured Françoise they're fine, and I brought her over to stay at my place this afternoon." He laughed. "My girls think she's pretty neat, and they're good friends already."

"It's a relief to know she's safe, Mike, thanks so much for being her . . . guardian angel, shall we say?"

"I'm happy to help her, poor kid," Mike replied. "I feel sorry for her. She's not had an easy time of it."

"I know that. Anyway, I feel better knowing she's actually staying with you and the girls. To be honest, I was a bit worried about leaving her alone at my place."

"I don't blame you, honey. I doubt that her parents would tell him where she is, but even if they did, under duress of some kind, she's no longer there now." His deep chuckle rumbled down the wire before he added, "Gone like a puff of smoke."

"Do her parents know she's with you? They'll worry if there's no answer to my phone."

"She's told them she's moving in with a friend, but she didn't say she was coming to my place. We thought it wiser her parents were kept in the dark . . . what they don't know they can't spill."

"That's smart of you."

"I thought we'd better phone you though, Val, to let you know where Françoise is, just in case you phoned her and there was no reply."

"I'm glad you did."

"And how's little old New York?" he asked,

sounding suddenly wistful. New York was his favorite city; he'd told me that so many times.

"Great, just great, and it's wonderful weather . . . Indian summer sort of weather."

"Enjoy. I'll call you later in the week. Meantime, here's Françoise," he finished, sounding brisk, businesslike once more.

"Mademoiselle Denning, please don't worry," Françoise said.

"I won't. But I told you to call me Val."

There was a small laugh, and she said, *"Oui . . .* Val. I feel safe with Mike's family. Olivier will never find me here. Because no one knows where I am . . . except you, Mademoiselle, I mean . . . Val."

"I'm not going to tell anybody."

"It will be better if you do not telephone *Maman,* I think."

"I understand, Françoise, and I won't. But you can call me anytime you wish. I'm going to be in New York for a good week, perhaps even two."

"Okay. Thank you for everything, and do not worry about me, Mademoiselle Denning."

"It's *Val,*" I half shouted down the phone, and we both laughed.

"Au revoir, Val," she said softly.

"Good night, Françoise, and be well. I'll phone later in the week."

V

After replacing the receiver, I leaned forward, my elbows on the desk, my head in my hands, thinking. The call from Françoise had brought me back to reality, my reverie about Jake and our lovemaking interrupted by her. My own life was suddenly rather sharply in focus, and I contemplated Jake's advice of earlier.

Before he had left for the meeting, he had suggested that I call my brother Donald. "Get it over with, once and for all," he had said, and there had been a stern look in his blue eyes. "Wipe that slate clean and forget it."

I knew he was right, and yet I hadn't been able to make the call. At least, not so far; but after all, I had been here for only a day. On the plane I had asked myself if I was *really* coming to see Donald and my mother . . . and not flying to New York simply because I wanted to be with Jake, as I believed.

Examining this thought now, I was able to answer myself; a resounding albeit silent *no* reverberated in my head. I *was* here in the city of my birth because of Jake, and that *was* the truth.

VI

Donald and my mother meant very little to me, and for all the obvious reasons. Nothing, nada, zilch, I muttered under my breath. And they had given me nothing, nada, zilch, and I had no intention of being at their beck and call at this stage of my life.

From this standpoint, Jake was right. I should get rid of all that old baggage, discard it, and start afresh without the burden of my past. But to do so I would have to confront them, my mother especially, and I had vowed long ago, and to her face, that I would never speak to her or see her ever again. And I hadn't. And I didn't want to now. I wasn't even remotely curious to know what these sudden overtures were all about.

The truth was, I had come to New York because Jake Newberg was coming, and *he* wanted me with him. And that was where *I* wanted to be, by his side, in his arms, in his bed, in his life, and in his heart. I wanted to be with him when we were working, relaxing, traveling, sleeping. Night and day for as long as I lived.

Chapter 17

I

When Jake walked in an hour later, I couldn't tell from his expression whether or not the meeting with the editor had gone well or not. He was poker-faced and his eyes revealed nothing.

After placing his briefcase on a chair, he walked over to me, gave me a bear hug, and kissed my cheek. "Hi, honey," he said. "Gotta get a Coke," and he walked off in the direction of the kitchen.

My eyes followed him. I couldn't help thinking how smart he looked today in the gray pin-striped suit, pale blue shirt, and darker blue polka-dot tie. Everything about him gleams, I thought as he came strolling back with the can of Coke in his hand, from the top of his blond-streaked hair to the tip of his highly polished brown loafers. I felt a little rush of pride in him. He had been gone all day, and ever since we had become involved, I was always surprised when I saw him after even only a few hours absence. He was so personable, so good-looking, and so well put together, it was always a bit of a shock when he strolled in nonchalantly, as he was doing now. He was the only man for me, the only man I wanted.

Sitting down next to me on the sofa, Jake said, "Why don't we go out tonight? I don't think you should cook."

"Whatever you want," I answered, and fixing my eyes on him intently, I asked, "What happened at the publishers? How was the editor?"

His face lit up. "He's a great guy, Val, you're going to like him. I wish you'd been at the meeting, but I'll get the two of you together real soon. His name's Bill Forrest, and he's very with it, very knowledgeable. Knows what he wants, how the book should look, what it should say, convey in terms of text and photographs. He's very enthusiastic about the project."

"So we have a contract," I asserted.

"Not yet. But that's pretty much a foregone conclusion, I think. Harvey agrees with me. But before we move on to that stage, Bill needs an outline. So what you and I have to do is break the book down into chapters and content, show him some more pictures, and then he'll make the deal, I guess. I told him we'd give him a little presentation next week."

"Will we have it ready?" I asked, a brow lifting.

"Sure. It's a snap as long as I have you helping me."

"Flattery will get you everywhere," I said.

"I sincerely hope so. Because I want to get everywhere with you."

"You have, silly."

He smiled, said nothing more, took a long swig from the can of Coke. Placing the can on the coffee table, he murmured, "We can work all weekend, sort the pictures, plan out the book. We'll be fine."

"I guess so—" I paused, gave him a fast glance. *"Jake?"*

He turned to look at me. "What is it? You sound concerned. And you look it."

"I am a bit. About Françoise. She phoned this afternoon, and she's staying at Mike Carter's apartment."

"Why? What happened? Don't tell me. I can guess! Olivier showed up."

"Not in Paris, at Les Roches Fleuries."

"Yes, that's what I meant. I suppose he's been giving her folks a hard time? Is that it, Val?"

"Apparently. But they've been pretty tough

with him from what I can gather. Nevertheless, Mike decided it would be better to move her out of my place."

"I see. Well, I guess that was shrewd of Mike. A smart cop might well put two and two to-gether and come up with five. We'd been staying down there, he could jump to conclusions, come up with the truth. Why wouldn't you or I provide some sort of help, give her shelter? A sharp *flic* might well figure that out. You and I would be easy to find in Paris, we're so well known. A cop wouldn't have any trouble locating us sooner or later."

I nodded. "True. I think Mike likes her . . . what I mean is, I have a feeling he's attracted to her."

For a moment Jake appeared startled, and then his expression changed, and he grinned at me. "And why not? She's a lovely-looking young woman, and she seems very sweet. And Mike's been a widower for . . . what is it, ten years now?"

"Yes, Sarah was killed in that horrible car crash ten years ago, when Lisa was four and Joy was two. They're teenagers now, and quite grown-up. Mike told me the girls are very taken with Françoise, he said they'd all become friends."

"Fast friends fast, heh?" He laughed.

I laughed too but made no comment.

"Yup, I guess she's better off with Mike at

Mike's. It would be hard for Olivier to track her down there."

"I hope you're right. You know, I do work for Mike—if Olivier makes the connection, he could show up at Gemstar."

"Yeah, that's true, but he sure as hell won't get anywhere with Mike Carter."

"He's a tough guy, I know that. A match for anybody," I answered.

"What a lousy world we live in," Jake muttered, swigging the Coke again, then slapping the can down hard on the coffee table.

I saw the flicker of anger in those deep blue eyes, and his mouth was drawn in a tight line. He was such a good man, so full of feeling for others.

He went on. "Wherever you look, people have such problems. Take Françoise—an innocent, loving young woman, beaten and battered about by some tough cop who goes ape when he drinks. Not fair, is it?"

"No, it's not, and I just hope she gets through the birth of the baby okay, that nothing goes wrong. Then once the child is born, she can decide what to do. Personally, I'm praying she stays in Paris. She might have a future with Mike."

Jake gave me a long, studied look, then leaned back against the sofa, frowning slightly. "What makes you say that?"

"I don't know . . . well, yes, I do. There was

a sort of . . . *connection* between them the day Mike took us to lunch, and she was so carefree, so *happy*. I couldn't believe it. I know it had something to do with Mike. And he looked . . . well, I guess it was the same for him. He was *happy* too. I haven't seen that kind of expression on his face for as long as I've known him, and that's seven years now."

"So they clicked, hit it off, but it doesn't mean there's a future there. Listen, she's married, and married to a maniac whose child she's expecting . . . better slow down, honey."

"I know, I know. But it would be nice if they—" I stopped, shrugged. "You know, got together . . . somehow."

Jake bent forward, kissed the tip of my nose. "Spoken like a true romantic, Val. And I agree, it would be nice for Françoise. Mike's a good guy."

II

Since Jake wanted to go to a nice neighborhood restaurant, I led him to Le Périgord on Fifty-second Street later that evening. I knew he would love it because he preferred French food—after southern soul food, that is. And I was right.

This was another of Grandfather's old haunts, and I'd been brought there for many special occasions in the past, and for over twenty years at that.

Georges Briguet, the proprietor, came over to greet us and seat us, and before we could even blink, two glasses of sparkling champagne stood before us on the table. To welcome us, Georges explained, offering us the Perrier-Jouët.

Jake quickly got into the spirit of things, and because I was happy to see *him* so happy and carefree for once, I went along with him. More champagne followed the first glasses. He ordered oysters for us both, and then roast duck, which was accompanied by a bottle of his favorite red wine, Saint-Émilion. We finished the meal with sumptuous floating islands in vanilla sauce.

"I was too thin before, I know that," I said to Jake at one moment. "But pretty soon I'm going to be too fat. Far too fat. I've got to go on a diet."

"You're fine the way you are, fine for me, that is," Jake murmured. "I don't like sticks."

I didn't say anything, since I'd just remembered how anorexically thin his ex-wife, the famous model, had been, a fact that had troubled Jake no end. I focused on her for a moment, wondering how she was, what she was doing. Still a top model, I knew that. They had been divorced for almost two years; God, how time was flashing by me at the speed of light.

"Did you call Donald?" Jake asked.

Lost in my thoughts as I was, I blinked several times before answering, "Er, no."

"You have to, Val." Jake looked at me closely,

intently, and covered my hand with his. He continued. "Not only for your sake, but ours. I don't
want you to have this situation hanging over your
head. Your past has always been a terrible burden
for you, I realize that as much as you do. I want
you to shed it once and for all, get rid of it. You've
got to be free, sweetheart."

"I want to be, Jake, honestly, but—"

"No buts, I won't take buts," Jake interrupted
me sharply. "Just pick up a phone and make a
date to see Donald. Alone. Then see your mother
another day. Let's do it while we're here in New
York, Val, it's such a good opportunity."

"Oh, Jake, you just don't know . . ."

"I do, and I'll help you. I'm here for you, I'll
even go with you to meet him, or we'll have him
to the apartment. You can see him alone if you
want, but I'll be in another room, a safety net for
you. *Please,* Val," he insisted in a low voice.

"I'll think about it. . . ."

"You'll see, it won't be so bad. Call him tomorrow morning, see him tomorrow. The sooner the
better."

"I can't tomorrow. I have lunch with Muffie."

"Oh, that's right, I'd forgotten. But lunch
isn't all day, Val. What about the afternoon? Or
listen, see him in the evening. Okay?"

"I don't know."

"Then see him on the weekend," Jake suggested,
determined to settle this.

"I thought we were going to work on the book."

"We are. And surely you're going to spend only an hour with Donald? It couldn't possibly take longer than that, could it?"

"You never know with Donald the Great."

"I've often wondered why you call him that?" Jake's blondish brow lifted quizzically, and he fixed his bright blues on me.

"Because my mother thought he was the greatest thing to hit the earth. The greatest thing since sliced bread, my grandmother used to say. My mother was always saying, 'Donald's great at this, Donald's great at that,' and I just got fed up. I guess we all did. And one day I said here comes Donald the Great, and Grandfather was tickled to death, and the name just stuck."

"I guess nicknames do. But surely it won't take longer than an hour, will it?" he asked again.

"Who the hell knows," I mumbled, and I shrank down farther on the banquette. I felt as though I were shriveling up inside. The mere idea of meeting with my sibling was something I could hardly bear to contemplate. I associated Donald with too many painful memories.

Jake said, "You're really trying to duck it, Val darling, and I don't think you should. Nor should you duck your mother. Face her head-on. You can do it, Val."

"I can't."

"Why? You're not afraid, are you?"

"Yes, I think I am," I whispered.

"Of her? Or of what she has to say?" Jake asked gently, taking my hand in his again, endeavoring to soothe me.

"Of what she has to say," I admitted. And then I sat up a little straighter, suddenly feeling better now that I'd admitted this to him, and just as important, to myself.

"Oh, Val, don't be. It's all in her, you know. I bet it's actually nothing to do with you. How could it have anything to do with you? You were only a baby when this started, from what your grandfather told you anyway. Isn't that so?"

I nodded.

"Listen to me . . . you and I have a lot of things going for us. But one of the most important is our shared integrity, that sense of honor, and our love of the truth. The truth in all things. I don't deal in lies, Val, and neither do you. I will always tell you the truth. Just as I know you will tell me the truth. Correct?"

"Yes," I replied, my eyes glued to his.

"Okay, then. I am telling you the truth now, Val. You've nothing to fear, nothing to be afraid of. Whatever your mother has to tell you, it's nothing to do with anything *you've* ever done. It's all about *her*. Don't you see? *It's to do with her.*"

I let out a long sigh.

"Do you want me to come with you when you go and see your mother?"

"I don't know that she'd like that. She might not open up under those circumstances."

"Well, it's possible, yes," he admitted. "But we won't know that unless we go visit her. Only then will we find out."

I had to agree with him. "It's nice of you to offer to come with me, Jake, it really is."

"I care about you."

"And I care about you too, and I know you're right in everything you say. I *will* phone Donald tomorrow, I promise, and I'll make a date with him. I think I'd rather hear what *he's* got to say before I do anything about my mother."

"Take it slowly, one step at a time," he said, and leaning closer, he kissed me on the cheek.

III

In the quiet, darkened room, in the vast four-poster that had been my grandparents' bed, Jake made love to me as he never had before. Nor I with him. Slowly, voluptuously, he drew me along the edge of ecstasy, as I did him, tantalizing, bringing each other to a fine pitch. And then ceasing all touching and kissing suddenly, we rested against each other to catch our breath.

"I want to draw this out, make it last forever," he

whispered against my hair. "And so do I," I whispered back, moving my fingers slowly up his stomach to rest on his chest.

Jake raised himself up on one elbow and kissed my eyelids, my cheeks, my lips, and my neck. He let his mouth linger on mine, devoured mine, and then kissed each breast. Slowly, he moved his lips down to that final resting place against my thighs, swiftly, surely, brought me up onto another high plateau. My legs were trembling, my whole body quivering under his touch, and I yearned to be part of him. And after a moment, as if he read my mind, he took me to him. We found our rhythm instantly, as we always did, and soared higher and higher together, and as our passion increased, he said tensely, "I love you, Val." And I said the same to him.

Much later, as we lay together, our arms and legs wrapped around each other, exhausted and sore, I said to Jake, "Always . . . it's for always. It's got to be."

"It will be," he replied; he held me closer, cradled me in his arms, and kissed my hair.

My joy and happiness at being with Jake so filled me with euphoria, it never occurred to me we might well be tempting fate when we spoke of always. But I was to remember this night later, and reflect on our words.

Chapter 18

I

It wasn't such a beautiful day after all. The bright
sunshine of early morning had given way to a
dull pale sky overladen with whitish clouds, but
it wasn't going to rain. At least so I had been
assured by Jake, who had been tuned in to CNN
for several hours.

And so I decided to walk to the Carlyle Hotel,
where I was meeting my old friend Muffie Potter
Aston for lunch. I said this to Jake as I went into
the study to kiss him good-bye.

Jake was seated at the old desk in the window
that had been Grandfather's, making notes on a
yellow pad and sipping a Coke from the can.

262 Barbara Taylor Bradford

"I'm off," I murmured, kissing him on top of his head. "I'll see you later."

"You're leaving early."

"I've decided to walk."

"All that way?"

"It's only twenty-five blocks," I said, laughing.

"And across First, Second, Third, Lexington, Park, and Madison," he pointed out, grinning at me.

"I need the exercise," I countered. "I feel like one of those ducks the French fatten for *foie gras,* and it's all those meals you've been feeding me, Jake Newberg."

"Mmmm. Nice and plump and the better for plucking." He leered.

"*Beast.* And I'm *not* plump."

He merely smiled in that enigmatic way of his. Or was it a smug smile this morning? I wasn't sure. I said, "Are you going to the agency later?"

He nodded. "Gotta get into those files Harvey's been filling up for years. I know there's a batch of my pictures in there, and they could be useful for the book. I'll mosey on over there at about one o'clock, have a bite with Harvey, and then get to work. It's a no-brainer; all I have to do is locate the files. After that it's just a matter of pulling the shots."

"I'll come back here after lunch," I said, edging out of the room.

"And you'll call Donald," he reminded me, giving me a stern look.

"Yes, I will. Bye."

"I'll buy you a Chinese dinner tonight," he shouted after me.

"I won't be hungry, so thanks but no thanks," I called back, smiling inwardly, and hurried through the foyer and out the front door before he could say anything else.

II

Since I hadn't gone window shopping in New York for years, I walked down East Fifty-seventh Street, making for Madison Avenue. As I turned onto this famous fashion street, I was amazed to see so many new stores and boutiques. It was a pleasure to stroll along at a leisurely pace, gazing in the windows at the latest clothes, shoes, and bags.

Not that all the styles appealed to me. They didn't. I tended to choose plain, tailored clothes in dark colors, because I knew they suited me. They were also much more practical for the life I led as a war photojournalist. My entire wardrobe was built on black, navy, and gray, a bit somber, I know, but easy to wear and easy to accessorize. Occasionally I went slightly crazy and bought something in white or cream, but never bright colors, because I hated myself in them.

Today I was wearing a lightweight wool jacket in black, cut to resemble a bush jacket, a style I loved, a white silk man-tailored shirt, and black gabardine slacks. I wore high-heeled black boots under the pants and carried a dark green Kelly bag Jake had given me for Christmas. As usual, my only pieces of jewelry were pearl earrings and a watch, a lovely old Cartier timepiece. This had been my grandmother's favorite and she had left it to me when she died.

I thought of the unique and very loving Cecelia Denning, whom I so physically resembled, as I walked along. Without her, and Grandpa, of course, I would have been a real mess, neurotic and damaged beyond repair, I've no doubt. And it was Grandmother who had introduced me to my closest friend, Muffie Potter, who had become my ally and sparring partner fifteen years earlier.

Muffie was a couple of years older than me, and she had lived in Washington, D.C., when we were teenagers, but we saw each other whenever she came to visit her grandparents, who lived in Scarsdale. They were friends of my Denning grandparents, and they also happened to be acquainted with Aunt Isobel, and so our friend-ship had everyone's stamp of approval.

We had remained friends ever since our teen years, even though our lives had gone in different directions. While I struggled with my camera on the front lines, shooting wars, Muffie had a high-powered job as an executive at Van Cleef & Arpels, the famous French jewelers on Fifth Avenue.

She had recently married Sherrell Aston, the renowned plastic surgeon; unfortunately, much to my disappointment, I hadn't been able to attend their wedding, since I'd been stuck in some hellhole in a misbegotten corner of the world, taking pictures of yet more human suffering.

Over the years we had always stayed in touch with each other by letter, card, fax, and telephone, and whenever we were in the same city, we met for dinner, lunch, or drinks, whatever we could manage. It was nice for me to have such a loyal best friend, and Muffie felt the same, I know.

There was something very special about her. The golden girl, I called her, because she *was* golden, inside as well as out, but especially in her nature. She was filled with sunshine and light-heartedness, so it seemed to me anyway.

Muffie was blond, blue-eyed, and very pretty. She had a serious side and was much wiser than most of the other people I knew, had a trenchant way of telling you what she thought about every-thing. Including your own life, if you were smart enough to ask for her advice.

But only if you sought her opinion. No gratuitous comments from her. She was far too smart for that.

I had called her yesterday to let her know we'd arrived and to make the date for lunch today. And then last night, when she got home, she called me, so that we could have a longer chat, catch up with each other's news.

After I'd returned to Paris from Belgrade, I'd called Muffie in New York to tell her about Tony's death. And so she knew all about my grief, and also how I felt later, following the nightmare of the memorial service in London. After listening to my outpourings over the transatlantic wire, she had agreed with me about Tony Hampton's extraordinary behavior. And then she told me to put the past behind me and move on.

When Jake and I had become involved romantically in the South of France, I phoned Muffie from Les Roches Fleuries to tell her about our budding relationship and to confide that our friendship had moved to a different plane.

I had wanted her to know that I had done as she had suggested, put the past behind me, buried the dead, and moved forward.

She was pleased I had taken her advice and delighted about Jake and me, because they had hit it off when they'd first met two years earlier. She had liked him enormously, and was approving of this new turn of events in my life.

And so for a while last evening we talked about

Jake, my feelings for him, and the future he and I might have together.

III

It was ages since I'd spent time with my best friend, and I was really looking forward to seeing Muffie. As I went into the Carlyle Hotel and through the lobby to the restaurant, I realized how much I'd missed her.

I was there first, but only by a few minutes.

I had just been shown to my seat, when Muffie floated in right behind me on a cloud of perfume, dispensing happy smiles, looking stunning in a suit of soft bluish-gray.

After we had hugged, exchanged loving greetings, and settled down finally on the banquette, she looked at me intently, her expression appraising.

After a second or two of this close scrutiny of me, she exclaimed, "You look fantastic, Val! I knew Jake would be good for you."

"Yes, he is. And he always has been, you know, looking back. He was never very far away when we were on assignment, looking out for me, protecting me, keeping me out of harm's way. Apparently he was in love with me then . . ." I left my sentence unfinished, simply gave her a long, knowing look and lifted a brow.

Muffie laughed. "*Men,*" she said, shaking her head. "If only he'd told you sooner, you wouldn't have become involved with Tony, and you'd have avoided all that awful heartache about him."

"Only too true. And listen, you look great yourself."

"A happy marriage works wonders," she murmured, smiling at me. Leaning closer across the table, she continued. "Do you remember what I once told you?"

"You've told me a lot over the years, Muffie. Which thing in particular?"

"That life can turn on a dime, that no one knows what's going to happen. Ever. Sometimes it's the bad stuff, but not always. Sometimes it's the wonderful stuff. Look at *you.* When you got back to Paris from London after the memorial service, you were miserable, downhearted, and angry. Now you're beautiful, blooming, in great spirits, and no longer angry."

"I am still a *bit* angry, Muffie. Inside."

"Oh, don't be, Val," she said very softly, getting hold of my hand, squeezing it. "It's just not worth it. Let it go. Anger's good only when you can express it, get it out. And you certainly can't do that, since you've nobody to express it to—Tony's dead."

"I know. And I think you're right. But—" I stopped when I saw the look on her face. I knew there was no point in continuing; also, she had a knack of making me feel as if I were whining in the way that Donald whined. I detested whiners, so why should I become one myself? I kept my thoughts to myself for once.

We ordered bottled water and sipped it while we looked at the menus. We decided on our food, choosing the same dishes, as we had so often in the past. We both settled on asparagus vinaigrette, grilled sole, and green beans. No potatoes, no bread, and no wine.

"I've got to lose weight," I said to her, grinning, and continuing to sip the water. "Jake loves food, and he's been fattening me up. Or so it seems to me. When we're on assignment, there's usually nothing very good to eat, and anyway, we don't have time to put much in our mouths."

"You don't look fat, you look . . . divine."

"Spoken like a true best friend, Muffie."

We talked for a while about our lives and how different they were. And then quite unexpectedly, out of the blue, Muffie said, "It's the oddest thing, Val, but I've been running into your brother lately."

"Donald!" I exclaimed, staring at her.

She nodded. "Donald the Great, as you used to call him. He always comes over and says hello, makes a point of it, actually, which is weird since I know you two aren't exactly close."

"To say the least!"

Muffie nodded, then laughed. "But he's turned

out to be quite good-looking, and he usually has this beautiful girl on his arm. From what I hear, he's doing well at the magazine."

I let out a long sigh. "He's in his element, gossip columnist to the stars. Donald's in pig heaven, what do you bet? Yep, that's one thing I'm certain of, *he's* got the job of his dreams."

"When did you last see him?"

"When he was in Paris about seven years ago. Actually, that's not correct. I saw him after that, at Grandfather's funeral, and he was positively awful, Muffie, don't you remember how he was going on about the will, for God's sake?"

"I do remember, and I also remember your mother that day. My mother always said there's less to Margot Denning than meets the eye. But actually, I think she's wrong. There's a lot *more* to Margot Denning, and that's at the root of your problem with her."

"What do you mean?" I asked, my brows drawing together in a frown, my eyes riveted on her face.

"I've thought a lot about your mother since the day of the funeral, Val, which is when I last saw her. I think she has a past."

"How could she have a past? She married my father when she was twenty-three, and I was born when she was twenty-five."

"Well, perhaps *a past* is the wrong phrase. What I really meant is that she has something to hide." Muffie's expression became thoughtful, and her blue eyes narrowed slightly as she said slowly, "My parents and most other people think your mother's shallow, but I don't believe that's the truth at all. Yes, she *is* concerned about her looks and clothes and jewelry and all that stuff, but there's a lot of depth there as well."

I gaped at her. "I'm sure you're the only person who believes that! My mother, so called, is as shallow as they come, and as cold as ice. You know Grandfather used to call her Iceberg Aggie, and the Ice Queen."

"She's a cold woman, no question about that. But by no means stupid. Margot Scott Denning is nobody's fool. Are you going to see her while you're here?"

"I don't think so."

"I heard she'd had a stroke, no, a heart attack, that was it. My parents told me."

"Two heart attacks, according to Donald."

"But she's not that old."

"No, she's fifty-six, actually."

"Is she really ill?"

"Donald thinks she's about to kick the bucket, but perhaps he's being overly dramatic, which is his normal way of behaving, if you recollect."

"Yes, he was always like that, full of histrionics. How old is he now? About twenty-five?"

"Twenty-six. Going on four. Very infantile."

She laughed.

And so did I. She always had that effect on me, brought out the lighter side of Valentine Denning, the not-so-serious side. I loved that about Muffie—her uplifting effect on me.

"Are you going to see her?" Muffie asked, her head tilted to one side. "I know how you feel about her, but I just wondered . . ." Her voice petered out, probably because she'd taken note of the dour expression settling on my face.

"Donald says she wants to see me, but I don't know that I will succumb to his blandishments."

Muffie threw back her head and roared, "*Blandishments,* what a wonderful word, Val, really wonderful!"

I grinned at her. "I guess it does sound a bit old-fashioned, and the phrase just jumped into my head. *Muffie?*"

"Yes?"

"I want to ask you something. . . ."

"Go ahead, you know very well you can ask me anything, and if I can answer you, I will."

"Were you trying to say that Margot Denning is more *complex* than most people think?"

"*Exactly*. I believe she's a sick woman as well. Mentally sick. And all of their married life I think your father was an enabler. Whatever it was that troubled her, disturbed her, your father aided and abetted her. Because he didn't have the strength or the willpower to fight her. To *oppose* her, that's what I mean."

"That could be. My grandmother always thought he was weak-kneed. That was the word she used constantly to describe her son. And Grandfather was disgusted with him all the time—Aunt Isobel, as well. They thought he was under my mother's thumb, and he was. *I* know that for a fact."

Muffie nodded. "I saw it too, with my own eyes, Val, you don't have to convince me. And of course he worked for her at Lowell's." She wrinkled her nose. "That was a sort of odd situation, come to think of it now. Don't you think so?"

"Yes. But he liked it. My father had a cushy life in that sense. I don't think he was all that bright when it came to business, and my mother provided him with a great job. Vice president of Lowell's Cosmetics, founded in 1898, a hundred years ago this year. My grandmother, Violet Scott, was the chairman, if you remember. She ran a tight ship, and so does my mother now."

I took a breath, let out a long sigh, went on. "When I had that huge row with my mother eight years ago, I told her I'd never speak to her again. But I did, at Grandfather's funeral. However, I barely exchanged a word with her, even though she tried to patch things up. I don't know why she wanted to do that."

"I witnessed *that* scene," Muffie exclaimed with acidity.

"There's something else, Muffie. When Aunt

Isobel came to Paris about a year and a half ago, she said something about the Scott women being tyrants. And she made a catty remark about Violet Scott."

"What did she say?"

"That my grandmother Violet Scott was a hard bitch, and added that my mother took after her. You know how outspoken Isobel is."

Muffie grinned. "Don't I just." After a moment she became serious. "Look, Val, you don't have to listen to your brother. If you don't want to see your mother, then *don't*. For heaven's sake, she's never done anything for you. Not to my knowledge."

"She's given me nothing, nada, zilch." I threw Muffie a knowing look. "Don't you think it would be a bit hypocritical on my part—seeing her, I mean?"

Muffie thought for a moment. "Well, yes, I guess so." She took a sip of water and asked, "Why are you even considering it? Because of the heart attacks?"

"Not really. How can I have any feelings for her? A woman who has never shown the slightest interest in me ever. Look, she knew I was shot in Kosovo . . . there was a lot in the newspapers about Tony's death and the fact that Jake and I were both injured at the same time. On television too. She never once got in touch with me to see how I was. But that's her. No interest whatsoever. It's Jake, actually, who's after me to see her."

"*Jake?* But why, Val?" Muffie sounded surprised.

"He thinks I ought to confront her once and for all, ask her why she's treated me the way she has, and most especially when I was a child."

"You won't find anything out," Muffie said in an authoritative voice. "She'll never confide in you. *If* there's anything to confide."

"But you said you thought she had a past."

"Yes, I do think there's something there, something in her background that caused her to behave the way she did, and with your father's acquiescence. But so what? It can't possibly have anything to do with you, can it? It may have made her *behave* peculiarly, but *you're* not the *cause*. How could you be?"

"I don't suppose I could."

"Don't expose yourself to her, to more pain. She broke your heart when you were a child. And you can be so tenderhearted, I know you."

"Not about her! I don't have any real feelings for her!" I exclaimed. "In a sense, she's like a stranger. She made herself a stranger to *me* when I was growing up."

Muffie nodded but made no further comment, since a waiter was placing a plate of asparagus in front of her. He brought my plate, and we began to eat. Automatically, our conversation turned away from my mother and Donald. As I said to Muffie, we had better fish to fry.

But later, I was to wish I'd encouraged Muffie to rattle on, express her thoughts more fully, because to be forewarned is to be forearmed. I should have also listened to her about not seeing my mother. But I didn't. Regrettably so, as it turned out.

Chapter 19

I

"Who's the Kevin Costner look-alike?" my brother Donald asked as he followed me into the sitting room of the Beekman Place apartment.

Without turning around, I answered, "That's my best friend, Jake Newberg. You'll meet him later. He's a photojournalist. We work a lot together."

"And sleep a lot together, I bet," Donald shot back.

I swung around and exclaimed irately, "You're already irritating me, Donald, and you've been here only a couple of minutes! Let's not forget that you've not come to discuss *my* relationships, but yours with your mother."

"She's your mother too, Val," he responded, then continued swiftly, almost apologetically. "And there's no need to be annoyed. I caught a glimpse of him as I walked past the study, and he *does* look like Costner."

I sighed, sat down in the chair, and made no comment.

Donald lowered himself onto the sofa and sat staring at me across the coffee table, not speaking either, just scrutinizing me intently as if he'd never seen me before.

I stared back.

Muffie was right. My brother *had* turned into a very good-looking young man. He took after my mother, had her black hair, the beautifully sculpted looks, the same perfect nose, high cheekbones, and smooth, high brow plus her light green eyes. But he wasn't tall and willowy as she was; it was I who had inherited those particular characteristics from her. But that was the only physical resemblance we shared. I was a Denning through and through.

It was Donald who was a Scott, her male clone, her spitting image right down to the widow's peak that was such a prominent and striking feature in them both. He was not built like her though; rather, he resembled my father in physique. Donald was not very tall, and he was small-boned, as my father had been.

Donald was studying me so closely, I began to

feel uncomfortable, and I said, "What is it? Why are you looking me over in this way? You seem to be memorizing every detail of my face."

He grinned at me, flashing those perfect pearly white teeth I'd always envied. "I haven't seen you for a long time . . . but I don't have to memorize your face, I know it well. . . ." He let out a long sigh and said in a low, almost inaudible voice, "You used to love me once, Val, when I was little."

Taken aback not only by his words but by his sudden mild demeanor, I was speechless for a moment; he was usually so combative with me.

"Well, you did, didn't you?" he pressed.

"Yes, you're right, I did," I admitted. "I loved you a lot in those days."

"Why did you stop?"

"I didn't, not really," I murmured, frowning. "It was your mother. She got in the way, put herself in between us, so to speak. Your mother took you over, and in so doing she pushed me out."

"She's also your mother," Donald said.

"This is the second time you've said that in the space of a few minutes! And no, Donald, she isn't my mother. She may have given birth to me, but she has never been a mother, nor has she shown me any motherly love."

"I know that," he admitted very quietly.

He had startled me again. I couldn't believe that he had actually agreed with me on something to do with our mother. But I didn't say a word. I couldn't help wondering why he had had this change of tune all of a sudden. I was immediately suspicious.

I said, "What's this all about, Donald?"

He shook his head, but he remained silent.

"Let's cut to the chase."

Donald sat back and shook his head again. "I don't understand too much, because she won't tell me. But basically it's to do with the will, her will. Mother won't tell me anything in detail."

"What do you mean, she won't tell you anything? *You* told *me* that your inheritance was somehow tied to mine. I don't get it."

"Neither do I, because she won't explain. But after she had her first heart attack, she told me to call you, to get you home, to get you to New York. But you refused to come. She wasn't too happy, I can tell you that, and then she had a second heart attack. When she was better, she got really forceful about my persuading you to come to New York. She told me it was *imperative,* she had to see you and that it involved a lot of money. That's all I know."

"I see. So it's all to do with Margot Scott Denning and her money."

"True."

"I'm not interested in her money. You can have my share. All of it, Donald."

"That's nice, thanks, I accept it," he said. "But

first you have to talk to her, *see* her. She wants to *see* you, urgently. Come on, sis, agree to this. Please, for me."

"Donald, why do you persist in annoying me when you need my help?"

He frowned, looking puzzled.

"You know very well I hate being called sis," I reminded him.

"Sorry, *Val*."

"So, is she at death's door or not?"

"No," he admitted. "Not *actually*. Not now. She seems a lot better, and the doctor says she can go back to work next week, but only part-time, for a few hours a day. She has to take it easy, and she has to rest a lot."

"That won't go down well. I used to think she was hyperactive, the way she moved around, rushed hither and yon when we were little. She was never still for a moment, and hardly ever at home, always in her office at Lowell's."

"That's true. Even when we were just small kids, work came first, I guess. And since Dad died, she's been really committed to business, a workaholic."

"Oh."

"Well, she misses him, Val."

"He's been dead for ten years, Donald! Has she become keeper of the flame? Is that it?"

He didn't answer, simply looked into the distance, at the space above my head.

The silence became drawn out.

Donald looked so miserable, so perturbed, I found myself feeling sorry for him. How I used to bully him. He had looked at me in much the same way when he had been a child. He'd been a nice little boy until she'd come along and ruined him. But I had loved him, he was right about that. Until he had been grabbed away by that monstrous woman who'd borne us both.

Taking a deep breath, I broke the silence when I said, "Muffie told me she keeps running into you these days, and that you always have a beautiful girl with you. Is there anybody special yet?"

"Well, yeah, sort of . . . there's a really great girl and I care about her a lot—" He cut himself off, settled back against the sofa, squinted at me in the sunlight. "So, you saw Muffie Potter."

"Yes, for lunch yesterday."

"Val, listen, I think you really must see her, Mother I mean!" he exclaimed with sudden urgency. "She won't open up to me until she's talked to you. If she's said that once, she's said it two dozen times. I need to know what this *will* stuff is all about, and only you can find out. Val, this is about my future."

"I hadn't planned on seeing her. Nor had I planned on seeing you, Donald. I came here on business with Jake, and it was he who pushed me into making a date with you. He feels I have to get to the bottom of it. Find out why she was so horrible to me when I was growing up."

"I guess you do, sis. I mean Val," he quickly corrected himself, obviously trying hard to be nicer to me than he normally was, to ingratiate himself. Well, he wanted something, didn't he? But unexpectedly he had such a pleading look on his face, I found myself saying, "I'm not going to actually promise I'll see her before I leave, Donald, but I will think about it. That I *do* promise."

This pleased him and he beamed at me. "Thanks," he said. "I'm appreciative. Anyway, we should both know what's on her mind, shouldn't we?"

"That's true," I acknowledged.

"When do you think you'll see her?"

"I didn't say I'd see her. But, okay, I will *phone* her. Before I leave New York. Let's forget it for the time being. Don't nag me, otherwise I might change my mind," I threatened, and instantly realized I'd reverted to my bullying of old.

He laughed, obviously thinking the same thing. "Fair enough. Now, when do I get to meet Costner's clone?"

"Is somebody talking about me?" Jake asked from the doorway.

I looked across, saw him leaning against the doorjamb nonchalantly, looking impossibly handsome, dressed in pristine blue jeans and a white cable-knit sweater. And I acknowledged to myself that he did indeed look a bit like the actor.

"Come on in, Jake," I said, standing up. "I want you to meet my brother, Donald, who's being positively sweet today, and not his usual obnoxious self."

Donald laughed, also rose.

The two men walked toward each other, met in the middle of the room, and shook hands. Jake said, "Would you like a cup of coffee or a drink, Donald?"

"Not right now, thanks, but maybe later, Jake."

Jake sat down in the chair next to me, gave me a long, questioning look, and asked, "So tell me, have you solved the problems of the world?"

"No," I answered quickly. "But I have promised Donald I'll contact his mother before I leave New York."

Jake nodded. "Why not do it now? Make a date to see her as soon as possible? Let's get this family stuff out of the way. You and I have so much work to do on the book."

"Are you two writing a book?" Donald asked, his face lighting up. "What's it about?"

Before I could stop him, Jake was telling Donald all about *Flowers of War,* his excitement and enthusiasm more pronounced than ever. There was no way I could curtail the flow of words, and naturally Donald was eating it all up, his eyes fastened on Jake intently. He was mesmerized.

I stood up and walked across the floor. At the door I said, "I'm going to get a cold drink. Either of you want anything?"

They both glanced at me and said nothing, simply shook their heads and immediately went back to their conversation. I shrugged and hurried down the corridor to the kitchen. As I pushed open the swinging door and went in, I couldn't help thinking that Donald had improved a bit. At least he wasn't as nasty as he usually was. In fact, he was almost civilized. Wonders never cease, I muttered under my breath. And then instinctively I wondered what kind of game Donald was playing.

II

Late that evening, when we were getting ready to go to dinner, Jake turned to me and said, "Give your mother a call now; arrange to see her tomorrow."

"Tomorrow!" I exclaimed, looking horrified. "It's too *soon*."

"Too soon for what?"

"To see her, Jake. I need time to prepare myself before I venture into her territory. And I must

286 Barbara Taylor Bradford

call her and then go over there at once, otherwise
I might—" I stopped and stared at him.

"Or you might lose your nerve? Is that what
you were going to say?"

I nodded.

Jake came across the room in a few strides, put
his arms around me, and brought me into his
warm and loving embrace.

"Listen, sweetheart, there's nothing she can do to
you now. Not anymore. You're no longer a little
girl at her mercy. You're a grown woman, a war
correspondent, a woman who has faced every kind
of danger, looked it in the eye, and stared it down.
You can see her *anytime,* Val, you don't have to prepare yourself. That's silly. Just pick up that phone,
dial her number, and tell her about Donald's visit
today—"

"She'll already know about that!" I exclaimed,
cutting him off. "He'll have told her everything."

"Okay. Maybe. Just tell her you'd like to see her
tomorrow. I'll go with you if you want."

"I do want," I said, and immediately felt somewhat foolish about my attitude of a moment
before. What was Margot Scott Denning going to
do to me? Nothing, of course. It was just that I
had so many bad memories of her and I always
felt nervous at the prospect of being in her presence. Not that I'd seen her since my grandfather's
funeral.

"All right," I agreed, "I'll do it now."

"Good girl."

I went over to the phone, picked it up, and dialed the number of the apartment on Park Avenue.

When she answered, I said, "It's Val. Donald says you want to see me."

"Yes, I do," she said quietly. "How are you, Valentine?"

How am I, I thought. What a damned nerve she has. That was practically the first time she had asked me how I was in my entire life. Instantly my suspicions spiraled into alarm. I said, "When can we meet? How about tomorrow?"

"Well, I—"

I cut her off coolly. "We'd better make it tomorrow afternoon. At about four. It's really the only time I have available."

"Very well," she said. "I'll see you at four."

"Fine," I answered, and hung up.

Chapter 20

I

Although *I* was nervous about meeting with my mother, and had originally wanted Jake to accompany me, at the last moment I suddenly realized I preferred to see her alone.

It had struck me early on Sunday morning that I probably stood a better chance of finding out more if I went to her apartment by myself. And so I explained this to Jake over breakfast, hoping he would understand my motivation.

He seemed a bit uncertain about my decision at first, as always protective of me, and then he quickly came around to my way of thinking.

Nodding, he sounded more positive as he said, "Okay then, Val, go over there by yourself, if you're more comfortable with that. As long as you stay cool and unemotional, you'll be fine. Just be businesslike and matter-of-fact."

I promised I would do this, agreeing with him that it was the best way to handle the situation. My mother had requested the meeting, I had agreed to go, and I would listen to what she had to say.

But, in point of fact, it *was* truly my call, and I could leave whenever I wished. It was as simple as that. And very reassuring.

Later that day, as I walked out onto First Avenue, looking for a cab, I told myself I must make the visit brief and to the point, for my own sake.

Lingering at that apartment where I had grown up so miserably would only exacerbate the deep-seated anger that lay buried deep inside me. Certainly I didn't want it to erupt, because that would not accomplish anything other than upsetting me, making me incapable of dealing with my mother.

She had continued to live at the rambling, traditional apartment on Park Avenue after my father's death. Obviously she was attached to the place, which she and my father had moved into when they had married in 1965.

As the taxi turned off East Fifty-seventh Street and started to go uptown on Park, I suddenly asked him to stop and let me off.

After paying the driver, I got out, relieved to be outside in the fresh air. In the cab I had suddenly begun to feel overly warm, even a bit claustrophobic, not to mention anxiety-ridden as well.

Breathing deeply, I walked up Park toward Seventy-third Street, where the apartment was located, endeavoring to dispel the queasiness that had settled in my stomach. For a split second I thought I was going to vomit, then I realized that what I was actually feeling was mounting uneasiness at the prospect of seeing my mother. I had never known what to expect, how she would react to me, or what she would say, and in consequence I dreaded being in her presence.

After walking steadily for ten blocks, the nauseous sensation began to diminish, and I suddenly started to feel much better.

Jake had said yesterday that my mother could no longer hurt me, and this was true. I was not that little girl she had been able to wound so easily with her cruel neglect and lack of love. I was a grown woman, thirty-one years old, a woman who faced danger in the extreme almost daily in her job. A woman who was self-supporting and independent. A woman fully responsible for herself and her life. I didn't need Mommy anymore, that evasive Mommy I had always longed for as a child and had never had.

My mother had been out of my life for the past fourteen years, so why was I tensing up again about seeing her? Because of the past, of course, I answered myself. As a child all I'd ever wanted was her attention, love, and approval. And they had been withheld. I had never understood why. I didn't understand to this day . . . and it was a question that nagged at the back of my mind, one of many.

In spite of my tenseness and vague apprehension, all of a sudden I became unexpectedly more confident about seeing her again. Although I was going to visit my mother for Donald's sake, and because of the pressure he had exerted on me to do so, if I were honest, it was also because *I* needed to see her. *For myself.* Jake was correct about that . . . wipe the slate clean, he had said. By confronting her, I hoped I could slay the demons, the demons that had haunted me for as long as I could remember.

II

She looked exactly the same as always.

Margot Scott Denning. Great American beauty.

And she *was* still beautiful. Black hair coming to a dramatic widow's peak on her proud, wide brow; light-green eyes below curving coal-black brows; chiseled features; a perfect nose; the wide mouth, bloodred against the pallor of her flawless white complexion. A face that had bowled men over, probably still did.

Tall. Thin as a rail. Elegant in a perfectly cut gray flannel skirt topped with a red cashmere sweater, with a matching cardigan as well, tied around her neck in the way women of her ilk were wearing them these days. The plain pearl studs at her ears, in place as they always were, as was the mandatory string of pearls. Legs sleek and long and shapely, encased in pale-gray, very sheer stockings. Narrow, immaculately shod feet in gray suede pumps.

My mother.

Fourteen years ago I had walked out of this apartment and gone to Beekman Place to my beloved and caring grandparents, who had taken me in eagerly, willingly, and with a great deal of love.

And in all that time, from that day to this, she had not changed. She looked exactly the same. It was not only uncanny, it was unnerving. Nor did she appear to have been ill. She looked to be in blooming health as far as I could tell.

She let me into the apartment herself and said hello in that low, cool voice of hers I remembered so well. But she made no move to embrace me, which didn't surprise me in the least. She had never been affectionate, and certainly not with me. And, of course, I didn't make a move toward her either. I merely responded to her greeting verbally, in a neutral voice.

I followed her into the sitting room.

It was a spacious, elegant room overlooking Park Avenue, and just like her, it had remained unchanged.

For a moment I felt as though time had stood still. My childhood years came rushing back . . . the suffering I had endured, the hurt of her neglect, my loneliness, my terrible sense of rejection. Everything I'd ever felt seemed to tumble all around me, a whirl of emotions in the pale afternoon sunlight that filled this beautiful room.

The decades fell away . . . voices long since stilled, faces long forgotten, all of them were suddenly here with me, echoes and images of the past jostling for prominence among the dust motes rising up in the air. For a second I felt dizzy and undone; I thought I would keel over.

Very swiftly, I pulled myself back into the present, blocked out that unhappiness and pain of my early years. I did not want to look behind me ever again. Peering at ghosts in the shadows was a waste. My eyes were fixed ahead, riveted on the future.

III

My mother sat down in her usual place, on a French *bergère* covered in oyster satin, positioned near a Louis the Fifteenth sofa in striped oyster-and-burgundy silk and close to the fireplace.

I did not fall into the trap of taking the chair where I had always been instructed to sit as a child. Instead, I remained standing near the fireplace, one hand on the mantel.

She sat looking me over for a moment or two, in much the same way Donald had yesterday.

I stared back at her unblinkingly, my face unreadable.

I knew I looked smart in my black bush jacket, white silk shirt, and black gabardine pants, and this pleased me. I was no longer filled with trepidation now that I was actually there. In fact, any nervousness I'd felt before had totally evaporated. I was completely calm, very cool, and in control.

"You look well, Val," she said at last in her well-modulated, uppercrust voice.

I nodded. "So do you. But I don't think we're here to discuss each other's appearance or state of health. Donald is very agitated. He says you keep alluding to your will and his inheritance ever since you had your first heart attack. But that you won't discuss anything with him. Until you've talked to me, that is. So here I am, on Donald's behalf, so to speak. Shall we get down to business?"

She was absolutely silent.

She simply sat there, gazing at the painting over the fireplace. It had always been there. A fabulous Boudin. And it was filled with the most extraordinary light; I recalled how fascinated by it I had been when I was a youngster. It was the sky that caught and held my attention today, now as then. It was the most perfect blue, a dazzling blue.

Pulling my attention away from the remarkable and very valuable painting, I looked across at my mother and got right to the point.

"I can't imagine how my inheritance is tied up with Donald's, but I think I ought to tell you now, right at the outset of this conversation, I don't want mine. Leave everything to Donald."

Rousing herself from her thoughts, and very visibly so, she sat up straighter and exclaimed, "That's not possible!"

"Of course it is. I willingly give it up. Rewrite your last will and testament. Make him the sole beneficiary."

"I cannot do that. And neither can you. *You* must inherit Lowell's. That's a fact that can never be changed."

"Why can't it be changed?"

"Because you are a female descendant of the founder of Lowell's, and only a woman can inherit Lowell's. This was The Tradition started by your great-great-grandmother, Amy-Anne Lowell. It was she who founded Lowell's in 1898 when she opened a chemist shop in Greenwich Village. She decreed that only her female descendants could inherit her company. And that's the way it has been since then. Amy-Anne left the company to her daughter Rebecca, who left it to her daughter Violet, who was my mother, your grandmother. And my mother left it to me. I in turn must pass it on to you. It is The Tradition in our family."

I couldn't speak for a moment, I was so thunderstruck. Finally finding my voice, I said, "And what would have happened if you hadn't had a female child? Only Donald? Or other sons instead of me?"

"In that instance, the wife of the eldest son would inherit the company. She would probably have to be just a titular head. The day-to-day running of the company would be left to others more skilled, those properly trained. But she would be the owner and the chairman. However, that has not come to pass yet, not in one hundred years, since there have always been female descendants of Amy-Anne Lowell."

I digested her words and asked, "Have you always known this? Did you know about the Amy-Anne tradition when I was a child?"

"Yes."

"Then why did you treat me so badly when I was growing up?"

She looked at me askance, frowning, the beautifully curved brows pulling together to form a jagged black line that suddenly gave her an ugly look. Leaning forward slightly, she exclaimed, "I did not treat you badly! How can you say such a terrible thing! You were beautifully dressed, well fed, and well cared for in this lovely apartment. You had your own room—and a beautiful one, I might remind you. You went to the best schools, had the most wonderful vacations." She shook her head denyingly. "You're absurd. And ungrateful, very ungrateful, and after all I did for you. *Really,* Valentine!"

"Don't *really* me in that tone, or use the word *ungrateful*. What you've just said is perfectly true, about the clothes, this apartment, the food, and the schools. But you did neglect me and shamefully so. You rejected me, you denied me motherly love, treated me with total indifference, and to such an extent, and so blatantly, some people around here at the time construed it as criminal, that indifference of yours."

"How dare you to speak to me in this way. I am your mother. I deserve your respect!"

I threw her a look of condemnation and said in a cold voice, "What's so surprising to me now is that all along you knew me to be your heir to Lowell's. I just can't believe it. Nor can I believe your gal . . . how could you ever *think* that I would want Lowell's under the circumstances, and after all you did to me. *You ruined my childhood.* And if it weren't for my Denning grandparents, I would probably be in a loony bin today because of you and your treatment of me. That's how wicked you were."

She sat erect in the chair, imposingly beautiful and as cold as ice. The Ice Queen, Grandfather had called her. How well the name suited. There was something inhuman about her.

I could tell from the coldness in her light-green eyes and the tight set of her mouth that she was angry; also that she had not understood what I was saying. She believed herself to be innocent of any wrongdoing. How appalling, I thought, she has no conscience. And instantly I recalled Muffie's words of the other day. She had said she thought my mother was mentally unbalanced. Perhaps she was right about that. Certainly my mother was seriously disturbed, I knew this deep down within myself. Because only a woman who was not normal could have treated her own child as badly and as unfeelingly as she had treated me.

Staring at her intently, I asked quietly, "Do you expect me to give up my career as a war photojournalist? Do you expect me to come back here and start working at Lowell's? Is that what you're getting at?"

She nodded. "Yes, Val, of course it is. And it is

the proper thing for you to do now. I have had two heart attacks already, and I think this is the right time for you to learn about the business, a business that one day will be yours."

She spoke evenly now, and it struck me once more that my words had meant nothing to her. They had not sunk in. Perhaps she had no conception of just how much she had hurt me when I was growing up.

Taking a deep breath, I explained, "But I just told you, I don't want Lowell's. Give it to Donald. He was always your favorite anyway."

"I cannot give it to Donald. I must follow The Tradition. That is the family rule . . . it has always been a . . . a *law* within the family."

I laughed hollowly, suddenly understanding so much. "Donald's not married, so there's no female in the immediate family. Other than *moi,* that is. Little old me, I'm the *one*. But you didn't bargain for that, did you?" I shook my head, finished scathingly, "You fully expected Donald to be married by now, didn't you, Mother?"

A flush crept up from her long neck to invade her face, and I knew my words had hit home. Her expression was one of embarrassment.

"You put all your hopes in Donald. You were always so certain he would marry young, and marry well, and you didn't give a damn about me. But you miscalculated. You never imagined that you'd have two heart attacks in the space of a couple of months at the age of fifty-six. It never occurred to you that you were anything but immortal. But you are indeed mortal, just like the rest of us. And you never expected Donald to still be a bachelor at twenty-six."

"You are quite wrong about Donald. He has a lovely young woman friend, Alexis Rayne, and I understand the relationship has become serious. I feel quite certain your brother will become engaged momentarily."

"I expect he will, once he knows the advantages," I exclaimed. "He won't be able to resist. He'll lasso her and drag her to the altar if he has to, just to get his hands on the money."

"How disgusting you are," she snapped in a shocked voice, giving me an angry look. "You were always mean to Donald."

"No, I wasn't. But *you* were *mean* to *me*. And I've never understood *why,* or what prompted your behavior toward me. So I'm asking you now. *Why?*"

"Don't be ridiculous, Valentine. I was never mean to you. Not ever in your life. All of this nonsense is in your very vivid imagination. Furthermore, you have the most extraordinary tendency to exaggerate, especially when it comes to your childhood, which was absolutely normal."

I ignored her remarks. I thought about pressing her further to explain herself to me, explain her behavior when I was growing up. But it struck me that this would be useless. At this moment anyway. Instead, I asked, "How is Donald's inheritance tied up with mine?"

"It isn't. Not in actuality, in reality. When I said that to him, it was just a manner of speaking on my part. I didn't want to explain to Donald about The Tradition, or my will, until I had had an opportunity to explain things to you."

"So what exactly *is* Donald's inheritance?" I asked more out of curiosity than anything else.

"Under my will Donald is well provided for," my mother answered. "He does receive a large amount of shares in Lowell's. And if he wishes, he can have an executive position there. I am leaving him this apartment, and all of the possessions in it, the art, everything." She glanced about her, waved her hand around airily.

True to form, I thought, gazing at her thoughtfully. Everything she owned was going to Donald. I was to inherit Lowell's because she had no alternative but to leave it to me under that curious family rule.

Although I knew I was repeating myself, I said, "I think you should give Lowell's to Donald, as well as everything else. I certainly don't want it, not under any circumstances."

"No, I cannot do that, and I just explained why a moment ago."

"Listen! I don't want it! And if you do leave

it to me, then I'll turn it over to him.
Immediately. Lowell's is meaningless to me.
You never told me anything about it, or
explained about The Tradition, as you call it,
when I was growing up. Neither did your
mother, my grandmother. And I was next in
line, after you. I can't understand why I was
never made to understand the importance of
Lowell's as far as I was concerned."

"You were too young."

"I see. And what makes you think I could possibly care about the company now? As for this
family rule, I personally think it's rather stupid."

"Amy-Anne Lowell did not think so," she said
slowly. "And neither would you if you had had
her early life."

IV

I heard the key in the lock and the door slam, and
I suspected it must be Donald.

And it was.

"Ah, there you are, Donald," I said. "Come on
in and listen up. I have a big surprise for you.
Your mother has explained the famous will. I am
supposed to inherit Lowell's. It's an old family
tradition dating back to Amy-Anne Lowell of
1898. Only girls get it, you see. But I don't want
it. I therefore give it to you, Donald."

"You cannot do that!" my mother cried heatedly, half rising from her chair, her face suddenly flushing.

Donald remained standing in the middle of the antique rug, looking from me to his mother, a stunned expression on his very handsome face.

"I don't understand," he said, speaking directly to her. "Don't I get any part of the business? Is that what Val's saying?"

"Shares, Donald. You will receive shares in Lowell's, and also my other investments will be yours," she answered in a placating voice. "This apartment, the art, everything I personally own is coming to you when I die." She patted the sofa. "Come and sit here, and I will explain about the will."

He glanced across at me, then did as she suggested.

Slowly, and very patiently, our mother gave Donald all the details of her will and spent quite some time explaining about The Tradition. The way she had pronounced this right from the beginning had made me realize that she was capitalizing it. But then, no doubt all the Lowell women before her had done the same thing. I had meant what I said to her. It *was* a stupid family rule. What if there were no female descendants? No wives or daughters of sons in any given generation? What would happen then?

I thought of asking her that and then immediately changed my mind. I was itching to escape; there was really no reason for me to stay. I had made my point. And it was obvious she was not going to give me any explanation for her treatment of me when I was little. I could not wipe the slate clean, as Jake had suggested. Nor could I slay the demons after all. So I might as well go.

After hearing his mother out, Donald turned to me. "You said you didn't want Lowell's. Do you mean that, Val?"

"Of course I do. I don't live in New York, I live in Paris, and I've no intention of moving. Furthermore, I have a *career*. I don't need another one. I certainly have no interest in Lowell's. I wouldn't know what to do with a cosmetics company."

"You could learn to run it," Margot Denning said.

"Fat chance of that!" I shot back. Looking across at Donald, I continued. "You'd better get married quickly. Marry that girl. Then when the time comes for me to inherit Lowell's, I'll just give it to her. It's as simple as that."

"Is it?" Donald stared at his mother.

"That has never happened in the entire history of Lowell's, but I suppose Val could do that . . . she *would* be passing it to a *female* member of the family. . . ." Her voice trailed off.

"But why does a female have to inherit?" Donald asked.

"It was a rule made by the founder of the company, your great-great-grandmother Amy-Anne Lowell. Her early life was terrible. She suffered horrendous physical abuse from her father and her brother. She was a punching bag for them when they were drunk. When she was fourteen, she ran away from Boston, where the Lowells lived. She eventually found her way to New York and worked mostly as a servant girl in the home of the rich of this city. When she was seventeen, she found a position with an old lady, a spinster lady, and she became her personal maid and companion-secretary as well.

"The old lady liked her, was very kind to Amy-Anne, and she left her some money when she passed away three years later. But much more important, she left Amy-Anne a handwritten book of recipes for creams, lotions, soaps, and candles. Amy-Anne knew they were excellent since they had been made up for the old lady, a Miss Mandelsohn, to her specifications. And Amy-Anne had used them, knew their quality.

"Miss Mandelsohn had brought the book with her from Germany when she immigrated to America as a girl. It's a long story how Amy-Anne opened her chemist shop in Greenwich Village, and I won't go into it now. But once she did, she made a vow to herself. She vowed that no man would ever have power over her ever again.

Nor over any of her female offsprings and her eventual descendants.

"Amy-Anne was most fortunate in her choice of husband, because he was a truly good man, devoted to her and their three daughters. And he was a chemist who helped her to succeed. Nonetheless, that rule remained. It was the law in the family: Only females inherit wealth and power. And it has been passed down from mother to daughter. It is The Tradition."

Chapter 21

I

"And there you have the whole story," I said to Jake, and leaned back against the floral sofa in the sitting room of the Beekman Place apartment.

"It's just amazing—I mean that she denies her behavior during your childhood," he murmured, frowning and shaking his head. "I think you're probably right, Val, she must be seriously disturbed to have treated you the way she did in the first place. And there's something else . . . where was your father when all this was happening?"

"Oh, forget him, he was a wimp!" I exclaimed. "Totally under her thumb. He was besotted with her, gaga about her, actually. I knew that, but

Aunt Isobel confirmed it to me a few years ago. She said my mother walked all over him, and he never objected. Aunt Isobel also intimated to me that my mother had affairs with other men, and I'm sure that's true. In a way, I'm sorry you didn't meet her, because she's really something—"

"I'll bet she is," he cut in.

"Yes, she *is* a piece of work, no doubt about that," I agreed. "But what I meant is that she's *very, very* beautiful. Glacial, mind you, but still beautiful. And you know what—she doesn't seem to have aged since I was seventeen. She's exactly the same in her appearance. Time passing has not left a trace."

"I thought she was ill?"

"I guess she made a rapid recovery from the heart attacks. Anyway, all I can say is that on the surface she looks fantastic. There's certainly no sign of illness. And not a line on her face."

"There's nothing like a sharp knife cleverly wielded by a brilliant surgeon," he said, and reaching out for the bottle of Beck's he took a quick swig.

"I wouldn't know whether she's had plastic surgery or not, Jake. But I doubt it. I think she has good genes, and, of course, she's taken great care of herself . . . to the point of being obsessed with herself and her appearance."

He nodded. "There are a lot of vain women in this world. But, hey, Val, you've done your best, tried to get to the bottom of your problem with her and without success. She's in denial, she'll never talk to you about your childhood. So, since you can't wipe the slate clean after all, then I guess you should just sling all that garbage out the window. Figuratively speaking. Get rid of it. And let's get on with our lives."

"You're right, as usual, Jake. I'll do just that."

"One more thing before we close this subject matter out. What about that rule . . . about only females inheriting the family company . . . it's the weirdest thing I've ever heard. Don't *you* think so?"

"I think it's . . . *daft,* but then, the full story of Amy-Anne is quite hair-raising, I'm sure. Being the punching bag for the Lowell men when she was a child must have been soul destroying as well as brutal on the body. She was probably pushed to the limits of her endurance, so who can blame her for not wanting any man to have power over her ever again? She obviously discovered that money is power, and therefore the best protection ever invented."

Jake rose, came over, and sat down next to me on the sofa. Taking hold of my hand, he gave me a long look that seemed oddly sorrowful, then cleared his throat several times.

"Is there something wrong?" I asked. I knew there was even before he answered. Being sensitive to his moods and his emotions, I could read him like a book. I was convinced he was troubled about something quite separate from my family problems.

Finally he answered. "While you were out seeing your mother, you had a call from Mike. He wants you to phone him back. He'll wait up for your call, he said."

"Something's wrong! What did he tell you?"

Jake sighed and his mouth drooped down at the sides. "It's about Françoise. She went into labor yesterday. Prematurely. She lost the baby."

"Oh, no! *No, Jake!* That's so terrible for her." I felt the sudden pinprick of tears behind my eyes, the rush of emotion in my throat. "Poor Françoise, oh, that poor girl, she's suffered so much. Now she's lost the child. . . ."

I shook my head and stared at Jake intently. "You should have told me when I first got back. This is much more important than my mother and my problems with her."

"I wanted you to get everything off your chest, it's troubled you for so long." He leaned into me, kissed my cheek, and finally released my hand. "There's not much you can do for Françoise from here, you're too far away. And that's why I let you rattle on about Lowell's. But now you'd better go call Mike, honey. He's waiting, and it's late in Paris."

II

"Jake just told me what happened, Mike," I said to my boss in Paris once we had exchanged greetings. "I'm so very sorry."

"Yeah, I know . . . it's tough for her, Val, and thanks for calling back, I appreciate it."

"So where is she? What hospital's she in? And even more important, how's she holding up?"

"She's doing fine, she really is. . . ."

I waited for him to complete his sentence, but he did not. I said, "Mike, Mike, are you there?"

"Yeah, yeah, sorry," he answered, sounding down in the mouth. He sighed and added in the quietest voice, "There's something I didn't tell Jake . . . the baby was born dead . . . she'd probably been dead for a few days, maybe even longer. . . ."

"Oh my God, Mike! Françoise must be devastated, beside herself with grief."

"She is pretty heartbroken about it, and she blames herself, because she says she should have left Olivier a long time ago. She's convinced he damaged the baby when he pushed her down the steps in Marseilles. She believes the baby would've been all right if she'd left him. Who knows . . . I told her she shouldn't castigate herself." He let out another weary sigh.

"Françoise is broken up about the loss of the baby girl."

"I can imagine. Can I contact her? What hospital is she in?"

"I put her in a private clinic."

"That was smart of you. Which one?"

"I'll tell you in a minute. There's something else you should know. I'm pretty damn certain that son of a bitch Olivier has been sniffing around your apartment here. Certainly he came up to the Gemstar office looking for you—"

"You're kidding!" I interrupted peremptorily, taken aback. "I'm glad I'm not in Paris. What's he like?"

"Good-looking, but I suspect he's one helluva thug. I don't think he'd have any compunction . . . about doing anything. Adam Macklin saw him, I was in a meeting, but I caught a glimpse of him when he was leaving. Anyway, he doesn't know you're in the States. Adam had instructions from me to say you were in the Bwindi Impenetrable Forest in Uganda. On special assignment. I doubt very much that he'll go looking for you *there*."

"You think he put two and two together, then? Is that what you're getting at, Mike?"

"More than likely. That's why I didn't take Françoise to the American Hospital here. Too obvious. And it would be the first place he'd look if he had any inkling or suspicion that she'd gone into labor prematurely."

"Why do you think he seized on me, focused on me?"

"You're a very obvious connection. Françoise told me that her mother had mentioned you when they went to Marseilles. Olivier heard your name that day. He knew you were staying at Les Roches Fleuries with Jake and were still there when Françoise came back to Saint-Jean-Cap-Ferrat with her parents. It's more than likely he checked the airlines, asked for the manifests when she disappeared. He saw your name and Jake's and, of course, *hers*. I'm sure her parents haven't given anything away. It's all deduction on his part, and let's not forget, he's a homicide cop and he's used to doing complicated investigations, tracking stuff down. And from what she's told me, he's an ace at it."

"Can I get in touch with Françoise tomorrow, Mike?" I asked, not wanting to hear anything else about Olivier. He scared me.

"Sure. I put her in a private clinic in Saint-Germain-en-Laye, just outside Paris. She's pretty safe there until she's feeling strong enough to come back to the city."

"What's going to happen to her, Mike? What are her plans now that she's lost the baby?"

"I don't think she has any plans. Not yet. And I honestly don't know what she wants to do in the future. The main thing on her mind had been to carry the baby to full term . . . she'd been having acute pains, other physical problems, and to tell you the truth, I wasn't too surprised when she suddenly went into labor. Nor am I surprised that she lost the baby . . . she's been under such physical and mental stress."

"She can't go back to Olivier," I announced. "She'd be sentencing herself to death if she did."

"I agree, and she agrees, and let's face it, he's already started tracking her."

"You and she must be careful, Mike, and I must too . . . because I'm a link to her—in his mind anyway. But she could come and stay here. When she can travel. He thinks I'm in Uganda, and he certainly doesn't know about this apartment. Françoise could stay here and fully recuperate. And at the same time she could do some hard thinking, decide what she wants to do, make some plans for the next few months."

There was a silence at the other end of the phone.

"Hello, Mike," I said. *"Hello . . ."*

"Sorry, Val, to go silent on you, I was just thinking that one through. It's not such a bad idea, having her come stateside. But I was hoping you'd be coming back to work soon. There are all kinds of assignments waiting for you."

"I plan to, Mike. In fact, Jake and I don't

intend to stay here much longer. We've been pulling some of our pictures together this week-end, trying to get the presentation ready for the publisher. And once we've done our stuff, so to speak, we're hightailing it back to France. But Françoise can stay here without me, that's not a problem. It's my grandfather's old apartment, very roomy, comfortable, and there's a maid who comes in several times a week. She'll be fine here. Also, my best friend lives in New York. Muffie Potter Aston, and Muffie will be happy to keep an eye on Françoise. Look, she'll be *safe* here, Mike, I'm sure of that."

"I believe you, and it may be just the solution she needs. I'll talk to her about it in a few days. She's too troubled right now, honey, and as I told you, heartbroken about losing her baby."

"Olivier's a bastard . . ."

"That he is . . . you asked about her plans, the future. The thing is, I'd like her to be in *my* future, and so would my girls. They've really taken to her, as I told you before, and I have a strong suspicion Françoise wants that too. But, well . . . listen, she's got that maniac of a hus-band to shed first, and that ain't gonna be an easy task."

"You're right. Anyway, let's think about my idea for a couple of days, and if you give me the number of the private clinic, I'll call her."

"Sure," he said, and rattled it off.

III

While I was on the phone to Paris, Jake had been busy in the dining room. Earlier, we had spread out the piles of pictures on the table, trying to bring a semblance of order to them. Now he sat making notes on a yellow pad, and when he heard me come in, he turned around.

"Mike's pretty upset, isn't he?" he said.

Leaning against the doorjamb, I nodded and answered, "Yes, he's very worried about Françoise. I guess he's really become involved with her in the last couple of weeks. I can't say I blame him, she's lovely looking and sweet natured. But that husband of hers presents a huge problem."

"And how," Jake agreed. "He's a bully and—"

"Mike called him a thug," I interjected.

"He more than likely is, and he could prove to be dangerous."

"I suggested to Mike that Françoise come to stay here at the apartment when she's up to traveling."

Jake looked surprised and exclaimed, "I'm not so sure that was a good idea, Val."

"We'll be going back to Paris very shortly, and there's no reason she can't stay here. Aunt Isobel won't mind, and Muffie will keep an eye on her."

Jake let out a long sigh. "You seem to have adopted her."

"Not really, but I do feel so sorry for her. From what she's told me, her life with Olivier Bregone has been a nightmare."

"And you probably saved her life that day at the villa, so you feel responsible for her now, no?"

"I hadn't thought of it that way," I said.

"This guy Olivier Bregone is a nasty piece of work, from what we've heard about him, Val, and I think if he becomes too frustrated about finding her, he'll lash out, and I don't want you to be one of his targets. I don't want you to get hurt."

I didn't respond, merely stood staring at him from the doorway, and then I explained. "When Olivier showed up at Gemstar, looking for me, they told him I was in Uganda on assignment."

"He's been to Gemstar!" Jake cried. "Jesus! That spells trouble to me already. You can't get so involved, Val. But tell me what happened?"

"Mike was in a meeting, but he instructed Adam Macklin to say I was out of the country, and there's no way he could know I'm here in the States."

"Want to bet?"

"Well, I guess cops can find out things if they really want to," I muttered.

"I don't think Françoise should come and stay here, Val, I really don't. Please be sensible about this. She has to work out her problems with her husband, get a protection order, divorce him, do whatever's necessary, and if you think Mike's become emotionally involved, then he should be the one helping her. You hardly know her."

"You're right, I guess. . . ."

Jake jumped up, crossed the floor, grabbed hold of me, and pulled me into his arms. "You're just too good for your own good sometimes, Valentine Denning! I've got to look out for you, and look after you, because you're the most precious thing in my life."

"Oh, Jake darling," I said against his shoulder. "Thank you for that. I feel the same way about you . . . I love you."

He held me away from him and looked into my eyes. "And I love you, Val. Very much."

IV

Leading me into the dining room, he pulled out the chair next to his and said in a more matter-of-fact voice, "I've begun to get a theme going here with the first batch of photos. Look." As he spoke, he began to spread them out a little more neatly.

After a moment of rearranging them, he continued. "Here are lots of your shots of children . . . children who haven't been injured . . . see, children with little bunches of flowers, with pets, with their siblings. Look at this one, this little boy with a scrap of bread held so close to his chest, as if he's afraid someone will take it away from him. It gets to you . . . in fact they all say so much, and they're very poignant."

"Yes, they are," I agreed. I remembered where and when I had taken most of them; the faces of the children were very touching. They were so sorrowful, so pathetic, heart-rending even, and yet there was something about them that suggested hope . . . hope for the future. They brought a lump to my throat, made me choke up. And if they affected *me* in this way, then surely they would move others. I wanted the book to be a success, most especially for Jake.

Chapter 22

I

Having confronted my mother and found out nothing, I decided to take Jake's advice and fling the family garbage out the window.

There was no point in attempting to talk to my mother again. As my grandfather used to say, there's nothing to be gained from flogging a dead horse, and this was true. My mother was in denial about her treatment of me when I was a child, and she probably always would be.

I could think of no way to convince her she had done wrong by me, and so my only course of action was to do nothing. I had to put it out of my mind once and for all, and move on.

This I did by throwing myself wholeheartedly

into the book project. Since Jake wanted me to write a great deal of it, I started by working on the captions for the photographs, intended for the presentation to the editor on Friday. "Practicing for the book itself," I told Jake as daily I bent my head over my yellow pad and drafted the lines I thought would best convey the feeling behind each picture.

After a couple of days I discovered how much I enjoyed writing the rather lengthy captions, and I was extremely flattered to hear Jake's words of praise when he read them at the end of each day.

While I wrote, he spent most of his time sorting and cataloguing his pictures, and also mine, which Mike had said we could take from the Gemstar archive in New York. "As long as you make a copy of each one and send back the original," he had reminded me on the phone from Paris.

On Wednesday morning we were very busy working at the dining room table, when the phone rang. Jake answered, and after listening a moment, said, "Oh, hi, Marge. Yes, okay. Wait a minute, let me find a pen."

Automatically I got up, handed him mine, and grabbed the yellow pad, placed it on the side table where the phone stood.

I went back to my chair and stared at the group of pictures I had spread out in front of me. I selected one and studied it for a moment. It was of a ragged-looking little boy, covered in grime, who was hunkered down next to his brother and his mother. They lay dead or dying on a dusty street in a Balkan village. Mounds of rubble surrounded them.

The images I had captured on film the previous year told their own story. What I wanted to do was use the back story, the story behind the photo for the caption. And I needed to do so in a cogent way, but also I had to choose exactly the right words. The whole idea was for the caption to have an emotional impact on the reader, and just as much as the images had.

"Okay, right. I'll call now," Jake was saying, and when he hung up, looked across at me and said, "You'll *never* guess who's in New York. Who just called me at the agency." His eyes fastened on mine, and he stood there, slightly bemused.

Knowing it had to be someone we didn't expect, or unlikely, I racked my brains. "Olivier," I answered, because I couldn't think of any other likely suspect.

"Don't be ghoulish! No, not Olivier, thank God. It's Fiona."

"Fiona!" I repeated.

"Yes, Fiona Hampton."

"I wonder what she's doing here," I muttered, frowning.

"I'm about to find out," Jake replied, and before I could say another word, he was dialing.

"Hey, wait a minute, let's not be rash here," I exclaimed, but he was already asking for her.

The next thing I heard was his cheerful "Hello, Fiona! How are you? And what are you doing in New York?"

He leaned against the antique mahogany sideboard, the phone pressed to his ear, nodding from time to time, listening intently, apparently interested in every word she had to say.

"Just a second, let me ask Val," he murmured into the phone, and looked across at me.

I sat up straighter in the chair and focused my attention on him. "What does she want?" I mouthed.

"Fiona would like us to have lunch or dinner with her. Which do you prefer, honey?" he asked.

"Are you talking about today?"

"Yep."

"Then let's make it dinner, since I'm really on a roll here with the captions. I'd like to keep working for a bit."

Nodding to me, he said into the phone, "Dinner is much better for us, Fiona, and why don't we meet at, let's see . . ." He stared at me, lifting a brow questioningly.

"Le Périgord on East Fifty-second. At eight o'clock," I suggested.

Jake repeated what I had just said to Fiona,

adding, "Yes, it'll be lovely to see you too. Until tonight, then."

II

"So what *is* she doing in New York?" I asked Jake once he was off the phone.

"She's here on a little holiday, she said. With a friend. Who she is bringing to dinner—"

"Male or female?" I interrupted.

"It's a man."

"*Oh*. So the grieving widow is no longer grieving."

"I never thought she really was grieving," Jake murmured, coming back to the dining room table, sitting down opposite me. "She was sad, yes, at the memorial, but looking back now, don't you think she was oddly contained?"

I nodded. "You're right, Jake, and there weren't too many tears flowing either during the eulogies or the rest of the service. Mmmm. Well, we'll see, won't we?"

"We sure will." He began to shuffle the photos.

I said, "By the way, how did she know you were in New York?"

"Don't you remember, she was calling me when we were at Les Roches Fleuries? Calling the Paris office, I mean. I kept trying to reach her, first in Dublin and then London. But she always had a machine on in London. I finally left a message that I was going to New York. I guess she got it, and decided to phone the Photoreal office once she arrived."

Once more I bent my head and began to write, trying to concentrate on the caption I'd been working on before Fiona's call. But she kept intruding, popping into my mind, and in the most insistent way.

During the year I had been emotionally involved with Tony, he had brainwashed me into believing she was a harridan and a difficult woman. But then I had discovered she was quite the opposite when I finally met her. Ever since that day I had often wondered if she had known about me, but I'd inevitably dismissed this idea. Married men didn't tell their wives about their mistresses. Or did they? Well, certainly not Tony Hampton, because there had been too many women in his life over the years. So many confessions would have surely caused a rift between them.

Gripping my pen, I began to slowly write on the pad, but within minutes Fiona was intruding again, and my concentration fled. Damn, I thought, why did *she* of all people have to show up in New York? That's all I need, a reminder of Tony Hampton and his double dealing, his lying, his cheating ways, the pain he caused me. And most probably her.

But as it turned out, Fiona's arrival would prove to be fortuitous, although I didn't recognize that until later.

III

Since black dominated my wardrobe, I wore black for dinner, and in doing so I stayed right in step with New York women, who never wore any other color at night.

But instead of my usual pantsuit, I was actually wearing a dress, and Jake let out a wolf whistle when I walked into the living room at seven-thirty on the dot.

"Oh, boy, don't you look great!" he exclaimed as the whistle faded away. "With those fabulous legs of yours, you should wear dresses more often."

"Thanks," I said, pleased with his reaction. The dress was simple, just a straight wool sheath, but it was stylish; with it I wore sheer black stockings and high-heeled black pumps. The pearl earrings my grandparents had given me, and a gold-and-pearl pin Muffie had rashly bought for my birthday two years earlier added just the right touches.

"Do you want a drink before we go?" Jake asked.

"No, thanks. And you're very smart-looking

yourself tonight," I said, looking him up and down and then leering theatrically.

He began to laugh and pulled me to him, held me close. "If you're not careful, we're going to end up in the bedroom not the restaurant," he muttered against my hair.

Pushing him away gently, I also laughed, then I took hold of his hand and said, "Come on, let's go. It'll take us a few minutes to walk up there to the restaurant, and we ought to arrive before they do."

"So let's go," Jake replied.

In the entrance foyer I picked up my black wool shawl and a small black evening bag, flung the shawl over my shoulder as we went out of the apartment, making for the elevator.

It was a lovely evening for early October, brisk but not really cold, and after a day inside working on the captions, it was refreshing to be outside.

Jake said as much as we walked along, echoing my own thoughts as we crossed Beekman Place heading for First Avenue. Neither of us was used to being as confined as we had been lately, since we were usually out in the field, wielding our cameras.

Linking my arm through Jake's, I asked, "What do you know about Alexander St. Just Stevens, the painter?"

"Not much really. Isn't he supposed to be today's equivalent of Picasso?"

"Yes, that's right, I believe he is."

"Why do you ask me about him?"

"Mike wants me to go over and see him, take a look at some of his work. Apparently he's halfway through a new series of paintings. He's preparing a big show to open in Paris. Mike has several magazines interested in spreads on him and his new paintings."

"I didn't realize he lived in New York. I thought he was English."

"He is, but according to Mike he's got a loft in New York and some sort of fancy estate in Mexico. I don't think he's lived in England for years. Mike said yesterday that he's currently at the loft in New York, painting, and he wants me to go and see him, get a feeling about the art."

"I can't help you very much, Val. I've seen some of his work, and I remember that it was very strong, that it makes quite a statement. I know several of his war paintings have been likened to Picasso's *Guernica,* which, as you know, Picasso painted during the Spanish Civil War in the thirties, and which Robert Capa photographed. Anyway, does Mike want you to shoot the art?"

"No, I don't think so. What he wants is for me to make contact with the artist, find out when the series will be finished, and hopefully get some sort of commitment from him. Mike wants us to have first crack at photographing it."

"*You,* I'm sure he wants *you* to do the spreads, otherwise why doesn't Mike send somebody else from Gemstar in New York to see the paintings?"

I shrugged. "I don't know . . . I guess he wants my opinion about the art itself."

"Well, I'm sure Alexander St. Just Stevens will jump at it. Artists, like everyone else, love publicity. It helps them sell their wares," he said, chuckling.

We were almost at the restaurant on Fifty-second Street, when I stopped a bit abruptly and looked at Jake. "I feel funny all of a sudden about seeing Fiona. Do you think she knows that Tony and I were involved?" I asked worriedly.

"I'm sure she doesn't know, so don't feel awkward, Val. And she was very pleasant with you at the memorial. Fiona's a lovely woman, take it from me, and very straightforward," he answered in a reassuring voice. "You always know where you stand with her, so please relax, Val."

"I'll try to, but it suddenly hit me this afternoon . . . the thought that she might know something. But you're right, she is very straight, that was one of the first things that struck me about her." I took a deep breath. "Okay, come on, then, let's go inside." I laughed as I slipped my arm through his and added, "She'd hardly be wanting to see us if she suspected anything about me."

"True," Jake agreed as we arrived at the door of the restaurant.

As always, Georges, the owner, was there to greet us, and he showed us to a lovely table for four in a quiet corner. Jake and I had just settled ourselves, when Fiona arrived, escorted by an attractive-looking man with premature silver hair and a fairly ruddy complexion.

Jake and I both stood up, hugged Fiona, and then were introduced to David Ingham, who I immediately realized from his accent was English.

Once we were all settled and drinks had been ordered, Fiona said, "It's lovely that you were able to have dinner with us tonight. We arrived yesterday, and today's our only free time in New York. Yes, it's lucky for us you were free."

Jake smiled, then asked, "And where are you going?"

"Connecticut," Fiona answered, and explained, "David's daughter is married to an American and they live in Greenwich. We'll be driving up there tomorrow evening."

David said, "Pamela, my daughter, and her husband, Frank, have a lovely house on the water. I know Fiona's going to enjoy the weekend."

"It's a pretty town," I murmured, glanced at Fiona and asked, "How're Moira and Rory?"

"Oh, thanks for asking, Val, they're both getting along fine, very fine indeed. They're adjusting now to Tony's death."

Jake said, "I did try to get hold of you in Dublin, you know, Fiona, but you'd checked out of the hotel by the time I called."

"Oh, don't be worrying about it, Jake, I was only phoning to say hello, to see how you were. And you both look wonderful, 'tis the truth. And what are you doing in New York, the two of you?"

"I had business here with a publisher," Jake began, looked at me, and took hold of my hand lying on top of the table. "And I insisted Val come along . . . she and I—"

"Oh, don't tell me, Jake, you and she . . . oh, that's so lovely . . . you're an item, then, are you?"

"I guess you could say that," Jake replied, laughing, motioning to the waiter, ordering a second round of drinks.

"I suppose you could say Fiona and I are an item too," David volunteered, glancing at us and then turning a loving smile on Fiona.

I thought she looked uncomfortable for a moment, but perhaps it was my imagination, because she instantly beamed at Jake and me and confided, "David's a very old friend, and he's been wonderful to me these last few years, what with Tony traveling so much and all. Anyway, he's proposed to me, and I've accepted, but we won't be getting married until next year. 'Tis a bit too soon right now, and we decided to wait. We thought that was the decent thing to do, although Moira doesn't agree, under the circumstances."

Jake stared at her. A puzzled look crossed his face. "What does that mean?"

Fiona gave a little shrug of her shoulders, and a faint smile flitted across her pretty mouth before instantly disappearing. "Well, Jake, surely you know Tony and I were married in name only for the last few years. . . ." Leaning across the table, she said *sotto voce*, "I couldn't compete with all of his other women. I didn't want to, if the truth be known."

I sat back in my chair, and my hand crept toward Jake's knee. I felt uncomfortable, awkward again. Jake took my hand in his and squeezed it. I knew he was trying to reassure me, but the moment Fiona had mentioned *other women* I had gone cold inside. Did she count me among them? Surely not, I told myself, eyeing her surreptitiously. Her expression was warm and loving; I decided there was nothing devious about this very charming and pretty woman with her halo of burnished red hair and beautiful eyes. Jake's assessment of her was accurate, I felt.

Jake had given his entire attention to Fiona, and now he was saying to her, "To tell you the truth, I didn't pay too much attention to Tony's private life, I'd enough problems of my own to contend with. And I'd no idea, none at all, Fiona, that your marriage was in name only. He never told me."

"Oh, no, he wouldn't, that was Tony," Fiona responded quietly. "He loved to play games with everybody. He always maintained they were harmless, but they weren't. They were most dangerous games indeed."

Thankfully, at this moment the waiter arrived at our table and handed around the menus. It was with a degree of relief that I opened mine and hid behind it, not wishing to be drawn into this particular conversation. I was worried about where it was drifting, what Fiona would announce next.

IV

Fortunately the conversation about Tony's women ended as everyone studied their menus. Jake pushed his leg against mine under the table, and when I looked up at him, he smiled and sent me a reassuring message with his eyes.

There was a bit of discussion about some of the dishes, and since I knew the restaurant better than anyone else at the table, I made a few recommendations. I myself settled for oysters and grilled sole, as did Fiona; Jake and David both ordered smoked salmon to be followed by the beef stew country style.

334 Barbara Taylor Bradford

With the orders given, Jake studied the wine list, ordered a bottle of Pouilly-Fumé and his favorite Saint-Émilion, and then, turning to Fiona, he said, "I'm sorry it's such a short trip for you."

" 'Tis very short, I'm afraid. David's got to get back to England. We'll be leaving on Tuesday, so it'll have been less than a week. We're staying with Pamela until Monday night, flying out the next morning. Directly to Manchester."

"*Manchester,*" Jake repeated. "Whatever for?"

Fiona burst out laughing, since he had said the name of this northern city in the most disparaging way. "Manchester's not so bad. It rains a lot in Lancashire, mind you. And we're flying to the north because I've bought a house in Yorkshire and I'm in the process of furnishing it."

"Are you moving from London?" Jake asked. He sounded surprised, and looked it. "You're not selling the beautiful house in Hampstead, are you?"

"Oh, no, not at all. I'd never sell that. It's too special, and part of me. But I will be living in Yorkshire in the summer, when the weather's always better. I bought a business there as well, you see."

"My goodness, Fiona, you're full of surprises," I exclaimed, staring at her intently across the table. "What kind of business?" Fiona fascinated me; Tony had never done her justice when he had spoken about her. More fool he.

"A restaurant and bar," she said. "David's in the wine and food business, always has been, and when he retires, he'll be running it with me. In the meantime, his son Noel will be working alongside me . . . Noel's a superb chef."

"Where's the house? *And* the restaurant?" Jake asked.

"The house is in Middleham, so's the restaurant, actually. It's a lovely place, Jake, 'tis indeed. You and Val have to come and stay with me and sample the food at Pig on the Roof . . . that's its name. Noel's a Cordon Bleu chef, you know—"

"And a *great* chef," David interjected, "even though I do say so myself. He's made good old-fashioned English fare his specialty. You know, steak and kidney pudding, roast leg of lamb, lamb stew, roast beef and Yorkshire pudding, game pies, meat pies, fish pies, bangers and mash—all the dishes that are so very tasty when properly made. I think Fiona's going to have a great success."

"So do I! I love that kind of food," I confessed. "It's really my favorite, and it's a good thing I don't live in England, I'd be as fat as a pig! And where's Middleham exactly?"

"North Yorkshire, just outside Ripon," David told me. "That's a lovely cathedral town in the Dales. Middleham has a very famous ruined castle, which used to be called the Windsor of the North, and it was exactly that. It was the stronghold of the great magnate Richard Neville, the Earl of Warwick, who brought up Richard III, and who put the Plantagenets back on the throne of England."

"It sounds like a beautiful place," I remarked.

"Oh, it is." He laughed and added, "Well, it *is* if you like uninhabited rolling moors strewn with heather and gorse, endless empty skies, flocks of sheep, and quaint old stone cottages. I'm afraid there's really not much there—"

"Except lots of horses," Fiona interjected. "There are a number of very famous stables around Middleham, and some of England's greatest racehorses have been, and are, trained there. You see, Yorkshire is truly horse country, Val, and in case you hadn't guessed, David's a Yorkshireman through and through."

"And you come from Middleham," I asserted, smiling across at him.

"No, actually, I don't," David answered. "I know it very well indeed, but I hail from Harrogate, which isn't very far away, of course. I'm taking early retirement next year, and moving to Middleham. I'll be working with Fiona in the restaurant."

"He's my business partner in it," Fiona suddenly thought to point out. "As well as my life partner."

V

Our first course arrived and everyone fell silent as the plates were put in front of us and the white wine poured.

I demolished my six oysters so rapidly, I felt slightly embarrassed, then realized that Fiona, too, had finished quickly.

The conversation turned to all manner of subjects during the main course. Fiona asked lots of questions about the book, and Jake and I told her what we were doing. Then she and I talked about the best shops in Manhattan, while the two men fell into a discussion about sports.

Suddenly it was time to look at the dessert menus, which we did. Fiona and I both ordered chamomile tea only; Jake went for a floating island again, as he always did here at Le Périgord, and so did David.

It was when we were sitting waiting for the desserts that Fiona dropped her first bombshell.

Quite out of the blue, and very unexpectedly, she brought up Tony again, when she said to Jake, "Tony was a charmer, a bit of a rogue, as we all know, but a very lovable one. Wouldn't you agree?"

She was looking at Jake and me. I nodded, afraid to say a word, and Jake said, "You're right, Fiona, I always said Tony had kissed the Blarney

Stone . . . I don't think I ever met anyone more charming than he was. And he was my best buddy, I loved him."

"And he loved you too," she said. "But he was also very jealous of you, Jake. He always wanted what you had or what he thought you wanted. He couldn't stand for you to get there first."

My eyes were on Jake, and I saw how startled he was. He sat there, staring back at Fiona, saying nothing.

Seemingly without a second thought, she hurried on. "Take the Robert Capa award . . . you won it, he didn't, and he never got over that. He always felt that you and Clee Donovan had one up on him."

Finding his voice at last, Jake murmured softly, "But Tony did win other awards, lots of them, and he was a world-famous war photographer, Fiona."

"Oh, I know, but he had set himself up in competition with you, so naturally he was jealous, because some of your awards were more important than his."

Obviously at a loss, not knowing what to say, Jake simply shook his head, leaned back in his chair, and sipped the last of his red wine. Although I knew him well, knew his moods and feelings, I couldn't define the expression in those bright blue eyes. It was unreadable.

Fiona said, "I'm not telling you this to run

Tony down, to denigrate him in your eyes, but I do want you to know the truth." She was speaking very softly, and then she glanced at me and said in that same quiet voice, "It was the same with you, Val. He was awfully jealous of you . . . professionally."

"Oh," I said in a low voice. I was relieved she had added the word *professionally*. I went on. "I can't imagine why. He was a much better photographer than I was." My heart was pounding against my rib cage; I wondered what was coming next.

"In some areas, yes," she replied. "Action. Wars. But your pictures of children are very moving, and your still lifes are superb. Didn't you recognize some of them in Tony's study that day . . . the day of the memorial?"

"Yes, I knew they were mine" was all I could muster, and I settled back in the chair, just as Jake had, and sipped the water.

It was at this moment that David pushed back his chair and excused himself, went off to the men's room.

Once we three were alone, Fiona dropped her second bombshell.

Looking from me to Jake, she said, "When your divorce was coming through from Sue Ellen, and you were about to be a free man, Tony moved in on Val."

I tried to stifle a gasp without much success.

Jake, totally unperturbed, nodded, and said, "I've figured that out for myself."

Turning her attention to me, Fiona went on, very quietly, in a subdued tone. "I knew all about you and Tony, Val, and I just want to say this . . . I'm not upset or angry, I never was. I just felt sorry for you, because I knew he was playing his usual games with you. As he had with so many other women before. He just couldn't help himself, 'tis the truth, Val."

Chapter 23

I

"Why did you invite them back for a nightcap?" I asked, giving Jake a hard stare.

Returning it with one equally as penetrating, and frowning slightly, he said, "Does it bother you, Val?"

I shook my head. "No, I guess not. Fiona's been perfectly sweet to me ever since she dropped her second bombshell an hour ago. And I believe her . . . I know she's not angry or upset with me, quite the opposite. I just wondered why you wanted to prolong the evening. It's already ten-thirty."

"Because Fiona obviously wants to unburden herself some more. Also, I'd like to ask her a few pertinent questions," he answered as he opened the refrigerator and took out a large bottle of carbonated water.

"There's quite a few *I'd* like to ask her myself, come to think of it," I remarked, and emptied the contents of two ice trays into the small silver bucket standing on the countertop.

"Then, why don't you, Val? She'll certainly tell you the truth, honey. I told you before, Fiona's always been as straight as a die."

"I'll think about it," I replied noncommittally as the two of us left the kitchen together and went down the corridor to the sitting room.

Fiona and David were standing at the big window, looking out across the East River, and they swung around as we came into the room.

"We were just admiring the view," she said. "And we can't get over the beautiful metal bridges, and the way they're strung with emerald-green lights. How lovely they look at night."

"When you're actually on the bridges, the lights are white, just like any other electric light bulb. It's the atmosphere that makes them appear green from a distance," I explained. "The emerald green is just an illusion."

"Like so many other things in life, eh, Val?" Fiona remarked pithily, throwing me a pointed look. "We're surrounded by illusions, aren't we?"

"Nothing's truer," I agreed, and I carried the

ice bucket over to the console table, where glasses, bottles of liquor, and liqueurs were arranged.

Jake was already hovering at this end of the room, and I gave him the ice bucket, then went and sat down on the floral sofa.

Looking across at Fiona, Jake asked, "Now, what would you like?"

"I think I'll have a Bonnie Prince Charlie, please, Jake."

He frowned at her, looking baffled. "I don't think we have *that*. . . ."

"Oh, silly me," she said, laughing lightly, shaking her auburn curls as if chastising herself. "That's just a nickname. What I'm referring to is Drambuie. It's a marvelous liqueur from Scotland, and you should try it sometime. It has a lovely spicy flavor."

Jake searched among the bottles, looked up a second later, smiling triumphantly and holding the Drambuie in his hand. "You're in luck! There's a bottle here after all, Fiona."

"Oh, good, and I'd like a wee drop over a couple of ice cubes, please, Jake. In a straight tumbler, not a liqueur glass."

I was curious about the drink, and asked, "Why did you call it a Bonnie Prince Charlie?"

"Bonnie Prince Charlie was the eldest son of Charles I, who was beheaded, and legend has it that when the prince fled to Scotland, he was aided by a member of the MacKinnon clan of Skye," Fiona told me. "As a reward for the man's help, Prince Charlie gave him his own recipe for his personal liqueur, and that recipe has been passed down over the generations. Actually, it's been kept a secret for three hundred years or more, and only the MacKinnons know what goes into Drambuie. But whatever the ingredients are, the drink *is* delicious." She smiled at me, and finished, "Have one, Val, you'll enjoy it."

"All right, I will." I looked at Jake and said, "I'd love a glass of water as well, please. Shall I come and help you?"

"No, no. Thanks anyway, but I can manage. And, David, what can I get you?"

"Thanks, Jake, I'd like to have a cognac."

II

Jake not only insisted on being the bartender, he was the waiter as well, taking Fiona and David their drinks, and bringing mine over to me.

I observed him surreptitiously as he moved with an easy grace around the long room. I noticed that his limp was barely perceptible. His leg had been steadily improving over the past few weeks, until it had suddenly acted up again the other day, worrying me. I was relieved to see that he was walking with such ease tonight.

As I watched him, I couldn't help thinking how good he looked in the dark-blue suit, white shirt, and blue-and-gray-striped tie. I rather liked Jake's sudden sartorial elegance, which had come into being in New York. It suited him.

Once he had poured himself a small cognac, he joined me on the sofa. Lifting his glass, he glanced around and said, "Cheers, everyone."

"Cheers," we all echoed, and sipped our drinks.

I liked the taste of the Bonnie Prince Charlie at once. It was thick and sweet with a tangy taste, almost spicy, as Fiona had mentioned. I took another sip, decided I could easily become addicted to it, and put the glass down on the coffee table. A wise move.

After a moment or two, Jake focused on Fiona, who still stood near the window with David. "Apropos of what you said in the restaurant earlier, about Moira thinking you and David shouldn't wait to get married . . . I'm inclined to vote along with her, Fiona, for what it's worth. I just wanted you to know that."

"You're absolutely right," David agreed. "I think it's ridiculous to wait . . . silly really."

Fiona's eyes swiveled to David, and she gave him the benefit of a loving smile, then looking over at Jake, she said, "Tony's been dead for only a few months, and—"

Jake interrupted her. "But your *marriage* has been dead for years. At least, that's the impression you gave when you were talking to us about it earlier in the restaurant. Actually, Fiona, you made me think your marriage had been a sham since Rory was born, or thereabouts anyway."

Fiona moved away from the window, came and joined us; she took a chair next to the sofa. David followed suit, sitting down in another chair within this central seating arrangement.

There was a brief silence as Fiona settled down, composed herself, and took a sip of the Drambuie. Finally she volunteered, "Things started to go wrong about three years after Rory was born, when Moira was five. By then we'd been married about seven years. I used to think it was the seven year itch, as they called it in those days, but it wasn't . . . it was just *an itch*. And it had always been there. I know that now, and it grew worse as he got older.

"You know, Jake, it's a terrible hard thing to be married to a man who can't keep his hands off other women. I suppose as long as you don't know, it doesn't matter . . . but, oh, dear, when you do know, how painful it is. Dreadful, I am thinking. And hard to live with, trust me on that, both of you. Well, David himself knows what I went through, don't you, darlin'?"

"I do indeed," David said with a quiet vehemence. He looked across at Jake and me. "I've been comforting Fiona for ten years now, and wishing she would leave him and marry me." He paused, then rushed on. "I've been widowed for fifteen years, and ready, willing, and able to marry her, to take her out of her misery. Needing to do so very badly, in fact. Because I love her. But Fiona wanted Rory to be a bit older before she took that final step."

Fiona nodded and exclaimed, "David's been a saint, waiting for me for all these years the way he has. And I don't know how I'd have managed without him."

Jake inclined his head, but he didn't comment and neither did I. There were all kinds of questions on the tip of my tongue, but I was afraid to ask them. I suppose because I didn't want to upset Fiona; also, perhaps I was afraid to hear her answers. Sometimes it was better to remain ignorant. What was that line? "Where ignorance is bliss, 'tis folly to be wise." I wasn't sure who wrote it, but it was very apt.

I leaned back against the floral pillows and tried to keep my mind very still. I didn't want to get upset tonight, especially in front of Fiona and David. And talking about Tony might exacerbate my anger, which still ran deep, ran to my core.

More than ever, I felt as though I had been lied to, used, and abused, as had Fiona. We're a gang of two, she and I, I suddenly thought, and smiled inwardly. It was a cynical smile at that. A gang of two hundred was more like it. Who *were* all those

women he had had? And where were they now?
As if I cared!

The others were talking quietly about Tony,
and their words washed over me for a moment or
two, and they truly didn't register because I was
lost in my own troubled thoughts. But eventually
I sat up straighter and began to listen more attentively.

"Is that really why you didn't divorce Tony in
those days? Because you had two small children
and wanted them to be in their teens before you
separated? Or were there other considerations?"
Jake probed.

"Other considerations as well," Fiona admitted
softly in her lovely lilting Irish brogue. She let out
a small sigh. "And why wouldn't there be, Jake?
Firstly, I'm a Roman Catholic, and with me,
divorce goes against the grain. I've always
believed in the sanctity of marriage, and once
you're married, it's for life, as far as I'm concerned. So there was my belief in marriage and
my religion to contend with. But secondly, I was
still very much in love with Tony, if I'm absolutely honest with you, Jake. And with you too,
Val. But 'tis awfully hard to love a man who
comes home with the smell of other women on
him all the time. So humiliating. And that's only
one of the things that erodes love, yes, it's the
truth, Val."

Swallowing hard, I nodded my understanding,

unable to say a word. I looked at this beautiful woman and I hated Tony Hampton with a vengeance, even though he *was* dead.

What a fool she'd been, and more fool I. At this moment I hated myself as much as I hated Tony. And I suppose that's why I hadn't wanted Fiona and David to come back for a drink. I had sensed she was determined to talk about him, and I didn't want to be cast in the role of his last mistress. But of course I was, and anyway, it *was* the truth. Might as well admit it.

Suddenly Fiona was addressing herself directly to me. "There were always a lot of women, Val, I just want you to know that. I'm not trying to upset you, please believe me, I just want to make you understand that by the time you came along, I was well and truly out of love with Tony. Because of all the other women who had gone before you. I was beyond hurt, beyond humiliation, beyond caring. It just didn't matter anymore."

"I know you're not trying to hurt me, Fiona," I reassured her.

A deep sigh trickled out of her, and for a moment she looked weary; finally, she straightened in the chair and hurried on. "I was biding my time, waiting for Rory to go to university, and planning to leave Tony. I'd been with David for six years by then. And we'd been best friends for four years before that . . . after ten years of knowing this lovely man, I knew I could have a good life with him, a happy life, and not one fraught with jealousy and lies, betrayals and humiliations. We were right for each other."

I nodded.

Jake said, "All the more reason to get married as soon as you can, in my opinion."

David looked very pleased to hear this statement uttered so forcefully once more, and although he refrained from making a comment, he nonetheless beamed at Jake.

Finally summoning all of my courage, I said, "Fiona, I would like to tell you my side of the story, tell you about my relationship with Tony. . . ." My voice trailed off weakly, and I wondered if I'd made a mistake, embarking on this saga. It was after the fact now. And perhaps she didn't want to hear it, and I wouldn't blame her.

Immediately she said, "I have a good idea what it was about, but why don't you tell me anyway, Val. I am thinking it will make you feel better, my dear."

Jake reached out and took hold of my hand, held it lovingly in his, and smiled his encouragement. "Talk to Fiona," he said quietly. "It'll be cathartic for you, honey."

After swallowing some water, I began. "It was like this, Fiona . . . when we met I wasn't interested in Tony because he was a married man. I thought he was a great photographer and a good friend, but that's all, a comrade-in-arms, as he always said about Jake and me and him. What you don't know is that I was really attracted to Jake when we first met, but he was trying to solve his divorce problems with Sue Ellen. Anyway, about a year before he was killed, Tony let it drop to me that he was in the middle of a divorce from you, and he asked me out." Staring at her, I took a deep breath, released it, and said, "But he wasn't, was he? It was a lie."

"Yes, it was a lie, Val," she replied gently. "We were never divorced, I *am* Tony's widow. But I would have given him one. However, he never asked me for a divorce in all the years we were married."

"*I've* got something to tell you, Fiona," Jake said, leaning forward slightly, pinning his eyes on her. "I was always somewhat emotionally involved with Val, from the first day we met. She didn't know this, because I never told her, which was foolish of me now that I look back. When Tony got entangled with Val, I was thrown for a loop, upset, and disapproving of his relationship with her. I told him so, and he immediately said he was on the level, serious about her, and that he was now separated from you." Jake took a sip of my water and continued. "And then later, this past summer, he was obviously in a sticky situation with Val, even though neither she nor I understood this."

"Yes, he was, Jake, I can see that . . . and it was because he'd led her on," Fiona murmured, nodding her head. "He'd told her so many lies."

"Yup, he had hoisted himself on his own petard. Then, when he came to Paris in late July, just before we went to Kosovo, he told me he was divorced from you," Jake finished.

"My God, he didn't do that, did he?" Fiona looked at us askance.

"Oh, yes, he did," I interjected with swiftness. "And he told *me* exactly the same thing. He also said we—he and I—would be married by the end of the year."

There was a total silence, and I wondered if I had said too much.

Fiona was very pale all of a sudden. Her freckles stood out starkly. She looked from me to David to Jake, and then she leaned back in the chair and closed her eyes. It occurred to me that she seemed wiped out, wearier than ever. And shocked. But a moment later she pulled herself together. She sat up and said, "I don't know why I'm so appalled, because he was capable of anything. But I must admit to you both, I am horrified he told you such terrible lies. It was unconscionable. How awful for you, Val, and you too, Jake. But mostly I am hurt for Val, who was the victim here."

In a whispery voice I asked her, "And how did you find out about me?"

For a split second she was startled, and then she answered, "But I didn't find out, Val. He told me . . . he told me he was having an affair with you, and that's why he was away so much between assignments . . . he said he was with you in Paris because you needed him to be there."

"But he wasn't!" I cried. "He was hardly ever in Paris with me. He always came home to London. *To you.*"

"No, no, he didn't, Val! Oh, of course he spent some time with us, he loved the kids and his garden and the house in Hampstead, but he was away an awful lot between his jobs."

Jake said, "Well, he certainly wasn't in Paris, that I *can* attest to."

Fiona murmured, "It was odd really, our life together. We sort of muddled along when he came home, certainly there was nothing between us any longer. He knew that David and I were close, and he didn't seem to mind, but I think he thought it would never come to anything. He thought I'd always be there."

David said, "Very simply, Val, Tony didn't want a divorce. He wanted to stay married to Fiona and have all of his other women as well. That lifestyle suited him."

Jake said, "But he made such a point to me about having to be in London, Fiona. I can't believe he lied even about that."

"If he wasn't with you, Fiona, and if he wasn't

in Paris with Val, then where was he?" David asked, sounding mystified.

"*I* certainly don't know," I said. "I've no idea where he went."

"I think I know . . ." Fiona began, and instantly broke off. A look of comprehension had crossed her face, and she now said in a sudden rush of words, "It's just come to me . . . how involved he was with Anne Curtis—"

"Oh my God!" I practically shouted, cutting across Fiona's words, and I brought a hand to my mouth. "*She* was in Beirut when I was there with Tony. You were in the States, Jake, and I wasn't involved with Tony then, but I remember at the time I thought she had designs on him. Yes, yes, and now I remember . . . it was when Bill Fitzgerald was captured by the Islamic Jihad."

Fiona looked so stricken, I thought she was about to burst into tears.

I said, "Oh, Fiona, do you think he was having an affair with me, and with her too . . . at the same time? You do, don't you? That's it, isn't it?"

For a moment all she could do was nod. But after a few minutes she spoke. "I'm so sorry, Val, but I'm afraid I am thinking that. And if it wasn't Anne, then it was certainly *someone* else . . . *somewhere* else . . . because he was hardly ever at home between jobs."

"What made him think he could get away with any of it?" Jake asked heatedly.

Shrugging, Fiona replied, "I've no idea. . . ."

"I suppose you have to be a little mad, a bit off the wall to think you can deceive the entire world—" I stopped, wishing I hadn't volunteered this comment. I no longer wanted to talk about Tony Hampton. I was sickened by this whole mess.

Jake said, "Tell me something, Fiona, do you think Tony *would* have committed bigamy and married Val?"

"I don't know, Jake. Perhaps he would. Other men have done it, 'tis a well-known fact that they have. And they got away with it too. At least, for a long time—until they were eventually caught."

"Or he could have found an excuse to break it off," I remarked. "Other men have also done *that*."

Jake raised a brow. "The mind of a man," he began, and stopped abruptly, looked away; he was uncomfortable.

David ventured, "All kinds of excuses would've worked. Such as: My wife is seriously ill, I can't leave her now . . . that's just one of them that comes to mind."

"And if the mistress throws a tantrum, or protests unduly, she looks like a bitch," I muttered.

David glanced at Fiona and murmured, "You may not agree, love, but I think Tony would have broken the law and married Val."

"And why not Anne Curtis, if she was the other one?" I asked.

Ignoring my comment, Fiona answered David when she said, "Maybe he would have committed bigamy with Val. He was impulsive and unpredictable. On the other hand, the 'my wife is desperately ill' excuse would've appealed to Tony. He might have used it, I am thinking. . . ."

"Listen, all of you! He duped me!" I cried, my voice an octave higher. "Because I'm a grown-up, a mature woman, I *can* accept that. But what I want to know is *why* did he do it?"

"Do you mean why did he do it to you? Or why was he the way he was?" Fiona asked me. "Do you mean why did he have so many women and tell so many lies?"

"*Absolutely.* I mean all of that, yes. You've hit it on the head exactly," I answered tensely. I felt uptight, filled with fury all of a sudden. I tried to relax, to ease the anger away.

She took a deep breath, allowed all the air to trickle out of her, and then slumped against the chair back. After a small silence, she said slowly but with total assurance, "He picked you, Val, because he knew Jake wanted you. I told you that in the restaurant. But it was also because you were fair game, gorgeous, and a challenge to him. But Tony was a born womanizer . . . through and through. And through again. I always suspected he was unfaithful to me on our honeymoon, you know, but I had no way of ever proving it. He was also very selfish, with an infantile need for instant gratification. If he wanted something, he wanted it *now*. Just like a child."

Fiona's eyes swiveled from me to David to Jake, and she shook her head sadly, just sat there, staring at us wordlessly. I felt so sorry for her because of the life he had inflicted on her.

No one said a word.

What was there to say?

But eventually Fiona spoke, explaining in a low, almost inaudible voice, "Yes, he was extremely selfish but he was also a very sick man. In his head. But not a bad man, no, not that . . . he was mentally disturbed in certain ways. I also think he was addicted to sex. I believe he needed different women all the time in order to . . ."

"Get it up," I said, unable to curb myself. "To get an erection."

"That's right," she responded, her eyes meeting mine and knowingly so.

"He was rotten to the core, in my considered opinion," David announced. "And you know it, Fiona. We all know it."

I was really surprised at David's courage. This quiet, laid-back man was impressing me more and more. He certainly knew who he was, what he believed, and he wasn't afraid to say what he thought, even at the risk of upsetting Fiona a little. He had earned my respect in just a few hours, and he was certainly much more worthy of Fiona than Tony had ever been.

"There's something else," David went on, addressing Fiona. "I know you won't misunderstand . . . and it's this. Basically, Tony didn't give a damn about your feelings, or the children's feelings either. Or Jake's or Val's. Or mine, for that matter, not that *I* really count in this domestic drama."

"But you do, David! You do!" Fiona protested, her voice rising sharply. "And he knew that. Tony knew I cared for you, and that you cared for me and his children."

"*Your* children," David announced very quietly. "He never had much to do with their upbringing. He was always away."

"But I got the impression from Moira and Rory that he spent a lot of time with them this past summer," Jake said in a puzzled tone, looking at Fiona and David, his eyes narrowing.

"He was at home for a couple of weeks . . ." Fiona replied. "Well, you know, Jake, they do tend to exaggerate a bit and fantasize. They wished he'd been there for months on end, but that was not actually the way it was. Even though they told you that perhaps."

David downed his cognac and got up. "Mind if I help myself, Jake?"

"No, go ahead, David."

David walked across the floor and then

turned around when he was almost at the console table. "Tony did what he wanted, took what he wanted, and to hell with the consequences. That was his attitude. Nobody else mattered. Oh, yes, he was a charmer, and lovely to us all. And talented. And he could spin the best yarns, take the best photographs, prepare the greatest meals, make us all laugh. And cry. We all loved him at one time or another. But he was a bastard nonetheless."

Fiona sighed. "He's the father of my children . . . and I did love him once, but 'tis true, what David's just said."

III

Jake's bright blue eyes settled on Fiona as he asked in a warm voice, "Why did you bring this up tonight, Fiona? Had you been planning it?"

Emphatically she shook her head from side to side. "Oh no, no, Jake, I hadn't been planning it at all. But when I saw you and Val together at the dinner table, saw the way you were . . . so very much together, so in love, I thought you should know the truth, know about the real Tony. I knew him better than anybody, and I suppose you could say I knew what made him tick, what went on in his mind. He was so complex. . . ." She sighed and shook her head again. "Well, there's nothing worse than having a tantalizing ghost hanging around, and I wanted you to know about him."

"There's a lot to be said for that, getting rid of ghosts," I exclaimed. "And I for one am glad we've had this chance to talk. I knew you were Tony's widow, not his ex-wife, the day of the memorial service. When I stood next to you in the Brompton Oratory, I just knew, Fiona."

"I don't want you to suffer needlessly, grieve needlessly, ruin your life yearning for such a man. I felt you should understand about him, know the truth about him. I have always put great value on truth."

IV

I had believed for the past few weeks that I had exorcised the ghost of Tony Hampton. And that Jake had too. But only after this very honest discussion with Fiona did I really feel truly liberated.

It struck me that Jake felt the same way. We didn't mention it or discuss it after they finally left just after midnight. We simply turned out the lights and went into the bedroom. But there was a carefreeness in him, a lightness that had not been present before. It was as if a weight had been lifted, and I certainly felt as though my shoulders were lighter, a terrible burden finally sloughed away.

Yes, Tony Hampton was gone from my life, and from Jake's as well. All I wanted now, tonight, was to lie next to Jake, make love to him, have him make love to me. I wanted to be with the man who truly loved me, and whom I loved with all my heart.

V

The past became dust. The present was passion.

Jake pulled down the strap of my nightgown and began to kiss my breast very tenderly. After a moment he looked into my eyes, and I saw that his were spilling his love for me.

He gently stroked my cheek with his fingertips and kissed my eyelids, and then he tugged lightly at my nightgown again and murmured, "Take this off, Val. Take it off."

I did as he asked, and eagerly so.

He slipped off the bed and shed his pajama bottoms, and as he stood there naked, looking down at me in my nakedness, I shivered slightly.

The room was dim except for the moonlight filtering in through the windows. And he looked so masculine in that pale light, my breath caught in my throat. Tall, lithe, broad of chest, his face finely etched, and those eyes such a vivid, star-

tling blue. He was all man; and his manhood pro-
claimed his desire and longing for me.

He lay down on the bed again and pulled me
into his arms, murmuring my name. He began to
kiss my breast, sucking on the nipple until it
hardened, became erect. And he entwined his
legs around mine and held me close, and I could
feel his hardness against me. And I wanted him.

The heat of passion and an urgent desire raced
through me, burned me up, and I cleaved to him,
holding on to him tightly. "Oh Jake, oh Jake, I
want you so much," I whispered against his
shoulder. "Now."

He pushed himself up on one elbow, looked
down at me, and said softly, "Oh look, look. Just
look at you . . . you're so beautiful, Val."

All his attention became centered on that
mound of blondish-brown hair at the top of my
thighs, and he bent over me, lavishing me with
kisses and tender touching until I opened up to
him fully. And as always he brought me to the
edge of climax, then stopped, took me to him
with infinite tenderness and care, fitting the
length of himself into me with expertise.

Swiftly and with precision we rose and fell
together, lost ourselves in each other, gave ourselves to each other. And as deep shuddering
began to overcome me, and I found myself spiral-
ing into ecstasy, he let himself go. He rushed
headlong into me, calling my name over and over

again as we came together, were fused together as one.

After our passion was spent, and we lay wrapped in each other's arms, I looked deeply into those clear blue eyes, and I saw that he was at peace with himself and with me. Just as I was.

Jake had said we were destined to be together. And he was right. It had always been so, from the beginning. We had simply missed our way for a short while. But I *was* his . . . his woman, his passion, his love.

And he was the only man for me, the only man I wanted. And that was the absolute truth.

Chapter 24

I

A week after our remarkable dinner with Fiona and David, my newfound inner peace and contentment suddenly shattered, blown to smithereens by several unexpected and unwelcome phone calls.

The bad news came filtering into the Beekman Place apartment on a cold but sunny Wednesday morning, thereafter etched in my mind as Bad Day at Black Rock, to remind me that the good things didn't last very long for little old Val.

The first call came from Mike Carter in Paris. My boss began by telling me that I had missed the boat with the famous artist, who'd retreated to his compound in Mexico to wield his magic brush in

a more congenial environment than a SoHo loft.
And then he had added in a dour voice that there
was serious trouble developing with Olivier, the
abusive husband. He had somehow discovered
that Françoise was staying with Mike, and was
apparently on the warpath, violent, threatening,
and out to make mayhem.

Before I got into what I knew would be a difficult discussion about Françoise, I apologized for
missing the great Alexander St. Just Stevens, who
had never even had the courtesy to return my
innumerable phone calls to him. Which was the
reason I had never had a peek at his paintings
before he had flown the coop for more exotic
climes.

I then addressed the problem of Olivier, cop on
the rampage.

"You've got to send Françoise here," I pushed,
only to be told by Mike that she did not want to
come stateside, as he called it.

"New York is too far away, Val, and she says
she won't like it. Especially since you're not going
to be there. And you're not, are you? You *are*
coming back to work next week, aren't you?"

After reassuring him that I was indeed returning to Paris and work, I decided to offer him a bit
of good advice. "If you haven't done it already,
get her a lawyer. And make sure he's not only
tough but has vast power within the French legal
system, you know, the right *connections*. That's

the only kind of legal eagle who'll be able to handle Olivier. That flic obviously has pull somewhere. And tell me, how the hell did he find out she's staying with you and the girls?"

"No idea. As for the lawyer, I *have* hired somebody, a powerhouse, a real shit, I'm told, and just the kind of guy she needs. Françoise is seeing him tomorrow. But I wish I knew where I could send her for a while . . . out of the country would be preferable. London would be great, but I don't know anybody—"

"Pig on the Roof!" I practically shouted down the phone, clutching the receiver tighter as an amazing brainstorm hit me.

"What the hell does that mean, Val?" Mike said.

I had to laugh, even though I knew this wasn't a laughing matter, and also that my laughter would annoy him. Taking a deep breath, adopting a more sober tone, I explained. "It's a restaurant, Pig on the Roof is . . . and it is being opened imminently by Fiona Hampton, Tony's widow. She also bought a house close by, and both are in Middleham. That's in Yorkshire. She told me she was looking for an assistant to help her pull both places together, especially the decoration of the restaurant. It just occurred to me that Françoise might be ideal, since she works for a decorator in Marseilles, or at least used to work for one."

"I don't know," Mike mumbled uncertainly.

"She would be safe there, I'm sure, Mike, and listen, Yorkshire's not that far from Paris. Fiona invited Jake and me to go and stay with her for Christmas if we want, and she said we could fly from Paris to Leeds-Bradford Airport, which is in a place called Yeadon. Or fly into Manchester Airport and drive to Yorkshire from there. Françoise would be in easy reach if you wanted to see her, Mike."

"It's a possibility, yes," Mike responded, suddenly sounding a bit brighter. "And could she live with Fiona Hampton?"

"I don't know, but under the circumstances, I would think so, yes. Fiona's one of the most understanding women I've ever met. Do you want me to call her? She went back to London yesterday."

"I'd better talk to Françoise about it first."

"It sounds to me as if you're heavily involved there," I ventured to say, and then stopped abruptly, deeming it wiser not to pry. Besides, as Jake kept telling me, the less we knew about that particular mess, the better off we were.

Mike was saying, "Well, yes, I am very involved. I'm in love with her and she with me . . . I want to marry her." There was a pause before he added, "She's the only woman I've loved since Sarah's death."

I wasn't a bit surprised to hear this declaration,

but the mere idea of this union made me excessively nervous, not the least because Olivier was definitely not someone to tango with by choice.

Taking a deep breath, I forced a cheerfulness I suddenly did not feel when I said, "I'm going to be bridesmaid, I hope. Or should I say maid of honor?"

Mike chuckled, promised to call Françoise immediately, and get back to me pronto.

After cautioning him to be careful about Olivier, I hung up.

II

I had no sooner put the phone down, when it rang again.

"Hullo?" I said, and was startled when my brother returned my salutation.

"I've got to come and see you, Val," Donald said in a rush of words and with no preamble whatsoever. "As soon as possible."

"But it's only seven-thirty in the morning! I haven't even had coffee yet," I protested, and wondered what had happened to Jake, who had gone out to the supermarket to buy milk.

"I don't mean this minute," Donald explained. "But later this morning. Please, Val, we've got to talk."

"What about?"

"The will."

"Oh, come on, Donald! We talked about that the other Sunday. You know how I feel. You can have everything, Lowell's included. I don't want her stuff or her business, and I explained that to you. And to her."

"But she says you *have* to inherit the business, she won't listen to me. I thought perhaps you could give it one more shot. Maybe work something out with her."

"Oh, Donald," I groaned, and sighed heavily. "She won't listen to *me*. You're her favorite. You used to be able to twist her around your little finger, so why don't you try doing that again?"

"She's stuck on this family thing, The Tradition, as she calls it, with two capital T's."

"Do you think that's a binding legal document? Or is it simply a tradition within the family, something started by Amy-Anne Lowell a hundred years ago?"

"I just don't know," Donald answered, his voice glum.

"It didn't occur to me to ask her the other day, but I wonder if it's written into the articles of incorporation? Try to find that out if you can."

"I will, but why do you want to know?"

The dumbness of this question took my breath away, but then, you didn't have to be a genius to be duplicitous, which was Donald's main claim to fame in the family. "Because if it's written into the articles of incorporation of Lowell's, then it has to be treated as a legal matter," I replied patiently. "But if it's just a wish, a suggestion, a desire put forward by Amy-Anne, then I guess it would be simple to break. Because it's not *legal*."

"She'd never let us break The Tradition."

"What's the matter with you this morning, Donald? Get with it! If there's no legal document, then I can simply decline to accept Lowell's. Or better still, I suppose I should accept it, then give it to you by drawing up the appropriate papers."

"You keep saying you'll do that. But *will* you give it to me?"

"Don't you trust me?"

"Sure I do," he muttered, sounding doubtful, I thought.

"Call up your mother, find out what you can, and meet me here at one o'clock," I ordered tersely, resorting to my bullying of old. "I'll take you to lunch at a local joint, and we can settle this damn thing once and for all. Okay?"

"Okay, sis."

"Donald!" I shouted. "Don't call me—"

He hung up on me.

Ungrateful little pig, I thought, and wondered why I bothered with him. Anyway, I didn't want Lowell's, that was the absolute truth, and he should have it as our mother's son. There was no one else, except for those distant Lowell cousins who received annual checks for doing nothing.

Desperate now for a blast of caffeine, I padded into the kitchen and filled a mug with coffee, adding sweetener. I didn't particularly like it black, but Jake hadn't returned from his errand to buy milk.

I stood standing at the kitchen window, looking out, thinking that it appeared to be one of those clear, crisp fall days. The sky was a blameless blue and the sun was already edging out from behind foamy white clouds. I always enjoyed the change of seasons, which is why I had never wanted to live permanently in a hot climate.

The sudden shrilling of the wall phone made me jump, and I grabbed the receiver and said hello, wondering who it was this time.

"Is that you, Valentine?"

I didn't recognize the woman's voice, and said, "Yes, it is, who's this?"

"Good morning, Val, it's Lauren, Jacques Foucher's wife."

"Hello, Lauren! How're you?"

"I'm fine, but I'm afraid Jacques has had a terrible accident. I was looking for Jake to tell him about it. Is he there?"

"No, he's out on an errand. He'll be back any minute, but please, tell me what happened."

"Jacques is badly injured, but he *will* recover. Eventually. He's in hospital, obviously, and he's lucky to be alive. He was on his way home last night, when he had a heart attack. In the car. He was driving, Val, and he hit a parked van, empty, thank God! And then he careened across the street and slammed into a brick wall head-on."

"Oh my God!" I said. "You're right, he is lucky to be alive. How bad are his injuries?"

"He broke his nose and his collarbone, and an arm and a leg, and of course he has a lot of contusions, bruises, some minor internal injuries. But that's about the extent of it."

"It could have been worse, let's face it."

"Yes, he could be *dead,*" Lauren said. "Anyway, will you tell Jake I'm at the office now, and I'll come in every day until you get back to Paris. When do you think that'll be?"

"Next week, of that I'm absolutely sure. But Jake might want to leave earlier now."

"It's not necessary," she replied. "Everything's under control, and fortunately Jacques is in the best medical hands. Please tell Jake I can cope with the agency, not too much is going on at the moment anyway."

"I know you can cope," I said, remembering just how efficient Lauren Crane was. English born, she was a successful agent running the Paris office of a well-known American talent agency. Like me, she had lived in Paris for a number of years and was a dyed-in-the-wool Francophile. She was Jacques Foucher's second wife, and he adored her and their four-year-old daughter, Jasmine.

"But how are you going to run your own office?" I now asked Lauren.

"I'm going to spend the mornings here at Photoreal," she explained, "and the afternoons at my own office. Since I'm dealing with New York and Los Angeles, the time differences work in my favor."

"I see," I responded. "And I'll have Jake call you the minute he gets back. It won't be long. And give Jacques my love, and tell him I hope he's feeling better soon."

"I will, Val, and thanks."

III

After we had both hung up, I stood drinking my coffee, continuing to gaze out across the East River, though a little absently now, I must admit. I was thinking of Jacques and trying to remember his age. I knew he was older than Jake, by about fourteen years I thought, which would make him around fifty-two. Still, that was relatively young to have a heart attack, wasn't it? Luck was running with him, I thought, just as it was with me and Jake in Kosovo. Our time wasn't up then, and neither was his last night. It's all to do with destiny.

When the phone began to ring again, I cursed under my breath and reached for the receiver once more. "Yes," I said somewhat sharply, which wasn't like me at all. But this unexpected early morning activity was suddenly getting to me.

"Val, 'allo, it is me, Françoise."

"Françoise, hello, how are you?" I asked, my voice instantly softening. "You must be glad to be out of the clinic and back with Mike."

"*Oui.* Yes, I am very happy with him. He is wonderful. But, Val, it is Olivier, he will grab me any minute and take me back to Marseilles, I feel this."

"Listen to me, Françoise," I instructed, "and listen carefully. You must get out of Paris after you have seen that lawyer tomorrow. And I think I can arrange for you to stay with a friend in England. How do you feel about that?"

"I will go. Mike explained it to me. About the Pig on the Roof lady. I am so frightened of Olivier. And so are my parents now. He is going to see them at Les Roches Fleuries. All the time."

"I'll bet he is! And I also bet he's got the phone tapped and the mail monitored. Stay away from them, Françoise, if you want to be safe."

"*Oui, oui.* I know this must be the way. They are worried about *me*."

"Things will turn out all right," I reassured her. "I'm going to phone my friend in London, and I'll get back to you. Or, rather, I'll call Mike.

That would be better. Just be careful, Françoise, and don't take any chances."

"I understand. *Merci,* Val. *Au revoir.*"

"Bye, Françoise, keep your chin up." As I put the phone back in the cradle, I wondered if she knew what that phrase meant. Too late to explain.

I walked out of the kitchen, now more baffled than ever by Jake's prolonged absence; I was heading down the corridor to the living room, when I heard the key in the lock. Then the door slammed.

As I hurried into the entrance foyer, I saw Jake struggling with three large bags from the supermarket. He was dressed in a heavy white fisherman's sweater, blue jeans, and a baseball cap worn backward. He looked a little flushed, or perhaps it was windburn.

"Hi, Kid," he said, grinning at me over the top of the bags. "It's bitchy out there, cold all of a sudden. Sorry I took so long, but I bought stuff for dinner tonight, to save time. I thought we could—"

"There's bad news, Jake," I interrupted, going forward to help him with the overflowing supermarket bags.

"What bad news? What's wrong?"

IV

Jake went immediately into the study to call Lauren in Paris.

I retreated to the kitchen to make fresh coffee and toast the bagels Jake had bought.

While the coffee perked and the bagels browned, I set up a tray with milk, sweetener, butter, and apricot jam. I added mugs, plates, spoons, knives, and napkins, and then stood watching the bagels, not wanting them to burn.

Earlier, I had planned a cozy little domestic scene. A blissful breakfast with Jake, since our sojourn in New York was soon coming to an end. I craved intimacy with him. All kinds of intimacy, and most especially the domestic kind. I asked myself why I needed this; then it had occurred to me the other day that domesticity with Jake made me feel safe, secure, and nurtured. Things I'd never really known. But today, unfortunately, life had intruded.

Once the coffee was ready, I put the pot on the tray, then peered into the toaster oven to evaluate the bagels. They looked perfect, and I lifted them out with a clean kitchen towel and dropped them on one of the plates.

As I carried the tray into the study and put it

down on the big coffee table, Jake hung up the phone after saying good-bye to Lauren.

"What a lousy thing to happen to Jacques," he said, walking over, sitting down on the sofa, and pouring coffee for us both. "The funny thing is, there's no history of heart trouble. Lauren says he had a checkup only two weeks ago and he was fine."

"Thank God he's alive," I said, flopping down next to Jake. "He could have so easily been killed. He had a narrow escape."

Jake nodded, buttered a bagel, and spread it with apricot jam. He bit into it and nodded his approval.

While he munched on it, I relayed the news about Françoise and the rampaging husband out to get her and Mike and his two daughters. And whoever else got in his way. Like little old Val, perhaps.

"Shit!" he exploded, almost choking on the bagel. "I knew that situation spelled trouble right from the beginning!"

"And then some," I muttered, and rapidly told him about my idea of asking Fiona to take Françoise under her wing for a few weeks.

"But you're doing it again, Val!" he exclaimed, impaling me with his blue eyes.

"Doing what?" I asked, feigning sudden innocence.

"Meddling, for God's sake!" he almost shouted.

"Having meddled once, and created a problem called Love with a capital L, certainly not anticipated by me, I feel I have to help them overcome the newer problem. The problem which that love has brought upon them. In short, the fury of Olivier."

"Mike's a big boy," Jake snapped. "He can take care of Françoise, and I don't want you getting mixed up in this any more than you already are. A guy like Olivier can easily go berserk, and if you get in his way, he'll think nothing about exterminating *you*."

"What you say is true, but calm down, Jake— please. All I want to do is put a call in to Fiona, explain the situation, and ask her if Françoise can go and stay with her for a while. Surely there's no harm in that?"

Jake let out a long, exasperated sigh, took off his baseball cap, flung it to the other side of the room, grabbed me, and pulled me into his arms. "You're . . . you're just . . . *incorrigible,* Valentine Denning, the most impossible, stubborn, interfering, meddling, beautiful, sexy—"

I stopped this flow of words by planting my lips on his. I gave him a long, soulful, passionate kiss, then slid my tongue in his mouth and let it linger there. Which was a big mistake on my part, because it only inflamed him, gave him all the wrong ideas.

Except that they were not so wrong, I decided as he slowly but deliberately began to make love to me on the overstuffed sofa.

What a lovely intimate breakfast it turned out to be after all, I thought, smiling to myself.

Chapter 25

I

When Donald turned up on my doorstep at exactly one o'clock, carrying a large bunch of expensive-looking flowers wrapped in cellophane and tied with pink ribbon, I was immediately suspicious. I had to curb the impulse to snarl at him.

Did he think I was a fool? Didn't he realize I saw through this ruse, this sudden loving gesture, the first one in years? *Flowers, indeed.*

He underestimated me if he thought I hadn't twigged that he was cozying up to me, being sweet and ever so friendly because I had suddenly become vital to his future.

But somehow I managed to swallow the acerbic words that had leapt to my tongue. I might as well be pleasant; I had nothing to lose. I laughed inside. Sex with Jake for breakfast was infinitely more satisfying than coffee with bagels for breakfast; our unexpected and wonderfully ful-filling lovemaking on the overstuffed study sofa had put me in a generous mood. And so I allowed Donald to get off unscathed.

Smiling sweetly, I offered him my cheek to kiss, thanked him for the flowers, and told him to throw his coat on the bench in the entrance foyer. After putting the flowers on the kitchen counter, I led him into the paneled study overlooking the East River.

"Where's the Costner clone?" he asked, glancing around.

"Having lunch with Gwyneth Paltrow," I said in a snippy voice, knowing that this would make him crazy. Donald the Great had always groveled at the feet of female movie stars.

"Is he really?" my brother asked, impressed, his eyes widening.

"Donald, come on! Don't be daft. I was kidding. Jake's gone to have lunch with the publisher. At the Four Seasons."

"You've got a publisher?"

I nodded. "Sure do. He apparently gave a terrific presentation, and the deal's made. They're drawing up the contracts now."

"Congratulations, sis."

"*Donald,*" I said threateningly, glaring at him.

"Sorry, *Val.*"

I pointed to the sofa where earlier Jake and I had enjoyed our delicious sexy romp and said, "Sit there and start talking. What did she tell you?"

He did as I said as I stood hovering over him, my eyes riveted on his face.

"She didn't tell me much—"

"What!" I exclaimed, cutting across his sentence. "You come here with no information, expecting me to welcome you with open arms. Is that why you brought the flowers? As a peace offering?"

"No, no. And you didn't let me finish!" he whined.

"Okay, shoot."

"Listen, Val, you don't let me get the words out. You've certainly reverted to your old self. You're so fucking bossy and bullying again, I can't stand it." He started to get up. "I think I'm going to leave and you—"

"You're not leaving, Donald," I snapped. "So put that idea out of your head. And please refrain from using bad language. You know it irritates me."

"Okay, okay. Let's get back to Mom. She didn't say much when I first got there. Just sat like Elizabeth the First on her throne, looking regal and imposing. Then she eased up after I'd stroked her ego and yabbered at her for half an hour. I finally managed to establish that there's no legal document. About The Tradition thing." He sat back, looking pleased with himself.

"That's good to know," I exclaimed, and beamed at him, hoping to encourage him to keep talking. "What else did she say?"

"She explained about The Tradition. And that's all it is, Val, a tradition started by Amy-Anne, who wanted to give the women in the family the power, not the men. But even though there was—*is*—nothing in writing per se, Mom says the Lowell women have taken it very seriously for a hundred years. It's kinda . . . like . . . well, I guess it's like their Bible." Leaning forward slightly, Donald looked up at me and confided, "Mom says that the women descendants of Amy-Anne believed that it would bring bad luck to the family if a woman stopped being the head of Lowell's. Maybe she believes it too?"

"Goodness me, Donald, where does that leave you?" I asked sweetly, and walked across the room, stood leaning against the fireplace, trying to hide the amused smile that had sprung to my lips.

"I'm getting engaged. To Alexis. She accepted my proposal."

"How fortuitous for you, Donald," I purred sarcastically, thinking what an opportunist he was. He wasn't wasting any time or taking any chances. But what did I care. It suited my purpose to give him the family business. I certainly didn't want anything to do with it. Nor did I want anything from her.

He said, "I think Mom wants to see you again, Val."

"What for?" I demanded, turning frosty with him.

"I don't know, she didn't say."

"God, Donald, you are dim at times! Why didn't you ask her?"

"I did. And stop being a *bitch*!"

I ignored this and said, "And how did she answer you?"

"She didn't, at least she wouldn't tell me her reason, except that she said something about owing you an explanation."

"No kidding," I murmured, wondering what had prompted this sudden need for truth-telling on my mother's part.

Donald nodded and sat back against the pillows.

I softened my attitude toward him and said in a pleasant tone, "Well, Donald, this is really good news for you. About there not being a legal document. That makes it so much easier for me to give you the company."

"I told her you wanted to do that, and she says she won't let you."

"I don't inherit Lowell's until she dies, Donald,

and when she's dead she won't be able to stop me handing the business over to you. Now, will she?"

"Mmmm. Yes, that's true, I guess."

"No guessing. It *is* true."

"You're going to have to see Mom again, Val."

"No way, brother mine."

"I'll go with you."

"I bet you would, under the circumstances," I said.

"Please, Val. Be nice. You used to love me, and when you stopped, I was really hurt. You damaged me when I was a child because you dumped me, withdrew your love."

"Cut the crap, Donald, you know she took you away from me the moment it suited her."

"Bad language, Val, *really*!"

"Donald, tell me something, why the hell do you want Lowell's anyway?" I asked, truly perplexed by this and genuinely wanting to know.

"Because you don't want it and it should stay in the family."

"But would you work there?"

"Sure as hell I would."

"But you've got your dream job on the magazine. You always wanted to be a gossip columnist. After all, you cut your teeth on gossip in the family."

"There you go again, being a bitch."

"Oh, stop using that word. You're getting monotonous. So tell me, why would you want to give up your column? Which, I hear from Muffie, is very influential, to go and work in an office every day, making and selling cosmetics that nobody's ever heard of or really cares about."

Donald looked at me alertly, his eyes narrowing slightly, and after a split second he said, "You don't know, do you?"

"Know what?" I asked swiftly, noting the sudden change in his demeanor, and wondering what bombshell he was about to drop.

"About Lowell's, and what's happened to the company?"

I shook my head. "How would I know? I spend most of my life shooting pictures of the dead and dying on the battlefronts of the world."

Donald stood up. "Let's go to lunch," he said, suddenly becoming authoritative, "and I'll tell you all about it."

II

He had intrigued me with his comment about Lowell's and I tried to pump him as we walked across Beekman Place and out onto First Avenue. But he wouldn't be drawn, and insisted on telling me about his fiancée, Alexis, whom he wanted me to meet before I returned to Paris.

To shut him up, I finally agreed to this, and

hoped Jake wouldn't mind that I'd invited them to have dinner with us on Friday.

By the time we arrived at Billy's, a place I liked for its fish and chips and great hamburgers, Donald was all over me like chicken pox, being sweet because of the dinner invitation, no doubt. And everything else I was doing for him.

After hanging up our coats, we were shown to a table in the second room, which I preferred. The restaurant had a warm, attractive publike atmosphere, with bare wood floors and tables covered in red and-white-checked cloths. Its informality and good food made it a favorite of mine, especially when I was in a hurry and wanted to eat well without a lot of fuss.

Donald said, "Let's have a glass of white wine to celebrate."

Frowning, I asked, "Celebrate what?"

"My engagement to Alexis," he answered, staring at me. "What did you think I meant?"

"I didn't know," I said, although it had just struck me that perhaps he was counting his chicks before the hatching, *if* he was now celebrating his entry into the business world.

When the waitress showed up at our table with the menus, Donald ordered two glasses of dry white wine and took the menu from her, as did I.

Once she had departed to fill the drinks order, he leaned across the table and said, "A lot of siblings wouldn't tell you this, Val, they'd let you go back to Paris in ignorance. But I'm not like that, and whatever you think, I've always loved you. I may not have always liked you, but loved you— yes."

I stared at him but made no comment. Let him hang himself, I thought, and sat back in the chair, wondering why he was suddenly making these protestations of love for me.

He said, "Don't look so suspicious. And *doubting*. I know you think I'm like Mom, but I'm not."

"Let me go back to Paris in ignorance of *what*?" I demanded.

"Lowell's amazing success. The company's become a gold mine."

"Lowell's?"

He started to laugh. "Yes, Lowell's. They've had an amazing success in the last ten years, thanks to Mom. The products are in all of the best stores in New York, and across the—"

"What stores?" I asked, leaning closer, pinning him with my eyes, now riddled with curiosity.

"The *best* . . . like Bergdorf's, Saks, Barney's in New York, Neiman Marcus, in fact, Lowell's products are distributed across the country. The line has become very popular with women in every city in America. Going to take Europe soon."

"Those little dinky bottles, the homespun

creams and lotions," I exclaimed, totally taken aback by this news.

"Oh, yes, Val, and you shouldn't sound so disparaging about those dinky bottles and homespun creams, as you call them. That's part of the success, according to our mother."

"What do you mean?" I asked, frowning.

At this moment the wine materialized, and the waitress asked if we wanted to order. I selected a hamburger medium rare with French fries, and so did Donald. With the lunch order out of the way, he lifted his glass. "Cheers," he said.

"Cheers," I answered, touching my glass to his. "So, Donald, tell me more."

"I was just saying that the dinky bottles, as you call them, are not really so dinky. And they haven't changed much since Amy-Anne started Lowell's. They're actually a modern version of the apothecary jar, in miniature of course, with the glass stopper and the plain printed label. And that's where the homespun bit comes into play. Did you know the labels on the Lowell products haven't really changed in a hundred years, Val?"

"How could I possibly know that?"

"I guess you couldn't, and I didn't either until quite recently."

"Been doing your research already, then, have you?" I asked, endeavoring to curb the sarcasm that frequently crept into my conversation when talking to my brother. But he missed it, as he so often did; or maybe he merely chose to ignore it.

He replied, "No, I haven't. But Mom sometimes talks to me about business when I go over to dinner, and she was telling me about a Japanese company recently that wants to import the products to Japan. And the president of this company told her that Japanese women love the plain old-fashioned apothecary bottles and simple printed labels that merely state the product, its purpose, and give the ingredients."

"You're kidding me!"

"No, I'm not. It's funny about the Japanese— do you know hundreds of thousands of them love Early American furniture?"

"What's that got to do with Lowell's cosmetics, Donald?"

"Nothing, I was merely making an analogy. But it's the old-fashioned apothecary bottle and the old-fashioned label that appeals to millions of women here too. Call it nostalgia, confidence in something that looks homemade, whatever . . . it's part of the secret, Mom says. The old-fashioned packaging apparently works better than ever, and by keeping to the simple bottles and simple labels, she's managed to keep her costs down. It's the same with the products . . . by limiting them, she's kept production costs down too."

"What do you mean when you say *limiting* them? I'm not actually following you," I said.

"Mom told me that when Dad was alive he wanted her to make a lot of other products . . . lipsticks, eye makeup, nail polish, that sort of stuff. But she wouldn't, she remained faithful to the line created by Amy-Anne. You know, the face, hand, and body creams, shampoos and bath products. That decision has played into the success of Lowell's today, because her costs have remained fairly reasonable. Also, she hasn't had to cater to fashion and its changes." Donald paused, took a big swig of his wine, and finished, "Where she has spent money is on marketing."

"How the hell did she suddenly turn this company around?" I exclaimed, and shook my head, totally baffled. "When we were little, there were always money problems, money struggles, as I recall."

"Things weren't that bad, were they?" Donald muttered, and looked at me questioningly over the rim of his glass.

"I think money *was* very tight at times," I responded. "But the only really nasty problem I can remember was when they wanted to let Annie go, and we both became so hysterical in the end, she wasn't fired. But I have a feeling our grandfather paid her salary for a while."

"Annie loved us, didn't she, Val? She was the best nanny."

"Yes, she was. . . ." I let my sentence trail away, thinking that without Annie Patterson

392 Barbara Taylor Bradford

looking after me from birth, I would have probably never survived in that household.

"Anyway, Val, to give you a final definitive answer about Lowell's success today, let's say it's all been in the marketing. Apparently Mom sent it to every top model, every Broadway actress, every movie actress, and every female celebrity she could think of. She had an old-fashioned carpetbag made, filled it with products, and enclosed a handwritten letter on Victorian-style notepaper. It worked, everybody fell for . . . the carpetbag, the *dinky* bottle, and the *homespun* products, as you just called them."

"So she's making millions?" I said, grinning at him. "Is that what you're trying to tell me?"

He nodded. "She sure is. She has a mail order catalogue. She's on the Internet. And Lowell's has a Web site too. And in about eighteen months, after she's launched the product in Europe and Japan, I think she'll go to Wall Street and do an IPO."

"My God, Donald, our mother's a veritable tycoon, and I never knew it!" I hoped he'd get my sarcasm, but I could tell he hadn't.

"I had no idea either. I've picked up stuff from her from time to time, but Alexis is a financial journalist, and she's the one who's filled me in with a lot of information lately."

"Do you mean in the last week, Donald?" I asked, eyeing him speculatively.

He shook his head. "No, I don't. I mean ever since Mom got sick, you know, had the first heart attack."

"Well, congratulations, Donald darling, I think you're going to inherit a great company and be very rich."

"You really mean that, don't you, Val? I can see you're not leading me on."

I stared at him and frowned. "Of course I'm not, why would I?"

He took a deep breath. "When Mom does the IPO next year, or in the year 2000, Lowell's could bring in between five hundred million to a billion dollars, give or take few hundred thou."

I gaped at Donald, unable to speak. Taking a deep breath, I said at last, "I'm gobsmacked, Donald, utterly and completely gobsmacked!"

He laughed, but I think more from the expression on my face than the words that left my mouth. When he stopped laughing, he said, "But I don't know what gobsmacked means, Val."

"Smacked in the mouth, in the parlance of the British," I explained.

III

It was after lunch that Donald broached the subject of seeing our mother. "Please, Val, let's go and visit her now. Get this worked out properly, before you go back to Paris."

"Donald, I'll give you the company when I inherit it, I've already told you that half a dozen times. I don't wish to see her."

"She said she wanted to see *you* again, to explain something, to come clean with you, I guess. So let's go up to the apartment. And at the same time, maybe you can reiterate your feelings about Lowell's. And me, I mean."

I looked across the table at him and saw him very objectively for a split second. He really was a handsome young man, twenty-six and very virile-looking. He has movie-star good looks, I thought, just like our mother. He wasn't so hard to take. If I were honest with myself, I guess I'd always been jealous of him because she had favored him above me and spoiled him. And he was a bit devious and gossipy, but not a bad young man, just human, really, like all of us.

I sighed and shook my head, and then I said slowly, "Donald, you can't imagine what a hardship it is for me to go and see her, really you can't."

"I guess I can," he answered swiftly. "I admit she wasn't always . . . *loving* with you, Val."

"So, at long last you're *finally* admitting that, Donald."

"I've always known it," he said, sounding defensive. "But we haven't really had a heart-to-heart conversation since we've been grown-up, have we?"

"Only too true."

"Look, I realize what a pain in the ass she can be," he said, "and how painful it is for you to see her, but surely it'll help if I come with you."

"Actually, Donald, what do you want me to say to your mother when we get there?"

"Our mother," he corrected me. "And I want you to ask her to have some sort of paper drawn. A paper that says if you want, you can give the company to me and that I, a man, can inherit it."

"You mean a legal document, is that it?"

He nodded. "Yeah."

"Don't you trust me?" I asked, swallowing a smile. I was playing with him now, and that wasn't really fair.

"Yeah, sure I do, that's one thing about you, Val, you've always been straight. But don't you think there ought to be a document? Look, God forbid something happens to you in your job, then what? I mean, who gets the company?"

"You have a point there," I said, leaning back in the chair, sipping my coffee. If I got killed covering a war somewhere, my mother would *have* to leave the company to Donald. "You," I said at last. "*You* would, Donald, or, rather, your wife." I paused and looked into the distance, then muttered, "Gee, I wonder how they work that out when there's a divorce?"

Donald said, "I guess there's never been one. Maybe we should ask Mom."

"No," I said, coming to a decision. "Let's not ask her anything. Let's go up there to see her, present a united front, and explain that we think there should be something in writing about me wanting you to have the company. Just in case I die in the line of duty as a war photographer."

"Okay," he said, and looked at me curiously. "I wonder what it is she wants to explain to you."

"I don't really need to hear what she has to say, Donald. I'm just going up there to make sure she does right by you."

"Why? Why do you care about me, Val?" he asked, looking at me intently, frowning.

"Because you're my little brother and I loved you a lot when you were a small boy, and besides, it's your *right*. We're almost in the year 2000 and we've got to move on from a rule made in 1898. It was a good rule, I'm certainly on the side of women, but it needs—"

"Updating," Donald volunteered.

IV

Donald took out his cell phone and called our mother, asked if we could come over, made a date for three-thirty, and then clicked off.

"That's all set," he said, slipping the phone into his jacket pocket. "Let's have another coffee."

"Okay." I glanced at my watch. "We do have a little time to waste. So tell me some more about Lowell's."

"Such as what?"

"Well, you've talked about the packaging and the marketing, but what about the products? I guess they're good, that people do like them."

He nodded. "According to Mom, they do, and I guess the success of the company proves that. Alexis loves them; she says the creams are very rich and very effective."

"You said Lowell's will be launched in Europe. Where exactly?"

"London and Paris to begin with. Mom hasn't really said. Listen, I don't know as much as you think I do. She's never said anything about Lowell's to me in the past, I've only just found things out since she had the heart attack, I told you that. Plus Alexis has filled me in a bit, since she's studied the financial side of all the cosmetic companies for her job."

"I realize all that, Donald. When we get there

I want to get straight to the point with our mother. You know, let's talk about the legal document for you right away. I don't want to start discussing other stuff."

"I understand. We'll go in and out. And there'll be no discussions, no explanations from her."

"Correct. I don't want to hear anything at all. And if she starts yammering at me, I won't listen."

But how wrong I was about that.

V

My mother was still under doctor's orders to take it easy, so she wasn't spending as much time at her office as she usually did.

When we arrived at the Park Avenue apartment, the door was opened by a maid in uniform.

"Hi, Florina," Donald said, nodding to her as he struggled out of his overcoat. "This is my sister, Valentine Denning."

The young woman stared at me with interest, smiled, took my coat, and said, "Pleased to meet you, Miss Denning."

"I'm glad to meet you, Florina."

A moment later my mother was walking into the foyer, looking staggeringly beautiful in a black wool jumpsuit trimmed with velvet with a large pearl pin on one shoulder. She was wearing very high heels, which made her even taller, but then, so was I today, and I matched her in height.

Her jet-black hair was pulled back in a chignon, and her face looked all cheekbones and eyes, and I wondered unexpectedly how she had ever coped with this amazing beauty. Had it been a burden? Had it ruined her life? I had no idea. It suddenly struck me that I knew so little about this woman who had given birth to me.

Chapter 26

I

"Hello, Val . . . Donald . . ." Margot Denning said, and with an airy wave of her hand toward the sitting room she added, "Shall we go in there and have tea?" Without waiting for our responses, she glided into the room.

I followed her, saying, "I don't want anything, thanks. Donald and I just finished lunch."

"Nothing for me either, thanks, Mom," Donald muttered as he trailed after me.

Naturally she went and sat in her usual chair, because she had been sitting there for years. She obviously knew she looked her best in that particular area of the room; certainly the lighting near the fireplace was flattering to her.

I went and took up a position near the fireplace, standing as I generally did, and Donald
came and joined me. He was apparently my ally
now since we were presumably presenting a
united front.

"I'm happy you came, Val," she murmured,
looking directly at me, smiling faintly. "I told
Donald I wanted to explain something—"

"Oh, but I don't want any explanations . . .
about anything. I haven't come for that reason.
I've come to do the talking, not the listening.
And I'm going to talk sense about Lowell's and
your will."

She stared at me, frowning. "We've had that
discussion already."

"But it was not to my satisfaction."

"There's nothing more to say."

"There's a lot to say. Donald has told me about
Lowell's as it stands today, and the success you've
made of it. You're obviously a very clever businesswoman. That's why I can't understand why
you cling to some antiquated tradition started a
hundred years ago. Donald tells me there's no
legal document backing up this tradition, so you
can very easily leave the company to him."

"I can't. A female descendant of Amy-Anne
Lowell's has to inherit."

All of a sudden it hit me why she was being so
stubborn, and I exclaimed, "Don't tell me you
believe all that crap about bad luck for Lowell's if

a woman's not holding the power." I began to laugh. "Oh my God, you do!" I went on laughing.

Donald gaped at me. Our mother was poker-faced. I noticed a vein pulsing on her temple. She remained totally silent.

I said, "Lowell's is no longer the same company it was. Its structure has changed radically. You're going into worldwide distribution imminently, from what Donald tells me, and next year you're apparently going to do an IPO on Wall Street. You've pushed this dinky little old-fashioned company into the twenty-first century, yet you yourself are still lingering in the past, clinging to an antiquated idea started by the founder."

"No I'm not!" she protested, her voice rising shrilly.

"Yes, you are. Please get it through your head once and for all. *I don't want your company when you die.* Leave it to Donald, who would love to be involved with it. And he's entitled, as your only son. He should be your heir. And he was always your favorite anyway. Forget about this tradition nonsense and act like the smart businesswoman you apparently are."

"Is that why you don't want Lowell's?" she asked.

"I'm not following you," I murmured, but I

was. I just wanted to hear what she would have to say.

"I mean because you believe, mistakenly, that I mistreated you as a child?"

"No," I replied, but I was telling a lie.

"The company is going to be worth millions," she said suddenly, obviously believing this would influence my decision.

"*Billions,* more than likely, Mother. But I'm still not interested. Thanks, but no thanks."

"Please, Val, reconsider."

"I can't."

"You mean you *won't,*" she snapped in her snooty voice.

"Look, I have a life of my own. I don't want a life you're trying to create for me, suddenly, out of the blue, after years of indifference and neglect."

"You're bearing a grudge . . . how ridiculous when there's so much money involved."

"I couldn't care less about the money."

"More fool you!"

I sighed. "If I said *okay,* I'll take Lowell's, leave it to me, what would it entail? Just out of curiosity, what would you expect of me now? What would you want me to do?"

I felt Donald tense, he was standing so close to me at the fireplace.

My mother sat up straighter in her chair and studied me for a moment.

I hated this close scrutiny of hers; almost frantically I wished I could escape, get out of her presence. I disliked her intensely, and I now regretted that I had come. I had done so because I wanted to help Donald, who wasn't such a bad guy after all. I thought he was getting the short end of the stick.

My mother said carefully, in that well-modulated, upper-class voice of hers, "I would expect you to come home, Val, to live in New York. And of course I would want you to work at Lowell's alongside me. I would train you, teach you the business, teach you everything I know. It would give me great pleasure, Val."

"You've had two heart attacks, unexpected because you've always been so healthy, and you're young. And so now you feel a bit . . . vulnerable, and it occurs to you that you need . . . a daughter. Is that what all this is about?"

"Don't be ridiculous! I want you to come home because this is where you belong. With me. In the business."

"This is certainly *not* where I belong," I almost yelled. Taking a deep breath and clinging to my control, I added, "We're not getting anywhere. If you won't change your will, I must certainly go and see my lawyer, have some legal document drawn that protects Donald if something happens to me. After all, I'm a war photojournalist, I could easily be killed when I'm working. I will leave Lowell's to him."

Donald said, "Thanks, Val."

Our mother was silent.

II

Florina came hurrying in with a large tea tray, which certainly curtailed the conversation for a moment or two. She placed it on the mahogany coffee table in front of the sofa and said to my mother, "Shall I pour, Mrs. Denning?"

"No, no, we can manage, Florina. Thank you."

Florina hurried out.

"No tea for me," I said. "I'm leaving." I walked toward the door.

Donald called, "Wait for me, Val."

"I'm in a hurry," I responded, but I paused in the doorway and turned. "Good-bye, Mother. So long, Donald. I'll see you around."

"No, wait, Val. I'll only be a second." Donald went to our mother, pecked her on the cheek. "I'll talk to you later, Mom."

I was halfway across the entrance foyer, heading for the front door, when she said, "But I want to explain!"

"I don't need an explanation. Not anymore," I replied without turning around.

"Don't you want to know why . . . I was never able to love you?" my mother asked.

This stopped me in my tracks. And of course her words were irresistible.

Very slowly, I walked back to the sitting room, stood in the doorway, leaning against the door-jamb. My eyes did not leave her face.

III

"Come in and sit down, Val. And I think you, Donald, should leave. This is private."

"Donald stays," I snapped.

"Yes, I'm staying," my brother said, surprising me, since he'd never argued with her in the past, or defied her.

"I'll stand if you don't mind," I said. "I'm sure this isn't going to take long."

Donald joined me by the fireplace. He stood close to me and reached out, took hold of my hand, as he had when we were small.

How often we had been brought to task for something or other in this very room. We had always stood in this exact spot and our mother had always seated herself in that antique French chair.

But today I was not afraid of her. And I was certain that Donald wasn't either.

Together, showing our united front, we waited for her to speak.

"This really doesn't have anything to do with Donald," she said, addressing me directly. "I *do* think it would be better if we were alone, Val. This is very private."

"No way Donald leaves. He stays."

Donald said, "I sure do, Mom," and squeezed my hand.

Margot Denning didn't say anything for a very long while. She simply sat bolt upright in the chair, her posture superb, her head held high, remote, her regality intact.

Finally, she said, "It all began a long time ago, when I was very young, just a girl. . . ." Her voice wavered. She stopped and steadied herself, gripped the arms of the French chair.

If I hadn't known better, I would have said she was suddenly emotional. But this wasn't possible, she had ice water in her veins.

Because I so disliked her, I said, "A very short story indeed. Well, so long, I'm off." I began to move toward the door.

"No, no, I was just . . . trying to formulate the words . . . to get things in order in my mind, Val. I was a girl, just seventeen, when I met a young man. His name was Vincent Landau and I fell in love with him, and he with me. Unfortunately, my mother did not approve of him, and his parents did not approve of me. We were from different worlds, you see. And I—"

"Why didn't your mother approve?" I asked, curiosity getting the better of me.

"Because he was Jewish."

"And his parents disapproved because you were a gentile?"

"Yes, but it was more than that. The Landaus were extremely rich, they owned a private bank, and they were aiming high for Vincent. They thought he should marry someone of his own ilk, someone in society. I was a nobody as far as they were concerned."

She paused again and Donald said, "So what happened, Mom?"

"Vincent was sent away to Europe, he was a few years older than me, and his father sent him to work in the Berlin branch of the family bank. Eventually—"

"I hope this isn't going to take too long," I interrupted. "Because I have an appointment, and I'm starting to run late. Can you cut to the chase?"

"Yes," she answered tersely, and leaned back against the chair. "Two years later Vincent came back to New York and sought me out immediately. We began to see each other in secret, and not long after we had resumed our relationship I discovered I was pregnant. I was nineteen. I knew if I told my mother she would push me into having an abortion, and so I didn't tell her I was pregnant until it was too late to do anything. Vincent was worried about his parents' reaction, but at the same time he was pleased. He hoped that once they met me and knew I was having his child, they would relent, accept me, allow him to marry me."

She paused, took a deep breath, and smoothed her hand over her hair.

I said, "But they didn't."

"That is correct. In fact, they were more furious with him than ever, and did everything to break us up."

"Did they succeed?" Donald asked.

"Oh, yes, they did."

"And you miscarried," I said.

"No, I didn't," she answered with a small frown.

"The baby was born dead, then?" I asserted.

"No, the baby wasn't born dead," she replied. "She was a beautiful little girl. Perfect in every way. But my mother was beside herself, bitter about Vincent's behavior, because she thought he should have defied his parents and married me. She didn't know how to cope, and she was also angry and frustrated. Here was I, not quite twenty, and the mother of an illegitimate child."

I began to feel cold inside and I became fearful. I didn't want to hear any more, but I knew I couldn't stop the flow of words from her mouth.

As for me, I was frozen to the spot, unable to leave.

Donald was saying, "So what happened, what did you do?"

We stood there together, he and I, holding hands, united for a short while, protective of each other, and I sensed that Donald was as apprehensive as I was. I realized I didn't want to hear the rest, because I knew I wasn't going to like it.

She said, "I settled down to being a mother. Vincent came to see me all the time, he loved us both so much, he loved little Anjelica. She was such a beautiful baby. So perfect. His presence kept my mother calm for a while, and she began to believe we would ultimately marry, and then out of the blue Vincent was sent to the Paris branch of the Landau bank. Soon after he left New York, his engagement to the socialite Marguerite Shiff was announced in *The New York Times*. I called him up in Paris and he admitted he'd been forced into the engagement.

"My mother made me put Anjelica up for adoption, and I had to do as she said, I had no alternative. I never saw my baby again. It broke my heart. Vincent came back to New York, and we did meet a few times, but we knew it was an impossible situation, quite untenable. So we said our good-byes. He killed himself a week before his marriage. He drove to his family's country estate, locked himself in the garage, turned on the ignition, and died of carbon monoxide poisoning."

"So you never saw your baby again, Mother, and your lover killed himself. But what does all this have to do with me?" I asked. I was icy inside now, very fearful.

"Please let me finish."

"All right," I responded, looking across at her. I thought she seemed pale all of a sudden and her expression was stark, her mouth taut. It was apparent she was having difficulty with this.

"I met your father several years later, and we were married. He was very kind to me, good to me, but I could never love him. At least, not in the way he wanted to be loved, not with the same passion I had loved Vincent Landau."

"And you couldn't love me either, is that it?" I exclaimed in a cold and angry voice. "Is that what you're leading up to?"

"I tried, Val, I really did try to love you. But whenever I looked at you, I thought of little Anjelica and my guilt overwhelmed me. I couldn't bear to think of her being out there without me, living with another family, being brought up by another woman. Losing Anjelica and Vincent shattered me completely, my heart was broken and I knew it would always be broken. I lived in a kind of netherworld for years. I was like a zombie in some ways, I suppose. I thought of Anjelica every day. She was never far from my thoughts. When Donald was born it was different, because he was a boy."

I was gaping at her, stunned, and so was Donald. Neither of us spoke.

"I'm sorry," she said at last. "So sorry . . ."

"*Sorry,*" I screamed at her, losing it completely. "Is that all you can say after thirty-one years of torture? *Sorry*. Well, thanks a lot, *Mother*. Thanks for the indifference, the injustice, the neglect, and that monumental lack of love and caring. I had a miserable, tormented childhood because of you! Oh, how you made me suffer, and all because of your selfishness, and your ridiculous self-involvement." I was shaking with rage, and it took all my self-control not to rush at her and strike her. "You talk about your broken heart, but what about mine? You broke my heart, Mother, you punished me because of your mistakes. My God, you're monstrous, wicked! No, more than wicked, it goes beyond that . . . you are evil!"

IV

Margot Denning was gaping at me, as stunned and devastated as I was. Her face was white, stricken, but I did not care. I had no sympathy for her. How could I? She had ruined my childhood and almost ruined my life, and if it had not been for Annie Patterson, our nanny, and my Denning grandparents, God knows how I would have ended up. In a straitjacket, perhaps. Or, worse, a coffin.

To deny maternal love to your own child, an innocent child, was cruel, inhuman, and unconscionable, and that was what she had done to me. I felt the tears rising in my throat, pricking behind my eyes, but I pushed them back. I was damned if I was going to let *her* see me cry.

Drawing myself up, I said, "And somehow, now, because you need me, you think you can lure me back into your orbit, into your world. Well, tough luck, Margot. I'm not buying your brand of shit today. As for Lowell's, if you don't want Donald to have it, who *is* entitled, by the way, I suggest you give it to that daughter you gave away so long ago. Little Anjelica. If you can find her after all these years."

V

Donald's face was crumpled up, as if he were going to cry, and he reached for me protectively and said, "Val, please let me—"

"No, I don't need help, I'm fine," I cried, and shook free of him, stepped away, stepped to one side.

Margot Denning was frozen in place like a marble statue in the chair, her face as white as bleached bone, so stark looking, her cheekbones appeared more prominent than ever, as though they were protruding from her face. She cried, "Val, I—"

"Don't say a word to me!" I screamed. "You've said and done enough these past thirty-one years." I was shaking all over and my heart was hammering in my chest, I was so outraged. I knew I was in danger of doing something violent if I didn't escape this room. "You are a reprehensible and destructive woman," I shrieked at her. "And when I think of my painful childhood, of the cruelty you inflicted on me by refusing to love me, to acknowledge my existence, I have only this to say to you: I hope you rot in hell, Margot Denning."

I stumbled out of the room blindly, my body racked by the terrible pain and anguish I'd bottled up for years.

Donald came rushing after me and got into the elevator with me. As we rode down together he endeavored to comfort me, to calm me, but without any success. I just couldn't stop shaking and I felt nauseated.

Donald must have retrieved our coats when he ran out of the apartment, and he wrapped mine around me when we got out onto Park Avenue. As he shrugged into his, he hailed a cab and bundled me into it, gave the Beekman Place address.

Riding across town, edging through the rush-hour traffic, I clung to him, buried my face against his shoulder, praying this awful shaking and feeling of sickness would go away.

But it didn't, and it took all my self-control not to throw up all over my brother. Donald kept trying to talk to me, to sympathize, to soothe me, but I just couldn't speak, and I refused to cry, although hot tears were very near the surface.

Once we arrived at the apartment building in Beekman Place, Donald helped me out, paid the cabbie, and put an arm around me as he maneuvered me across the lobby and into the elevator.

At the front door of the apartment I began to fumble in my bag for the keys, but I wasn't doing too well, and Donald took the bag away from me, found my keys, and opened the front door.

Still helping me, both his arms around me, we went into the apartment together.

Jake must have heard us, and he came out of the study, exclaiming, "Hi, where've you been—" But the words died on his lips when he saw me half crumpled over, clinging to Donald as if my life depended on it.

"My God! Val, what's wrong? Are you sick, darling?" he cried, rushing into the entrance foyer.

Letting go of Donald at last, I moved forward and stumbled into Jake's arms, filling with relief as I did. He looked into my stricken face and cried again, "You're as white as a sheet, what is it?"

I stared back at him, struck dumb, unable to utter a word.

Looking over my head, he asked my brother, "Donald, what the hell's wrong? What happened to Val?"

"Let's get her inside, let's sit down," Donald muttered, and at once Jake did as he asked, half leading, half carrying me into the study. I collapsed on the sofa and Jake sat down next to me after pulling off my coat and throwing it to one side. He wrapped his arms around me again.

"Come on, let's have it, Donald! Why is Val in this terrible state?"

Donald sat down in the chair opposite and began to tell him.

And I began to weep, finally letting go now that I was safe with Jake.

VI

I wept all through Donald's excruciating narrative, desperately holding on to Jake, clinging to him. As he listened to Donald, he stroked my hair, tightened his grip on me, but did not interrupt my brother with questions. He simply listened and digested everything.

When Donald finished, Jake exclaimed in an

angry voice, "I've never heard anything so disgusting, so despicable in my entire life. It's monstrous, and your mother must be a monster. Or mentally ill."

"A monster," I mumbled through my tears.

"And mentally ill in certain ways," Donald ventured.

Unexpectedly, I began to sob brokenly, and I couldn't control myself. I cried for a very long time, sobbing out the tears that had been filling me up for years. Ever since the day I had been born, in fact. That's how long she had punished me for not being Anjelica.

Part Three

A QUESTION OF
$\mathcal{T}$RUST

Chapter 27

I

Paris, November · "I'm glad Françoise has settled in so well with Fiona," I said to Mike Carter, leaning back in the chair, crossing my legs.

"I am too, and there's absolutely no way Olivier can find her, I'm convinced of that," Mike responded, looking at me intently across his desk.

"I agree, I'm sure she's safe. It was a good idea of yours to charter a private plane."

"It was Fiona's idea, not mine, and she arranged everything with a local charter company. Her point was, private plane, no manifest, no way Françoise could be traced through the airlines. And it was a point well taken, Val. And much appreciated by me. I'm so grateful for your introducing us to Fiona."

Mike rose, walked across his office at Gemstar, and closed the door, then returned to his desk. He was a big, burly man with a barrel chest and thick dark hair tinged with gray at the sides. His craggy face was open, honest, and kind, reflecting his character, and his dark eyes were full of humor and wisdom. Intelligent, hardworking, and supremely loyal, he was the best boss I'd ever had, and a truly good friend.

He said, "As I told you on the phone, I flew over with her—"

"Was that wise?" I interjected, frowning. "What if Olivier has a PI tracking your movements?"

Mike let out a belly laugh. "You think of everything, Val. And I do too, I must confess. I took a circuitous route to Le Bourget, and traveled alone. So did Françoise, also alone. I doubt anyone could have followed us."

"And Fiona welcomed you with open arms from what you and Françoise have told me."

He nodded. "She's a terrific gal, and we got on well. More important, she took Françoise under her wing, and I think it's all working out very well. Françoise loves decorating and designing, and she's really been able to make inroads on the restaurant, it's going to be finished in record time.

Fiona wants to open it before the Christmas holidays."

"That's great, and I'm so relieved Françoise is okay. Listen, I hate to bring up Olivier, but what's happening with *him*? Any information?"

"A bit, yes. Apparently he's working on a big murder case in Marseilles, to do with drug dealers and the worst bunch of criminals around, the scum of the earth, in fact. So that's keeping him busy, since he *is* the crack homicide cop down there. The lawyer I hired for Françoise has been in touch with him, and so Olivier knows she's taken out a restraining order, filed for divorce, and moved out of Paris. I think he'd like to get his hands on her if he could, and if he knew where to look. But as I said, he's really caught up in that case, and he's vital to the investigation, seemingly. Therefore his bosses are not going to let him off the hook all that easily, so that he can go searching the world for his estranged 'wife. I've been in touch with Armand and Simone, and they haven't heard a peep out of him or seen him lately. They know nothing about him other than that he's working on the murder case. There's been a helluva lot of press coverage about the case, and he's always mentioned, and in glowing terms, I might add."

"I'm presuming Armand and Simone have no idea where Françoise is staying."

He grinned. "In a pig's eye they don't! What do you think I am, honey, stooopid?"

I started to laugh. "Oh, Mike, you're a card! Anyway, let's keep our fingers crossed, let's hope he stays tied up with the murder case, that he's far too preoccupied with it to hunt down Françoise."

"From your mouth to God's ears, honey," Mike replied, and shuffled the papers on his desk, glanced down at them, then looked up, squinting in the sunlight.

"No wars," he said, "nothing dangerous, that's what you told me when you got back two weeks ago. This rule still holding, Val?"

"Absolutely, Mike. Very honestly, I'm burnt out. And I don't want to risk my life for a picture anymore, nor do I want to go out of town on a job."

"Unless it's with Jake, right?"

"That's correct. I do want to go back to work now, take on some assignments, but providing they're interesting—and local." I gave him a long look and went on. "I'm tired of all the junk that's flung around in war, Michael. Tired of all the lies, all the deceit, all the nonsense that goes on with the military and the politicians. And on both sides. I've seen too much. Too much death, too much destruction." I sighed heavily, shook my head. "Frankly, I don't think I could take it any-more. And I *know* I don't want to experience that awful fear, the panic inside, that sick feeling when I have to look at the dead, the dying, and the mutilated. Or deal with those who are alive but frightened out of their wits, so terrified, they're incapable of saving themselves.

"You know, Mike, there's nothing glorious about seeing the dead in their Sunday clothes, killed by surprise, after a special lunch or a religious service, or a day's outing with the family. And I'm weary of picking my way through rubble and broken glass, mud and blood and . . . dead bodies. I suppose what I'm trying to say is that the devastation of war has devastated me."

Mike was silent for a moment, and then he said quietly, in a serious voice, "I know exactly what you mean, Val. And you *are* burnt out. That doesn't surprise me either. You've covered too many wars already in your young life, and it's time for a change. So—" He paused, shuffled through the papers on his desk once more, and said, "I think this story might appeal to you. . . ."

"What is it?"

"It's a fashion shoot, and no, don't pull a face like that. This could be interesting. Behind the scenes of Paris haute couture, mainly three houses . . . Balmain, Lacroix, and Givenchy. The designing and preparation of the summer collection for 1999. It's got glamour, beauty, and intriguing people. You could make it into something interesting, Val, and very easily. It has potential, and it can be a lot more than just a few pretty pictures."

"I'll think about it. Anything else?"

"Well, I am hoping that the famous painter will let us shoot his big canvases in Mexico, but that's a few months off."

"Alexander St. Just Stevens? Who never returned my calls. I don't think so, and what kind of a name is that anyway?"

"It doesn't matter what the guy's called, Val, he's a genius," Mike said, and laughed at my expression. He went on. "I have a movie shoot you could do with your eyes closed. And incidentally, before I forget to ask, how's the book coming along?"

"Wonderfully, Mike!" I exclaimed. "Jake and I put quite a lot of effort into the selection of the pictures in New York, and he's been working on it in Paris for the last few weeks. He's had time, actually, because he's not been out in the field."

"Oh, hell, that's right! Jacques is still in hospital. How's he doing?"

"Really great. His broken limbs are mending, thank God, and the doctors at the hospital have been treating him for his heart. He's going to be fine, but he's going to have to take it easy. He'll never go out in the field again, and he was hankering after that. It's an office job, and *permanently,* for Jacques Foucher, I'm afraid."

"So Jake's been running the agency, has he?"

Mike asked, and chuckled. "I bet that's not pleased him too much."

"Not really. On the other hand, he has had time to work on the book."

I got up. "I won't keep you, Mike, I know what kind of day you have, and listen, I'll do the haute couture shoot. Why not? Anyway, I've got to earn a living, you know."

"Don't we all, Val."

I grinned at him, went to the door, paused, and swung around. "Listen, let me know when you want to come to dinner, and I'll cook up a storm for the three of us."

His face lit up, and he asked eagerly, like a kid: "Would you make a pot roast? A real American pot roast, Val?"

"Sure I would, just name the night, and we're all set." I stepped into the corridor, then turned, stuck my head through the door, and added, "And for dessert it'll be homemade apple pie and ice cream. How about that?"

He grinned and gave me the thumbs-up sign.

II

After the meeting at Gemstar with Mike, I went home to my apartment on the Left Bank.

By the time I got back to the Rue Bonaparte, Janine had gone for the day, but she had left the place as immaculate as always, gleaming brightly and filled with fresh flowers.

The whole apartment smelled faintly of beeswax, lemons, potpourri overlaid with the scent of cinnamon, and pinecones, a mingling of fragrances that evoked the fall to me.

I had done the marketing earlier, and I went immediately into the kitchen to start dinner. I had always liked clay-pot cooking, and since it was such a cold, damp day, I had decided earlier to make my version of *poulet grandmère,* using a clay pot called a Römertopf. My chicken casserole was based on a whole chicken, along with a mélange of winter vegetables such as carrots, parsnips, turnips, onions, leeks, mushrooms, and a handful of chopped celery. All of these went into the pot with the chicken, which I had left in the refrigerator marinating in chicken stock, tomato juice, and a mixture of herbs when I had gone to Gemstar.

As I prepared the vegetables for the casserole, I thought of the last couple of weeks since our return to Paris. Once again Jake and I had fallen into a pleasant routine, which worked for us, since we were both addicted to order. Every day we worked on *Flowers of War* because we had to meet a December deadline for the publisher. My dining room had always doubled as an office, with a big English partners desk in the bay window and my filing boxes hidden inside an antique armoire set against an end wall.

And so when Jake went off to his photo agency every morning, I settled down to complete the captions and edit the main body of text. Jake struggled with this every day at the office, or at night at the apartment, and he was making excellent progress. Once he was relatively satisfied with the pages he had written, he passed them to me for editing and polishing.

When Jake had been a Rhodes scholar at Oxford, he had majored in European history, and he was much better educated than I was, and certainly better equipped to write the book, since he was a historian. But this aside, the book was his idea and I felt he should be ultimately responsible for the text, that it should reflect his point of view.

The good thing was that we were working well together on this project, just as we did out in the field when we covered wars. We were making great progress, beginning to see the light of day; the book would be finished sooner than expected, and we now hoped to accept Fiona's invitation to go to Yorkshire for Christmas.

Jake was living at my apartment with me, although he made frequent trips to his own place to check things out, collect his mail, and bring back fresh clothes.

In the beginning, when we first returned from New York, he had been concerned that Olivier might be loitering about, lurking near my place looking for Françoise. And even though Janine had assured us things had been quiet in my absence, he insisted on moving in. I was glad he had; I certainly didn't argue. His presence pleased me, and we quickly settled into that pattern of normalcy, of domesticity, which I craved, needed to share with him.

With all the vegetables now ready, I placed the chicken in the clay pot, added the thick, herb-flavored stock and the vegetables, then put the pot in the cold oven, a necessity for clay-pot cooking. I turned the oven on and went into the dining room to set the table. Once this chore was finished, I hurried into the living room; after turning on the lamps, I found a box of matches and lit the fire that Janine had left ready, the grate filled with paper, wood chips, and logs. It was already growing dark outside and it had started to rain. To my way of thinking, there was nothing more welcoming and cheerful than a roaring fire on a night like this. Jake would appreciate it, I knew that.

How nice everything looks, I thought as I sat down on the sofa, enjoying the surroundings that had been so lovingly created by my grandfather. And at that moment of quietness in my busy day, it was not long before my thoughts turned to Margot Denning.

III

After the confrontation with my mother, I had bottled it all up again—the rage, the hurt, the anguish. I had done so in order to survive.

But there were times when a pall hung over me, and I continued to be haunted by my disturbed past, by the terrible injustice meted out to me by that woman who called herself my mother.

My childhood had been a tragedy, that was the only word for it. How sick she had been and probably still was . . . unable to love me because of her love for the illegitimate daughter she had given away, had abandoned to her own fate. She had been saddled with a guilt that burdened her down, a guilt that ultimately must have ruined her life. Because it became a morbid and obsessive guilt that dominated her and submerged all rational thought. I had come to believe that Margot Denning *was* irrational, among other things.

I wondered if she had ever tried to find that abandoned child, Anjelica. And I also wondered about *her,* wondered what had happened to her, and where she was today. Somewhere out there I had a half sister, a sister who had probably had as bad a childhood as I.

I had discussed some of these thoughts with Jake, but I really tried hard not to burden him with my pain. Anyway, there really was nothing anyone could say to give me comfort, or help alleviate the agony I experienced at times.

Nor could I simply stick a Band-Aid on my psychic wounds and hope they would eventually heal. They wouldn't, at least not all that easily, and not for a long time. But now that I had a grasp of the truth at long last, perhaps I could do something to heal myself. I hoped I could.

The only thing I had not asked my mother during our confrontation in New York had to do with my father. And it was actually a twofold question—had he known about her involvement with Vincent Landau and her illegitimate child? And why had he condoned her cruel behavior toward me when I was a child?

Troubled and perplexed, I had finally called her before leaving New York, and she had immediately come to the phone to speak to me. No doubt she thought I had changed my mind about Lowell's.

When I launched into the questions about my father, she had obviously been taken aback momentarily. There was a silence before she had finally answered in a clipped tone, "No, I never told your father about Vincent and Anjelica. What was the point? That part of my life was over, finished."

I had then posed the most pertinent question of all. Why had my father followed her lead and virtually ignored me all my life until the day he died?

Her answer flowed so easily down the wire, and instantly; she hadn't even had to think about it. "Peter didn't want children, he believed they would get in the way of our relationship. He wanted me all to himself, you see. I suppose he resented you, and Donald too, even though you were both fathered by him. He thought you were a nuisance. And I know for an absolute certainty that he was jealous of you."

"Jealous!" I had retorted. "That's a laugh under the circumstances. And tell me, why did you bother to have kids at all?" I knew the answer before she spoke.

"For Lowell's, of course. I needed an heir. Or perhaps I should say an *heiress*."

I hung up.

Who could deal with a woman like that? Later that morning, when I had related everything to Muffie over our farewell lunch at Le Cirque, she had been as upset and as angry as I was myself.

But there were moments when I dwelt on Margot Denning, as I was doing now, trying to fathom her out, to understand her, as I struggled to slay the demons of my blighted childhood. And in the process I hoped I could help myself and my mental health.

On the surface I was calm, controlled, and functioning very well on a daily basis. But I was aware that I was needy, and in a variety of ways. I was insecure about Jake, afraid of losing him, and I craved his nurturing. And sometimes I was assaulted by an irrational panic that something terrible would happen to him and I would be left alone. And on those days I asked myself if I should visit a psychiatrist. But I kept changing my mind about that, strangely ambivalent about taking this step. And on the whole, I did manage to cope, and so I never did go to a doctor for help.

IV

My brother and I had talked about Peter Denning before I left for Paris, and Donald said right from the outset that he had not been a normal father. "No Little League for me, or any of that other stuff!" Donald exclaimed. "Have you forgotten? We didn't do anything together, none of those typical father-son activities. Oh, nosiree. And listen, don't you remember, they even left us to our own devices with Annie when we went on vacation. She used to call them 'the lovebirds' and we'd laugh about them."

"You're right, I had forgotten. But your mother fussed about you, Donald. She was always singing your praises and listing your virtues."

He was quiet for a moment, looking somewhat

abashed, and then he had agreed. "That's true, Val, she did do that," he had answered in a quiet voice.

Donald and I had grown closer during my visit to New York, and he was pleased that Jake and I had taken to his fiancée, Alexis. She was a nice young woman and very pretty, but most important, she was clever and street smart. Jake and I both agreed on that, and we believed that Donald had made a good choice for himself.

Ever since my return to Paris, my brother had stayed in touch with me, and I was beginning to realize this was not merely out of self-interest on his part. In fact, Donald had more than proved that he cared for me. I would never forget how well he had looked after me when I had fled our mother's apartment the day of the row. This rapprochement pleased me, and I was glad we had a normal relationship at long last.

Chapter 28

I

Yorkshire, December · "We get quite a lot of tourists in the summer and autumn, and even in the winter," David Ingham told me as we walked together down a narrow cobbled street, doing some last-minute Christmas shopping together.

"I can well imagine why," I answered, smiling at him. "This is magnificent country. I don't think I've ever seen anywhere like it." As I spoke, I lifted my eyes to the higher moors that rose above the quaint little town of Middleham in a grand and majestic sweep. "I went for a walk with Françoise the previous day and I couldn't get over it . . . the country is so beautiful in its starkness, in its emptiness."

"Aye, by gum, it is, lass!" David responded, and then immediately began to laugh.

"What is it?"

"I can see you eyeing me again, Val, wondering about my accent. But it always happens to me when I get back here. I sort of lapse into Yorkshire talk, as I call it."

I laughed with him and remarked, "But at least I can understand *you*. When Fiona and I were out marketing, I needed a translator in some of the food shops, especially the butcher's. Yorkshire dialect is a bit odd, isn't it?"

He nodded, "Aye, it is, and even those who have been brought up here, like me, can't always make out what some of the dalesmen are saying. And you're correct about the countryside, Coverdale is probably the most beautiful of all the Yorkshire dales. Did you get some nice pictures yesterday?"

"I did, especially of Middleham Low Moor and those steep, bare hills beyond. It's very bleak country indeed, but breathtaking. I also got some great shots of the castle ruins."

"I'm hoping it snows," David said. "You'll be amazed how the moors look then, like a giant white patchwork quilt because of the higgledy-piggledy drystone walls. Their distinct patterns look like seams on a quilt. And the castle ruins are eerily beautiful."

"I can't wait for Jake to get here to see this place. He's going to fall in love with Yorkshire, just as I have, and with Fiona's house." Glancing at David, I squinted in the bright morning sunlight and murmured, "That's a strange name, isn't it . . . *Ure* House?"

"It does sound a bit peculiar, I'll grant you that, although not to the locals. You see, the river Ure runs through here, which is obviously how it got its name in the first place. It was built at the turn of the century, and it's always been called Ure House, and I think Fiona felt a little funny about changing the name. Superstitious, I suspect."

"She's done a fabulous job with the decoration, David."

"Hasn't she just!" he agreed, sounding proud. "And Françoise has really helped to pull the restaurant together. Pig on the Roof has acquired a bit of Continental charm, I must admit, but we all love her touches, Frenchified though they might be."

"So do I. And listen, thanks for all you've done, David. You and Fiona. She's so much calmer than when she stayed with me in Paris."

"She's doing fine, although I have a feeling she gets nervous from time to time about that husband of hers."

"Jake might have some news when he gets here tomorrow. He was planning on calling her parents. He's always been quite close to Simone."

"Not from his office, I hope!" David exclaimed sharply, glancing at me.

"No, from a pay phone. I just hope that Olivier hasn't got a private investigator watching Mike, or me and Jake, for that matter."

"That gets to be very expensive, so I doubt it," David reassured me. "And from what she's told us about him, he sounds like a conceited bugger. He more than likely thinks he can do better than anybody else, when the time is right. I understand he's still caught up in that murder investigation."

"He is, according to the French newspapers."

"Anyway, don't worry about investigators. I doubt there are any on your tail, as I just said, and there's been no one snooping around here. Also, Jake and Mike are coming by private plane to Yeadon, which is the best way, the safest, in my opinion."

"I guess I sort of took a chance," I muttered, frowning to myself. "But at least I didn't fly. Thank God for the train."

"Now, shall we go in here?" David suggested, and explained, "I want to get a couple of extra gifts." As he was speaking, he pushed open the door of a shop that had a collection of carved wooden sheep in the window. "Best place for slippers," he added as he bundled me inside.

He was right about that, I soon realized as I browsed around the shop. It was a boutique really, and it specialized in a variety of items made from sheep's wool. Most of all, I liked the slippers

David had mentioned. Each pair had been hand-made and hand sewn from sheep shearings, the hide turned on the outside, the fluffy white wool on the inside.

I immediately bought a pair for Jake and Mike's two daughters, who were flying in tomorrow with their father and Jake. I knew that Lisa and Joy would love them, and that the Fair Isle sweaters which were on display would also appeal to the girls. After a short discussion with the saleslady, I settled on medium-size sweaters for the two teenagers, who were fourteen and twelve. Not sure of what else I might need at the last moment, I finally took a couple of lovely hand-knitted scarves, two more pairs of slippers, a knitted vest which I suddenly spotted for Jake, and a heavy cream-colored fisherman's knit sweater for Mike. I had brought gifts for Françoise, Fiona, David, and his son Noel from Paris; perfume and silk scarves for the women, Hermès ties for the men, Jake and Mike included.

II

Armed with our shopping bags full of gifts, we walked back to Ure House at a steady pace, chatting in a desultory fashion as we walked.

David, who was full of folklore, local legend,

and genuine history, kept me well entertained as he spoke about Middleham and its historic and illustrious past, when the castle had been the stronghold of that great feudal baron Richard Neville, the Earl of Warwick.

"And what a man he was," David told me. "Handsome, persuasive, rich, charming, brave, and courageous. And powerful. At one moment in his life, and in the history of England, he was the most powerful man in the land. The uncle of Edward IV, who was Edward Plantagenet of the House of York. The prized White Rose of York, a true prince of the blood and one of England's greatest kings. Thanks to Richard Neville, who put him on the throne of England and brought an end to the War of the Roses, and ruled the land, the real power behind the throne.

"And here he lived at Middleham Castle, known in those days as the Windsor of the North, and it was at the castle that he raised Richard of York, who married Neville's daughter, and also became, for a short while, Richard III of England."

"Jake will love all this historical stuff," I exclaimed. "I find it fascinating myself, and Jake will just eat it up. He was a Rhodes scholar and majored in British and European history at Oxford."

"So Fiona told me, I was very impressed indeed," David said. "I shall be eternally grateful to Jake, you know, Val."

"Oh, why?" I asked, raising a brow, glancing at him.

"Because he was very straightforward with Fiona in New York. It did her good, I'll tell you that. We're going to get married in the New Year. I wanted to do it immediately after we got back from New York, but she was a bit reluctant. We even talked about tying the knot at Christmas but changed our minds because we knew we would open Pig on the Roof on December fifteenth. I've taken a couple of weeks off from my job in order to help out, and it's going very smoothly so far. Much to our delight, we've done record business." He came to a halt and stood looking at me.

I also stopped walking and stared back at him. "What is it, David?"

"And what about you and Jake? When are you two going to get married?"

I shook my head. "I don't know. Jake hasn't asked me."

"Such a grand lass like you, he'd better not leave you hanging around too long. Somebody else'll snatch you up."

"That's not likely, David," I answered swiftly, and laughed as we set off walking again.

"What, a gorgeous lass like you! Don't be daft, Val!"

III

Ure House stood a little up the hill from the center of the picturesque little town, nestled in the fold of the lower moors. The higher undulating moorland swept around it like a giant Elizabethan ruff, just touching the edge of the sky, which was a lucid blue this morning and scattered with wispy clouds.

But how easily these northern skies could change, I had discovered after being here for only two days. When the thunderheads blew in from the seacoast of East Yorkshire, the sky turned black as night and looked eerily lit, as if from behind. And the fierce and icy winds brought sleet and rain from the North Sea and a decided change in the temperature.

Ure House was set back from the road on a patch of green grass, with a semicircle of trees growing behind it. The house was surrounded by a low wall made of local gray stone, and a paved stone path cut through a neat front lawn, stopped at the front door.

Beautifully proportioned, the house was built of a different gray stone, which Fiona had explained came from the ruins of Middleham Castle. At least the stones on the front façade of the house. Low and rambling, it had a sloping slate roof, many windows, tall chimneys, and a door made of heavy oak painted white and trimmed with black wrought-iron hinges.

When I first saw it two days before, I had thought at once of my grandfather. He would have loved Ure House because it was ideally suited to the moorland landscape, designed to blend into those bleak, implacable moors, and yet able to stand on its own without being humbled by the breathtaking scenery. The architecture was somewhat similar to the stone houses of the Cotswolds that my grandparents had both loved, as did I.

As we walked up the path together, the door suddenly sprang open and Fiona stood there, smiling at us cheerfully, her fiery halo of red hair brought even more into focus by the emerald-green twinset she was wearing with her tailored gray slacks.

"You two look as if you've bought up the whole town!" she cried, eyeing our packages and then coming forward to help us.

"Val raided the sheep boutique," David told her, grinning.

"And so did you, it seems, my lad," Fiona shot back. "But I'm glad to see you've both been supporting the local industry." She glanced at me and added, "The one thing they've got in Yorkshire is a lot of sheep. Now, you both look as if you could do with a wee drop of something. Soup or a drink, which will it be?" she asked as we trooped into the front entrance hall. It was warm, welcoming with its stone floor, terra-cotta-colored walls, and moss-green-velvet draperies at the windows.

Although I didn't like to drink much at lunchtime, I said, "I wouldn't mind one of those Bloody Marys you make, David. They're so delicious. And you can't even taste the vodka."

He laughed good-naturedly and said, "Am I being accused of stinginess with the vodka, Val? Oh, dear, that's not good."

I began to laugh too, and explained, "No, not at all. I'm not a big vodka drinker, and what I meant was that you put in all those wonderful spices, and I don't notice the taste of the alcohol."

After hanging up my coat and his own, he and I followed Fiona, who had walked on into the living room. This was a long room with four windows that looked out onto the moors, and a huge stone fireplace was built at one end. A highly polished wood floor was covered with a large cream rug patterned with green-and-black scrolls, and this picked up the color of the green-and-black-striped silk draperies at the windows.

The walls had been painted a funny green, which Françoise had informed me was called eau de Nile, literally water of the Nile, and it was created by putting a lot of gray into the pale-green paint. I had discovered that

Françoise was a fount of information about design and decoration and had quickly come to understand how useful she must have been to Fiona with the decor of Pig on the Roof.

The room was comfortable, yet it had elegance without being overly pretentious. Two over-stuffed cream sofas faced each other near the fireplace, and antique tables, brass lamps, and several good paintings completed the setting.

David went out to the small bar that opened off one end of the living room to mix Bloody Marys for us all, and Fiona and I moved toward the fireplace. I sat down in one of the armchairs, and she went and stood with her back to the fireplace.

After a moment she said, "We can have dinner alone tonight, Val, if you like. David's going down to Pig on the Roof to play 'mein host,' and Françoise wants to help Noel in the kitchen, you know how she loves cooking. Anyway, when you got here on Monday you said you needed to talk to me, and tonight is as good a time as any. Before the others arrive tomorrow."

"That's great, Fiona, thanks," I responded, and then I thought to add: "It's nothing to do with Tony, I just want you to know that."

She gave me a funny little smile and murmured, "I think it would be fair to say that we've exhausted the subject of Tony Hampton, don't you agree? Is it Jake you want to be discussing, Val?"

"No, it's not, actually. I wanted to talk to you about my mother, about something that happened between us in New York. I've struggled hard with the problem, tried to understand her, and I've hit a blank wall. I thought if I told you a few things, you might be able to give me some insight. . . . I don't know what makes her tick. You're so wise, Fiona, and understanding, and I'm sure you can help me."

"I'll certainly try, Val. 'Tis my pleasure."

"Oh, there you are, Fiona . . . Val!" Françoise cried from the doorway and came hurrying into the room. She was now fully recovered from the loss of the baby and the spousal abuse, at least physically. I did not know how she was coping with the psychological damage, because she had not talked to me on that level as yet.

But she looked wonderfully fit and healthy, and seemed more relaxed. Her entire demeanor was different than it had been in Paris. There was no question in my mind that this was because she was so far away from the dreaded Olivier, cop with an agenda.

She came across the room, kissed me on both cheeks French-style, and then kissed Fiona, whom she obviously adored. I had spotted that on Monday afternoon when I had arrived from London and walked into this warm and friendly house.

Fiona said, "Did you and Noel get the tree finished, Françoise? I can help this afternoon if you haven't, I am thinking."

"No, no, it is not necessary, Fiona. Noel finished it an hour ago. I helped him. . . ." She began to giggle. "I have never seen a tree like it. Oh, *mon Dieu*!"

"It's full of little pigs, isn't it?" Fiona said.

Françoise nodded. "But what funny pigs!"

"Don't tell us any more, you'll spoil it for us." Fiona glanced around as David came back into the room carrying a tray of drinks. She said to him, "Moira phoned when you were out shopping with Val. She's coming for Christmas after all. She'll take the train to Harrogate with Rory on Thursday morning."

"Is she bringing the boyfriend?" David asked as he placed the tray of drinks on the coffee table.

"No, and seemingly that's the whole problem, David. They've broken up, and so she now has nowhere to go, since they were intending to spend Christmas Day with his parents. I gather she had really wanted to come up here to us, and that's when the rift started. They quarreled about it."

"I'm sorry it blew up," David murmured to Fiona as he handed me a Bloody Mary. "He seemed like such a nice boy. But I must say, I am pleased she's going to be with us. I feel we should

all be together as a family at Christmas." He gave
Françoise a glass of white wine, handed a Bloody
Mary to Fiona, and took the last one for himself.

"Cheers, one and all!" he said.

"Cheers."

"And to our extended family, Françoise, and
Val," Fiona graciously added.

IV

After lunch, which consisted of hot tomato soup
with croutons, quiche Lorraine, green salad,
and Stilton cheese followed by coffee spiced
with cinnamon, I helped Françoise to clear the
table.

As we were carrying the dishes into the spacious kitchen, Françoise said, "Shall we go to the
ruins . . . it is such a nice walk, Val."

I nodded, smiling at her. I had noticed that she
had a funny way of saying my name, as if she still
wanted to call me Mademoiselle Denning.
"That's a terrific idea, and perhaps it'll help to get
some of the calories off, although I doubt that."

"You will have to go on a *régime* after
Christmas. So will I," Françoise added.

Once the dishwasher was stacked, we put on
our heavy coats, wrapped scarves around our
necks, and set out to walk to the ruins of
Middleham Castle, close to the town.

Françoise didn't say much on the way to the castle, and I remained silent myself. I hadn't realized Rory and Moira were coming, since Fiona had never mentioned them before today; and I had not bought presents for them in Paris. It was a good thing I picked up some extra items at the sheep boutique, I thought as I shoved my hands farther into my pockets and increased my pace to keep up with Françoise.

"I miss *Maman* and *Papa,*" Françoise eventually volunteered, staring straight ahead as we walked at a brisk pace down the hill.

"Yes, I know you must. But it is wise to play it cool at the moment, Françoise. They know you are safe and well and being looked after by friends of ours. And that's all they care about. They don't need to know exactly where you are."

"*Oui.*" She sighed and glanced at me out of the corner of her eye. "The day I met you at Les Roches Fleuries I wanted to die. Now I want to live. I hope Olivier doesn't find me. If he does, he will kill me. I know he will."

I did not respond immediately.

Françoise said, "Val, you must believe me . . . that is the truth."

"Yes, I think you're right. But you must trust me when I tell you that Olivier will never find you. How can he? Your parents don't know where you are. You came here on a private plane.

Mike and Jake are coming on a private plane tomorrow. Please, Françoise, try to relax."

"I am trying, but—" She broke off, shook her head. "I worry . . . I worry so much. What if he has an investigator looking?"

"Did Olivier have a lot of money? Spare cash?"

"Non," she said swiftly, shaking her head emphatically. "He had no spare money. Only the money he earned as a flic."

"Believe me, there's no investigator looking for you. Olivier can't afford one. And please, trust me, trust my judgment."

"Oui, oui, I do, Val."

V

As I wandered with Françoise through the roof-less chambers of the once-glorious Middleham Castle, I stared up at its shattered battlements and wondered about those who had lived here long ago. The great magnate Richard Neville, his wife, his daughters, and the young princes of the blood. And I thought of the splendor of old that was gone, lost forever in the dust of time passing. Weeds and tufts of grass pushed up through the broken walls, and birds built their nests in ancient crevices and sheltered corners of the massive ruins.

Centuries ago, great nobles and their ladies,

dressed in rich and elegant clothes, had walked amid these splendorous halls, where banquets and sumptuous entertainments had been held. And here had lived the most powerful in the land . . . here they had worked and played and plotted together. Made love, given birth, quarreled, fought, and made up. And died.

How hard to imagine as I glanced about me. Frost covered the hardened winter ground, bits of gray stone lay all around me, remnants of those walls that had crumbled long ago. It was a stronghold no more, had not been for eons.

Dead, all of them, and buried. Their lives forgotten by most. And what had their lives been all about in the long run? And why did those lives matter now? They didn't, did they? *Ashes to ashes, dust to dust* . . . one day Françoise would be dust, and so would I, and why did her life and mine matter? One day we would be gone and nobody would care. Yet while we lived we fought so hard to have what we thought we should have . . . what mattered to us . . . what we conceived as being ours. . . .

What had they been like, all those who had inhabited this place? So many ghosts here, flitting through the ruined chambers . . .

"Val, Val, is something wrong?"

I stopped in my tracks and turned to her. "No, I'm fine. Why?"

She said quietly, "Are you weeping? There are tears on your face."

I touched my cheeks with my fingers and realized they were wet. She was right, and I was surprised. I shook my head. "I was thinking about the people who had once lived here. All of them dead these hundreds of years, and I was contemplating their lives. All that they suffered, enjoyed, lost and regretted, longed for and attained. And all the things they never had. Lives lived, then snuffed out. Just like that. Gone in a flash. We are here for such a short time. And then we are dead and nobody cares . . . why does *any* of it matter? Why do we bother? Why do we struggle?"

She stared at me thoughtfully, and then after a moment she answered slowly, "I think . . . because we are human."

"Yes," I agreed. "And perhaps we always see . . . *hope*. Hope for ourselves and our lives. Hope for something better."

Chapter 29

I

The night had turned icy cold and it had begun to snow. I stood at the living room window, looking out at the moors, watching the flakes float down, delicate and crystalline in the moonlight. The high-flung sky was like the inside of a bowl turned upside down, jet black, hung with bright stars and a clear silver orb of a full moon.

Fiona had built up the fire and turned the central heating, and now, as she hurried in with the coffee on a tray, she exclaimed, "Thank God we had the foresight to put in a heating system. These old houses are impregnable, built like fortresses, but they can be cold. On a night like this the extra heat is very welcome. Come, Val, have a cup of coffee and let's settle down for our chat."

"It was a lovely dinner, Fiona, thank you," I said as I walked across to join her near the fireplace.

"You're welcome, but it *was* only cottage pie." She laughed and poured our coffee.

I sat down on one sofa and she took a seat on the other, so that we were facing each other. It was warm and cozy in the room, with the fire hissing and crackling in the hearth, and the lights turned low. The soft mood was conducive to intimacy and sharing, not that we were shy with each other after our conversations about Tony in New York in October.

"You don't know anything much about my life," I began, looking across at her. "So let me tell you about those years before I came to live in Paris."

She nodded. "That's a good idea, I'd like a bit of background, Val. I'll be able to understand things much better."

And so trying to be as succinct as possible, endeavoring to avoid embellishments, I told her the story of my childhood growing up in New York. I gave her enough details for her to fully understand how I had been brought up, and told her about those people who had been part of my life: my mother and father, Annie Patterson, Donald, and my grandparents.

When I had finally finished, I sat back, gazing at her intently, waiting for her to say something.

Fiona looked ineffably sorrowful, and her eyes were moist. After a long silence, she said in a low voice, "How tragic, what a sad childhood you had, Val. And how dreadfully sad for your mother, she missed so much, missed all the joy of you, of your early years, when you were a little girl, and then those wonderful teen years." She shook her head. "And how terribly hard for you, heartbreaking really. How you must have suffered."

I exclaimed, "It's a wonder I'm as sane as I am, when you think about it, Fiona! I know my troubled past has done all sorts of things to me, but somehow I've managed to cope and lead a relatively sane life, although I also accept that I am damaged in certain ways . . . psychologically damaged."

"I suppose that's true, but you did have that lovely Scottish nanny. And your grandparents were wonderful to you, and of course you had a little brother to love until your mother stepped in, broke the two of you up, so to speak. 'Tis a shame she did that."

"Yes, it is, and I foolishly blamed Donald for it when it wasn't his fault. And I realize now that I must have been very jealous of him in those days. After all, she was forever favoring him. It was like a knife in my side, although Annie did try to assuage my hurt, dry my tears, make me feel wanted."

"You're lucky to have had her, you know.

Those early months and years are so important in a child's development. The child must know it's loved, feel that love, have that nurturing, that cuddling and caring. Thankfully Annie gave it to you, was there for you, to love you, make you feel safe."

"Yes. And yet I do still crave nurturing, you know. . . ." My voice trailed off, I didn't want to mention Tony or Jake at this point in my story.

I told Fiona everything. I told her about my mother's love affair with Vincent Landau, about her illegitimate daughter, Anjelica, the child whom she gave away, and about Vincent's suicide a week before the day he was to wed the society heiress Marguerite Shiff. Finally I finished: "My mother said she couldn't love me because of her guilt about Anjelica, about giving her away."

Fiona sat there, staring at me, her shock and disbelief written all over her face. Eventually she roused herself, shook her head from side to side, and exclaimed, "I'm appalled! Absolutely *appalled*. What that woman did to you is unconscionable . . . that she could treat her own daughter in such a cruel way, it's just beyond understanding, beyond belief. She has to be bonkers, off the wall."

"Yes, I think she was, is, more than likely mentally ill, disturbed. In New York that day, I told her she was wicked and added she was beyond wicked, that she was evil. And in a way I think she is evil . . . but there's also something else, something very odd about her. She's so very beautiful, Fiona, movie-star beautiful, but, oh, God, is she cold. Icy cold. My grandfather called her the Ice Queen." I let out a long sigh. "When I asked her why my father had followed her lead and behaved toward me in exactly the same way she had, she told me he didn't want children, that he abhorred them. She said he was jealous of me, and of Donald as well, because he didn't want to share *her*. We were a nuisance, totally unwanted as far as he was concerned, so she said anyway. I guess we were in the way. But he was a wimp, and she walked all over him." I paused and looked into the fire for a second or two, and then I said to Fiona with a small frown, "Yet she was able to love Donald, you know. She took him away from me when I was eleven and he was six . . ." I left my sentence unfinished, stared at her helplessly.

"Because he was probably rather cute by then, and he was perhaps a useful accessory for a woman like her, and then again, she knew it would hurt you if she split you up."

"But why would she want to hurt me?"

"I just don't know, Val. I think it would take a psychiatrist years to get to the bottom of your mother's troubled psyche, to find out what motivated her, what made her tick. And what makes her tick today. I will say this though, among other things, I think she's probably rather stupid."

I frowned on hearing this. "But she's not, she's become a very good businesswoman, something of a tycoon, in fact."

Fiona raised an auburn brow and exclaimed, "Really!"

I told Fiona about Lowell's, how it had been started in 1898 by Amy-Anne, and about her rule, commonly known in the family as The Tradition. "So you see, she has to leave it to me. There's no legal document apparently, but that's the family rule. The company's now worth millions, and its value will only increase next year if Lowell's makes a public offering. But I don't want it. I refused my inheritance. I told her to leave it to Donald."

Fiona looked startled momentarily, and then she broke into delighted laughter. "Good for you, Val! But you wouldn't do anything else but that. You have far too much integrity. Anyway, getting back to my remark about your mother being stupid, I really do think she might have been both stupid and a little weak when she was a younger woman. And that has nothing to do with being clever in business."

"Stupid and weak in what sense?"

"Look, she had an illegitimate child, and her mother had allowed her to keep the baby for months. Why not simply adopt the title of Mrs.

and pretend to be a young widow? Your mother wasn't well known, so who would know the difference? She behaved in a very stupid way, and she was weak in her handling of her mother, your grandmother Violet Scott. They could have worked something out between them. Then there's Vincent Landau, what kind of jackass was he? He was just as stupid and weak as your mother, in my opinion. He should have either defied his parents and married her, if he loved Margot so much, and to hell with the consequences. Or he should have married his society fiancée and kept your mother on the side as his mistress, and supported her and Anjelica. Or, if she didn't want that, he could have simply provided for them financially. And why did he commit suicide? None of it really makes sense. I don't understand . . . like you, I'm baffled, Val."

"I've wondered lately . . . if it's all a bunch of lies."

"But why would she lie to you?" Fiona looked at me alertly, her eyes widening.

"I suppose she felt she had to try to explain to me why she couldn't love me, and maybe she thought it would be a much more sympathetic story . . . an innocent young woman forced to give up her illegitimate child, et cetera, et cetera, and becoming guilt ridden thereafter."

"You could have a point, but no, I don't think she lied. There's something about the story that

has the ring of truth. But you know, Val me darlin', you shouldn't be trying to fathom out your
mother, her mental state, her personality disorder, and what was at the root of her behavior
toward you when you were a child. It's basically
of no consequence, because knowing *why* she did
what she did won't change anything. That's all
water under the bridge now. And anyway, knowing won't help you, now, will it?"

"No, I don't suppose it will," I replied.

"You must forget all about your mother and
worry about yourself, Val darlin'. Get yourself
truly well inside, so that you can move forward
the way Jake said you should."

"But how . . . I don't know *how* to do that,
Fiona," I said.

"By forgiving your mother. You must have the
courage and strength to do that, to empty your
heart of your hatred for her, your condemnation
of her. It will be your forgiveness of her that will
set you free."

I didn't speak. I merely gazed at Fiona, digest-
ing her words, trying to heed her wisdom.

Rising, she came over, sat next to me on the
sofa; she put her arms around me, held me close,
as a mother holds a child in distress. "She did terrible things to you in your childhood, Val, but you
must let them go . . . they're simply not worth
holding on to. They're of no value now."

Unexpectedly, I began to cry, the tears spurting

out of my eyes and falling down my cheeks unchecked. I hadn't known I was going to become so emotional, and I tried hard to take hold of my swimming senses. But I didn't do very well, and soon I was sobbing uncontrollably, as though my heart would break.

But slowly the weeping did eventually subside under Fiona's calming influence. Finally I extricated myself from her arms and sat back. I offered her a weak smile. "I'm sorry," I said. "I didn't know the floodgates were going to open like that."

"I know you didn't, but perhaps it's just as well they did. There's nothing like a good cry to make you feel better."

I nodded and groped for a tissue in the pocket of my jacket.

She said, "It's not going to be easy, because you've struggled with the problem of your mother's behavior toward you for your entire life, but now it is time to expunge it. And always remember this, Val, forgiveness, like the truth, *does* set you free. Trust me on that."

II

The moors were covered with a giant quilt of white by the following day. Jake and Mike, along with Mike's two daughters, Lisa and Joy, arrived at Ure House in time for tea on Thursday. It was

Christmas Eve, and there was already a festive feeling in the air. Fiona and Françoise had decorated most of the downstairs rooms with holly, and a large sprig of mistletoe dangled from the brass chandelier in the entrance hall.

The tree stood there at the back of the hall, tall and stately, a dark green fir that awaited its Yuletide decorations. The dressing of the tree was planned for later that evening, and I told Jake about Fiona's plans as the two of us went upstairs to our bedroom.

The moment Jake walked into our room he exclaimed with pleasure, "This is great, Val! And just look at that bed! I've never seen one so inviting."

I laughed and agreed with him. The four-poster dominated the room, was piled high with fresh white linen pillows and a plump duvet in an antique linen cover. "It's very cozy," I pointed out, "I've been sleeping in it for the last couple of nights. And isn't it great to have a fire in the bedroom?"

He nodded, walked across the room, and looked out the mullioned windows that offered a panoramic view of the windswept, snow-covered moors. He shivered slightly. "I bet it's kind of cold up there."

"But beautiful, Jake. You're going to love this place, and it's so full of history. David's been filling me in. It's fascinating."

"So he told you about the Kingmaker, did he?" Jake asked, joining me by the fire, putting an arm around my shoulders.

I frowned. "I'm not sure who you mean? He did tell me about the Earl of Warwick—"

"That's him," Jake said, interrupting me. "He's one of my favorite characters in British history. Quite a guy, he was." Jake tightened his grip on me and added, "I'm glad we're here, Val, and Fiona's wonderful, the way she's planned this old-fashioned family Christmas for all of us."

"She's been very loving to me, Jake," I confided, and then I told him about our heart-to-heart talk of the night before.

Jake listened carefully, as he always did, forever attentive and concerned about my problems. When I'd finished, he asked, "And do you think you *can* forgive your mother, Val?"

"Yes, I do. Because there is nothing else *to do*. Anyway, I believe that everything Fiona said is true. If I can see it in my heart to forgive my mother, then I myself can go forward into the future, putting the past behind me."

III

Christmas Eve at Ure House was only a foretaste of what was to come for the next few days—a typical Yorkshire Christmas.

Fiona and David gathered us all in the big living room later that evening and served eggnog, chilled white wine, and champagne, along with hot sausage rolls and bite-sized cheese tartlets. After our first drink, we all trooped out into the entrance hall and started to dress the tree.

"Everything's silver and gold," Fiona explained, showing us the stacks of boxes in one corner, "so no one can make a mistake. Just hang *something* and anywhere you want."

There was a lot of banter and laughter and everyone enjoyed the traditional activity of hanging the ornaments. And as she said, it was impossible to make an error.

The smells emanating from the kitchen were delicious, and at one moment I breathed in the aroma of chestnut stuffing and goose roasting in the oven, and my mouth began to water. A bit later Noel appeared. David's son was a younger, taller version of his father, and he came out dressed in his white chef's uniform and toque. Waving his wooden spoon, he announced, "Your goose is cooked! Well, almost."

"My goose was cooked the moment I met Fiona," David quipped, and we all laughed.

"Back to the kitchen to finish up," Noel said, and disappeared, but not before he'd admonished us to hurry up with the dressing of the Christmas tree.

I was hanging a silver pear, when I paused to

listen. In the distance I heard the church bells ringing out, and how beautiful they sounded on the still night air.

Fiona explained, "There's a service at the church tonight and it's lovely. But there's also one tomorrow for those who'd like to attend."

Almost immediately after this the carolers were at the front door of Ure House, and the strains of "Silent Night" rang out. This time we all stopped what we were doing and listened, marveling at the beautiful young soprano voices.

Fiona and David went to the front door when the carol was finished and invited the young people in for eggnog and tidbits and a chance to warm up by the fire. And after their little respite from the cold, they sang "The Twelve Days of Christmas" before leaving to wend their way through the neighborhood.

I stood to one side, watching everyone, pleased to see the happiness on their faces. Mike was relaxed, joking with Jake, who couldn't stop smiling tonight. Mike's girls, besotted with Françoise, were laughing and helping her to hang golden cherries and apples on a high branch. Rory was draping tinsel with Fiona, and Moira was talking to them with great animation, and David, like me, was standing on the sidelines, the quiet observer. But I could see from the expression on his face how happy he was, and contented. And his eyes never left Fiona.

I realized as I stood there that I had never had a Christmas like this in my entire life—so family oriented, old-fashioned, and full of love.

IV

The dinner was superb.

It had been chiefly cooked by Noel, since Pig on the Roof was closed for the Christmas holidays. But Fiona, Françoise, and Moira had helped out during the day. I had been shooed away, but at least I'd volunteered to pitch in.

Once the meal was ready, Noel went off to change out of his uniform, and when he came back, he, Rory, and Moira hurried into the kitchen and brought out the first course: smoked salmon, foie gras, and potted shrimps. "Something for everyone's taste," Fiona said, glancing around the dining room table. She had set it herself that afternoon, and the beautiful china, crystal, and silver gleamed on the antique lace cloth. White winter roses arranged in a silver bowl sat in the center of the table between silver candlesticks with white candles. A perfect setting for the dinner.

After the salmon from Scotland, the potted shrimps from Morecambe Bay, and the French pâté de foie gras, the roast goose was served with its chestnut stuffing, roast potatoes, steamed vegetables, gravy, and applesauce.

We all kept telling Noel how delicious it was, and he just beamed and beamed, looking pleased. It was true, and he was a great chef—as well as a pleasant young man with an easygoing, carefree manner; he was interested in everyone.

Halfway through dinner, David startled me when he looked across at me, Mike, and Jake and remarked, "I hope you'll find time to go into Leeds in the next few days to look at the wonderful new art at the museum there."

Mike asked, "The paintings are that good, are they?"

David nodded. "Absolutely, and if you do wish to go, I'll drive you into the city. It's about an hour and a half from here. You'll get a wonderful surprise when you see what's hanging there."

"Who's the artist?" Jake asked.

"A local lad, a kid from Leeds who is immensely talented. Well, he's no kid anymore. He's a man. But he originally hails from Leeds, and his name's Bill Smith. But the rest of the world knows him as Alexander St. Just Stevens."

"He's from Leeds?" I said, staring at David, and then Mike and I exchanged glances.

Mike said, "I didn't know that, David. Is it common knowledge?"

David shrugged. "I'm not sure, to tell you the truth. We all know in Yorkshire, of course, because he's from these parts and something of a character. He was born in a poor neighborhood

of Leeds, studied at Leeds College of Art before
going to London, where he was a student at the
Royal College of Art. It was around that time
that he changed his name, adopted a posh,
upper-class accent, and became a bit of a fancy,
rather eccentric dresser. Reinvented himself
when he was a student, and never looked back
from that moment on. But he's a genius, no two
ways about it, and the paintings he has given to
his hometown are mind-boggling. He's been
extremely generous to the city where he was
born. And everyone appreciates him and his
art."

"We'll be gobsmacked, will we?" I asked.

"You certainly will, as will I, Val, yet again. His
paintings have that effect on everyone," David
responded.

Mike said slowly, "It's an odd coincidence,
David, but I wanted Val to go and see him when
he was in New York. Unfortunately, he'd left,
gone back to his place in Mexico before she could
visit his loft. I have several magazines wanting
photographs of his new series, which he's painting for the Millennium Art Show to be held in
Paris in 2000."

Looking from Mike to me with great interest,
David said, "Then you should see the paintings in
Leeds, Mike, and you too, Val, if you're going to
be photographing the new series."

"I'm not sure that I am," I said, frowning at

Mike, and then I added, "But Alexander St. Just Stevens does sound like an intriguing character."

"Oh, he is," Moira volunteered. "Very colorful, isn't he, Mum?"

Fiona nodded. "Let's try to go to Leeds together," she suggested.

We agreed we'd like to make the trip to Leeds if we could, and Alexander St. Just Stevens became the topic of conversation for the rest of the meal.

V

"What a lovely evening," I said later to Jake as we headed upstairs and went into our bedroom.

"Yes, it was, and especially because we were together, Val." Pulling me into his arms, he kissed me on the cheek and then reached into his pocket. Slowly turning me around so that my back was to him, he hung a string of pearls around my neck and said, "Merry Christmas, honey."

I looked at him in surprise, touched the pearls, and ran to the mirror to look at them. Swinging to face him, I exclaimed, "Jake, they're beautiful! And you shouldn't have. But thank you, I love them."

He grinned at me. "They're not the best, not South Sea pearls, but they are good ones."

"As if I care about that! They're gorgeous," I responded, and went to hug him. "Your gifts are downstairs in that pile near the tree," I explained. "Shall I creep down and get them?"

"They can wait until morning." He laughed.

I nodded, then touched the pearls again and turned once more to regard myself in the mirror. As I admired them, I promised, "I'll wear them always, Jake."

"Not on the front lines, I hope."

"I'm not going to be on the front lines, and neither are you," I replied. I did not realize I was tempting fate again.

Chapter 30

I

Paris, March 1999 ⋄ We went back to Paris after the New Year's celebrations, but Jake waited for over two months before dropping his bombshell.

One afternoon, at the beginning of March, I was minding my own business, feeling happy and contented as I worked at home, sorting through a batch of Polaroids of paintings by Alexander St. Just Stevens. Mike was still on my back about the British artist, urging me to go to Mexico to do the shoot. As I sat there, studying the shots, I wondered how to talk Jake into coming with me, *if* I did accept the assignment, when suddenly he was standing there.

He must have entered the apartment quietly,

because I didn't hear him come in, and then there he was, as large as life, leaning nonchalantly against the doorjamb.

"Hi!" I exclaimed, grinning at him. "I was just thinking about you."

"And what were you thinking?" he asked with a faint smile.

I took a deep breath and decided to plunge. "Mike's still after me to do the shoot in Mexico, you know, of the paintings by St. Just Stevens, and I was wondering how to talk you into coming with me. *If* I accept the job."

"Do you want to do it, Val?" he asked, scrutinizing me intently and shifting slightly against the doorframe.

"To be honest, I'm not sure. It could be interesting, certainly the art is just . . . *mind-boggling,* as David said, and as we saw for ourselves in Leeds. But I don't know, it's such a long trek to Mexico."

"But nice weather at this time of year."

"True. Anyway, what are you doing home so early? I thought you had an important meeting at the agency with Jacques Foucher and the guy from *Vanity Fair*."

"Yeah, I did, and we had the meeting."

"Did it go well?"

He nodded, then walked into the dining room, which served as my office, and came to a stop just before he reached my desk.

I stared at him, a brow lifting quizzically. "What is it?"

"Val, there's something I want to talk to you about."

"What? Why do you look so serious all of a sudden?"

There was an almost imperceptible hesitation on his part before he said, "I'm thinking of going back to Kosovo."

For a split second I thought I'd misheard. But I knew I hadn't really. I was so stunned, I couldn't speak for a second, and I just sat there, gaping at him like a fool. When I could finally speak, I said in a faltering voice, "But you promised you wouldn't go back there."

"I didn't actually *promise,* Val, I merely said I *thought* I wouldn't go back to Kosovo."

"Jake, it's me you're talking to, and you're splitting hairs!"

"No, I'm not. I said I didn't *want* to go back, that I *thought* I wouldn't, but I never made you a promise."

"And now you're saying you do want to go, is that it?"

"Yes. Because I have to, Val."

"No, you don't, there's no earthly reason why you should go back to that lousy war." My voice rose slightly as I added a bit shrilly, "You'll get killed."

"I won't. I'm not like Tony Hampton, I don't take risks."

"No, I guess you think you're like Robert Capa, who didn't take risks either according to you, and made sound judgments before he rushed into the fray. But even so, Capa got himself killed in Indochina by stepping on a land mine. So much for sound judgments."

"I must go Val, really, it's important to me that I do—"

"Why?" I cut in peremptorily, and in a harsh voice.

"Because I'm a Jew, that's why. I can no longer ignore what's happening in Kosovo, what Slobodan Milosevic's up to, in all good conscience, I can't. I have to go and take photographs of the atrocities . . . of the killing and murder, torture and mayhem that's occurring there right now. This war is escalating, and before you can blink, NATO will intercede, they have to, because Milosevic is perpetrating genocide."

I couldn't move or speak for a moment, and I knew then that whatever I said I had probably already lost the battle to stop him going. I finally managed to say in a low voice, "But, Jake, genocide has been committed in other countries in the world. And you didn't—"

"This is different. This is happening in Europe, and I'm of European stock, and I feel compelled, impelled to go. I was born of German

Jews, and this is a repetition of what happened in Nazi Germany in the thirties, and I just can't stand by and let it happen without lifting a finger. I should say, lifting a camera."

"I bet if you talked to your mother, she'd tell you not to go."

"I'm not a little boy needing his mother's permission," he said in a suddenly snappish tone. "And no, she wouldn't tell me not to go, she'd tell me, yes, Jake, go, get over there and take the pictures. Prove that this monstrous man is a criminal, that he should be brought to trial as a criminal."

"I didn't mean you needed permission," I said weakly. "You misunderstood me."

"Listen to me," he said, leaning forward slightly, resting his hands on the edge of my desk. "My grandmother Granmutti Hedy and my grandfather Erich Neuberg fled Nazi Germany in 1937 because they knew only too well what was going to happen to them if they stayed. My mother's parents Ernst and Anna Mayer were just as smart and left Germany in 1935, also fleeing racial persecution. Hitler was already on the rampage. And frankly, Milosevic is of the same ilk. He is waging an ethnic war against the Kosovar people, and it is a criminal war."

"Oh, Jake, I understand what this means to you!" I said. "Intellectually, I do. Truly, I do. But emotionally, I don't want you to go, I'm so afraid you'll be . . . *hurt.*"

"It's just seeping through to the world that Milosevic is prepared to act like Hitler, and Stalin . . . he's going to fight a war against a *whole people*. Jesus, Val, he's already doing it!"

"I realize it's about ethnic cleansing, and that it's wrong—" My voice wavered, came to a stop, because I saw the look on his face. His expression was stubborn; his blue eyes blazed with passionate intensity.

Jake said, "I can't help but think the Nazi era is being repeated in Kosovo. That this terrible, primitive kind of fascism is making a comeback, and I don't believe the world can accept that. I just have to stand up against genocide, Val. *I do!* Almost all of my grandparents' relatives were murdered in the Holocaust, and on both sides, Neubergs and Mayers, and Steiners in Munich, on Granmutti Hedy's side."

"Please don't go to Kosovo," I whispered, leaning back against the chair. I felt sick inside and I was terrified, because I suddenly had a terrible premonition that something unspeakable was going to happen to him. I loved him so much and I had to try to stop him from going, and I had to do it now, before it was too late. "I'm begging you not to go, Jake. For my sake, for our sake. For our future's sake."

"Oh, Val darling," he said quietly, "you know

I have to do this. I couldn't live with myself if I ignored my conscience. You've seen the newspapers every day, watched television . . . it's growing by the minute. And you'll see, by the end of March, before this month is out, NATO will have to go in and bomb. We have to intervene. And I want to be there, Val, taking the pictures that might help to change somebody's perception of this war. That's one of the reasons I became a war photographer, I wanted to make people really *see* violence and terror and wholesale slaughter. It's a sea of sorrow and blood over there."

"If you go, it's over between us," I threatened, using the only weapon I had left.

He ignored what I said. "Come with me, Val."

"No, I just can't, Jake, I'm totally burnt out. I can't go. I don't belong there on the front lines anymore."

Nodding his understanding, he walked around the desk, bent over me, and kissed me, hugged me tightly. I choked up, yet somehow managed to push back the tears. But my voice wavered as I said, "Oh, Jake, please, please stay . . ."

Releasing me, he looked down into my face and gave me a small boyish smile. "I'm going to be fine, Val. Really I am, you must trust me."

II

And so he left.

He flew out three nights later to Belgrade.

I was all alone in the apartment, suddenly lost and helpless without him, after seven months of emotional and physical closeness and involvement.

I kept shaking my head, wondering to myself how this had happened. It had all been so sudden, so fast; he had told me what he was going to do, and then he had gone. Toting his cameras and his big bag, in which he had packed his combat boots and flak jacket.

He had gone back to Kosovo, where Tony Hampton had been killed and where my life had changed forever, and because of this I was superstitious. I knew that this place did not bode well for me, and I knew he would be killed. And it was something I could not bear to contemplate.

There *was* one thing in his favor. I knew he was not rash or foolhardy, as Tony had been, and I hoped and prayed that he would use his good judgment and wisdom once he was in harm's way.

Yes, I wished him well, because I loved him with all my heart. But deep within myself, at my core, I was hurt, because he had chosen his cause over me. And that was hard for me to accept.

III

It was Mike who convinced me to take the assignment in Mexico. Although I was at first reluctant, I finally decided my boss had a good point. I would be far away, busy working, and so less inclined to sit and worry about Jake. Of course I *would* worry, I knew that only too well. But he was right, inasmuch as Acapulco was at the other side of the world. CNN was broadcast there too, but I didn't have to turn it on.

The project was quite complex, and since we had finally received Alexander St. Just Stevens's permission to fly to his compound, fairly elaborate arrangements had to be made. "You'll need a couple of assistants," Mike had said a few days before, and had suggested two of the junior photographers at Gemstar in New York. They were nice kids and competent, but I turned them down.

"I'd like to take my brother Donald and his fiancée, Alexis Rayne," I said to Mike, explaining, "She's an excellent journalist and so is Donald. I need somebody to make notes, keep a written record for me, and in general act like journalists who would be writing the story. Also, they can both help me set up the lighting, assist with that kind of thing. And they wouldn't be all that expensive," I'd thought to add.

Mike had agreed, I suppose because he realized how much I was hurting about Jake and he wanted to make me feel better. He was also aware I'd patched up my rift with Donald, and I knew he was in the mood to encourage family affection these days.

In the first few days that Jake had been gone I had cried myself to sleep at night, but eventually I had managed to pull myself together. I had to be grown-up about the situation, act like the mature woman I believed myself to be. I was thirty-one years old and responsible for myself, and I had to earn a living. I had bills to pay, commitments to meet, and floating around like some mad Ophelia wasn't going to get me anywhere. It would get me nothing, nada, zilch.

And so I packed suitable clothes for working in a hot climate, a few outfits for relaxation time, and all of my best cameras. I also loaded up on film, enough to last me for the two weeks I would be taking photographs of the art by the eccentric Alexander St. Just Stevens. It was quite a story really, an amazing success story about talent and genius propelling a poor boy, born in the slums of Leeds, to great heights. Fame and fortune. Success and wealth. The public would eat it up, Mike was right about that. They loved anything stamped money, success, power.

Janine had been working today, and she had helped me to get my packing finished and put everything in order in the apartment. She had promised she would come in several times a week, as she usually did, to keep the place as immaculate as always until my return.

I wasn't very hungry that night, but since she'd made me a veal stew with vegetables, I decided to eat a little of it while watching television. I sighed to myself as I reheated the stew. I knew that as long as I was in Europe I would be tuning in, looking for the war coverage from Kosovo.

I stood, stirring the pot, my thoughts miles away with Jake. He was somewhere in Kosovo, probably Priština, which is where Jacques Foucher said he had gone. When the phone on the wall began to ring loudly, I jumped out of my skin, startled.

Hoping it was Jake, I grabbed it. "Hello?"

"*Il est mort, il est mort,*" a strangely hoarse woman's voice whispered down the wire. I did not recognize the voice.

My heart missed a beat, and I clenched the phone tightly, swallowing hard. "Who is dead?" I demanded. "Who is this? Who's speaking?"

"*Il est mort,* Mademoiselle Denning. Olivier Bregone is dead!"

"Oh, my God, it's you, Simone!" I shrieked, filling with relief. "I thought it was somebody calling me from Kosovo to tell me Monsieur Jake was dead."

"I am sorry, Mademoiselle, if I gave you the fright."

"You certainly did! Now, please start again. Is it really true? Is Olivier really dead?"

"*Ah, oui, Mademoiselle, oui.* I do not wish anybody dead . . . but I am relieved he cannot any longer make the life of my Françoise difficult. She is free."

"But how do you know this?" I asked swiftly, the journalist in me taking over. Rumors, suppositions, they did not work for me.

"It was on the television. Tonight. He was shot to death by one of the criminals in Marseilles. One of the drug lords," Simone explained in her excellent but stilted English.

"Honestly, Simone, it's a relief that he can't bother Françoise anymore."

"*Oui. Mademoiselle*, please make the phone call for me to Françoise. I want her to know. Better, give me her number so I can speak to her wherever she is."

"Simone, I'll call her and ask her to get in touch with you. I think that's best."

She chuckled over the phone and said, "Ah, you do not trust me, Miss Denning. You are perhaps not sure I am I."

"Oh, I am, Simone, honestly, I am sure it's you. I recognize your voice." This was the truth, I did, but I also wanted to be absolutely certain Olivier was really dead before I handed out phone numbers that might fall into the wrong hands.

"Very well, I wait to hear from my daughter. Her father and I are here at Les Roches Fleuries."

After she had hung up I called Mike at home. Joy answered and immediately passed the phone to her father when I said it was urgent.

"What's up, what's wrong, Val?" Mike asked as he came on immediately. "Is there a problem?"

"I just had a phone call from Simone. She says Olivier Bregone is dead, that he was killed in Marseilles, shot to death by one of the drug lords down there."

"Jesus Christ!" Mike exclaimed. "How does she know?"

"She saw it on television. Can you check it out? Let's be positive it's true before we tell Françoise."

But he didn't get right back to me. In fact, Mike didn't call me for over an hour, and then, when he did, he was not entirely sure that Olivier Bregone was dead.

"Listen, Val, I talked to a contact of mine at Interpol who knows everyone there is to know in the police and justice systems throughout France, and he's made a couple of phone calls for me. Now he's waiting for his contacts to get back to him. But his first reaction was that it's more than likely true. He said he was sure the television network wouldn't run a phony story, which is what you're getting at, isn't it?"

"Yes, it is."

"Okay, we won't call Françoise in Middleham

for the moment. Let's hang in there, play it cool, Val, and as soon as my guy gets back to me, I'll call you pronto."

We said our good-byes, and I went back to the kitchen, where I washed the pan, the plate, and the cutlery, and made myself a cup of tea. I then sat down in front of the television and made myself miserable watching CNN, which had a great deal of coverage on the war in Kosovo. And I worried about Jake.

It was almost ten-thirty when Mike did finally phone me again, and he was triumphant. "Absolutely true, he's dead all right, Val. Shot to death by one of the crooks, just as Simone told you. The Marseilles homicide department confirmed it to my guy from Interpol. Shall I tell Françoise?"

"Oh, Mike, yes, you make the call. It's better coming from you," I exclaimed, hearing the relief mingled with eagerness in his voice. "Tell her to call her mother, please, Mike, and let her know I'll phone tomorrow before I fly off to Mexico."

"I will. Thanks for everything. And, Val?"

"Yes, Mike?"

"Please try not to worry about Jake. He's going to be all right, he'll make it."

IV

Acapulco ⋅ The Hacienda Rosita had to be seen to be believed. It was undoubtedly the most beautiful property in the area, a compound composed of a series of villas, guest cottages, a huge studio where Alexander St. Just Stevens painted, a building where kitchens were housed, and a house where the domestic help lived.

All of the buildings were of white stucco, very Spanish in feeling, and beautifully designed and built. Inside the main villa, where the artist lived, the floors were of white marble, as were some of the walls; the rooms were filled with distinctive antique pieces of Mexican origin, many of his own paintings, and eye-catching accessories and lamps.

These buildings were perched high on a cliff, just outside the town, and the view from any part of the grounds was spectacular. Far below, the brilliant azure sea glittered, and the gardens were filled with a riotous profusion of flowers, plants, flowering shrubs, and trees.

The entire compound was surrounded by a very high wall, guarded at the main gate and the back service gate by armed guards.

I have to admit that I was startled when I first saw the gun-toting guards when we drove into the property the day I arrived, over a week ago now. I had been picked up at the airport in Acapulco by

Len Wilkinson, the painter's personal assistant, and it was the genial and courteous Len who had explained: "The guards are necessary, Val, because there's so much of value here, quite aside from Alexander's paintings. So why make the place a temptation to thieves? The guards keep the unwanted at bay, believe me, they do."

I had taken to Len at once. He was from Leeds, and as he had volunteered himself, "I'm part of the Yorkshire Mafia that surrounds our hero." He'd had a twinkle in his eye when he'd used the word *hero,* and I knew at once we would get along, that there was no pomposity or pretension in him.

Donald and Alexis had arrived two days before I did, and they had brought with them the lights and other equipment I needed for the shoot. As it turned out, nothing I'd requested had been superfluous, and I soon realized the two of them worked well together. I remembered how much I liked Donald's fiancée; she was charming, willing, energetic, and sure of herself, the kind of young woman who was reliable, and who was going places. She was also pretty and stylish, and obviously well brought up.

On the afternoon I arrived, Len Wilkinson had taken me straight to the large sun-filled villa I was sharing with Donald and Alexis. "See you later for dinner. At nine o'clock," Len had said before disappearing through the front door.

Donald had greeted me warmly, obviously

pleased to see me, and Alexis had immediately volunteered to help me unpack. I was grateful that she had, since I'd traveled from Paris to New York by Concorde, spent the night in the Beekman Place apartment, and then flown out to Acapulco on Mexicana Airlines that morning. I was used to travel, but I felt bushed the first day I arrived; all I had wanted to do was lie down and go to sleep.

"How on earth will I stay awake until dinner at nine?" I asked Donald, who had laughed and said, "Have a nap once you've unpacked and we'll get you up later."

"If you say so," I agreed, and set about emptying the big bag I'd brought, while Alexis put my clothes on hangers.

Once this had been accomplished and everything had been hung up, Donald, Alexis, and I went out and sat in the garden for a while, drinking iced tea.

They couldn't wait to fill me in, and I had listened in amazement as Donald had explained the setup at Hacienda Rosita.

"It's quite a place," Donald had confided, "and you're going to like Alexander, he's kind of neat, very eccentric though, and a flashy dresser."

"But he's very handsome," Alexis had volunteered.

"And a womanizer," Donald had added, winking at me.

I had nodded. "Yes, I do know a few things

about him. I did a bit of research before I left Paris. He's had several wives, several mistresses, and there are innumerable children."

"And they all live here," Donald had told me with a huge grin.

"The first wife can't possibly live here, Donald," I had answered, laughing. "She died long ago."

"True, but you know what I mean. They're all here. But there's no one special that I know of at the moment. They're all exes. You know, ex-wives, ex-mistresses. Better watch out, Valentine, he's got an eye for a pretty face."

"You don't have to worry about protecting me, brother mine," I had retorted. "Just keep an eye on Alexis."

"Oh, he's not interested in her," Donald had muttered, and had broken into amused laughter again. "He's looked her up and down already, and turned away."

"Well, thanks a lot for those few kind words," Alexis had exclaimed, and punched my brother on his arm.

V

That discussion was now a week old. I had quickly settled in at the Hacienda Rosita, and so much so, I wondered if I could ever bear to leave.

It was the most beautiful spot and so calm and tranquil. The weather was temperate, warm and balmy during the day, cooler in the evenings. The sky was always blue, the sun was always shining, and I felt rejuvenated there.

I knew everyone now. The Yorkshire Mafia was made up of several old friends of Alexander's from his student days, and that was one of the things I liked about the artist. He seemed to have a strong streak of loyalty in him. Len Wilkinson was the *capo di tutti capi*, as Alexander liked to call him jokingly, using Sicilian Mafia parlance. And Len was indeed the boss of all bosses, in charge of everything to do with the painter's business transactions, his art exhibitions, and the sale of his paintings.

Len was of medium height, fresh-faced and silver-haired, an attractive man with an attractive wife. Jennifer Wilkinson was also an old friend from the painter's earliest days in Leeds; then there were two former fellow students who hadn't made it themselves in the world of art, and who helped Alexander move canvases, prepare them, frame the giant-sized paintings in plain wood, mix paints, and assist him any way they could. They all enjoyed working with Alexander, and it was easy to understand why. He was kind, respectful of them, and always courteous.

For all his eccentricity, flamboyance, and womanizing, he was at heart a good man, dedicated to his work, a devoted father, and nurturing of the women who had once occupied a place of importance in his life.

As for the art, it was extraordinary. The new series of paintings was overwhelming. Each one had strength, energy, power, and brilliant color. They really were mesmerizing, and took my breath away. They would take the art world by storm, of that I was absolutely certain.

For a whole week I had been photographing these marvelous paintings, which I considered to be masterpieces and in a class of their own. They were huge, dominating, and dramatic, and I knew my photographs would do them justice.

But today I was going to start taking pictures of Alexander St. Just Stevens . . . at work in his studio, in his white marble villa with his small children, and out in the grounds of the compound with his friends from Yorkshire. All of these settings could not be covered in one day, as I had explained to him, and he had agreed to spend the next few days with me, posing for the camera.

VI

I brushed my hair back in a ponytail, tied a piece of ribbon around it, slipped on a pale blue T-shirt, then stepped into a pair of white cotton shorts. I decided to wear a pair of comfortable tennis shoes, old but clean, since I would be scrambling around all over the place, and on my feet all day.

"I'm leaving, Donald," I called to my brother, who was still in his room.

The door flew open and he exclaimed, "Oh, that's right, you're having breakfast with the maestro this morning. Be careful, Val, he's devouring you with his eyes more than ever. This guy definitely has the hots for you."

"I'm sure he doesn't," I said evenly, aware that Donald enjoyed teasing me.

"But he does, Val," Alexis remarked, coming out of the room.

I frowned. "Honestly, you two, you've got sex on the brain."

"No, he does," Donald said. "His eyes are lascivious."

I burst out laughing, "Donald, what an expression! You *must* use that in your column."

"Do you think so? I will for sure."

Alexis then said to Donald, "Let's have breakfast now, and afterward we can go and meet Val at ten, as she said we should last night. Is that still all right, Val?"

I nodded. "That's about right. Alexander invited me to the studio for coffee, not the villa, so meet me over there at ten."

"Okay." Alexis bit her lip, hesitated slightly

before saying, "Look, are you going to photograph any of his women or not?"

"I'm not sure he'll sit still for it. Why?"

"I just think it adds a bit of . . . color, spice, if you like, to the story."

"But this is about the art, *great art,* as a matter of fact and about the painter. It's not about his love life, his women, and his four kids."

"Six altogether," Donald interjected. "Two are away at college."

"Thanks a lot, Donald, for reminding me, but I hadn't forgotten, honey."

"I just thought he might like to be photographed with his . . . extended family. It sort of makes him more . . . *human,*" Alexis said.

"You have a point," I answered. "I'll think about it and decide later."

Picking up my cameras, I added, "Don't forget to bring all the equipment, Donald. Even though that studio is so well lighted, I want to create the same feeling we had the other day."

Donald nodded. "No problem, sis."

I smiled at him. "Thanks, Donald."

My brother began to laugh.

"What's wrong?"

"I've been calling you sis all week, and you haven't screamed at me once."

"It doesn't bother me anymore," I said, meaning every word.

Chapter 31

I

I thought of Jake as I walked through the garden of the guest villa, heading in the direction of Alexander's studio. He was never far from my mind, and I fretted about him, worried about his safety. Often I turned on the television at night for news of the war in Kosovo but switched off almost immediately. Chaos and mayhem reigned over there.

Mike, good friend that he was, stayed in daily contact with Jacques Foucher at Jake's photo agency and sent me updates by fax. For the moment Jake was alive and covering the war from Priština. And so I held my breath, got on with my work at the villa, and prayed for his safety.

I had liked the subject of my photo shoot right from the beginning. At forty-five, Alexander St. Just Stevens was considered to be the world's greatest living artist, often called the Picasso of the Millennium. But to me his paintings were much more exciting, had more visual impact, and they were full of life and vibrant color.

Alexander was an extremely good-looking man with a strong, well-defined face. His dark hair was tinged with white prematurely, and the silver wings at his temples seemed to make his green eyes all that more piercing as they gazed out at the world from beneath thick black brows. Tall, well built with a wonderful physique, he was tanned and fit, and something of an athlete, enjoying tennis, swimming, and deep sea fishing.

I knew full well he was a womanizer. I hadn't needed my brother to inform me of that. His passion for women, and his many involvements with them over the years, was well documented in the newspaper and magazine articles I'd read for my research before coming here. And in a sense his passion for the female sex reflected somewhat his passion for his art, his work.

Len Wilkinson had told me that Alexander often painted for days on end without cease. And I had noticed myself that the artist had an unusual energy and strength, visible in everything he did.

Although I had pooh-poohed the idea that Alexander was eyeing me speculatively, Donald had, in fact, been accurate. My brother didn't miss a trick. His lively, observant eyes were everywhere, and since he was working alongside me on a daily basis, he saw everything.

But I deemed it wiser to claim ignorance, pretend I was unaware of Alexander's interest in me, and so keep a lid on the situation. But it did worry me at times, because I knew he was more than merely attracted to me. I felt he was actually becoming involved with me, even though I had not encouraged this.

On the other hand, in the past nine days we had spent an enormous amount of time together, in the same environment, working, eating, and relaxing. We had come to know each other extremely well, without there being any sexual intimacy, of course. And we had discovered we were compatible, understood each other, and enjoyed being in each other's company.

There had been a lot of socializing in our free time. Alexander had invited us all to dinner at the villa every night; we also had lunch together during the photography sessions. But even though two ex-wives and two ex-mistresses lived within the compound in their own villas, they had not been included in these social occasions. Len and his wife, Jennifer, were always present, as were Neal Lomax and Kevin Giles, Alexander's devoted assistants who worked with him in the studio. Marcia Dermot, Alexander's secretary, was often there as well, but not always, since she had a three-year-old daughter.

Alexander lived alone at the main house, the white marble villa. It was there that he did his lavish entertaining, although I knew he often worked in the studio long after we had all gone to bed. He was obsessed with his art; it was his life, he told me.

It was Jennifer Wilkinson who had explained that there was no one special in Alexander's life at the moment. However, this had been an offhand remark, not pointed in any way. And I had merely nodded, made no comment whatsoever.

When I arrived at the studio, I paused for a moment and looked up at it. Poised as it was close to the edge of the cliff but within the encircling outside wall, it looked grand and imposing in the early morning sunlight.

Walking on, I pushed open the heavy oak door and went inside, and, as I usually did, I remained standing in the doorway, admiring this extraordinary interior.

The studio itself was one vast room with a wall of glass that soared to the ceiling and overlooked the sea. This glass wall moved up onto the ceiling to form a wide skylight, which cut through the roof at one end to allow more light to enter the space.

At another end, a raised platform, a kind of stage, was used to display the finished paintings, some of which were huge. Behind this stage there was a fully equipped kitchen, a bathroom, and a bedroom where Alexander frequently slept when he was working at night.

A second platform was built at the opposite side of the studio. Here light flooded in through the skylight as well as the wall of glass; Alexander painted both day and night on this platform, and overhead ceiling spots flooded the area with artificial light after dark.

I hesitated in the doorway. There was no sign of Alexander, and the studio was quiet. "Hello! Hello!" I called and walked into the room, glancing around.

"Is that you, Val?" Alexander's voice boomed out, and he suddenly appeared from behind the stage. His face was covered in shaving soap and he was holding a razor. Bare-chested, he wore a pair of white cotton slacks badly smeared with paint, and tennis shoes that were equally as messy.

"Who else but little old me," I said, laughing. "Good morning, Alexander, I hope I'm not too early."

He glanced at his watch and shook his head. "No. Anyway, *you* could never be too early for me. Give me a minute and I'll be right with you. They've already brought breakfast over from the kitchens."

"I'll wait for you on the terrace," I said as he disappeared.

I went outside; the terrace was on the far side of the studio, quiet, secluded, and hidden from the rest of the buildings in the compound. It overlooked the sea, and there was a table with a sun umbrella attached, as well as four chairs. I sat down at the table to wait, and within a couple of minutes Alexander came out carrying a large wooden tray. He was now properly dressed in white cotton slacks, pristine tennis shoes, and a white Mexican shirt.

II

"I've been working," he said, putting the tray down on the table.

"All night?" I asked, looking up at him.

He shook his head. "No, since dawn. I wanted to finish something—something special, I think. I'll show it to you later."

He served the coffee and motioned to the basket filled with thick slices of home-baked bread and pound cake, and slices of toast.

I shook my head. "I'm not hungry," I murmured, and sipped my coffee.

Alexander also drank his coffee, then buttered a piece of toast and munched on it. And we sat together in a compatible silence for a short while.

Finally I said, "Would it be all right if we started shooting in the studio this morning? I mean, could I do the first shots of you with the finished paintings?"

"Yes, if you wish, Val." His green eyes rested on me for a moment before he said, "I'd like to keep the pictures of me to a minimum, Val, if that's all right with you?"

I nodded. "Okay, but I would like to get a couple of shots of you painting, as well as standing next to the ones you've completed. And also—" I stopped, hesitating, suddenly wary of continuing.

"You're not going to ask me to pose with my former wives and mistresses, are you?"

I was silent.

"I know my ex-wives are somewhat reluctant to be photographed, and certainly Danielle and Carole are extremely shy. They too prefer *not* to be featured in the story."

"Well," I began, and stopped.

"Well, what?" he asked softly.

"I guess I can understand that, but—" I paused

again and stared at him. "I guess I thought it would add a human touch to the story."

He smiled at me, and very knowingly so. "Listen, Val, I've led, still lead, a somewhat unconventional life. Many people think I'm crazy to have everyone living here at the compound, but it's none of their business, and I consider it best for the ladies and my small children. They are all safe, protected, well looked after, and taken care of all the time. They can come to no harm here. But I am not too certain about advertising my lifestyle to the world."

"I realize that, Alexander, but I thought that perhaps a photo of you with the children?" I raised a brow.

He shook his head. "Oh, no, I don't think so. The world is full of crazies, you know that, and I don't want to expose my children to the possibility of kidnapping."

"But they live here with you in this highly protected compound."

"True." He sighed, gave me a long, penetrating look, and finished, "Let me think about it."

A silence fell between us and I did not want to break it. I needed a moment to collect my thoughts and rethink some of the photographs I'd planned on taking. I glanced away, stared up at the sky. And then I stretched slightly, turned my face to the sun, and closed my eyes for a few minutes.

At last I sat up straighter in the chair and turned to Alexander. "I'm sorry if I've asked too much, but the photographs are so important, and the feature is going to be appearing worldwide."

"Oh, I know, and I want you to do the pictures, Val, but I prefer to keep my private life out of this shoot."

"I understand," I responded, realizing I was not going to win this one, and I didn't want to antagonize him by pressing further.

Alexander suddenly said, "I've enjoyed having you here. You like Hacienda Rosita, don't you?"

"I certainly do!" I exclaimed, my enthusiasm apparent. "It's beautiful, peaceful . . . a paradise. And there aren't many of those left in this world."

"Why don't you stay on a bit longer?"

"I wish I could, but I've got to leave at the end of the week. Got to get the pictures back to Paris."

"If that's the only reason you have to go, I can easily send Neal. He'd love a trip to Paris."

I stared at him speechlessly.

He said, "I like you, Val. When I first set eyes on you, I knew you'd do me good."

Still I didn't say anything. I just looked at him, and I wondered what he would say next.

"We've had some good talks this past week, Val," Alexander said in his mellifluous voice. "I've never opened up to anyone the way I have

with you, at least not since I was an art student in
Leeds." He offered me a warm smile. "And you
know all about those days now, about my whole
life, about me and what makes me tick. And I
know *you,* and what you're all about, and that's
quite unique."

"I feel the same way, Alexander. You're a wonderful listener. . . ." I began to laugh. "You're
the possessor of all my secrets. I think I've really
bent your ear, talking so much."

"I did my portion of talking too, and I'm glad
you stayed up late with me, sharing so many
things. It's not often that happens to me these
days."

"I think we've become truly good friends, don't
you?"

"I hope we have." He leaned forward and
pinned his eyes on me. "Stay a bit longer, Val.
You've brought something special here."

"I'll think about it," I replied, not knowing
how to answer him. It was true, we had confided
a great deal in each other. We'd talked about our
childhoods, our lives, and those we had loved. We
had become exceptionally close, although that
wasn't so surprising under the circumstances. We
had been thrown together, and we had clicked.

III

It was a long day.

I shot endless film of Alexander in the studio and with his two assistants. We worked well together, and it was a smooth shoot, with Donald and Alexis backing me up. They were efficient yet relaxed about things, made no fuss.

We all had lunch together on the terrace and then went on working until early evening. Finally we packed it in at seven. I was tired, but Alexander was still full of energy and vitality. He insisted on cocktails on his terrace at the villa, a swim in the pool before supper, and after we had eaten we sat and watched a movie in his screening room, eating popcorn and laughing at the comedy he had chosen.

At midnight I said, "I'm on my last legs, I've got to go to bed." I got up and started to leave the screening room with the others.

He nodded, and I knew he wanted to walk me back to the villa. But Donald and Alexis sidled up to me, and that was that.

When we got back to the guest villa there was a fax from Mike. In it he told me that Françoise was finally back in Paris and that all was well. He had not mentioned Jake, and so I assumed that he was still alive and in Kosovo.

Later I fell asleep easily, because I was so exhausted. And I had a dreamless sleep for once, awakened refreshed and rested the next morning.

IV

Toward the end of the week, Alexander asked me to meet him in the studio for a drink. He said I should come alone, because he wanted to show me something.

I'd had a good day with him, taking some marvelous pictures of him with the Yorkshire Mafia, and I looked forward to our drink as I now walked down the path to the studio.

The main room was empty when I went in, and as I always did, I called out, "Alexander, I'm here!"

He appeared instantly, coming out from behind the platform where the large paintings were displayed. He had a bottle of champagne in one hand, two glasses in the other.

"There you are, Val!" he exclaimed, hurrying forward, smiling hugely. "A drop of the old bubbly first, and then the unveiling."

"Unveiling," I repeated, looking at him alertly. "Don't tell me there's a picture I haven't yet seen?"

"Yes, there is. And it's just finished, that's why I haven't shown it to you before."

Placing the glasses on one of the tables, he

poured the champagne, gave me a glass, and took one himself. Lifting his flute, he touched it to mine and said, "Here's to you, Val, may you live a long and happy life."

"And to you, Alexander, may you enjoy the same."

Putting his arm around me, he led me over to the far side of the studio, to the platform where he painted. We went up the steps, walked toward an easel that was covered with a large white cloth. He positioned me where he wanted me to stand, then walked over to the easel and pulled off the cloth.

I stared at the painting. I was stunned. Alexander had painted a portrait of me, in his own very special style, but it was very obviously me. I stood against a seascape, and I looked extraordinary.

"Alexander, it's just beautiful! I don't know what to say . . . I'm so flattered. But how could you paint me? I mean, I didn't sit for this."

"From my memory of you, Val. After all, you've been with me practically night and day for two weeks now. Your face is engraved on my mind."

"I am so flattered," I said again. "It's . . . wonderful. What an honor to be painted by you."

"I'm happy you like it." He took hold of my

hand, led me down the steps, and out onto the terrace overlooking the sea.

After we were seated on a long rattan sofa, he said, "Stay here, Val. Let Neal take the pictures back to Paris."

"You know I can't do that. Anyway, I want to see the feature through to the end, and I've still got work to do on preparing it."

"I was thinking the other day . . . how you can know someone all your life and yet never know them. And then meet another person and know them *instantly,* know all about them. I feel that way about you, Val."

I stared at him but I didn't respond. I had no words.

"Did you know that King Hussein of Jordan met, fell in love with, and became engaged to Queen Noor within twenty days?"

I shook my head. "No, I didn't."

"So can you understand it when I say this . . . I've fallen in love with you."

"Oh, Alexander."

"Please stay here with me," he repeated.

"You know, I don't think I'm cut out to be your mistress, or anybody's mistress," I said softly and sat there, frowning at him.

He laughed. "I've always said that when you

marry your mistress, you create a job vacancy and—"

"That's not an original line, somebody else said that before you."

"Yes, and I knew him."

"Oh, Alexander," I said again, and simply shook my head, totally at a loss.

"But it would be different with you. I would be faithful. I wouldn't be looking for someone to fill the job vacancy."

When I still remained silent, he moved closer to me on the sofa and took me in his arms. He kissed me tenderly and I found myself responding, returning his kisses, and my arms went around him.

Pulling away, he looked deeply into my eyes. "Stay here with me."

I was incapable of speech.

"We don't have to sleep together tonight, if that's what you think this is leading up to. I'll be patient . . . if that makes you feel more secure about this old devil."

"You're not old," I said, finding my voice at long last.

"You need a lot of loving, Val, to heal those hurts of yours. I can heal them with my love, you know. *And you're so good for me.* Say you'll stay here at the hacienda."

I didn't answer him, and so he folded me in

his arms and held me close, and we sat there for a long time on the terrace.

I knew he was sincere, and I did find him attractive and compelling, not to mention sexy. Yes, I could easily become involved with him, maybe even fall in love with him and be happy at the hacienda. We could probably have the best life together.

The problem was, I loved another man. Truly loved him. I was committed to him, and he was my destiny. And that was why I would have to leave.

Chapter 32

I

Kosovo, April ◦ It was a cold day even though spring had come to this blood-soaked land, and the sun shone, rode high in a pale-blue sky filled with white puffball clouds. And despite the bitter wind, it was a pretty day. But few people noticed that.

Jake had been right about NATO intervening in the war. The air strike was on and bombs had begun to fall on March 24. NATO was still in the fray, and I suspected the battle would last a long time.

I was in Priština, the capital of Kosovo, looking for Jake, which is where he had been a few days earlier. Jacques Foucher had given me all the information when I had arrived in Paris, having flown from Acapulco to New York, and from there to Paris on the Concorde.

After a night at my apartment on the Left Bank I had filled a small backpack with film, put in an extra camera, a few toiletries and a change of underwear, plus two clean T-shirts. When I left for Belgrade, I was wearing my combat boots and flak jacket, and thus was able to minimize my luggage, travel light, be mobile at all times.

The streets of Priština were filled with masses of rubble; people were hurrying through the streets, dodging Serbian bombs and gunfire, trying to find somewhere safe to hide.

So many had apparently left, were moving on foot and cart and tractor toward the borders of Albania and Macedonia, hoping to be allowed to enter these countries. But luck was running out now for all these refugees who were fleeing Milosevic's terror.

It was a hellhole here.

The barrage of gunfire was deafening, and dust rose up from the rubble to choke me. I had a camera slung around my neck and the backpack was on my shoulder. Traveling light worked, I decided as I hustled along, dodging the crowds as best I could.

There were so many people moving through the streets, it was hard to spot anyone, although

I'd kept my eyes peeled for Jake ever since I'd arrived that morning.

Suddenly and unexpectedly I spotted Hank Jardine, an American war correspondent with one of the cable networks.

"Hank!" I screamed, and began to run toward him. "Hank, wait! It's me, Val Denning!"

He was hurrying down the street ahead of me with his cameraman, and it was the cameraman who heard my voice and grabbed Hank's arm. The two men swung around, and Hank waved when he saw me, looking surprised.

I caught up with them and exclaimed, "Hi, guys."

"Hi, Val," Hank said.

The cameraman smiled at me and said, "John Grove."

"Val Denning." We shook hands and then I addressed Hank. "I'm looking for Jake. Have you seen him?"

"Sure did, about two hours ago. He was with Clee Donovan, and they were down by the Red Cross tents. About ten minutes down this road. The tents are set up at the edge of a field."

"Were they wounded?"

"I don't think so. But I'm not sure."

"Thanks, Hank. Are you heading that way?"

"No, I'm going over to talk to some of the Kosovars who have been wounded. I want to do a couple of interviews."

"Thanks," I said again, and hurried off on my own. It worried me that Jake and Clee were at the Red Cross tents. It didn't bode well, I thought.

I began to fill with anxiety, and as apprehension got the better of me, I started to run, pushing myself forward, dodging people, intent on getting to the tents as fast as I could.

I was panting and out of breath by the time I came to the field where the Red Cross tents had been set up. In the distance I could see several K.L.A. soldiers talking in a group, and a couple of Red Cross doctors close by. *And Clee Donovan.*

I came to a standstill for a moment, and my heart stopped. Oh my God, something had happened to Jake. I just knew it. This place was unlucky for me. It stank of death.

I took a deep breath and began to run again, and as I continued sprinting hell-for-leather down the road, I spotted Jake.

"Jake! Jake!" I screamed, rushing forward, my feet flying along the road, my heart racing.

He heard me and swung around.

"Val!" he shouted, raising an arm, and then he began to run toward me.

We met in the middle of the dusty road.

I stumbled into his outstretched arms.

We clung to each other, and I began to sob with relief.

"Oh, thank God you're all right, that nothing's happened to you," I cried, my voice cracking.

"I told you I'd be all right, that you should trust me," he said, holding me away, looking into my face. An amused smile made his mouth twitch, and he said, laughing, "Your face is dirty, Val."

I gaped at him, uncomprehending for a second, and then I yelled, "What the hell do you expect it to be in this muck hole!" But I started to laugh myself.

He held me close again, saying, "Val, oh, Val, it's so wonderful to see you, and this has just been the worst few weeks. I sure am glad you weren't here, it's been very rough, pretty damned lousy."

I drew away from him, stared into those very bright blue eyes of his, and murmured, "But I'm here now, Jake, with you. Where I belong. Here in your arms. On the front lines. Or wherever you want me to be. Just as long as we're together."

Staring at me, he said, "And I want you with me, Val. But not here, not here anymore. I've sent out enough pictures, done what I set out to do when I came. I was planning to get out just before you arrived."

"You mean you want to leave Kosovo?" I asked, looking at him intently.

"Yes, I do. Let's go and say good-bye to Clee." He put an arm around me and we headed on down the road toward the field.

Abruptly, Jake stopped, looked down at me, and said, "There's just one more thing, Val."

"What's that?"

"You just said you belong with me . . . does that mean you'll marry me?"

"Yes, I will," I said, looking up into his face, smiling at him.

"I'm glad," he said as he smiled back.

He took hold of my hand and held it tightly as we set out across the muddy field, and I knew that at last I was safe from harm.